Force Ripe..

..Like a Julie mango pick before time

CMcKenzi
Jan 2016

Force Ripe

A Novel

By

Cindy McKenzie

Praise for Force Ripe

"Force Ripe is a powerful and poetic account of a type of Caribbean childhood that has been covered up for too long. Cindy McKenzie's fresh and heartfelt writing brings the authentic perspective of a girl, painfully alive. This narrative is an important and moving contribution to Caribbean and international literature on familial abuse - without the imposition of adult judgement. The disturbing honesty and reality of the life portrayed only makes it unforgettable. McKenzie is to be commended for her courage, talent and diligence."— **Oonya Kempadoo**, author of *Buxton Spic, Tide Running and All Decent Animals*

"Cindy McKenzie's novel, Force Ripe, is a literary gift to Grenada, an inspiration to children, and a powerful lesson to parents everywhere. This novel touched my soul. Its magic is in the simple but profound observations of Lee, a young girl facing the challenges and dangers of a harsh existence that no child deserves. It's an unforgettable journey of abandonment, betrayal, and painful secrets. The story rings so true, the details so vivid.— **Dunbar DC Campbell**, author of *Blood of Belvidere and The Bianca C Still Burns*

"Force Ripe is more than a story. It is a deeply poignant and moving account of the effect of displacement and the culture of migration on the island child. The story is striking because it is very ordinary and at the same time extraordinary..."— **Akima Paul-Lambert**

"Cindy Mckenzie's Force Ripe lived up to the book's title. Set on a Caribbean island it was written in easy to read dialect about a young girl who had to handle grown up situations way before her time. It felt very much like a V.S. Naipaul classic theme where all of the Caribbean's social ills creep up on the main character for a sinister Murphy 's Law attack... I would recommend Force Ripe simply because of the intensity and passion within the pages and the poignant experience walking with Lee."— **Marsha Gomes-Mckie,** *Caribbean Books Foundation review*

"Force Ripe is easily the best Caribbean Novel I have ever read. It taps into and captures that evasive 'something' that we often try to make sense of... our essence...our soul...our identity as Caribbean people. I LOVE the use of language and I lived through every line...compelling... colorful, so dynamic, so rich, so entertaining so truly Grenadian. Force Ripe is captivating, you go to bed with the characters and wake up in the middle of the night to read and reread again and again.— **Wendy Crawford Daniel**, author of *Unveiling Island Passion*

The First West Indian book I've read for which I strongly believe a Literary Prize deserving! Everyone should read "Force Ripe" – a MUST READ. Simple, yet powerful language. Bravery, mastery, skill, creativity, and pure guts **Claudia Hood Halley—** *UWI Open Campus*

"How brave Lee was. I walked with her to the end and felt kindred to her journey. McKenzie's descriptions are compelling and commanded my brain to follow."— **Patricia Wallcot**

ISBN-13: 978-1517069681
ISBN-10: 1517069688

For my children: Brendon, Gino and Kamilah. My parents; without whom I would not be, nor this story made. And my Aunty Lena, who shared family stories.

Not to know your family story is bad. Not to want to know it is worse, for to pass on ignorance to someone is like passing on a curse.

Nena Camille Yarbrough

Prologue

First Memories

Mommy get up and open the door for Daddy. The breeze blow inside before him. It make cold bumps on me skin. The door creak. It always creaking. It old and rotten. The hinges rusty, rusty. And breeze does pass through them holes in it.

Daddy kick out he shoes by the door. Mommy raise me up from the bed and put me down on the floor, by me brother. I start to cry. Mommy say *shushh, shushhhh. Go back and sleep.* The cry go away.

Daddy pass over me brother, then me. He kneel down by me and kiss me. Daddy beard tickle me face. Daddy not smelling nice. When Daddy climb on the bed by Mommy, the bed creak too. Just like the door. Creeeak. Creeeak. Creeeak. The bed old and the spring rusty. The house old too. It shape just like the capital L in me name. It have grass in the yard. A coconut tree on the bank.

We in the front room facing the road. Auntie Helen and Auntie Louise in one room with their children. Me three uncles staying in the next room.

I wake up before everybody. Outside getting bright. Light peeping through the holes in the door. It have a almanac with a lady posing on she motorbike hang up on the door. The breeze flap the plastic blind in front the door. It tickle me brother but he en wake up at all. He sleeping sound, sound. He foot under the bed. And he snoring loud loud, just like Daddy.

Mommy and Daddy sleeping still. Daddy lie down on he side. He knees pointing up to he face and he hands

1

clasp between he knees as if he praying. I want to go and lie down by Daddy but Mommy take up all the space on the bed. I shake Mommy. She open she eye. *Go back and sleep, chile. It early still.*

I pull out the potty from under the bed. It nearly full with pee. Pee splash up on me *bambam* when I stoop down.

I watch me brother sleeping with he mouth open. He dribbling on he pillow. The dribble make a big wet circle, like the one Teacher V teach us to make on we slate. A fat mosquito rest on he face. He slap it. The mosquito dive inside he ears. He slap he ears hard. But the mosquito get away.

I take me time and put back the potty below the bed. I lie down on me back and watch the light leaking through the holes in the roof. The holes look like dots and sometimes the roof does make noise as if somebody sprinkling gravels on it. I watch the holes until me eye seeing doubles.

Outside bright. Auntie Helen cursing in the back room. Me two uncles who looking same ting, does cuss too. And so they does stammer bad. *You doh doh doh doh hear ah sa-sa-sa-say doh touch me bla-bla-blasted ting!* And the next one say *so so so so wha-wha-what youuuu go do me? Eh, eh?* Daddy say how them is twins. He say they so bad they kill they mother when they born. She is Daddy mother too, but Daddy have a different father. Daddy does always tell me how I look just like he mother. She name was Baby

And Auntie Helen does talk loud. And she always cursing she big sister, Auntie Louise, for using she ting. *WHY YOU DOH GET YOU MAN TO BUY MILK FAH YOU BLASTED CHILREN?* And me other uncle saying, *stop dat fu-fu-fucking noise dey eh. Every fu-fucking morning all you*

2

you you ma-ma-makin fucking noise! He does stammer worse than the twins.

Auntie baby start to cry. The noise wake up Daddy. He *stupse.* Knock the partition. KOKE KOKE KOKE KOKE KOKE! *Watch, stop all you flipping noise dey nuh!.* Auntie and them get quiet quiet.

Mommy wake up and make tea. She put mine in me little pink cup - the bite-up one with the plastic peeling off. Then Mommy go to work. She working by some white people in Bathway.

Daddy is a bus driver. He have to go down in Sauteurs for the bus so me and me brother walk down to school with him. He give me a *jackey* so I could ride on he back when we passing through the cemetery. I so fraid, I grip Daddy neck tight tight. I squeeze me eyes tight too. When me brother ask for a jackey too, Daddy say, *Boy you too big for dat boy!* Me brother vex vex. He vex with Daddy. He vex with me. He stretch he mouth long. And he watching me bad eyes. But break-time he still pick bread and cheese flowers from the tree in the cemetery for me.

Daddy does not come home so much. Then Mommy go away with the plane. Me and me brother go and stay with Mammy and Papa in a big house. We have a big bed for weself.

Chapter 1

Mammy and Papa

All of us in the kitchen: me, me brother Rally, Mammy and Papa. Mammy is we great-grandmother but Papa is not we real great-grandfather. We don't know we real great-grandfather. We don't even know we real grandfather. But we lucky, because we have a real nice Papa.

Mammy and Papa living together long. Mammy say me and Rally living with them since we mother go in Aruba – three years now. Mammy say I had three years when she go. Rally had four years. Sometimes Mammy does say, "You doh see all you mother doh even want all you? You en see how she leave all you an go!" Mammy say she go and look for greener pastures. But Miss Kay does say how we in the same boat like a lot of children in Celeste. We in the same boat like she grandchildren — mother gone to look for greener pastures.

Miss Kay house full up with children. And she house only have three little rooms. But she does make space for everybody. And I bet if me and Rally have to sleep over by her, she making space for us too - even if she have to put us under the bed! Mammy say that's why Miss Kay strong like a horse so, because she have to work like a donkey to mind all she children. And all she grandchildren too.

I kneel down on the sofa by the window watching the rain. Since last night it falling. And it falling heavy heavy, like mud on the galvanize roof. Rain water skating down the roof of the main house, and falling on the steps. It gathering up all the leaves and dust and everything else, and running down the concrete drain in the yard with them. Then straight in the callaloo row. The callaloo row run under the cashew tree, behind the kitchen. And so I like to hear the rain falling on the roof, especially in the night. It does make me feel to wrap up tight in me blanket and stay in me bed.

The kitchen separate from the main house, just like everybody kitchen in Celeste. Everybody cook on coals or firewood. The wood does make too much smoke to cook inside. The kitchen have two sections: the back and the front. The back have a fireside and a counter. Mammy does call it she dresser. That is where she does peel yam and bananas, knead flour to make dumplings and roll out she dhal puri. It have a shelf below the counter with all Mammy burn-bottom pots and skillets, and a shelf over the counter with curry powder, masala, ghee, saffron, pepper-sauce, coconut oil, and bottles with all kind of things that don't look good to eat. And every day, when Mammy finish cooking, she does take she old piece of kitchen knife and scrape out all the saffron and banana stain from the counter. Then she does scrub it down nice and clean, ready for next day.

We do everything else in the front section: eat, clean nutmeg, shell peas and shell parched cocoa for Mammy to make cocoa balls for tea.

Papa always sit down by he little table; the old rickety one by the window. It have big holes and crevices on top it, where wood-ants eat they belly full. The plastic tablecloth have pictures of red mangoes and it full of cuts and round spots where hot plates of food melt it up. Papa have a rusty biscuit tin in a corner of the table; it full with ha'pennies, pennies, nails, pins and all kind of old things. It have a old dent-up enamel cup in the corner too, with he old shaving things. And everything old and rusty rusty, but Papa not throwing them away at all. Mammy wooden mortar - the one she does use to pound cocoa and spices in, it under Papa table.

I sit down on me little stool - Mammy does call it a *pirha*. I have on me red long pants and me green shirt. Mammy say I could wear them in the house now, because they getting too small for me. And they stain-up too. And me hair rumple. The cornrows and them get loose now. They looking puffy puffy. But school on holiday so it staying so until Miss Kay daughter feel sorry for me and plait it. Mammy have Indian hair and she can't do nothing with me hair. She say me hair coarse like fibre and she don't know where I get that hair from. When you watch Mammy, you go never think me is she grandchild. But me and Daddy have same hair. Just like me and Daddy have same eyes!

Mammy always make cocoa-tea when rain falling. She say that cocoa does warm you up. Sometimes Mammy does make real Red Rose tea from the green box with the red rose on it. She does make it in the little enamel teapot. Black-sage, sweeten with brown sugar is tea. And when Mammy boil cinnamon stick or *bwaden leaf*, and dash a little bit of milk in it, it does look just like the soapy water from the wares basin. But she does call that tea too. Once it hot, is tea.

And Mammy does not say, "Come and eat all you breakfus," like Miss Kay. She does say, "Come and drink all you tea, eh". Even though we eating bakes and salt-fish too.

Papa watching out the window. He don't touch he breakfus yet. He never touch he cup until he tea cold enough to drink. He just sit down there watching the rain.

"What Mammy! It en look like I could make it up today, nuh," Papa say.

"It en look so, boy! That rain look like it mean business today!" Mammy say.

Papa scratching he leg inside he water-boots. He have on he mountain clothes already — he old stain-up shirt and long pants. But Papa does call he pants trousers. He is the overseer in Plaisance and Bologna Estate. He does go up every day to feed the cows. And to make sure the workers and them pick up the nutmeg and pick the cocoa when they in season. And sometimes Papa does bring me and Rally with him.

Mammy sit down by she table, with she plate on she lap. She table bigger than Papa table. And it full-up of all kind of things too: a bowl of eggs from the hens in the yard, a bottle with money for when the Coke truck or the fish car pass, a milk tin with spoons, knives, forks and even cockroach eggs and *tootoo* in it, and bottles with dry corn, peas, sorrel and ochra seeds.

Mammy mash up she *bluggoe* with she short little fingers, Put some in she mouth. She always cook bluggoe and fig for sheself. And she does pound seasoning peppers, hot peppers, onions and garlic on a flat stone, dash some salt in it and mix it up with coconut oil to make she fresh chutney to eat with she bluggoe and fig. And Mammy don't have a single tooth in she mouth, so when she chewing, she whole face does move up and down like a little tractor.

A piece of hair escape from she bun and fall down she face. She tuck it back behind she ear with she greasy fingers.

"Well stay home today nuh, Papa," I say. I wish Papa stay home. If Papa stay home, all of us go be home, in the kitchen, with we bakes and cocoa-tea, and the rain falling nice nice on the galvanize.

"Well it look as if ah go have to stay home, yes. Dat rain en giving me chance today!"

Rally sit down on the sofa eating quick quick, as if somebody chasing him. He biting off big chunks of bakes and blowing he cocoa-tea, W*heeew! Wheeew! Wheeew!*

Belle curl up by him. Mammy get Belle from Miss Kay when she mother-cat drop four kittens. Belle have orange fur and green eyes. Rally always picking her up and petting her. He does even put Belle in the bed with us in the night. But I does push her down. She does rub up on me leg and I don't like that.

Rally pick up his cup and blow it again. *Wheeew! Wheeeew! Wheeew!* He take a big mouthful and spit it right back in the cup.

"You beggar! Dat tea hot oui, boy!" He hang out he tongue for the breeze to cool it.

"Well wait for it to cool nuh, man," Papa say.

Rally still hanging out he tongue for breeze, like a dog. Cocoa-tea is the hottest tea. Is just as if the cocoa does lock up the heat inside the cup, so breeze can't pass through.

Rally blow again. He take a little sip. He in a haste, because he meeting up he partners, Boyboy and Lano. Boyboy is Miss Kay grandson. And Lano living with he grandmother, Miss Sangie. She does have Shango dance in she yard.

"Well what do dat rain so? We well say we go *nana* dat ripe fig today." And Rally vex because the rain spoiling he *parrie*.

"What ripe fig?" I ask him.

"Me and Lano and dem see a nice *doomsie* bunch down by the ravine. Ah sure it well ripe by now."

"Stay dere and bawl doomsie bunch! Ent Papa tell you aready, not to go in people ting?" I turn to Papa but he still gazing out the window and scratching. The mountain on he mind.

"Well nobody en taking it and it go jus stay dere and spoil," Rally say.

The rain still pounding the roof. When rain falling, me and

Rally does sing *Rain rain go away, little Tommy want to play*. But I don't want the rain to go nowhere.

"Heh. Dat rain serious boy!" Papa say. He look down at he plate as if he just seeing it. Papa does eat like a bird, but Mammy always fulling up he plate too much.

"You want more bakes, Reenie? Mammy give me too much, man."

"Yes tanks, Papa."

Reenie is me auntie in England but Papa always calling me Reenie. And he does say Reenie nice nice!

Papa break he bake in two. He hands shake just like when he shaving. He give me a piece and he give Rally the other piece. I put mine on Rally plate too.

The tea not hot again, but it too strong. Mammy always making she cocoa-tea too strong. I prefer Miss Kay cocoa-tea. Hers milky and thick, like porridge. And when she making it, we could smell the bwaden leaves and cinnamon all the way from we kitchen.

I don't even know the rain stop until I hear the whistle from the road. Me special whistle. I could hear that whistle from anywhere. I could hear it from down in the bottom of the garden, even if the donkey braying, all them cocks crowing and the cow calling Papa for she food. And when I hear me whistle, is like something does take me. I does leave anything I doing and run full speed.

I jump up from the pirha. I knock down me cup. The tea fall on the floor. It spread quick quick and disappear between the flooring. It go fall and soak up in the dust under the kitchen.

"Eh eh! What taking you so, Peeya!"

Mammy spit out Peeya so hard, some of she food pitch out from she mouth with it. I don't even know what Peeya mean. I used to wonder if is somebody who does pee in bed. But I does not pee in me bed. Mammy never call Rally names like that. She does call him *Beta*. And when she say *come Beta*, it does come out soft and nice – like sweet potato pudding. But she does spit out *Peeya*, just like she does spit out coconut husk from she mouth – after she suck out all the milk from it. She does spit it out just like she does spit out nuts – after she suck out all the sugar from the sugar-cakes.

And Peeya does hit me hard like a stone. But this time I don't go behind the kitchen. I don't go in the room downstairs and cry with all them box of books that full of dust and cockroach. And all them bats hanging up in the ceiling. I fly out the door just like how them bats does fly out the window when light come inside the room. Because me Daddy come.

Chapter 2

Daddy Come

Daddy come! Daddy come! I pelt out the kitchen. Hop up the steps between the kitchen and the house, two by two, gripping my *hula hoop* slippers hard hard with me toes. I dash into Daddy so fast, he drop the bag of fish back in the trunk of the car to catch me. He raise me up in the air. I have six years now and I getting too big for Daddy to toss up like he used to. But I still bend back me feet so I wouldn't dirty he nice, clean clothes. Daddy always looking nice in he bellbottom jeans, tight tight jersey and he Clarks boots. And he always look as if he just come out by the barber. Mammy say he is a saga boy, that's why he was always dress up dress up so.

"What say now Lee?" Daddy squeeze me and kiss me.

"Nuttin," I say and I wiggle and hug Daddy back. I press me face in Daddy neck until I giddy with he Pears soap smell, mix up with cigarette and cologne. Sometimes Daddy face does tickle me, but it clean and real smooth like Papa face when he take a shave.

"So you good?" Daddy smile and he gold teeth sparkle just like the gold dust in the cliff by the kitchen. Rally does scratch it out to put in he trap to catch ground dove.

"Yea, ah good." I grip Daddy neck when he bend down to pick up the fish again. Daddy have a friend name Cheekie who is a fisherman and he does give Daddy fish to bring for us. Once, Daddy bring a big piece of turtle, full of blood. Mammy tell Daddy he better bring it back where he get it because she don't want it in she house. And I glad Daddy take it back because when I see all the blood, me belly started to feel real sick, like when I want to vomit. Sometimes Daddy does bring letters from the post office for Mammy or a parcel with clothes or toys and sweets for me and Rally, things that we mother send from Aruba.

Daddy living down the road in the same little house with he brothers and sisters, but he does hardly come up by us. He driving bus and Taxi so he always busy. "Busy chasing woman," Mammy does say. So when he come and see us, I does glue on to him like sticky cherry. And when Daddy go I does feel just as if Daddy take away something from me, so I always crying.

"Whey your brother?" Daddy ask me.

"He in the kitchen drinking he tea." I know Rally glad when Daddy come, you know, but he does never run to Daddy like me. I know he just pretending though.

Daddy carry me down the steps and stand up in front the kitchen door. I never see Daddy go inside the kitchen yet. He say he don't have time with Mammy. He say that she didn't like him for we mother so she make a lot of trouble for him. He say Mammy didn't like niggers and that he didn't know why she didn't go and stay around she own Indian people, down in Samaritan.

"What say now Millie?"

Daddy use the big voice he does use for Mammy, as if he want her to know he wasn't making no joke with her. He give me the fish to bring for Mammy.

"Ah there. Just so so," Mammy say, her voice sounding poor-me-one poor-me-one, as if she sick or something, and she want Daddy to feel sorry for her. But Mammy was always saying bad things about Daddy behind he back.

"What you mean you there so so?" Daddy not smiling at all. He put he face serious serious. Daddy say he don't have no time for no hypocrite people, so he finish with Mammy long time.

Mammy put the bag of fish in the special wash-pan she have for fish. She have a special one for when Papa kill a hen for Sunday lunch too. Daddy does bring the fish already clean so Mammy just have to season it. And when you see she frying it later, the smell does turn all the cat and them into little thieves.

"So everyting aright Norman?" Everybody else does call Papa Uncle Norman or Mr Norman. Daddy is the only person who does call Papa by he name so. And Daddy doesn't use the big voice for Papa neither. He does speak to Papa as if them is real good friends. And I like that because Mammy always talking to Papa rough rough, as if he is a bad person--as if he always fretting her.

"Well ah dey man," Papa say. And Papa grinning as if he real glad to see Daddy. Papa looking like a real *sillybilly* because most of he front teeth missing. And I waiting for Mammy to say something. I waiting for her to bark "What you grinning at so?" But she don't say nothing. She just sit down there rocking like a little fishing boat, with she hands in she lap.

Daddy pat Rally head from in front of the door. Rally used to have big long plaits but they had to cut it when he started to go to school. Mammy was real vex when they cut it. She still have the hair in a plastic bag in a drawer.

"You good, little man?" Rally duck he head, as if he don't want Daddy to touch him. And I don't know why he always vex with Daddy so.

"All you want to go for a spin?" Daddy ask. He does never stay long. He always just dropping something to go again. And he would take us for a ride when he going up to the junction to turn the car. Sometimes Rally come too, but this time he busy to go and meet up he partners and them, so he shake he head.

Inside Daddy car clean clean. And it have something stick to the dashboard and it make the car smell like when Mammy squeeze ripe lemons to make juice.

I sit down in the front with him and he drive up the road real slow. Rally like when Daddy speed up the road kicking up dust all about the place. Then he does go and boast how Daddy car fly up the road like a jet. But I like when Daddy take he time. None of we friends daddy have a car. Mammy say some of them don't even have a daddy.

After Daddy turn round the car, he cruise down the road like a taxi driver. And I feel just like a little tourist. And Daddy singing along with the song on the radio, *Ah, ha, ha, ha, stayin' alive, stayin' alive. Ah, ha, ha, ha, stayin' alive, stayin' alive.* Daddy dancing up he shoulders so I dancing up me shoulders too. "Dat's the *Bee Gees*," he tell me. And I like to hear the *Bee Gees. Ah, ha, ha, ha, stayin' alive, stayin' alive.* I singing with Daddy until he stop in front of the house. I climb over and sit down on Daddy lap. He hug me and I stick me face in he neck. I want to leave me nose right there. I want to stay right there singing in the car with Daddy.

That is my special time with Daddy. That is the time when Daddy does tell me things. Daddy have six other children besides me and Rally. We have two older sisters. And we have two brothers and two sisters who younger than us. And the four of them born the same year. And all of them have a different mother. But I know I special.

One day I run up from the garden in me short pants and when Daddy stoop down and brush off the leaves from me legs, he said. "You must take care of your legs, you know Lee. You must not let them get scratch-up and bruise-up at all. You must have nice legs like you mother. Men like women with nice legs." And Daddy told me I must never take money from men. "Never!" He said and looked at me serious serious. And I wonder if he talking about Uncle Cheekie too, because when me and Rally went by him to eat we lunch, he always give us twenty five cents each to buy snow ice. And we does take it. Daddy said that people always wishing bad things on me so I must be careful. And I don't know what Daddy mean, but I does hear Mammy saying the same thing too. She said that Daddy was spoiling everybody girl children. She said that once, Mr Randolph from down the road nearly kill Daddy for he daughter. Mammy said how men go spoil me too. How they go make me see trouble, because "You doh see how she look just like him! *Pee pee* him!" People always saying I look just like Daddy too. Daddy face long and he have deep deep eyes. And he nose straight straight. People say Daddy children could never lose – just look at their eyes.

Me and Daddy sit down in the car for a long time just listening to the radio. The rain pass and the sun trying to come out, but the clouds blocking it. And everybody that passing have to stop by the car and call Daddy. "Feneh. What say Feneh! How tings going man?" Everybody know Daddy, because he driving bus.

A reggae song start playing and Daddy singing "T*he harder dey coome, harder dey fall, one an'all. Jimmy Cliff,*" he say.

Then Daddy get quiet quiet. As if he thinking real hard about something. I twist he gold chain around me finger.

"Lee, ah feel ah go make a turn you know." Daddy say it real quiet. He say it just as if he talking to heself. And Daddy not looking at me at all. He looking out the window.

Me heart drop down in me belly, just like when Rally trying to climb on Papa donkey, Melba, and she start to back kick and I 'fraid she go knock him down dead dead. *What Daddy talking about? Make a turn?* I know that Daddy not talking about going down the road to make a spin. I know he not coming back and see me tomorrow. I swallow the little lump that just come up in me throat like a hard piece of dumpling.

"Ah want to go and see you mother." Daddy turn round and he watching me with he deep deep eyes. And I feel something gathering up behind me deep deep eyes that I get from Daddy. And me head swell up. I hear Melba kicking up inside me chest. And I wish Daddy just stop talking. I just want Daddy to sit down in the car sing with *The Bee Gees* and *Jimmy Cliff.* I don't want to hear him talking about going nowhere. I just want to sit down in the car with Daddy and smell he nice perfume.

"I want to spend some time with you mother." Daddy say. And I know Daddy not just going down the road. He going and leave me. I turn me face outside, but Daddy hold me face and turn it to him. And I don't know who tell Daddy to do that, because he make tears start to full up me eyes. And I know if I just open me mouth, the tears go burst out and the piece of dumpling in me throat go turn to stone and choke me.

"I might stay for a little while. But doh worry man, Daddy soon come back. You know Daddy won't stay away from you for long, eh."

A little while! What a little while is? I only see Daddy once in a while and every time he go I have to wait long long for the next time. And Daddy wouldn't just be down the road or driving he bus or liming in town. I don't know what Daddy mean by a little while, but a little while sound like a long time. Daddy hug me tight and he give me the biggest kiss he even give me, as if he think that go make it pass.

The cloud let the sun out now, but Daddy go and burst the swelling behind me eyes and tears start falling down me face like rain. *Daddy going away just like we mother. I go never hear me special whistle again.* Hiccups heave up from me chest. Tears bounce up with snot pouring out me nose and soak up Daddy shirt. *Good! Who tell him to say he going?* He take out he nice clean handkerchief from he pocket and wipe me face.

I listen to Daddy car going down the road until I can't hear it again. And Mammy still shouting from the kitchen. *"Peeya, you en coming and finish drink you tea?"*

Chapter 3

Celeste People

Saturday is mountain day and me and Rally like to sit down in the veranda and watch people passing.

I does wake up before the sun rise up over Piton mountain, and the big cock start to crow behind the kitchen. Papa say the cock is he clock, but Mammy always wake up before them.

I jump up and shake Rally.

"Rally, wake up. You en hear cock crowing aready?"

"Mmmmm. Leave me alone nuh. It early still." Rally groan and cover back he face with the sheet.

"Boy wake up nuh boy!" I shake him again but he pull the sheet over he head.

The sun coming inside the bedroom already. I wrap up me sheet around me and go out to the veranda. The wind brush me face. It still feeling wet. I rub me eyes, and wipe out the *caca jé* with the end of me blue nightie with the white tear up lace. The one I had for long long.

Rally come out rubbing his eyes. He sit down by me on Mammy's sofa, *bridle* all around he mouth and caca jé in he eyes.

"Boy wipe you face nuh!" I tell Rally.

"Gurl leave me alone nuh."

Papa room door half-open. Belle squeeze out from the room, meowing. In the night when I push Belle down from we bed, she does jump through the little window between we room and Papa room. And she does sleep with Papa.

Belle go straight by Rally and rub up on he leg. He

18

pick her up and she meow and curl up on he lap.

Papa gone up in Plaisance already. On Saturdays me and Rally don't have to go with him. Only if he picking cocoa. He have to feed the cows and milk the one with the calf. And he does bring down milk for Mammy to boil with cinnamon. I real like cow milk. I like how it does make a skin on top when Mammy boil it. And how it does leave a white moustache on me top lip.

On Saturdays, everybody does get up early and busy doing their work. That is when you could hear Miss Joyce calling out, "Dave! Boy get up and come and sweep de yard nuh!" Or "Shirley pass you backside an empty the posey before ah come an put a lash in you little ass eh girl!" And you could smell Miss Joyce's rice porridge boiling away on the fireside in she little kitchen. That time in the morning, you could smell Miss McKie black sage tea too. And Miss Ralda fish cakes frying in coconut oil. And so me mouth making water for some.

At this time in the morning, when you walking up to the mountain road, all kinds of smell does come out together with the sun: the garlic bush with the pretty mauve flowers that does make me belly feel sick; ripe guavas with *congorees* inside them; over ripe bananas rotting under the trees; honey from Mr Honeyman's bee hives; nutmegs and cloves and hog plums, the bright yellow ones that does pave the mountain road. Mammy say they poisonous, and that's why even the birds and them not touching them. And all that smell and them does mix up in my head make me giddy.

Trip trop, trip trop, trip trop.

"Mr Elias donkey comin up eh," Rally say.

The big garlic bush in front we house blocking the view but Rally know the donkey and them by how their hooves hitting the road. Sometimes we does play a game, guessing which donkey coming around the corner.

Mr Elias donkey is the biggest jack in Celeste. Papa say that everybody in Celeste does bring their jenny donkey by Mr Elias for jack. When Melba start galloping and kicking up when Papa trying to ride her, and not even Rally could go near her, Papa say that's when she in heat. And he does bring her by Mr Elias for jack. And Miss Kay husband does bring he jenny to Mr Elias too.

"Monning Miss Milleey," Mr Elias call out. He sit down high up on he donkey, he old mountain hat flopping down over one side of he face and he don't even turn he head to look in the veranda.

Little Joel sit down in front him, holding the rope with two hands. Joel grinning and waving at us. I wave back at him. Joel eyes make him look as if he always sleepy. He younger than me. He grandmother went to England, just like we grandmother. People say Joel mother is a *stupidee.* She doesn't go nowhere. She never even go to school. So everybody wondering who Joel father is. Joel grinning and waving until the donkey bend the corner, behind the giant avocado tree.

After everybody pass to go up the mountain, I put on me home clothes to go in the kitchen. I could smell Miss Kay bully bakes from the bedroom. Miss Kay does make the best bully bakes. She does put a lot of coconut milk in hers and they does come out nice and smooth - not like Mammy rough rough ones and them. And she does roll them out on she dresser with a bottle that have little bumps on it, so the bakes does have little round holes on them.

Mammy always telling us we must not go in people house when they eating, especially so early in the morning, but Miss Kay is not people. She is we neighbour.

So I put on my slippers and pretend I going behind the house, and I follow me nose, full speed to she kitchen.

Yvette and Boyboy outside sweeping the yard. They have a lotta goats and in the night, they does tie them in the yard. So every morning, when the bigger boys go and tie them out to graze, Boyboy and Yvette have to sweep up the goat mess and heap it up under the soursop tree. Their grandfather does use the mess for manure in he garden.

Boyboy have on he old khaki school pants with a big big hole in the back. And Boyboy don't have on no underpants, so I could see he bambam through the hole. Boyboy barefeet too and goat mess stick up between he spread-out toes.

The ground a little wet so the goat mess still soft. Yvette stick a lump of mess in piece of broom and swing it at Boyboy. The mess hit him right on the back of he head. Yvette younger than Boyboy, but she bigger than him.

I want to laugh at Boyboy. But he looking real vex.

"What you tink you doing gurl!" Boyboy swing around and give Yvette one lash with he bush broom.

"Boyboy! Behave youself eh," Yvette cry out. She rub she bambam through she dungaree pants. Then she fling another piece of mess at Boyboy again. She peel back she thick black lips and grin at him. And Yvette teeth look just like the little pearls on the string on Mammy dressing table.

Boyboy give her a lash with the broom again. It hit Yvette right on the back of she leg. Right on she *coucou pé.* Yvette leg and them tough tough and bruise-up, like a boy. But the broom stip naked so it sting her real bad.

"Aw aw! Ah go tell Mammy eh. You see how you head big as a breadfruit! Yvette say. And she rubbing she coucou pé.

"Tell her nuh. Tell her nuh." Boyboy say. And he sizing up Yvette. He chest heaving up and down. "You see how you black as coals. You ole tar baby."

Yvette real dark in truth. She is the darkest one in all Miss Kay grandchildren. She is the darkest girl in Celeste. And she look different from Boyboy and she brother Dwaine and she sister Dalia. Yvette have big, round eyes and when you see she want to do some mischief, they does start to jump. She big and strong, just like she grandmother, Miss Kay. And she could climb tree and play rough, just like them boys.

I stand up on the cliff watching them and listening for when Mammy call me. Me and Rally does never fight like them. Sometimes Rally does follow Mammy and call me names, but we does never fight with one another.

"Mammy. Mammaye. Tell Boyboy to behave heself eh". Yvette and them does call their grandmother Mammy, just like us. And their mother in Aruba like we mother too.

"What he do you now?" Miss Kay squeal from the kitchen. Ah giving him one cut-ass in he backside this morning," Miss Kay voice so sharp and loud that it could pitch all from she kitchen all the way to Mammy kitchen, just as how the smell of she spicy cocoa tea.

"Come inside now and get all you breakfus." Miss Kay say.

Rally run over and meet me.

"All you smell Mammy bully-bakes eh?" Boyboy say. He know how we like he grandmother bakes. We like all Miss Kay food.

Miss Kay just taking out the bake from the iron pot when we reach the kitchen. She put the bake on the flour-bag towel on the dresser. A lot of cups line up on the kitchen counter like school children in assembly. And smoke rising out from them.

"A A! Whey all you going wid dat speed?" Miss Kay

say, smiling when she see me and Rally. "All you doh fine ah have enough mouths to feed aready? Eh?"

Miss Kay does always say that but we know she joking. I squeeze in by Yvette, on the big wooden bench at the front of the kitchen. Rally stand up by the door.

"All you come. Come and take all you tea before fly fall in it."

Miss Kay take out another plate. She put two pieces of bakes on it and put it next to the twelve plates sitting down on the long counter.

"Come *doodoo*. Come and take dat for you and you brother," she say. "Mouths never too much for me to feed. Come. Come and take dat."

"Mammy how you could give Dalia more bakes than me?" Yvette ask. And she looking in everybody plate.

"Watch girl, stop you damn nasty habit there eh," Miss Kay say. She still break a small piece and put it on Yvette plate. But Yvette still not satisfied.

"Gie me some in you tea nah Dwaine-Dwaine,"

Dwaine does not like cocoa-tea, so he let Yvette take some from he cup.

"Girl how you lickerish so!" Miss Kay stupse.

Miss Kay always shouting and quarrelling with them. But in the evening she does sit down on the cliff in front the house with Dalia and Dwaine sit down on she knee, and she does tell them Anancy stories. And she does sing for them. And sometimes, she does let me sit on she knee too. And on Sundays, especially when the sun real hot, she does bring all she grandchildren over by Mammy to give them their Sunday scrub down. She does bathe me and Rally too. She does strip all of us naked and scrub us down with *sumache* bush to give we skin a good cleaning-- all man and their brother; scrub us until all the *laquas* come out like little dirty dumplings. Then rub us down with carbolic soap and rinse us under the stand pipe until

23

we skin start to squeak. Until she get she own stand pipe in she yard.

Mr Hugh, Miss Kay husband does sit down in the back of the kitchen, by the fireside. Mr Hugh is a little man. He even smaller than Papa and he looking weak weak - as if breeze could throw him down. And he always looking vex. He does just watch everything under his eye, like a snake, to see who doing what for when it was time to share licks. The only time Mr Hugh didn't look vex was when he sharing licks. When he beating Boyboy and them, he does get strong strong, as if he have powers.

"Rally! Beta!" I could hear Mammy calling.

I don't wait for Mammy to call me name. I jump down from the bench quick quick.

"Tanks Miss Kay. We goin. Mammy callin us." I say. And I dash home even though is bad manners to leave people house as soon as you full up you belly.

Chapter 4

On The Veranda

Every evening, six o' clock on the dot, Mammy does listen to the death news. She does sit down in the veranda, on she special sofa that Mr Jonjon make for her. The sofa low low and it facing the road, so Mammy could see everybody who passing. Mammy legs does stretch out on the wash-out linoleum with little red balls inside little yellow boxes. And she bambam does spread out and take up almost the whole sofa.

Sometimes Mammy does make Rally sit down with her. "Come Beta." She does say. "Come and give you Mammy a kiss nuh." Then she does pull Rally down on she lap, hug him to she flat chest, press she soft, wet mouth on he face and kiss him, kiss him, kiss him. . And I know Rally does smell the rancid coconut oil and sweat in Mammy hair, because he does squinge up he nose. And as soon as Mammy let him go, he does run in the hall and wipe he face on he jersey. He does wipe it, wipe it, wipe it!

"Beta, put on the radio for Mammy to hear the death news nuh. Bring it in the veranda." Mammy say.

Mammy face look orange from the sun. And she glasses making circles on the wall. And the circles and them dancing.

"Ah coming just now Mammy," Rally say, but he still sit right where he is. Kite season in the air and he busy making he kite. When kite in season, Rally does stay out for the whole day with Boyboy and Lano and them.

Sometimes he doesn't even come and eat, until night take place and me throat get dry calling him.

Kite flying is serious thing. When is kite season, all the boys does gather in the yard in front Maymay house to make their kite. They does use flex, from coconut branch, bamboo or stick. And they does have kite flying competition. But the best part is going and nana a kite when it fail. Rally is like a chicken hawk. He always on the look-out for a kite dancing in the sky. Ducking down the hill in slow motion; like them Chinese in them Kung Fu movies in Griffith Cinema. Diving down behind a tree over the hill. Then he going after the kite when it fall, skating down the hill. Diving through bush. Scrambling up any tree, like a monkey. And I bet he jumping over barb wire and all, if he had to, to get that kite. He didn't care if he rip up he pants or *gashay* he backside. And them kites does sing loud in the night. Sometimes people does go and cut them, fuss they making noise. Papa and all does go out with he search light and he cocoa knife to cut them.

When me and Rally lie down in we bed, we does listen to the kite and them. Rally know everybody kite.

He does say, "Listen. Listen eh. You hear that one?"

And I does say, "Um hm.

"You hear how it sounding heavy. Like a engine? Da's Booffie kite. Hear da one. You hear it? Listen nuh!"

And I does strain me ears.

"You hear how da one sound just like a *mybone*? Da's Manni own. Langalay own sound like a horn. You hear it? And da's Boyboy own."

Boyboy kite sound just like Belle, when Mammy lock her outside and she crying to come in. And I does listen to Rally until I fall asleep with the kite and them singing in me ears. Mybone. Engine. Horn. Belle crying.

"Lee, bring the radio for Mammy for me nuh," Rally

tell me.

"Me bring the radio! Is you she tell oui!"

"If you bring it ah go make a nice mybone kite for you."

I bring the radio. But I know Rally must make me kite for me.

The radio is the same red colour as bird cherry. It have two shiny gold knobs and some holes where the people voice does come out. And it stand up on four little leg on top the cabinet.

I turn the little knob until it clicks, like when you bite a dumpling. The voice inside the holes say, "...announce the death of Ms. Maisie Hypolite, from Florida in St. John's."

I hold the radio careful careful and I put it down on the wall. Careful careful.

"Eh eh. Who tell you to bring radio Peeya? Watch her nuh! You doh see how she mouth lang!"

I bring the radio for Mammy, but she have to make me shame. Sometimes she does say how me mouth long like a pig snout. And if I stay in the toilet too long she does say how me belly long as twine. And something does hurt me in me chest. But when Mammy say, "Beti oye, come and thread the needle for you Mammy nuh," all the name and them does fly straight out of me head, and I does run real quick and thread the needle for her. And scratch she back for her. And bring she teeth for her too.

"A a. Mammy you doh hear who dead?" Papa say.

He sit down on he old wrought iron chair by the gate. All the paint rub off from the chair, where Papa does rest he arm. The brown cover on the seat cut-up cut-up, as if Papa bambam have razor in it.

"Who dey say?" Mammy ask.

"Well ah tink he say Ms Maisie dead," Papa say. And he stretching he neck to the radio, just like a *morrocoy*.

27

"Who Maisie? Not Maisie down in Florida!' Mammy push she head near to the radio too, even though it right in front of her.

"*Ms Maisie Hypolite will be buried at the Florida cemetery.*" The man on the radio saying.

Outside starting to get dark and Mammy glasses stop dancing on the wall.

Mammy and Papa friend, Mr Fin, just reach down from the mountain. Just as how Mammy does listen to the death news every six 'o' clock, just so Mr Fin does go up in the mountain every 'fore day morning. And he does not come down till night time. Papa say he didn't know how la Diablesse don't go with Fin yet. Papa say la Diablesse is a woman with one human foot and one cow foot. He say how la Diablesse does take people soul in the night.

Mr Fin tie he donkey, Butch, on the electric pole by the road. Butch does graze on the patch of grass until Mr Fin ready to go home.

Mr Fin put down he cutlass on the step. The cutlass make a noise. Pling. Pling. Then he sit down in he usual seat on the floor, right in front the veranda gate.

"*Bon jé* Fin boy, you doh hear?" Mammy say.

"So who kick de bucket now ma?" Mr Fin ask Mammy.

"Dey say Maisie gone oui boy. Well ah doh have long again nuh. Hmm."

"Well all ah we behin you know. Not you alone," Mr Fin say.

"Bring de food for Fin nuh", Mammy call.

Mammy didn't call no name but I know is me that does bring the food. And where you see Rally studying he kite, nobody could make him move. So I don't wait for Mammy to say it twice. I jump up and run for the food. I nearly fall on top Rally.

"Gurl watch whey you goin nuh!" Rally say.

"Well sorry nuh!" I say.

And vexness start to spread on he face. He could get vex easy too much.

"A a. Tank you doodoo," Mr Fin say when I give him the bowl of rice and dhal. Mr Fin hand look as if he dig up yam with them and he never wash out the mud. Everything about Mr Fin look as if they doesn't see water. He hat and he old stain-up clothes look as if you could scrape out the muck from them.

"Bring a spoon for me please eh doodoo," Mr Fin say.

"You doh see is a *cocoyaya* what dey! What he go eat with, eh? He finger?" Mammy bark at me.

I run back in the kitchen to get the spoon and I mash Belle. She meow and jump in Rally lap.

"Cocoyaya, you can watch whey you puttin you foot!" Rally shout. He pick up Belle and rub she fur.

"Me is not no cocoyaya. An ah go tell Daddy eh! He done tell you not to call me name aready."

Belle meow again she watch me with she green eyes.

"You caan see she always lying down in people foot?"

I feel sorry I mash Belle. And I feel sorry I does push her down from the bed too.

I bring a dent up spoon for Mr Fin, just like the dent-up bowl Mammy have special for him. I hold me breath when I reach by Mr Fin because he smelling rank, like a ram goat.

"Niiice chile. You is a niiice chile man!" Mr Fin say. And I smile for him. And I hold Mr Fin niiice chile and me smile tight tight. I hold it just like I does hold me Joe Gum in me mouth without chewing it. So when Rally chewing up his and all the sweetness gone, I does still have mine in me mouth, holding the nice sweetness.

"A a? What nice chile? You doh see is cocoyaya wha dey?" Mammy say. And just so Mammy just come and grab it from me, just like when me teacher make me spit out me Joe Gum before I swallow all me nice sweetness. And she snatch back the smile Mr Fin give me too.

I sit down on the floor by Papa room door, watching Mr Fin eat. I can't see him good because he black as night, but I could picture him gobbling up the food, quick quick, just like Miss Kay dog Blackie. As if he afraid Mammy go change she mind and take it back. He spoon up every grain of rice and then he scrape the bowl with his crack-up, muddy fingers and lick them too.

But that's the only thing Mr Fin does do fast. He does walk slow. Come down from the donkey slow. And Mr Fin does talk as if he searching for he words and them in the dark, with a searchlight with dead battery.

"Papa, boy? Ah tink ah going to dat funeral tomorrow you know." Mammy say.

"Well yes," Papa say, in he sing-song soft pawpaw voice."

"Ah will have to go down and stay by Uncle Alfie," She say.

"You go sleep down then?" Papa ask. He scratching he leg through he socks. Papa always scratching he leg. Grup. Grup. Grup. Papa legs had a lot of bumps on them. He legs look as if he get cold bumps - some big big ones and then they forget to go down. They just stay on he legs and get hard hard and real rough.

"Well whey ah getting bus to come back dat hour?"

"Well yea. Dat make sense." Mr Fin just jump up. He was nodding away.

"We could make it without Mammy for a night man. What you say Reenie?" Papa watching me and he grinning. He grinning and scratching. Grup grup grup.

"Um hm," I say. But I wondering who going to make tea for us. And who go light the lamp in the night when Mammy go in she funeral all down in Florida. Down St John.

"Eh eh. Move from there Peeya!" Mammy say. "Somebody talking to you?"

Mammy didn't see me sitting down by Papa door.

"Well leave her nuh. She en doing nothing," Papa say. Papa say it careful careful, as if he fraid he words go pelt across the veranda and hit Mammy in she face. Break she glasses. He say it as if is egg he laying and he afraid it go fall and break.

And I sit down there, a cry *jooking* me eyes. Rally in the hall with he kite. Belle on the floor by him. And I waiting for Mammy to pick up Papa words and pelt them back like stones.

Butch bray. Grazing and plopping down donkey mess by the road. Mr Fin get up. Cutlass scrape step.

"Ah makin a move down de road eh."

Gate scrape floor. Rusty bolt in hole. Papa still scratching. Grup grup grup.

Chapter 5

Me And Papa

Papa don't go up to the mountain because Mammy going to the funeral down in St John. He just go down in the garden by the house to feed the cow. Papa does call the cow Betty. She big and fat and Papa say she dropping just now.

Rally go with Boyo and Lano to tie out their goats and I stay and watch Mammy get ready for she funeral.

Mammy put on she mauve funeral dress and she little white shoes, like the shoes nurses wear.

"Beti, go and bring Mammy teeth for her nuh," Mammy call.

I run in the hall, climb up on a chair to reach the bottle with Mammay false teeth on the safe. The teeth and them floating in slimy water and the bottle had *lallie* in the bottom. I hold the bottle real careful while I climb down the chair; if I throw it down Mammy go call me a stupidee.

Mammy dip she hand in the water and take out the teeth. She pour some powder in the drain on the teeth and then she press one down on she bottom gum and one on she top gum. And as soon as Mammy put on she false teeth, they full up Mammy mouth. They full up she face and just so Mammy look like somebody else.

Next Mammy powder she face and then she put on she white hat with the flowers on it, and the piece of netting falling over she face. And she fasten it with hair pins. She tie up she money in she white handkerchief, with the little red flowers all round the corners, and push it down inside she bosom.

Papa come back just as Mammy ready to leave.

"Behave all you self eh," Mammy say, even though is just me alone that there. And she teeth clack clack together. And Mammy mouth look as if it full up with something she want to spit out.

"Ah go ask Ken to come and keep all you company tonight eh," Mammy say. Then she fix she handbag on she shoulder, ready to go.

"A a. Doh worry youself. We go make it man," Papa say. He sit down in front of the kitchen floor pulling out he water boots.

"Well ah go see all you tomorrow eh," Mammy say and then she leave she Alcolado and powder smell all over the house when she go.

"Reenie, come and pull out Papa socks for him," Papa call.

I like to do things for Papa but I don't like to pull out he socks at all. Papa socks always wet wet and they does stick up on he foot. And they smelling wet and dirty, just like he water boots.

"Ok Papa. Ah comin just now eh."

I downstairs the house, digging up the boxes of books that me auntie leave when she go back in England. I could only go in them when Mammy not there. If Mammy see me she go ask me what I digging up there for.

The books and them old old and full of dust. The pages brown and feel as if they go rip if I touch them too hard. And they spotty spotty, as if flies mess up on them. The smell does tickle me nose and make me sneeze, but I like to take them out of the box and pack them up, one on top the other to make a tower. And I like to watch the pictures and try to read the words.

"Reenie, you comin?" Papa call me again.

I run to the kitchen. I pinch Papa socks with the tip of me fingers. I stop breathing. Pull out one sock. Then the next one. Quick quick. And I fling them on the step in the sun. Then I start to breathe again.

"And when you finish go an bring me shaving box for me eh," Papa say. "Ah tink ah go take a shave today."

Papa rub he face and I could hear he face grating on he hand. When Papa don't shave, the little white hairs does turn to prickle on he face. And he face does feel rough like *zebapique* bush.

I skip up the steps to the veranda and then to Papa bedroom. The wooden shaving case old! One hinge break and the other one ready to fall out. I hold it real careful and walk down the steps, one at a time. I put the case on Papa table. Then I bring the basin with some water for Papa.

"Take you time eh," Papa say.

And I taking me time but me hand trembling and the water shake up and fall on the floor. And I glad Mammy not there.

"But Reenie you is a good gurl oui," Papa tell me when I put down the basin on the table. Papa does never make me eyes and me chest hurt like Mammy.

I sit down on me little pirha watching Papa take out he things from the shaving box and rest them down by the basin: the straight razor, Gillette shaving stick, the brush, Palmolive soap stick and a new razor blade from the little packet. He hand shaking like a leaf. Next, Papa take out the piece of leather strop, and rub he razor on it until the razor get real shiny. After that, Papa splash some water on his face. Rub soap on it. Papa been using that soap long long, but it still look as if it would never finish. He have some new ones in he room, with shiny new paper, waiting patiently for that one to finish. I wonder if go ever get to use it.

The soap make fluffy, white froth when Papa rub it on he face. It look like ice cream and it smell nice! I want to scoop up some with me finger and lick it up, just like me and Rally does lick up the butter and sugar when Mammy making cake.

"Hold the mirror for Papa now Reenie."

I hold up the mirror for Papa. The mirror have red plastic around it and a picture of a lady on the back. And the lady look as if she watching me. She eyes look the same colour as the sea. She eyelash look as if she put black mud on them. She hair look like wash-out yellow, like me little, old baby blanket. And she lips thin thin, like the white lady up the road. It have a name on the bottom of the picture. *Lucy*.

"Hold it up a little higher Reenie."

I hold up the mirror. Me hands getting tired. And Lucy only watching me watching me.

Papa drag the razor on he face. He hand still trembling bad. I watch the razor make a road on he face and the grating noise make cold bumps on me skin.

"It smooth now eh," Papa say, dragging he hand all over he face, when he finish.

"Um hm." Papa face don't feel like he shoe brush again. I run inside for the Limacol, for him to splash on he face.

Outside looking dark early, because every time the sun try to shine, the clouds blocking it. Me, Yvette and Marie playing hopscotch in the road. Rally still out with he friends and them. Mammy not there so I stay outside longer.

"Reenie, you ain' comin and scratch Papa back for him today?" Papa call.

I like how Papa words does came out soft, like over-ripe pawpaw. Even when Mammy cursing him with she sour *gospo* words and them, Papa words does still come out soft.

"Ah comin just now Papa," I answer, even though game nice and I not ready to go inside yet.

"Marie leh we go home now eh," Yvette say. "We go play again tomorrow eh?" They run home.

Papa bedroom tiny. The bed narrow narrow, and I sure if Papa turn too hard in the night, he go fall down on the floor. He have a big trunk by the bed-foot - like the trunk in Mammy room - with all he new clothes that he son in England send for him. Papa say that's he funeral clothes, but I never see Papa go to a funeral yet. He always in he stain up old clothes. And when he change he old clothes, he always put on he blue and white pyjamas, the ones with the stripes that make him look like a zebra. And he have a lot in he trunk you know, but every Saturday Mammy does wash them, and Papa does put on the same old one again.

Papa little dressing table have all kinds of things on it: Limacol and Alcolado. Papa does rub them on he skin after he bathe and sap he head when he have a headache; Canadian Healing Oil – Mammy say it good for sprain; Vaseline Petroleum Jelly and tins of Vicks Vapour rub and a lot of other rusty, dusty, old things.

I pour some coconut oil in me hand. Whole evening the sun shining in Papa room so the oil warm. And it smelling so nice I feel to lick it. I always feeling to lick things that smelling nice. When the rain fall on the hot dust in the yard, I does kneel down on the ground and lick it.

Mammy does make she own coconut oil. Then she does grate nutmeg in it, and put mash up mace and cloves, Vicks and camphor in it. And when me and Rally have cold and fever, she does rub us with it too.

I rub the oil on Papa head and scratch it with he little black comb, with the mash up teeth. Papa head round. The top clean clean. But he have a row of soft grey Indian hair at the back of he head. I rub he head until it shiny and smooth like a marble.

"Scratch Papa back for him now Reenie," Papa say.

I raise up Papa pyjama shirt and scratch the side he pointing. Papa skin look like the piece of leather he does rub he razor on. I rub coconut oil on it too and then I scratch it with the comb so me finger nails won't full up with dirtiness from Papa back.

"Here Papa?" I ask him.

"A likkle to the right. Go down a likkle bit. Lower down. Aahhh! Dat's it! Yees, right dere Reenie. Aaahhhh!"

I scratch Papa back until the comb teeth make long tracks on him.

"Dat's it. Boy, scratch sweet oui! Scratch it a likkle more."

I scratch Papa back until it get red and he say, "Dat good now Reenie. Dat good."

I leave Papa scratching he legs and go in the hall. Papa always scratching he legs. When he in the kitchen eating, is *grup, grup, grup*. In he bed, *grup, grup, grup*. I glad Papa dosen't ask me to rub he legs, because I fraid to touch them. I just pour the oil in he hand for him and he does rub them for heself.

Chapter 6

Under The Table

Outside black as pitch. Papa in the veranda, even though Mammy not there. Mr Fin don't stop that evening either. He just slow down to ole talk with Papa a little bit, then Butch trot down the road, clippity clop, clippity clop, with Mr Fin legs bouncing against Butch big, full belly.

Me and Rally in the hall, me favourite room in the house. I sit down by the little mahogany table, by we bedroom door. Mammy have a table in every corner of the hall and all of them have a vase with plastic flowers on them. The flowers and them cover with dust and fly mess.

Rally on the floor by the new cabinet with the glass door, that Mammy buy one Christmas, from Kirpalani's store in Town. The cabinet full of new wares: plates, teacups and saucers, shiny silver spoons, knives, forks and all kind of glasses-- tall ones and little shot glasses, a big set with pictures of aces, queens, kings and jack cards, a set with gold and silver rims and another set with pretty pictures of birds, flowers and ladybirds on them. But the only time Mammy does use anything from the cabinet is when she have a special visitor, like the priest from she church or Miss Kay daughter from Canada. Then she does send me for a glass from the cabinet, to give them some soft drink.

"Doh run and break me glass you know Peeya!" Mammy does say. And I always take the one from the set with the Kiskadee birds, with the pretty brown feathers and yellow chest. I like them the best. Otherwise, the wares just there gathering dust and cobweb, until

Christmas when Mammy wash them and pack them right back in the cabinet.

"A a, you come man," I hear Papa say the same time I hear the footsteps on the veranda.

"Mammy say Miss Millie go to funeral so she sen me and stay with all you tonight."

Ken living down the road and he does come and help Mammy and Papa sometimes. He short and stumpy and everything about Ken black; even the palm of he hands. He hands so dark you could hardly see the lines in them. Ken eyes black as starapple seeds. And they always moving about fast, fast. He skin always shiny with sweat and he feet hard as the road, because he and shoes not friends at all.

Rally on the floor counting he marbles, putting the old ones in a old sock Papa give him, and the shiny, new ones and the *cocoateas* - the ones that look like cocoa and milk mixed up - in a special tin.

I reading me *Nelson's New West Indian Reader*. It had cockroach eggs on it when I take it down from the shelf. It used to be me Auntie Liz book.

Auntie Liz is me mother sister. They have the same mother but different father. She's the one with the long straight hair in the picture on the partition. And she skin look white as Queen Elizabeth the Second, in the picture that next to Auntie Liz.

Mammy have a lot of pictures on the partition. In one of the pictures, Auntie Liz look dress up as if she going to a dance. She have on a white mini dress with black dots on it. Mammy call it a polka dot dress. And Auntie Liz timble-heel shoes pointy pointy. The toes pointy. And the heel so pointy I was sure if Auntie Liz walk in the hall with them, they boring holes in Mammy board flooring. And Mammy always looking at that picture and saying, "She prutty eh! You doh see how she white like the queen!

Dat's me pruttiest grandchile!"

It have a small picture of me grandmother before she go to England - looking real happy with she big wide smile. But me favourite picture is the one with Auntie Liz, me mother, Uncle Lionel, Uncle Lennie and Auntie Reenie. All of them dress up in their school uniform. And me mother have on a beret.

Papa look just like a spirit standing up by the front door with all the darkness around him.

"Ah tink ah goin in now. All you will go in just now eh. And don' forget to out the lamp nuh,' he say.

Ken come inside the hall when Papa go in he room. He sit down on Mammy new Morris chair with he sweaty self. He lucky Mammy not there because she doesn't even let me and Rally sit down on the new chairs. Mammy buy them the same time she buy the cabinet. Mammy keeping them for special visitors, just like the pretty glasses in the cabinet.

"Ah beat Lano an dem backside today!" Rally telling Ken. Showing off he marbles.

Ken laugh. "Ah know. Boyboy still vex," he say. "All you playin tomorrow again?"

"How you mean! Ah ready for dey backside. Ah giving dem real blows!" Rally say, and he jingling he sock of marbles.

Rally could pitch marble real good. He does grip he *ta* - the one he using to pitch - between he stumpy little thumb and the finger he used to suck, and pitch real hard. He could aim so straight, sometimes he does hit three marbles out of the ring in one go. He like to play for take, and when he win, he does walk around with he sock of marbles tied to he pants loops, bouncing up and down he leg; showing off.

I put me head back in me book. *The Caribs had round, flat faces*. I watch the picture of Auntie Liz. She face round and flat too, like a Carib. *The Caribs were fierce, warlike people and the Arawaks were peaceful.*

"What dey mean by fierce?" I ask Ken.

Ken get up from the new chair and he come and sit down on the chair by me. He smell like a goat.

"Dat mean they like to fight," he say. And he looking in me book as if he reading. Ken doesn't go to school again. He leave school in standard six so he could help he mother and father work land.

"Dem Carib and dem was cannibal you know. Dem wretch and dem used to eat people and all oui!" Ken say.

How people could eat people? I don't understand that but I like reading about the Caribs and them. I like watching the pictures in the book too. In one picture, the Caribs and the Arawaks fighting with cutlass and knife and all kinds of weapons. And in another picture the Caribs jumping over *Leapers Hill* when the French chasing them. That is right by me school. And I imagine them Caribs and Arawaks walking about and fighting in the same pasture behind the school, where we does play during break time. We teacher say that's why tourists always coming up there. She say it is a historical site.

We does watch the tourist and them in their straw hats and their cameras around their neck, taking pictures. Some of the men have on sandals and socks, in the big hot sun! And the ladies look as if they draw on their lips with pencil crayons. And is as if they never see children like us before, because they always taking out pictures of us. But people always telling us we should never let tourists take pictures of us, because we don't know what they doing with them. I wish I was brave like the other children, who does run up to them and pose with their hands on their waist and grinning their teeth for the camera, because the tourists does give them money: shiny twenty-five cents or fifty cents that they use to buy snow ice and popcorn in the Snackette.

Blackie, Miss Kay dog, bark down the road. Blackie does bark at everything. If a fowl pass, Blackie barking. If a fly pass, Blackie barking. I never see a dog that like to bark so! Blackie does even bark at he own shadow.

Rally teasing Belle with the sock of marbles; putting it in front of her then pulling it back. And Belle springing after it.

The hall look dim all of a sudden. It look as if the kerosene in the lamp finishing. Papa let Rally light the lamp as Mammy not there. Mammy always full up all the lamps before they run out of kerosene. Maybe the wick need changing.

Rally drag the sock on the floor again and Belle leap after it. She catch it. Rally pull it from Belle claws.

Ken still sit down on the chair by me. He smokey sweat smell in me nose.

The lamp blinking. The shadows on the partition growing. Moving.

Something on me leg. Crawling up on me leg.

Oh gosh! What on me leg dey?

I shake me leg. The thing stop. Is not a cockroach. It pressing down on me leg. Cockroach does tickle. It crawl up by me leg again. It crawl up between me legs. Me skin raise. It crawl under me panty leg. I want to get up but I feel just like when I stay on the toilet too long and me legs sleeping.

When I jump up, I run in the room and sit down on the pail. The pee not coming out. I force and force. A little bit drip out. It burning me like when I wash up with Lux soap. I want to go and wash up in me little basin behind the house. But outside dark and I fraid. And I fraid to ask Rally to go with me. He go ask me what I want to go outside in the dark night for.

Belle come in the room. She come up by the pail and rub up on me leg. I don't push her away.

Rally come in the room and pick up Belle.

"Wha' happen to you?" He ask me.

"Nuttin."

"You goin an sleep aready?"

"Um hm."

I sit down on the pail until me leg fall asleep.

Ken sleep on the bed with us. He sleep in the front. Rally sleep in the back, close to the partition. And I in the middle. I wish I could exchange with Rally. I jam up close, close to Rally. And I glad he sleeping sound, so he can't say, "Go up some more nuh gurl!" Because I don't want to go up some more.

Me eyes open whole time. And Ken perspiration in me nose.

I dream Daddy come back from Aruba and when I tell him about Ken, he push Ken over the precipice in Celeste. The high high precipice- the one where all the kites does stick up in trees, twine tie up between vine, tail hanging on the branch and them, because all them boys fraid to board. And Ken bawling, "Ah din do nuttin Mr Feneh! Ah din do nuttin!" And he falling down the precipice.

When I wake up Ken gone. Rally snoring. Me nightie wet. The bed soaking too. I go outside and stoop down over me little basin of water.

Chapter 7

Red Water Boots

Mammy sit down on the pirha, naked as she was born, with the bath pan in front her, between she legs. And she legs open wide wide, as if she catching fly! The only thing covering Mammy naked self is she hair. She look just like a mermaid, with she hair spread out on she back and all down to she *bamsie*.

On Saturdays, Mammy does bathe outside in the yard. Me and Rally does put water in the bath pan and leave it out in the sun to warm up. And when the sun move, we have to move the pan round the yard to catch the sun.

"Beti come an scrub Mammy back for her nuh", Mammy call from behind the house.

"Ah comin Mammy," I say. I downstairs again in Auntie Liz books. And even though Mammy always making me shame, I still running and do everything she say.

"Come, Beti. Take the corn stick and scrub Mammy back."

Mammy gather up she hair and put it over one shoulder. She hair fall over she flat *taytay*. Mammy taytay so flat, they look like two ripe zabouca that fall down from a tall tree and flatten on the ground. And she bamsie flat flat too, as if she does sit down too much.

The concrete feel wet and warm under me bare feet. I gather up the front of me dress and stick it between me legs, so it wouldn't get wet. And I start to scrub Mammy back with the old corn stick.

Mammy legs and she arms tough and dry like the skin on a fowl foot, but she back and she bamsie look soft and smooth, like baby skin.

"Scrub it hard nuh," Mammy say.

So I scrub harder.

"Yes, harder. Go up some more. Yes, scrub it right dey. Scrub it hard. Scrub it hard."

And me hand tired! But I scrub and scrub. I scrub Mammy back with all me little strength, but she still want me to scrub it harder, as if she can't feel.

"It good now?"' I ask Mammy, because me hand tired and the hot concrete starting to burn me feet.

"Soap it up for me now," Mammy say, and she rub the Carbolic soap on she panty and give me to soap she back. And I don't know why Mammy doesn't use a rag because I don't like to touch she panty at all.

I rub she back until it full of pink froth. Then when I bend down to rinse out me hands in the bath pan, me eyes fall between Mammy legs. I pull back me head quick quick, before Mammy say I rude. One time when I was rubbing Papa back, I see he little squinge-up willie too, but it didn't have no straight grey hair like Mammy.

When Mammy finish bathing, she wipe up sheself with the dress she just take out. The same dirty dress she have on whole week. Even though she have a whole set of new towels in the trunk. Then she put on the dress and go inside.

I in the back of the house emptying out the soapy water from the pan and watching it run down between the fence, pass the cocoa trees and down to the pear tree.

Rover start barking. Rover come from a worker on the estate where Papa is the Overseer. Rover look like a real wolf dog. He have grey fur. He ears black, and he have black patches on he belly and he legs. The day Papa bring Rover home he say, "Rally boy, look what Papa bring for you." And Papa grinning at Rally. And I know Papa say that, because he know how much Rally like animals.

"Miss Milleeey. Ah passin." Porridge call from the road.

I empty the water real quick, turn down the bath pan and dash up in front the yard.

Rover barking and running up the bank of the yard. He know Porridge so he not growling. He just barking to let us know somebody in the yard.

"What you have today?" Mammy ask him. She just come out from she room and she have on she Saturday dress. It not as old as the ones she does wear to go in the mountain. But she don't have on shoes. Mammy does never wear shoes when she home. She don't have on she glasses either and she looking real nice, with she wet hair hanging down round she face.

"Man ah have everyting today!" Porridge say, coming down the bank, with he grip on he head.

Porridge does pass round on Saturdays selling all kinds of nice things. And he does stop by every house - by Miss Jean down the road, even though she don't have to buy nothing because she children in America; by Auntie Jeanette veranda, to show her the new church shoes because she like to dress up real nice when she going to church; and then he stop by Miss Kay before he reach by us.

"Come down, come down," Mammy tell him.

She sit down on the bench in the kitchen combing she wet hair. She put coconut oil in it and she combing it from the back to the front, so all she hair fall down over she face. Then she comb it to the side, over she left shoulder.

Papa by he table with a big grin on he face, waiting for Porridge.

Porridge take he time coming down the steps. He

holding on to he old grip with one hand and the side of the house with the other hand. He does carry he grip on he head without holding it, just like how Mammy does carry she bucket of nutmegs. And he always have on he khaki shirt-jack inside he khaki pants, pants waist tie up with a piece of string and pants legs roll up, as if he going and cross a river. He old brown shoes look too big for him and he brown hat look like something rat bite up.

I does smell Porridge even before reach by the kitchen; just like I does smell Mr Fin before he even reach the veranda. Porridge smell as if he clothes come out under a mattress, with old bedding.

I plant meself on the step. I restless, as if me bamsie full of *jigger*. I can't wait for Porridge to open up the grip, to see all them nice things he does have. Rally behind the kitchen interfering with the chickens and making the mother hen vex.

Porridge put the grip down on the kitchen floor and he sit down in front the door. He take out he hat, put it on the floor and scratch he head - it bald like Papa head, with some grey hair sticking out on the top.

"Papa, how tings man?" Porridge ask.

"Well ah dey holding on boy," Papa say, smiling.

"Well what else you go do? You have to hold on yes Pa. You have to hold on."

Mammy ask Porridge if he want some juice.

"Well yea mammy! Dat sun real hot today!" Porridge say. "It go cool me down a likkle bit."

"Beti, come an take some juice for Porridge," Mammy say.

I have to pass over Porridge foot to go inside the kitchen.

"How you do darlin? You good?" Porridge ask, as if he just see me. He grinning like Papa. And he looking real funny because he face wrinkle up like a force ripe mango skin. And he don't have no teeth. And Rally say he sure a rammer pass on Porridge nose, fuss he nose flat.

I pour out some juice in a white enamel cup and little bits of dirtiness float up on top. Mammy does sweeten the juice with brown sugar and she doesn't even strain it. She does just skim out the lime seeds with a spoon. One time I even see her taking out the seeds with she fingers.

"Dat's a nice gurl," Porridge say when I give him the cup. He gulp down the juice, gluck gluck gluck, in one go, he throat moving up and down like a snake.

"Ahhhhh! Ah feel better now. Tank you eh doodoo." Porridge give me the empty cup.

"You want some food?" Mammy ask him.

"Well yes man, if you have," he say.

And I know he done eat by people down the road already, because *Never Refuse* is he next name.

Mammy raise up sheself from the bench, as if she raising something real heavy.

"Oh bon jé oh! Dat knee go kill me oui mama!" She hold on to she knee.

"Aa. You knee givin trouble too? Mine does play it want to knock me down sometimes. But ah not givin up for it at all. Put saffron on it. Dat's what does give me a ease up oui!" Porridge tell Mammy. And when she give him the plate, if you see grin! "But Miss. Millie you is a good lady you know."

And I there waiting for him to open the grip but he eating slow slow. And I wondering how Porridge go eat the dumpling, but he cut them up as if he gum is teeth!

"Well girl, let me pinch you a likkle gossip nuh," Porridge say. And he start telling Mammy about he neighbour, who daughter come out from England. And how the woman work so hard under the cocoa to send she daughter in England. Now she come back and build a big

big mansion, while she mother still living in a little shack, all the way behind God back! Then he tell Mammy about how Miss Mary daughter pass well, because she getting married to "a school teacher oui!" And Mammy put in she two pence, saying how the teacher go "lif up she head from the mud." But Porridge say he hope she don't forget the mud she come out from. Then they talk about that good-for-nothing boy up the road, who don't want to work at all. "All de boy good for is to take he mother two pence when she sell she nutmeg. And de boy doesn't even help de woman to pick up de damn nutmeg you know! Ah Lord!"

And me jigger jooking bad. I itching for Porridge to open the grip. The last time, when Porridge pass, he had some red water boots in he grip. I wished Mammy buy them for me but she only buy something for Rally.

"Dat back and neck nice boy. Where you get nice meat so?" Porridge ask when he finish eating and scrape the bowl clean.

"By Mr Belton shop. He have some nice one this morning," Mammy tell him.

I don't like the stew chicken because Mammy cook it with all the fat and the skin, and all the oil floating on top of the gravy.

Then at last, Porridge open up the grip. And me eyes pop in me head. Porridge old grip just like a real treasure chest that you does see in pictures. He have all kinds of things in it and he know where to put he hand on everything.

"You have more in dose nice black panties today?" Mammy ask. And I know Mammy have one amount of new panties in the trunk in she room. Some of them still in the packet. So I don't know what Mammy asking Porridge if he have panties for. And she does never throw away those old raggy ones.

"How you mean if ah have panty. Ah have everyting inside here! Just say wat you want."

And he start to take out things from the grip: sheets, tablecloth, dungaree trousers, shirts, shoes, then he pull out a plastic bag full with panties. And I wondering how all that thing fit inside that little grip.

"Ah have black, blue, red. Any colour you want. Just say."

"Give me two in the big black ones."

"Ah have razor blades for Papa too. And ah have some nice water boots for the likkle one too," he say. "Come doodoo. Come and try it on."

He move some more things, then he pull out the water boots. And me little heart start to dance up. I jump down from the sofa. Me eyes stick on the water boots.

"Dey nice eh. You like dem?" Porridge ask me.

"Mm hmm," I say. He grinning and I grinning more.

The water boots bright red, like them hibiscus flowers. And they shining.

"Try dem on nuh doodoo," Porridge say.

I watch Mammy. She not looking at me. She finish plaiting she hair and she two long plaits lie down on she chest like an *Apache Indian*. Mammy watching Porridge but she not saying nothing.

I take the boots and sit down to try them on. The plastic feel smooth like glass and it smelling strong, like new balloons. I push me left foot in. Mammy say you must always try on the left side first because the left foot bigger than the right. I wiggle me foot in it. Stamp stamp, for me foot to go down. It fit me real nice. I put on the other side and I stand up for Porridge to see. Mammy watching but she still don't say anything yet.

"They nice eh? And it look like dey make dem jus for you, doodoo," Porridge say. "Walk round in the yard and see how dey feelin nuh."

So I step over Porridge and walk up and down the steps. Me eyes stick on the boots. And I grinning like a Cheshire cat. I imagine skipping down to the garden with Papa in me new boots; playing the potholes in the road when rain fall; walking in mud and all kinds of things in me water boots.

"You Mammy go buy them for you man," Porridge say.

"Fah who?" Mammy ask. "Fah that Peeya!"

I sit back down. Me heart stop dancing too.

Papa sitting there like a little lamb, watching Porridge and scratching he legs. Grup, grup, grup. I wish that Papa could buy them for me but he never have money. Any money Papa get from working in the mountain, he have to give Mammy.

Rally come in the kitchen when Porridge packing back the things. Mammy send him for she purse to pay for the panties and the green top he ask her for. I put down the water boots and I go downstairs with something jooking me chest.

That evening when I open the door to go and get the oil to rub Papa head, the sun shine on something red and shiny by Papa table. Me heart start to prance up and down.

That evening, I don't even go outside and play. I oil Papa head until it get shiny like the water boots. And when he say scratch he back, I scratch it until he tell me that enough. Me hands never even get tired.

"You coming wid Papa to see de calf tomorrow?" Papa ask. "You should see little Carrie, man. She frisky and she strong for so! You go put on you new boots eh."

Whole night I praying for tomorrow to hurry up.

Chapter 8

Indian Dance

I stand up by the road waiting for the Coke truck to come back down. I have the money in me hand and I skipping as if I have jigger in me feet. Every fortnight the truck does come up in Celeste to drop soft drinks for Auntie Sille shop and it stop by any house that have a an empty case out in the yard. But you have to look out though, because the driver, Mr Joe, doesn't waste any time waiting for nobody. And if I miss the truck, Mammy would call me a stupidee. And she go have to ask Jacko to buy the drinks for her when he go in Sauteurs.

Jacko is the driver for Mr and Mrs Goodman, the white people up the road. Mammy said he is their chauffeur. Mr and Mrs Goodman living in the big house with the swimming pool. And they have servants and three big dogs. They always had a lot of people going by them. One time they invite Mammy to a party and Daddy came to drop off some people. One minute we standing up with Mammy, next thing people start running and making noise. Then Daddy just grab me and Rally, push us in he car and drive off. Vex vex, like a bull. Afterwards, we hear people saying how the maid give Daddy some food and how Mr Goodman box down the plate of food out of Daddy hand and give Daddy one kick. They say Mr Goodman lucky they hold Daddy back, otherwise he woulda get it in he backside. Daddy say Mr Goodman is a wicked man!

As soon as I hear the truck and I see it bending the corner, I stick out me hand to flag it down even though I know Mr Joe could see me, and all the cases, big and bold by the road.

Mammy buying drinks for she Indian Dance. She buy three cases of Carib and three bottles of Clarks Court Rum from Mr Belton shop in Sauteurs already. She have them under the table in the hall, with the bottles of Johnny Walker whisky that Papa bring home from Mr Ramsingh shop. And Mammy announce the dance in she church already. She does go to the Presbyterian church in Samaritan every other Sunday or when something special happening. Mammy say this dance going to be a big one and that all of she people coming so she making big preparations.

Mr Joe slam the brakes and the truck pelt up gravels all on top the kitchen. As soon as he stop, Jummo, the helper, jump down from the truck like a cat. He pick up the empty cases, one in each hand, and throw them on top the mountain of cases on the back of the truck. Then he spring up on the truck again, like a monkey.

"Auntie Millieee," Mr Joe call from the driver seat.

"Oh boy!" Mammy answer from the kitchen.

"What for you today?" he shout to Mammy.

"Mammy want a case a Coke and a case a Fanta," I say same time as Mammy shout "Gimme a Coke an a Fanta." Mr Joe see me standing up right in front of he eyes with me money in me hand but he still asking Mammy what she want as if he think me is a stupidee!

Then he say, "You good darlin?" All the time I stand up there waiting and he doing as if he eyes just fall on me. "You brave man!" He say and smile at me. And I stand up there grinning and waiting for me favourite part, to give him the money.

Mr Joe don't come out of the truck. He just open the

door and rest he stumpy legs on the wheel. He pants legs pull up and I could see he red socks. He have on brown Clarks shoes like Daddy own, but his look real old. Mr Joe big belly sit down on he lap and he chin touching he chest as he press he little book on he knee to write.

"A Coke and a Fanta, in the back there," He shout for Jummo.

Jummo pick up the empty cases, heave them to the side of the truck, then jump down. He swing the full cases over the side and drop them on the bank of the road, as if they still empty. Then he jump back on the truck.

"What happen to you boy!" Mr Joe shout at Jummo. "Put them in the veranda for Auntie Millie nuh man."

So Jummo jump down again, pick up a case in each hand, and drop them down so hard, the bottles and them shake up and knock up one another. And I fraid they go break.

"Twenty-four dollars," Mr Joe say. He tear out the piece of paper and I give him the two new twenty dollars and wait for the change.

"So Auntie Millie, you all set for Saturday?" Mr Joe ask Mammy.

"Yea boy! Ah have everyting in order," Mammy answer.

"Well we go see Saturday den," he say and he hand me the change.

"Tanks Mr Joe." I say.

Mr Joe start up the truck but he doesn't speed down the road because Miss Kay and Uncle Dudley have soft drink cases out in their yard too.

Saturday morning Papa get up 'fore day morning, early early. Even before the cock and them start to crow, so he could slaughter the goats. Papa is a butcher and people always coming and get him to help them slaughter their cows and pigs, especially around Christmas time.

Mammy choose the two big rams. They look like the goats in the *Three Billy Goats* story. She say they still young so their bones not hard yet. And they have a lot of meat too.

Rally get up early too. He is Papa helper. He neck and neck with Papa, watching every move Papa make - from the time Papa tie up the rams, cut their throats and skin them. He passing the butcher knife to Papa, bringing buckets of water to wash down the blood and whatever else Papa ask him to do.

Me, I stay in the kitchen, peeping through the window and closing me eyes tight tight, when I can't stand to see what Papa doing. When Papa call me to come and help bring the meat inside and I smell the blood, me belly turn inside out. And me knees get weak.

The kitchen full of chopping, pounding, pots bubbling, talking, laughing and the whole place smell like curry and pepper and onions and all kinds of spices. And people passing by shouting, "Woy, dat curry smelling real good boy!"

Mammy and Papa is the only Indians living up in Celeste, so Mammy bring up some ladies from she church to help her cook.

I on the sofa watching everything. I have on me old home dress and me head-tie. Miss Kay daughter plait me hair in little cornrows and they look nice and neat, so I have to leave on the head tie until later. And I ready for when Mammy call me to go for some firewood from the back of the kitchen or to pick some peppers from the tree in the yard. I like the smells and all the noise in the kitchen, and how Mammy looking real happy, talking and laughing with she people.

Auntie Rita stir the rice in the big skillet then she pour the dhal from the iron pot in the big clay bowl so she could use the pot again. She is Mammy cousin. She short like Mammy, and round round. She have a big big bosom, and she does walk as if it too heavy for her. She have brown eyes and a big mole under she nose. The first time Mammy bring me by Auntie Rita and Uncle Prince, I remember how Auntie Rita watch me from head to foot, and how she say, "But Auntie Millie, she en take nuttin from your side at all nuh! She is pee pee she father oui!" But if you watch Mammy, you would never think she is me great-grandmother at all.

Mammy put Sister Deharry in charge of the dhal puree. Sister Deharry tall and thin like a stick. Mammy say she is five years older than her, but Sister Deharry look older than everybody. She have eleven children and Mammy say she have the most grandchildren in Samaritan. She grey hairs peeping out from under she head-tie, and she toes spread out like a fan under she dress.

Sister Deharry have long, bony fingers, and the rolling pin move real smooth over the dhal puri. She rolling and passing them to Lyntie to toss on the *tawa*.

Lyntie tiny! And she skin smooth like a Ceylon Mango. She have on a long green dress and she have one plait hanging down she back just like a cattail flower. I wish I have long hair like hers so Mammy could rub it with coconut oil and plait it like a cattail too.

"All you doh know who get married de other day?" She ask. She talking so much, she forget to turn the puri.

"Lyntie, study what you doing nuh!" Sister Deharry tell her. So she turn it quick. The puri puff up, but I could smell it burning.

"You know she can't stop talking already. Ah sure dat girl eat parrot bambam!" Auntie Rita say through she nose.

"Oh gosh, sorry! Lyntie say. She pick up the wood pallette and she waiting for the next one.

"All you know Miss Bella second daughter?" Lyntie ask.

"You mean de ugly one who does walk funny?" Auntie Rita ask.

"Yea, de one with the funny foot. Well de girl get married the other day oui!" Lyntie say. But she remember to turn the puri this time before it burn.

"So who married her then?" Sister Deharry ask. She stop rolling and she watching Lyntie, waiting for the answer.

"You mean Bella Ramsawan daughter?" Mammy ask. Mammy cutting up young pawpaw to put in the pot of mutton. It cooking on the fireside behind the kitchen since early morning.

"She married to dis ole man down St John oui! He wife dead and dey say he full a money. He have a lot of nutmeg land." Lyntie say.

"A a! Well who de tink she woulda ever leave she mother house!" Auntie Rita say.

"Well she doh play lucky nuh! She mother doh have to worry about nuttin again." Sister Deharry say. "Ah wish one a mine could pass well so!"

Rita put the puri on the plate. The pile getting so high it look as if it go capsize.

"Hm! Lucky!" Lyntia say. "Mammy better doh think she making me married no ole man just because he have nutmeg land nuh! I want to go in England and study nursing."

Everybody want to go in England or America. Yvette mother in Aruba, but she want to go in America. Marie want to go in England. And I wondering how come all me mother brothers and sisters in England, but she in Aruba.

All where you turn, it have a pot on fire. Mammy does cook every part of the goat - the head and the balls and all. Papa roast the head and feet and then he scrape off the hairs for Mammy to make *manish waters* with them. Then she wrap-up the goat balls in banana leaf, tie it with a string and put it under the hot ashes to bake. She say that's only for the men and does make sure Rally get piece, as if he is a man. And so the goat balls look soft and nasty, but I still want to taste it.

"Gimme a taste nuh," I tell to Rally.

"You doh hear Mammy say da's not for you."

"Jus a likkle piece nuh", even though it don't look like nothing to eat.

"Look, look!" Rally say. And he give me a little pinch.

But as soon as it touch me mouth, I spit it out.

"Oh geed!" I dash behind the house to wash out me mouth, over and over and over.

By the time the bus load of Mammy people reach, everything ready. Mammy spread new table cloths on the tables and the ladies lay out the food.

The men set up their band in the veranda to practice. They have banjos, an accordion, the tassa drum and a dholak drum. And the ladies beat the tambourines.

I wonder why Mammy never even invite Miss Kay to she dance, because they good good friends. Still it have a lot of limers. They come from up the road and down the road and from Marli, La Mode and even Chantimelle. Anywhere it have music and food, the limers does find their way there and hang about by the roadside to watch and see if they lucky to get some food too.

By the time outside get dark, the dance in full swing with Mammy people singing their Indian songs, dancing and clapping. The women gather in the centre of the yard, hands on their hips, waist swinging, feet stamping, shuffling, clapping and ankle bells jingling. The men drinking and singing real loud and when it was too dark they move inside. And the whole house full of people and music and the smell of curry goat.

Papa look real jolly wearing a new shirt from he trunk and he crimplene pants. They still crease up and smelling like camphor balls. He even put on he leather shoes; the one he does polish every Saturday, shine with he shoe brush and then put back under the dressing table.

Rally stay out in the yard with Lano and Boyboy. He showing them how to do the Indian dance and they laughing and trying to do it like him.

I in Mammy room by the window, watching everything. I bathe and Mammy let me put on me nice red and yellow dress.

The hall full of colours. The ladies have on pretty-colour saris, gold bangles, a lot of beads hanging round their necks, rings on their fingers and even on their noses. And the men have on pretty-colour shirts.

The music so nice and I wish I could dance too. I want to go in the middle of the hall and spin around and show them me pretty dress. I want to show them how I could do the Indian dance, because sometimes when Mammy feeling jolly, she does dance in the kitchen and I does watch her good.

Mammy on the Morris chair clapping she little hands and stamping she bare feet. She singing and clapping and next thing she in the middle of the floor, she hand on she belly and she waist going left to right. Side to side. She shuffling she feet and turning around, real slow. Just so Mammy turn into somebody else.

One of the men spin her round and round. And Mammy laugh and laugh and laugh. I never hear Mammy laugh so yet. I wish Mammy never stop laughing.

"Beta, come and show dem how you could dance nuh," Mammy call Rally. He stand up in the veranda watching.

"Yes Sir Rally. Show us what you could do," one of

the men say. Rally run on the floor, put one hand on he belly and the other one on the back of he head, how Mammy showed him. Then he do a fast fast little dance and dash outside. And everybody clap and laugh. I wish Mammy call me to dance too so everybody could laugh and clap for me too.

When the dance over, and Mammy people pack up and go, Rally and he friends by the road eating and tempting the limers. They moving in closer to see if it have left-overs.

"Eh, Rally, pass some roti nuh?" Somebody call out.

"And some rice and curry-goat too?"

Then Mammy come outside.

"Whey all you going? It doh have nuttin for all you."

It still have a lot of food there, so I don't know why Mammy say that. She always giving the neighbours things. When Miss Dora send she grandson for some kerosene to put in she lamp, Mammy does send Rally for the big gallon bottle to pour some for him. And when Miss Joyce send for "a likkle bit ah milk please," or "a piece a onion to put in de pot," Mammy does always send some for her. But it look like she rather leave the food to spoil. And then in the morning she giving the pigs instead.

Mammy even sing a little song for them. *Nigger come for roti, all de roti done!* But Rally and he friends change up the words, and say *nigger pick up a machine gun and all the coolie run.*

Chapter 9

Daddy Come back

The sun just starting to go down. Mammy gone and bring some bitter bush for Miss Dora, because she have the cold and fever. And Papa down in the garden feeding the cow. I did not go with Papa because I have to hold the hose in the barrel for it to full up before the water stop again. Sometimes Mammy does put a heavy piece of wood on the hose to hold it down, but we still had to watch it because as soon as you turn your back, the barrel fulling up fast fast and overflowing.

The hose jump out of me hand when I hear it. Water pitch on the floor and hide between the floor boards. I sure is Daddy whistle I just hear. But how I could hear Daddy whistle if he all overseas in Aruba? Maybe is a bird. Then I hear it again. Then I hear a car door close. Me heart jump out of me chest same time the hose jump out from me hand. I close the pipe fast and speed out of the kitchen. And up the steps.

"Daddy come back! Daddy come back!"

Daddy car in front of the house and he stand up there waiting for me. Well me feet turn to wings. I take off like a jet plane and fly into Daddy with full speed. Good thing he leaning up on the car because I nearly knock him down.

Three months since Daddy gone. Now he just stand up right there leaning up on he car, in he brand new clothes, smiling and he gold teeth shining.

"What say now Lee?" Daddy ask. Daddy squeeze me and kiss me and kiss me. And I wrap up me legs around

61

Daddy waist. I glad I wash up and change me clothes already because I don't even bother about bending back me feet. I just grip Daddy neck tight and press me face down hard.

"So you good?" Daddy ask. I don't even answer Daddy. I fraid to speak, because something stick in me throat, like a piece of dry coconut. And I could feel the water fulling up behind me eyes, like the barrel in the kitchen. And I know that if I only open me mouth, it go overflow like the barrel.

Daddy try to hold me so he could see me face but I latch on to him like the yam vine on the breadfruit tree. So Daddy just hold me, just so.

"So you glad Daddy come back?" Daddy ask. He still leaning up on the car holding me.

"Um hm," I still don't open me mouth, because the piece of coconut still in me throat.

Then I see Rally speeding up the road.

"Look Rally comin," I say. And the piece of coconut just slip down. I let go Daddy neck so he could put me down if he want. In case he want to raise up Rally too, even though he too big for raise now.

Rally run by Daddy and lean up on the car by him. He stoop down and hug Rally with one arm. And is a good thing Daddy don't raise up Rally because he clothes full of mango stain and he feet dirty with dust!

"So what the man say?" Daddy ask him.

"Ah dey," Rally say.

Rally push he hands in he pockets. He take them out. He put them in he pockets again. And he only watching the ground.

"Wha happen man? You en growin or what. You letting Lee come and pass you down!" Daddy say, rumpling Rally head. Rally laugh. He kick the ground with he bare toes. He take eight years April gone and I taking seven in July, but we almost the same height.

"Come on, let's go for a spin up the road," Daddy say.

And I ready to cry again because I know going for a spin mean as soon as we come back, Daddy going.

Me and Rally fit in on the front seat. Daddy speed up the road. He zoom pass Miss Dora house, Miss Joyce house, up the hill, pass Mr Broko and then he turn in the junction. Rally sit down on the edge of the seat, holding the dashboard. And he grinning and waving to everybody we pass. But Daddy drive back slow. When we reach by Miss Joyce house, Daddy stop to talk to she husband. She run out and shout, "You come back boy!" So Miss Joyce cornmeal porridge smelling nice. I could smell the bwaden leaf and the *belgamot* in it.

All she children gather up by the window, watching as if is first time they see a car in their life.

When we reach back, Rally jump out as soon as the car stop. But I stay in the car with Daddy.

"Your mother send some nice tings for all you," Daddy say. "Let's go and see nuh."

Daddy take out a big black bag from the trunk and we go in the veranda. When Daddy open up the bag, the whole place smell sweet.

"I have someting for you," Daddy say. He take out something from one of the bag pockets and give me. It fold up in soft red paper, like toilet paper. When I open it, is a picture of me mother. The only picture of me mother that Mammy have is the one with me mother in she school uniform. The person in the picture Daddy give me don't look like her at all. The lady in the picture have on a blue halter-back dress and blue high heel shoes to match she dress. She have a big afro and she looking fair fair. She fingernails long and red; the same colour like she lips.

Rally full up he pockets with sweets and run back down the road to meet Lano.

As Daddy getting ready to go Papa reach up.

"Everyting aright Norman?" Daddy ask Papa.

"A a. Well we didn know you comin man," Papa say. "So how Gloria?"

"She good man," Daddy say. Daddy stand up talking to Papa, but I could see he ready to go.

"I have to make a spin now." And as soon as Daddy say make a spin, the piece of coconut fly back up in me throat.

He stay in the veranda and put the bag in the hall.

"Daddy when you comin back?" I ask him. I don't want Daddy to go. He just come and he going already.

Daddy pick me up again. "Doh worry man, you go see Daddy all de time now."

He put me down. I didn't hold on to he leg. Mammy around the corner coming and Daddy see her but he just go in he car and drive off.

I run down the road behind the car, until it bend the corner down by the standpipe, until I can't see it again.

Sunday morning, Mammy don't have to call me twice to wake up for church. All the children in Celeste going to same church as their mothers or their grandmothers, except me and Rally. Mammy does go to the Presbyterian church and we going to the Catholic church. And we have to make first communion, so every Sunday, we have to go to service and then Sunday School in a dark dark room at the back of the church.

I never like getting up so early and walking all that long way to Sauteurs, but I like dressing up in me nice church clothes. And I could not wait to pass by Daddy, because we have to pass right in front he house, to go to church.

Mammy let me and Rally put on we new clothes. I put on me new red dress with all the little green flowers on it and elastic in the waist. Rally put on he new blue and white striped shirt and he gun-mouth pants.

We leave home half past six. The grass still wet with dew. And the breeze feeling wet too, when it touch me face.

We pass Miss Kay coming up the road with she bucket of water on she head, and she singing ...*Morning has broken, like de first mor-or-or-nin'*. Miss Kay don't even hold the bucket on she head. She have a branch in it for the water not to shake up and fall out when she walking up the stony road.

"Mornin Miss Kay," Me and Rally say it same time.

"Mornin chilren. Mornin. What! All you look nice dis morning oui!'

Me and Rally smile and we watch weself. Me black church shoes shiny, and it have a pink rose on the front.

"Come on, walk on fast. It late aready," Miss Kay say. And she start to sing again ... *black bird has spo-o-o-ken like the first bird...*

When we reach the junction, I run in front of Rally to go and see Daddy. He living in the same little room with he brothers and sisters. Daddy car not by the road, but I run up the bank and knock Daddy door.

"Daddy! Daddey!" I call. Nobody answer.

"Girl come on nuh. You en see the car en dere," Rally say.

But I knock and call Daddy again.

"Lee gurl, come on. We go reach late you know."

"Who tell you Daddy en dey!" Me voice start to get shakey and I ready to cry. I peep through a hole in the door but me eyes just bounce up with darkness.

I peep through the door again when we going home after church. No Daddy. Monday morning I look for Daddy when we going to school. No Daddy. The evening, after school, Daddy not there. The next morning, Daddy still not there. Everyday for the whole week, I looking out for Daddy, but is just as if Daddy gone away again. And every time he not there, me chest does hurt and I does have to swallow the cry before Rally call me a cry-baby.

Friday, after school, we play all the way up the road. We stop by Croft Hill to stone *pwadoo*. When we reach by Miss Netta we try to keep quiet and pass quick before she hear us. But she in front she door in she little board house, waiting for us. And Miss Netta blind as a bat but so she could hear! She knock she stick on the stone in front the door.

"Aye aye! All you cong ang gring song waker cor ge."

Miss Netta does talk like a dummy. She tall tall. She face long. And she have two long long teeth in front she mouth, like a Dracula.

Rally and the other boys run down in the yard for the paint pans. Yvette go with them too. Me and Marie stay up by the road. We fraid Miss Netta bad. We put we bags down on the bank and help *joeg* the water, but we don't go down in the yard at all. After Rally and them bring the water, Ms Netta pick up the big bottle of Crix biscuits from the floor, by she foot. She stick she long, bony hand inside the bottle and take out some mash-up mash-up biscuits. All the boys take the biscuit, but Rally give away his. Miss Netta always digging up she nose or scratching somewhere. And I sure is the same hand she does use to pick up the biscuit to give people so I don't want no biscuit!

"Gurl gimme the biscuit if you doh want it eh!" Yvette tell Marie. "What caan kill go fatten oui!" Yvette does eat anything.

Daddy place just around the corner from Miss Netta house, and even though whole week Daddy not there, as soon as we burst around the corner, me eyes start to make beast looking for Daddy car. When I see Daddy car there, I break out in one speed. I nearly burst me backside when I bump me big toe. I jump over the drain in front the house. Dash up the bank, up the steps. The steps not rickety again. Daddy change the board. The top door open.

"Daddy?" I call and I pound the bottom door.

"Mmmm." I hear from inside. That don't sound like Daddy.

"Daddy you dere?" I call again.

"Mmm. Pu- pull -de door- Lee," Daddy talking as if it hurting him.

I pull the door and the hinge and them cry.

The room paint in green, a light green, like the colour of banana leaves. The little table still in the corner. Daddy shoes line up on one side and he clothes hang up on nails on the partition. It have a bag on the floor, like the one he bring the clothes for us in. The room smell like paint and clothes. And it smell just like the surgery.

Daddy lie down on the bed and he cover-up with a sheet. I nearly bawl when he turn he head and face me. Daddy face swell up big big, as if bees sting him up. One of Daddy eyes almost close down. And he face bruise-up and purple.

"Wha happen to you Daddy?" I ask. Something sour come up through me throat and in me mouth.

Rally come up on the steps behind me.

"Ah fall off a bike man." Daddy groan and when he raise up the sheet, me belly drop down to me toes.

Rally move closer to the bed. "Aw!" Rally say.

All Daddy have on is he underpants. He whole body, from he chest down to he legs gashay. Daddy look as if somebody drag him up and down Celeste road, naked. All I could see was big purple patches all over him. It make me body hurt me, as if is me who bruise up so.

"It hurting Daddy?" I ask. I don't know what to say. I

don't know what to do. I can't even hug Daddy or give him a kiss. Daddy groan. He move he head. He groan again.

"Um hm."

"Rally you comin or what?" Boyboy call. He and the others outside waiting in the yard.

"Ah comin just now," Rally say, but he watching Daddy. He feeling real sorry for Daddy.

"We goin you know man," Boyo say.

"Well go nuh if you cyan wait!" Rally tell him.

"Lee, take-a–Phen-sic on the ta-ble for me." Daddy tell me.

I take the Phensic, rip the paper and put it in Daddy mouth. He swallow it without water. And I wonder how he could swallow that big tablet without water, because even when Mammy cut up a little WL tablet in two, I have to force to swallow the little pink piece, no matter how much water I drink. It have a glass of water on the floor by the bed. I pick it up and try to give Daddy, but he groan and put he head back down.

"All-you–could-go-on. Daddy takin a rest now," Daddy tell us. "Pass by me tomorrow eh."

Rally and the others stop and pick tamarind by Mr Georgie place. They chase butterflies, push flex-grass up in the butterflies' bambam, then let them go. I wonder if it hurt the butterflies. And I wondering how them boys could do that.

I not playing. I only thinking about Daddy. Who go look after Daddy? How he go get food? He could not even get up. Who go empty the potty for him?

The butterflies try to fly away, but the grass sticking in their bambam so they can't fly. The just fall on the ground. *Rally and them wicked too much!* I bet Daddy get up from the bed he go fall down like one of them butterflies. But I glad he can't go nowhere.

Chapter 10

Auntie's visit

Outside dark already so I don't see the car pass up. I just hear it.

I wash up in me little basin already and well grease up with Vaseline, powder me chest with Johnson's baby powder and put on me nightie. And I in the hall combing Suzie hair.

Suzie used to be me Auntie Liz doll. She so big that me old baby clothes that I find in a little brown grip, on top the shelf in we bedroom, could fit her. She have red hair and when I put her lie down on she back, she does close she blue marble eyes, as if she sleeping in truth.

I have two other dolls but I does hardly play with them. Jill missing a hand, two fingers on the other hand, and one eye. And Chrissy face stuff up with cloth, because one day I take Mammy kitchen knife to cut a little hole in she mouth, so I could feed her. I squeeze she soft little face together, and cut. And the knife slice right across she face, all past she ears!

Mammy, Papa and Mr Fin in the veranda. The death news just finish so Rally bring the radio back in the hall. Mammy so busy talking, she didn't bother to tell Rally turn it off.

"Ah wonder who come dey Fin?" No answer.

"Fin? A a. Not sleep you sleeping dey aready?"

"Eh. Nah man." Mr Fin say. And I bet he shaking he head as if he trying to shake out the sleep.

"This is the voice of the BBC with another episode of,

THE HEIR APPARENT," the man on the radio say, in he stylish voice. And he voice sounding as if it coming from all the way down inside he belly, then pouring out smooth smooth like eggnog. I don't even understand the story good but the man voice *bound* and *compel* me to listen. The story sound real, as if the people and them really talking to one another in truth. A lady running away to meet she fiancé, and she saying something about love. She voice come out from somewhere soft and silky, like one of Mammy new handkerchief. A man vex with the lady. And I could hear the vexness in he voice because he voice sounding as if he hawking up the words from he chest, like cold, and spitting them out. And I could even see the vexness on he face and all. And the horse clippity, cloppitying down a stony road, through an alley. The people and them sounding so real, I right there in the buggy with the lady. I there watching the horse going down the alley.

When the story finish, I put down Suzie on the floor and I go and stand up by the front door, so I could see the car when it passing back.

"Ah wonder who pass up dey?" Mammy ask.

"Must be dem Goodman and dem people man," Mr Fin say.

Mr and Mrs Goodman always have people going up by them.

"Not Jacko who pass up den?" Mammy ask.

"Nuh man. Dat's not Jacko car," Papa say, because he know Jacko car good.

"Well how it en comin back? I fine it stay up dey long man," Mammy say.

Maymay just coming down from the mountain, with she bucket on she head. I don't know how Maymay could bring that big enamel bucket without holding it, but she two hands by she side - one with she cutlass and a little bunch a bluggoe in the next one. Papa say, Maymay does work like a man. How she does cut down trees and burn coals better than any man he know. And all when Maymay reach by she old shack, between we house and Miss Kay house, she coals smell mix up with stale sweat and all kinds of dirty smell, still in me nose! Sometimes Papa burn coals down in the garden, and I like how the smoky smell does stay inside me nose. And even when it feeling as if it go stifle me, I still want to breathe in some more.

The car cruise back down. The driver slow down by we house, as if he looking for a house but he not sure which one. He start to move off again. He stop, reverse and he park up right in front we house. The driver come out the gray car with TAXI on the front.

"Good night. Good night," the man say.

I move closer to the veranda gate, because I dying to see who there.

"A a, Peeya how you fass so? Somebody come to you?" Mammy spit out, as if she spitting out little stones she find in she rice and dhal.

I move back by the front door.

"Good night," Mammy answer.

Papa straining he neck to see too. "Ah wonder who dey Reenie?"

"Ah doh know nuh Papa. It have a lady and a man in the back," I tell him and I move up by the door again. But I stay behind the door, in case Mammy find some more stones to spit out.

"Lee who come dey?" Rally ask me. He run out in the veranda. I follow him and we climb over the wall together to see.

The two people sitting down in the back keep watching the house.

The driver open the back door. A tall, tall man come

out. He holding a long black cloak over one arm, like the one Papa does put on to go in the mountain when rain falling. I can't see he face.

The driver pass round the back to open the other door. A lady come out from the other side and stand up in front the yard.

The car trunk too full to close good, so it open like the trunk in Mammy room

"A a! Fin, who is dat? Mammy ask.

"Well ah doh know. Ah can't see who dey."

"Beta put on de light nuh," Mammy say. Rally run back inside and switch on the light in the hall. Mammy does hardly use the electric light. She always light the kerosene lamps so she would not waste current.

The lady walk down the steps sideways, like a crab, using the light coming through the front door. She holding she coat on one arm and she hat in the other hand - the one that holding on to she right knee every time she take a step - as if it hurting her real.

The cliff feel warm under me bare feet. The whole yard and the veranda wall does feel warm in the evening. And I like how it does feel, but I run back inside by the door so me feet won't get dirty. I don't want Mammy to send me back behind the house to wash up again. Rally stay on the bank so he could see better.

"Well who dese people Papa?" Mammy ask.

"Well how ah go know?" Papa answer, squinging up he eyes to see in the dark. And scratching, grup, grup, grup.

And Mr Fin see people coming inside you know, but he wait until the lady reach right by the gate to get up. Then he stand up on the side watching like a stupidee. And Papa mouth open as if he catching fly.

The lady walk inside the veranda.

"Mammy?" The lady say it as if she still not sure she

in the right house.

"A a, well who is dat? Beta put on the veranda light let me see nuh."

Rally still outside so I put on the switch. And light spread all over the veranda like daytime. And I see the lady standing up there watching Mammy. She have on a blue skirt that fall below she knee and a blue blouse with little flowers on it.

Papa stretch he neck like a *gaulin*. He eyes coming out of he head and he still catching fly.

"Clarice? Is you wha dey?" Papa watching the lady in she face and grinning, with he *no-teeth-a-prampram*, looking like he silly billy self.

"Clarice is you?" He say again, holding the lady hand, and shaking it. And grinning.

"Yes Papa, is me! Well Papa and all know me and me own mother don't even know she daughter! Is me Mammy!" The lady say, turning to Mammy.

Mammy squinging up she eyes behind she glasses and look harder. Then she face fall down. She fold she arms. She unfold them. Then she put them in she lap. And all that time, Mammy just sit down there staring at the lady, as if she get *dotish*.

"Mammy, is me, Clarice," The lady voice start to tremble, as if she go cry now.

Then Mammy get up, in slow motion. She plant she feet on the floor. Make sure they on the floor. She press one hand on the wall to take purchase, then stretch out the other arm towards the sweet smelling lady in the veranda.

"Clarice is you? Is you Clarice? Me one piece ah chile?"

"Yes Mammy! Is me." Tears rolling down the lady face and wetting up she nice blouse.

And then Mammy and the lady hugging up one

another, and crying.

Mammy screw up she face with a cry. So Mammy good at making sheself cry. Mammy could make sheself cry anytime she want. And if she want, she could full up a bucket with tears. But sometimes Mammy does cry, and not a single drop of water does come out. And just like that she cry does stop. Just so! Daddy say how is crocodile tears she does cry.

The tall man and the driver bring the suitcases inside. The tall man have to bend down to pass through the door.

Rally trying to help drag the suitcases from the veranda to the hall.

"Woy, da man tall oui," Rally say. But he don't say it loud for the man to hear.

The lady hug Papa. Papa still stand up there grinning. "Well you din say you was coming. If ah did know you coming, ah wudda bring down dat nice, young bunch ah bluggoe for you man. Mammy din tell me you coming."

The lady in the veranda, who smelling like the Lady of the Night flowers by Miss Kay, and there sharing hugs and kisses like sweets, is me grandmother. Mr Fin and all, in all he *renk* mountain clothes, get hug too. And I know she clothes go smell like him now, but I edge up closer waiting for mine.

"Well look at how me grandchild get big nuh!" She say, when she reach me. She squeeze me tight tight. Me face press in she chest. I never get a tight hug so in me life. Daddy does hug different. When Daddy hug me, I does feel as if me is the only person in the world. But me grandmother hug me as if she lose me long long. And now she find me, she fraid she go lose me again. She squeeze me as if she fraid I might slip out from she arms and disappear. And she smelling so nice I want to stay right there, with me face in she chest, for the whole night. But she let me go to give Rally he share.

Then everybody start talking same time. I sit down on me grandmother lap with me nose in she bosom, just like a doctor bird in a hibiscus flower.

The next morning when me grandmother unpack the suitcase, I sure England smell even nicer than Aruba. The Morris chairs cover up with new clothes, tins of biscuits, Cadbury chocolates, and some chocolates in shiny gold paper name Ferrero Rocher and pretty little tins of fruit cake. Cake in tins! I never see cakes in pretty tins so.

I behind the kitchen sweeping the yard, when me grandmother ask, "Lee you want to go to Sauteurs with you granny?"

If I want to go in Sauteurs? I finish sweeping quick and I dash behind the house to bathe. The water cold, and the breeze cold too, but I don't even feel it. But I glad Mammy have a inside bathroom though, because I sure me fancy grandmother, with she sweet smelling self, have a big house in England, with a nice bathroom and toilet inside.

We walk all the way to Sauteurs - me Grandma Clarice and the tall man, Grandpa Tony. Grandma Clarice stopping to say howdy do, and me skipping down in me nice new frock and me *coksie* shoes.

When they come out from the bank, Grandpa Tony, who is not me real grandfather, give me a whole new dollar for meself. I buy eggnog and milk toffees in the Snackette.

We go home on the bus with the name *DIGNITY* paint on the front of it. The one Mammy always take when she going down Samaritan. She know the driver good.

Grandma Claris sit down by the window, watching and pointing at houses and asking Grandpa Tony if he remember who used to live there. When we reach the cemetery, she point a grave to show me where she grandmother bury. And although she tell me that is pure stupidness, I bite all me ten fingers, so spirits don't follow us.

Chapter 11

The Shango Dance

We play cricket in the road until the sun go and hide behind Carriacou Island, then all of us sit down on the bank in front Maymay house. Mammy and Grandma Clarice and them on the veranda talking, so they don't call us inside yet.

Boyboy team lose so he well vex.

"All you could cheat too much!" He say.

"Eh! Who does cheat like you boy!" Rally say. And he laughing, but Boyboy not making no joke. He vex to burst.

Darius stumbling up the road. He is Maymay boyfriend.

Maymay living in the little old shack behind the bank. People does call her Madmay. The only time I ever hear her talk is when she cussing Darius or cussing for sheself. And so she nasty! She have all kinds of old rubbish in she yard. She does even keep she *tootoo* cover down in paint pans, and then when she ready, she does open the pan and let go she mess - *jack iron*. Then everybody have to close up their windows and all man have to take cover because the whole place stink stink.

Darius always drunk when he come up by Maymay. Every time he take a step he missing a fall.

"Chilren a-all yoou goo-goood?" And Darius words and them stumbling out from he mouth in slow motion, just like how he walking.

When Darius come by Maymay, it does be real ruction. So all of us stop talking and we waiting to see what go happen next.

He stumble down the bank to Maymay shack. Fall on the door. The door open a crack. Maymay and all does have to squeeze inside because the door can't open good.

"Whey de fuck you goin, eh?" Maymay say. And she slam the door in he face.

"Ooman wha doo you! Hoow you meean whey ah goiiing?" Darius say.

"Ah say whey de fuck you goin?"

Is full moon night but the moon don't come out yet. We can't see nothing but we listening. Something fall. Bang-a-lang-a-lang. Clang! Clang! A knock. Clack! Clack! Door slam. Blam! And Maymay cussing. Then Maymay shouting. 'Oh God! Oh God!' And Darius saying "Ooman huush you fuuucking mouth nuh ooman!" Earthquake passing. The shack shaking.

Rally and Boyboy and them killing their self laughing.

"Boyboy! Yvette!"

Miss Kay calling.

A drum beating down the road.

"Dey starting up boy! All you comin in dance tonight?' Lano ask.

"How you mean?" Boyboy say. He not vex again.

"Stay dey and say how you mean! Mammy go give you!" Yvette say.

"You comin?" Lano ask Rally.

"If Boyboy comin ah comin too," Rally say.

"Well all you could come wid me," Lano say.

"Yea man. Leh we go nuh! We go listen for when Mammy callin us, eh Lee," Rally say.

"Ah fraid oui!" I say.

"What you fraid? We go stay on de bank and watch," Lano say.

"I en comin nuh. You tink ah want licks!" Yvette say.

"Eh! Jus down dey we goin. So we woun hear if Mammy callin us den?" Boyo say. And he stupse. "Man leh we go nuh man."

I could smell the oildown cooking in the big cast iron copper in the yard. The road full of people. Lano say how people does come from Chantimelle and La Mode and even all the way from La Baye, for the Shango Dance.

We follow Lano through the fence in front of the house. Miss Sangie little house have two rooms, a front room where Lano and he big brother does sleep, and the bedroom in the back, where he sister and Miss Sangie does sleep. Lano three big sisters gone in England and meet their mother. And every time he see a plane passing, he saying, "Jus now I going in a plane jus so, when me mother send for me." Just the other day a boy in me class go and meet he mother in America. And Rally friend Victor going in Canada and meet he father. How come we mother not sending for us too!

We settle by the sugar apple tree, on the bank of the yard. It have people everywhere - Shango Baptists in the yard and limers in the road.

Masantoes stand up all round the yard like little soldiers, blazing and smoking. The wind trying to blow them out and the kerosene fumes fulling up we nose.

When the big dark cloud move away, moonlight spread over the yard. Some of the Shango women make a circle in the centre of the yard. They have on white gowns with red and yellow cloth around their waists and around their heads.

The drums start to get louder and the women start to chant to the drums. A Shango woman come out from inside the house with a calabash, holding it as if is eggs she have in it.

"Dat's Rita with the sheep blood" Lano say. "They

does drink it you know."

Sickness boil up inside me belly, like the time Daddy bring the turtle meat with all the blood in it.

Another cloud block the moon again.

"Well I can't see nuttin," I say.

"Leh we go up some more," Lano say. We squeeze through the crowd to get closer to the front.

The cloud drift away and it get bright again. The women passing the calabash around the circle and drinking from it in truth. *How they could drink sheep blood?*

Then somebody scream and people start pushing and shoving to see. Then people start to scatter and it sounding as if they getting licks.

"Wha happening dey Lano?" Rally ask.

"*Tambran* whip in dey backside!" Lano say. And he laughing. He say when people come too close the men does beat them with tamarind whip. And tamarind whip is the worst thing to get licks with.

I jam up close to Rally and I hold on to he old khaki pants loop. The crowd move up closer again, pushing nearer to the edge of the bank. I feel meself moving too. I grip Rally loop tighter and hold on to the sugar apple tree. The tree naked as it born. And all the soil pulling away from it, so the roots naked too.

The women chanting louder.

Hake kede gede! Hake kede gedege! Haleleuia! Hake kede gedege!

The drums beating faster. Louder.

The moon come out again and the yard bright bright. The women and them dancing round in the yard.

Hake kede gede! Hake kede gedege! Haleleuia! Hake kede gedege!

"All you watch eh! Watch dem get de power eh."

Lano say.

"Ah want to see Rita," Boyboy say. "They say she does fly on de roof when power take her."

"Boy, yea boy! And she does dance on de roof and speak in tongues too oui," Lano say.

I want to see too, but I listening for Mammy. And I want to pee.

Hake kede gede! Hake kede gedege! Haleleuia! Hake kede gedege!

The women start to jerk up, as if they getting fits. They open up the circle and Rita in the middle jerking. Jerking. Jerking. She throw sheself on the ground and start to beat up like the fowl does beat up when Papa cut out the head.

Somebody scream again. Real loud.

Me skin raise. Me blood crawl. I feel cold. *Oh God!*

"Rally ah fraid!" I say. Me knee shaking.

People pushing to the yard and then back to the road, like the waves in Boucherie.

"Licks in dey backside!" Boyboy say.

Yvette move back. She eyes open wide and they shining. She mouth open too.

"Stay dey and say licks in dey backside. Mammy go show you licks in you backside!" She say.

"And you! So is me alone den?" Boyboy tell her.

A scream again. Cold bumps raise up on me. And I could hear me name. Somebody calling me name. I strain me ears and listen. *Maybe ah hearing things.*

"Rally leh we go home nuh!" I sure I could hear me heart beating louder than the drums.

Rita jump up and start to spin. And jerk. And spin.

"Yveeette! Boyooooooo!" Miss Kay shouting.

Yvette don't wait for another call. She fly home.

"Dat's the best part. She go fly up on top de roof now eh! Watch!" Lano say.

81

"Rally ah fraid! Leh we go home." I pull he loop.

Rita scream. Then I hear me name again, as if a spirit calling me.

"Ah goin home oui," I say, but I still holding on to Rally pants.

"Well go nuh! Ah want to see oui!"

Rita scream again. A cloud cover the yard. I sweating and squeezing me legs to hold the pee.

The crowd pushing again. We start to skate down the hill. Me hand slip out from Rally loop. I push through the crowd. I shove meself through them until I reach the road. I don't even look back. I fly home like a bat out of hell. One side of me hula hoop slippers fling out. I just keep running, me bare foot pounding the road, like the drums.

I dash in the veranda and plant meself on the floor, by Grandma Clarice. Not long after, Rally bolt inside as if somebody chasing him. He almost trip over me.

"What do you Beta?" Mammy ask.

Rally breathing hard and fast. "Nuttin."

Another howl from down the road sound just like a pig getting slaughtered.

I still sweating. Me whole body start to tremble when Mammy tell us to go outside and wash we feet. I fraid to even get up. I sure them spirits behind the house waiting for us. So I well glad when Grandma Clarice ask Mammy, "Why you sending the children outside in this dark?" And she tell us to, "Go and wash up in the bathroom you hear."

Grandma Clarice and Grandpa Tony sleeping on we bed, so me and Rally sleeping on the floor. Whole night, I lie down in the same position. I curl up on me side, facing the partition, with me hands over me ears. And I dream about me cousin - the one people say dealing with *De Lawrence.* I dream he holding me foot in one hand, a knife in the other hand, and he going and slice under me foot. And I fighting to call Mammy. I fighting to call Rally. Grandma Clarice. But he put the knife on he lips, like Teacher Vee, when she telling us to keep quiet. And he saying "Shusssssshs! Don't call Mammy." When he let go me foot, I fly up on the bed and squeeze meself between Grandma Clarice and Grandpa Tony. And me heart still beating like the drums.

Chapter 12

The Revelation

In the night, when Mammy and them sitting on the veranda talking, I does sit down on Grandma Clarice lap, listening to she stories about England.

Grandma Clarice words does sound nice and new, just like all them things in she suitcase. She does talk about the days before she go in England. How they used to live up in the mountain and how they had to walk miles to go to school in Sauteurs, without shoes. How Mammy grandfather come from India. He was an indentured labourer in Trinidad. Then he come in Grenada and he buy an estate, all up in the mountain. And how Mammy was supposed to get married to an Indian man she father choose for her, but she go and make a child for a negro man. Then she father put her out. He cast her out of the family, so when Grandma Clarice born, Mammy could not give her the family name.

"And that's why I had to carry McLean, even though I never know my father," Grandma Clarice say.

"And I was damn lucky getting a man to pick me up with two children."

Grandma Clarice have three children for Grandpa Tony, so I know she talking about me Auntie Liz in the picture, and me mother Gloria, because Grandpa Tony is not their father.

"When he go in England in 1959, he promise he go send for me. But I used to worry because I used to hear about all the men who leave their women and children, and when they reach in England, they never turn back!

84

They throw big stone behind them. Not a single word from them again! Not a penny to buy a pound a sugar!"

"Hhmm!" Grandpa Tony suck he teeth as if meat stick in them. He always sucking he teeth or picking them with matchsticks.

I watch Grandpa Tony from the corner of me eyes. He is the biggest man I ever see in me life. He big like a giant. He even too big for the Morris chair in the hall. When he sit down on it, he knees does reach all up by he chest, so he have to sit down on a wrought iron chair from the veranda.

"These men and them does get bright too much when they go overseas. They does forget what they leave behind. But he keep he promise," Grandma Clarice say.

Grandma Clarice hug me to her. Me face press against hers and every time she talk, I could smell the smoked herring she eat for supper. Even though she suck a dinner mint after.

The first morning when Mammy ask her what to cook she say, "Some fig and smoked herrings would be nice. If you know how I was longing to eat some of that eh!" And I feel like turning me face away because every time I smell it, me belly stirring up, making me feel as if I want to vomit. But I press me face in she chest instead, so I could smell she perfume.

"Exactly one year after he go in England, he send a ticket for me to go up and meet him. In those days we didn't go by airplane like now. Is the banana boat we had to travel on. We spend seventeen days on the sea. Seventeen days in that boat! And if it wasn't for this lovely lady I met from Barbados, I don't know how I woulda make it! Hmm! And I used to worry about me children. All I could think about was my children."

After Grandma Clarice go in England, she take up four of she children and she leave one alone behind. She leave me mother alone behind.

"Am sorry sorry I had to do leave Gloria, but I had to leave somebody behind to help Mammy. Mammy was a old lady."

And we mother leave us with Mammy too and Mammy more old now. She have sixty-five years. I wonder how I go feel if me mother send for Rally and leave me alone with Mammy. Maybe me and Rally woulda be in England too if Grandma Clarice did send for me mother.

The night before Grandma Clarice and Grandpa Tony go back in England, all of us sit down in the hall. Except for Mr Fin. He in he usual seat by the gate. Even Papa sit down in the hall. He in the corner in he striped pyjamas. Rally on the floor with Belle.

The big Home Sweet Home lamp lighting on the cabinet. Moths flapping around it. Rally catch one. He drop it in the flame and watch it fight to get away. But the flame eat it up. Rally like to do things like that. Sometimes he does lasso lizards with long flex grass-tied in draw-knots - give them to Belle, and watch her torment them.

Maymay must be outside cooking, because the wind bring a nasty smell right over to we veranda and inside the hall.

I had on me new pink nightie that Grandma Clarice bring for me and I sit down on the Morris chair next to her.

Grandma Clarice telling us more stories about England. How she started working as a cleaner in a hospital.

"I used to clean toilets. Scrub floor, wash bedpans, so I could send money for Mammy to mind my children."

The room quiet, except for Papa scratching, grup, grup, grup. Everybody listening. An owl hooting from the Mango Lung tree on the other side of the road.

"But I used to help the nurses on the ward. I used to watch what they doing and I even used to help them. It was me who used to help them lift up the patients to change the sheets on the beds. Then one day the Sister call me to her office and I was so frighten. I thought I was in trouble. But she just wanted to thank me. She asked me if I wanted to work on the ward as an assistant nurse. She said she was watching me all the time and she knew that I could do the work. Well I was not qualified. I never go in secondary school or nothing. But I knew the work well and Sister knew I could do it. That is how I started to work as an assistant nurse. That Sister! She was the nicest lady I knew. And she was white you know!"

Mammy arms folded on she chest looking straight at Grandma Clarice. Then she start crying trouble. She start saying how she work hard in the mountain to mind all Grandma Clarice children and pay for land with she nutmeg and cocoa money.

And all the time Grandpa Tony just there sucking he teeth and giving he little chorus, 'umm hmm' or 'ah ha' or 'what boy!' But when Mammy say that he open he mouth.

"What you talking about woman! What happen to all the money we sending every month to pay for the land?" He say.

"Money? What money you sen to pay for land?" Mammy ask, and she watching Grandpa Tony as if he mad. She unfold she arms. She fold them up again.

The owl hoot again, as if it calling another one. Belle ears prick up and she looking out the window.

"How you mean what money? The money we sending ever month!" Grandma Clarice answer.

"A a! What money you send? Is me nutmeg money what paying for the land oui!"

"How you mean is you nutmeg money! So what happen to all those postal orders you does get in the post office every month?" Grandma Clarice talking louder. She her chest heaving up and down.

I know Mammy does get letter from Grandma Clarice every month, when she go in the post office. I does see when she take out the light blue envelope, with the heavy blue stripes, from she bag and sit down in the kitchen to read it. Then she does send me and put it under the plastic tablecloth on she press. She had a lot of blue envelopes under the table cloth, with pictures of Queen Elizabeth II on them.

But Mammy don't answer. She not watching Grandma Clarice again. She watching the darkness straight in front of her, through the door. Mammy shadow dancing on the partition with the flame, and she nose look pointy, like the witch in *Hansel and Gretel* storybook.

I ease up and sit down on Grandma Clarice. She unfold she arms and hold me. I feel she chest moving, up down. Up down. I hear Mr Fin cutlass scrape the concrete. He going home. He say good night. Nobody don't answer.

When Grandma Clarice start to talk again, she take she time, just like I take me time to pick up the eggs in the fowl cage, just like Papa does take he time to sharpen he razor on the piece of leather strop, before he shave.

"You have not changed at all, have you? After all these years, you still the same!" Grandma Clarice looking straight at Mammy. She arms fall down from me and I wonder if I should go back in me seat.

Mammy looking at the partition and rocking like a fishing boat.

Belle meow and crawl back in Rally lap. He rub she back. I waiting to hear what Mammy going to say, but she don't say a word.

"I can't believe that my mother is still such a wicked woman," Grandma Clarice say. She say it as if she was talking to sheself. "Remember how you used to beat me?"

Grandma Clarice say. She words not sounding nice and new again.

"Hum! If ah remember!" Grandpa Tony say. As if is he Grandma Clarice talking to him. He shake he head. He staring outside in the dark too.

Mammy rocking like when she get some bad news.

"You used to beat me for everything. I will never forget! Never! You used to beat me with anything you put your hands on."

Mammy look at Grandma Clarice from the corners of she eyes as if she wondering what Grandma Clarice was talking about. As if she want to ask her who she talking about.

"Yes, you!" Grandma Clarice say, even though Mammy don't say a word.

Papa quiet now. No grup grup grup. The owl stop calling, as if it listening too. I watch Mammy shadow on the wall, how she mouth moving in and out like a frog.

"One time I had to run away to go to my school fair. When I reach back home, that woman beat me eh! She beat me with a piece of wood until me whole body swell up like bread that have too much yeast."

"Ah remember very well," Grandpa Tony say. "You think that woman was easy! Hmmm."

"But that was not enough! No sir!"

Grandma Clarice words coming out like prickle bush in the yard.

"She dig up ah ants nest!"

Mammy fishing boat rocking harder.

Me heart start to beat fast. I waiting. Waiting to hear what Mammy do with the ants nest. I know how vex ants does get when you just walk on their nest by mistake. I know how they could gang up on you and bite you up. Ants could even make a big man cry. So I waiting to hear why Mammy raise up the ants nest after she done beat up

Grandma Clarice so bad already.

Papa chair scrape the floor. He bedroom door creak. The rusty bolt grate.

"That woman tie my hands behind my back." And Grandma Clarice body trembling like a banana leaf. "And that woman, my own MOTHER, make me kneel down in that ants nest!"

Me mouth full up with sour spit. Grandma Clarice press she face on mine and I feel the water running down she face.

"She put me, she own DAUGHTER! She own flesh and blood, kneel down on a GRATER! In ah ants nest."

I swallow me spit. But me mouth full up again. *What Grandma Clarice talking about?* I remember the time I fall in the road and bruise up me knee, and gravels stick in it; how I bawl down the place when Uncle Dudley wife wipe it and pour spirits in it. And the neighbours does beat their children all the time, but I never hear nobody put their children to kneel down on a grater in ants nests yet. I try to imagine me grandmother kneeling down in an ants nest and the ants crawling all over her and she can't ever brush them off because she hands tie up behind she back. I try to imagine the grater teeth digging she knees, bursting into she skin, boring she flesh. And I can't imagine it. But I could imagine Mammy watching Grandma Clarice kneeling down there and saying "you little wretch you!"

Mammy still don't say a word. And I thinking Mammy does treat me bad, calling me nigger and cocoyaya and cursing me. But I real lucky.

Tears rolling down on Grandma Clarice face. I could taste tears on me face too.

"How could a mother do that to her own child? How could anybody do that to a child, eh?" Grandma Clarice say. "What could child do to deserve that?"

"Ask me that!" Grandpa Tony say. "Hm! Ah tell you she is a wicked woman! Hm."

Mammy still rocking, as though if she rock hard enough Grandma Clarice and Grandpa Tony go disappear.

The room feeling like when rain fall on the hot pitch. I wonder if Rally could feel it too.

Then Grandma Clarice shake me.

"She ever do that to you? Mammy ever do that to you Lee?" She ask. Grandma Clarice look as if a rain cloud just cover she face.

I shake me head. If I just open me mouth the cry go burst out. The wind blow away the rain cloud from Grandma Clarice face.

"Lee, you granny so sorry she had to leave your mother. But I had to leave one behind. I had to leave somebody with Mammy."

But how come she leave we mother with Mammy, when Mammy do that wicked thing to her.

"Every day I does pray that your mother will forgive me my child. God knows I does pray hard for her to forgive me."

I wipe me face with my nightie. Grandma Clarice cry real quiet. The tears rolling down and falling inside she bosom. She not smelling like the Lady of the Night flowers then.

Rally was sleeping on the floor; Belle spread out by him.

A moth fly in the lamp and the wings burn like a dry leaf. The flame die down then get bright again.

Grandma Clarice blow she nose in she handkerchief. Then when she look at me she say, "But if I did take your mother to England I wouldn't have such a lovely granddaughter like you now, would I?" And I waiting for Mammy to say "Eh! What lovely granddaughter?" But it's as if Belle get Mammy tongue.

Chapter 13

Temporary Sojourn

I sit down on the step with me bowl of green peas soup. It still a little warm and it thick, with a lot of peas and dumplings. Just how I like it. I cut up me dumpling and just putting piece in me mouth, when I hear Daddy car. By the time I hear me special whistle, the bowl on the step and I in the road, like lightning.

Daddy car park up in front the little house he just finish building. Mammy give me mother the spot and Daddy and he friends cook up a lot of food and they help him build up the house.

Daddy taking out suitcase from the car when I dash into him. It have a lady in the front seat. When she come out, I see she is the same lady in the picture that Daddy give me, in the black frame with a white cruise ship at the back.

We mother in Aruba five years now. Daddy did say he building the house for when we mother come but he never tell us when she coming. I stand up there and I don't know what to do with meself. Gladness spread over me like the warm, soapy water in the bath-pan, when I bathing in the yard on Sundays.

Rally come up behind me. He don't know what to do with heself either, so we just stand up there watching one another. He have he hand in he pocket, and I skipping from one foot to the next in me rainbow colour hula hoop slippers. And I glad I just take out me socks and shoes, so me feet still clean.

The lady stand up there watching us too.

"So all you not coming and give me a kiss then?" She say.

She stand up by the car door, with she handbag in one hand, and the other one opened out like a hen opening she wing. And I run under the wing, like a little chicken. Rally follow me. I wipe me face with me dress, in case it have peas soup on it still. And I latch on to me mother leg, me face pressing in she jeans. She smell even nicer than Grandma Clarice. Nicer than the Lady of the Night flowers, that does sweeten-up the nights. And she hug not like Daddy hug, but I like it too.

The little one bedroom house, right next to Mammy house, not empty again. Daddy start coming home all the time. He paint the house in a nice, light blue colour, like the sky on a Sunday afternoon. He cut the grass, trim the wayward fence in front the yard, and me mother plant flowers. The hibiscus in front the yard is me favourite. I like them even better than the daisies in Mammy garden that I does make chains and bracelets with. Then all the bright red flowers burst out, and we little house look just like a picture in a story book.

Me mother make inside the house look pretty too. She put up new blinds in the windows. She put pictures on the partition and plastic flowers on the table. She put new sheet on the bed and a big pink bedspread with green and yellow peacocks on it. And the dressing table full of me mother things: bottles of perfume and all different colours *Cutex* nail polish; eye shadows; lipsticks; face powder – the same colour as grind cinnamon. And everything smelling nice!

We have two homes now. And we have a whole new Mammy too. But we don't know how to call her. We calling we great grandmother Mammy already, so we couldn't call her Mammy too. She say we could call her Gloria, but every time I open my mouth to say it, it not coming out. So when she call us, we just answering "yea". And when she ask us, "Who you answering "yea?" we does say, "Nobody."

Now I have me own mother to bathe me even though I could bathe meself; and to wash me hair and plait it in neat little cornrows, and put pretty bobbles and ring combs in it. I glad I don't have to go and ask Miss Kay to plait me hair again.

Rally does still sleep over by Mammy, because he have the whole bed for heself now. And every night I falling asleep on the bed with Daddy and me mother, but when I wake up, I on the floor in the front room. And me mother in the little kitchen frying fishcake, or in the yard outside washing clothes - she hands squishing in the soapy water. And when she hang up the clothes, every time the wind blow, I could smell the Breeze soap.

Sometimes I does sneak back in the bed with Daddy before he get up. But one morning I nearly kill Daddy. He just come out from hospital and I lying on the bed with him. I have to be real careful because Daddy just have an operation and he still have stitches where the doctor cut he hernia. Me mother call me from the kitchen, so I going to see what she calling me for. But as I open the bedroom door, a big, ugly, black thing jump at me. "Yaaaahhhhh!" And the thing mouth open and the teeth big and stick out like a Dracula teeth. I nearly pee meself. I jump straight back on the bed. I land right on top Daddy! Then Daddy holding he belly and groaning, and a red spot spreading on Daddy short pants. And it spreading on the sheet. And Daddy twisting up he face and grinding he teeth. And me mother stand up there looking as if she want to cry.

"Lord look how I nearly make you kill you father nuh!" she say.

Then I start to cry, because Daddy twisting up bad and I thinking something bad go happen to him. After a while Daddy say he alright, but he don't look alright. He still groaning and me mother still saying, "Oh Lord! Look how I coulda kill the man nuh!" The mask Daddy play carnival with still on the floor saying 'yaahh.' And something burning in the kitchen

Then Daddy and me mother get married. I never see Daddy go in a church in he life yet, but they get married in the Catholic church in Sauteurs. And I glad. Maybe that mean Daddy go come home all the time. And maybe me mother won't go away again.

Me mother look real nice in she fancy, white wedding dress, with a lot of shiny things on it. It spread out like a fan and it sweeping the floor, so some ladies have to hold it up behind her, when she walking. And she curly hair falling down on the sides of she face, under she white veil.

Daddy look like a real star boy, in he tight tight jersey - with a jacket over it. But he bell-bottom pants too long and they cover he Clarks boots.

Rally in he suit and he pointy cockroach killer shoes. The suit make him look like a real little man. And he only watching heself and dusting off he suit. Fly couldn't pass near him.

I looking nice too. Me mother comb me hair up in one, on top me head with a pink ribbon in it, with one twist by me left ear and one by me right. Me dress is same colour as eggnog. It have a lot of frills and little pink flowers on it. Me shoes is same colour, with flowers on the front too. And I even have a little bag to match.

All Daddy and me mother friends come in the wedding, but I only know some of them. Uncle Henry and he wife Auntie Eva, who Daddy does bring us by down in

Mt Craven. They don't have children but their house always full of children. And Auntie Eva does give us Dixie biscuits and Fanta in a glass with little, blue diamonds on it.

Uncle Cheekie, who living near we school, who we does go by and eat we lunch. And first time I ever see Uncle Cheekie dress up so, because he always in he old fisherman clothes.

And Micky and Sally from England. They living up on a cliff, by a precipice. They have two children named Jimmy and Jenna. All of them speaking nice. And Jimmy always asking, "Why Mom or Why Dad?" Once, when he playing near by the edge of the cliff and Sally say, "Jimmy I don't think it's a good idea to play so close to the edge darling." Jimmy ask, "But why not Mom?" And Sally say, "Because you could hurt yourself darling and that would make Mommy and Daddy really sad. Do you want to make Mommy and Daddy sad sweetie?" And I thinking if is Miss Kay, she just saying, "Boy move you backside from dey if you know what good for you eh! You tink ah studying you when you break you blasted neck behind dey!" And it don't have no but why Mammy nothing nuh! You just moving you backside from there because even if you break your blasted neck over the precipice, you still getting licks in your backside.

And if you see people! The church yard full. The road full. People stand up on the steps and all, blocking the way, so they could *maco* the wedding. Daddy is a bus driver so everybody know him. And everybody want to see if the *cock sparrow* getting married in truth. Everybody come to the wedding except Mammy and Papa.

One Sunday after the wedding, Daddy and me mother lock up in the bedroom. Sun hot, and we outside in the yard playing. Lano say how they "doin ting." Lano older than us and he know about a lot of things.

Rally jump and say, "Ah bet you ah could climb up the window and peep!" And he push out he little pinkie finger to bet. Lano pushed out he little finger too and say, "Ok, les bet." They hook and pull. Rally tip toed up to the window, like an Apache and start to climb up. All of us stoop down by the corner of the house watching and ready to make a dash if anything happen. Rally hook he fingers on the windowsill and scrape up like a cat. We see he head reach the window sill, neck stretch up, then we hear the slap. We dash down under the house. Rally dash down behind us. He holding he face. I could see he well frighten you know, but hear him, "Woy boy! Daddy hand smelling ah salt fish oui!" And all of them laughing, but I afraid Daddy go beat Rally, because sometimes Daddy does get real vex with him. One time when I tell Daddy how he calling me nickname like Mammy, Daddy give him two belt. Two real hard belt in he backside. He fly down behind Mammy kitchen and dash inside the donkey stable. He rip off he pants and spend the whole evening rubbing he bambam, and vex like a bull. And I feel sorry I tell Daddy.

Carnival time come and we mother bring us in Sauteurs to watch the mas bands. Mammy never bring us to carnival. We does only see the *shortknee* bands when they come up in Celeste. And all of us afraid of the shortknee, especially me. From the time I hear the willows rattling down the road by the stand pipe, me heart starting to beat drum. Me knees starting to tremble and I running and hide.

We stand up in front Mr Benjy shop, by the Kwaesay - me, Rally and we mother. Daddy playing shortknee too, so he in a band. The fancy mas bands pass. The wild Indians is me favourite, in their straw costumes, making their *oo loo loo loo loo* noise and waving their wooden machetes in the air. Then the shortknee bands reach. They cover from head to toe, jumping, chanting '*pay de mass a penny*' and throwing powder on people. Then people start bawling and running like they mad. Somebody say fight break out down the road. How Chantimelle shortknee fighting with Mt Rich shortknee. Then the Mongoose Gang start to chase them. People grabbing their children and running. Vendors picking up their trays and running. Me mother pulling me and Rally and running up the back road to the pasture. And I could hear bottles breaking and people bawling. And me shoe falling out but me mother dragging me up the hill so I can't get it. Me shoe stay in the road.

And after carnival, Christmas come. And we little house smell of fruit cakes, sorrel and ginger beer, like everybody else. And Christmas Eve night, we go in Town. I never see Town bright so. Lights all over the place, all the shops open and full of toys, and all kinds of shiny things. And people walking about and shopping and looking happy.

Me mother buy a mouth organ for me, and a doll with green eyes and brown hair. And Rally get a car and a mouth organ too. And children throwing up Starlight sparklers in the air and running. One fall on me and burn me on me hand, but I so happy I don't even cry.

Then Christmas gone and Daddy don't come home so much. We don't go to the beach on Sundays or the cinema. Sometimes Daddy don't come home for the whole weekend. Rally hardly came over to the little house. He say we mother like to bawl in people head too much!

One Saturday evening, me mother ironing we school uniform, when Daddy come home. I drop me doll on the floor. Daddy raise me up but he put me down quick quick again, as if he busy to go again. He don't say anything to me mother and she don't even watch him.

I sit down on the floor watching me mother. She don't look slim again, like when she just come. She arms look fat and she hair get long. She plait it in two – one on each side, and it reaching by she shoulders. Sweat gathering up on she forehead and under her nose. She nose look just like Grandma Clarice nose, round and fat. People always say how I have everything like me father, but I know I have me mother nose. Rally have Daddy nose.

Daddy go behind the house to bathe and when he come back inside, he tell me to go outside and play. Daddy sounding vex. And I don't like when Daddy vex. When he vex with me mother, the house does sound vex too. Things does bang up in the little kitchen, doors does slam, and the flooring does shake with all the vex walking. When Daddy vex, something does swell up in me chest. And something does make me want to stay inside by me mother, until Daddy car door *blam* and he speed down the road. And then the swelling does go down.

I go under the house. The house sit down on tall tall pillars, so I could even stand up under it. And I could hear them moving about over me. And me mother saying, "Leave me alone nuh man. Jus leave me alone eh!" And the thing making me chest go up and down. Up and down. Then footsteps. Thump. Thump. A drawer open. It shut. Daddy shaking he pants – he always shake he pants before he put it on. Shoes hit the floor. Footsteps again. Bedroom to front room. Front room to bedroom. Daddy say something. I can't hear good. And me mother talking loud.

"Why you en get you woman and dem to do it for you!"

And I never hear me mother talk back to Daddy so. Me chest going up down. Up down. Up down. I edge up on the side of the house and stand under the front window.

"Who you tink you talking to?" Daddy say.

He voice make me run by the door and push it open. And I see when Daddy hand hit me mother across she face. And I feel as if Daddy hit me too because everything hurting me. I stand up by the door and I afraid to move. I stand up there watching Daddy. Daddy stand up there watching me mother, and he hand stand up in the air as if it want to hit her again. Cry rising up inside me like the steam from the iron me mother pressing on Rally khaki pants. When Daddy turn and he see me, he hand fall down. Then he bend down, pick up he shirt from the floor, shake he head and go back in the room.

She still pressing the iron down on Rally pants. She ironing and water rolling down she face and falling on the pants. I crying too and I want to go inside and hug me mother leg. Maybe she go raise me up and hug me like Daddy, but I don't know how to go and hug she leg.

Daddy come out of the bedroom, he slam the front door. The cabinet shake. The glass sets knock up one another. He slam the car door. I listen to he car speeding down the road, pitching up dust and stones, and I wait for the swelling to go down.

"Ah don't know who tell me to come back here!" Me mother saying. "Ah don't know why ah come back here to see trouble under all you father. Ah sorry I ever come back here!"

And Mammy in the back of the house saying, 'Ent ah tell you the boy is a good for nuttin! But you didn't want to hear!"

Daddy bring us to Pearls Airport with him. I watch the plane fly away with me mother, just like a g*eegee*, after it thief a baby chicken from the mother. I wish I could stone the plane, just like me and Rally does stone the geegee.

Chapter 14

Telling Me Mother

Daddy does only come and sleep in the house and go again. Sometimes when I wake up early, before the sun peep inside we room by Mammy, I does see Daddy and a woman going in the car. A different one every time.

One day, when I come home from down in the Mango Row, I see Daddy car in front the house. I didn't hear me whistle so I didn't know Daddy come. I drop me bag of mangoes and run straight inside. I throw meself on Daddy. He catch me, but he don't ask, "What's happening now Lee?" He bend down tying he shoe lace, and I could smell Lux soap on he skin.

Then I hear the room door open. When I turn to look, I see a lady coming out. She coming out from me mother room. The room me mother take she time to make look nice; that still smelling like she things.

I know the lady, but as soon as I see her, something pull me from Daddy. And I feel behind me neck get tight tight.

The lady name is Gleeta. Daddy have a child with her. He name is Terry. Gleeta have nice hair. It long like me mother. She skin look like milk fudge. She lips red like cherry. She fingernails long and she hands look as if she doen't do no work. And she have nice eyes too.

Once when Daddy bring us to see Terry, Gleeta give me and Rally snow-ice and biscuit. Then she go in Aruba, like we mother, and leave Terry with she sister. Daddy have six other children, besides me and Rally, but Terry is the only one he does bring to spend weekends with us.

Terry is the one who me mother cabinet fall on and almost all she glass and Pyrex dish break. And Mammy like Terry better than she like me. And he is not even she grandchild.

And I like Terry mother, but I sorry I like her. What she doing in me mother room? In me mother house? I watch her walking out of me mother room, smiling and saying, "Hello Lee," with she Glow Spread Margarine voice, and something fly up inside me head. I don't know what, but it fly inside me and make me mad like a dog that have rabies. And I feel like jumping on Terry mother and scratching up she face. And ripping out she nice long hair, for me mother. Me eyes turn to fire and I give her one cut-eye; I sure it burn up she fudge skin, and melt up she Glow Spread voice. And if cut-eye could kill, she dead dead!

The thing inside me start to bawl, as if I getting crazy.

"AH tellin me mother! AH TELLIN me mother! AH TELLIN ME MOTHER!" It make me jump up and stamp up. Daddy try to hold me but I fling meself flat down on the floor. I roll. I bawl.

"Ah TELLIN me mother! Ah tellin me mother!"

And then I feel something on me bambam.

Daddy does beat Rally sometimes, but he say he get so much licks when he little, so he don't like to make anybody skin burn them. And Daddy never hit me in me life yet.

The slap stop the bawling. It pick me up from the floor and put me in the corner. I watching Daddy and hiccups heaving up in me, and I still can't believe Daddy just slap me!

"Come come, Lee," Daddy say and he bend down to pick me up. And I see the sorry in Daddy eyes, but I drag meself in the corner under the table. *Sorry can't pass it nuh.*

"Come nuh Lee. Come by Daddy." Daddy try to pick me up from under the table. I could smell the Hacks sweets on he breath. I close up meself. I want Daddy to come and get me but I want him to go, he and Gleeta. She standing up outside, by the car.

Daddy stand up by the table. He legs bend right back. Mine does bend back so too. I watch he Clarks shoes walking away from the table, the lace dragging on the floor behind him. He finish tying he lace and he go outside. When Daddy close the front door, I feel as if the door close right inside me. Then the car door slam, and when I hear the car revving down the road, something burst inside me. *How Daddy could jus leave me and go with he woman.*

The bawl come back. I bawl as if Daddy never coming back. I kick the table. I bawl for me mother. The plastic bowl with the plastic fruits tumble over. The fruits roll under the cupboards in the kitchen. The twenty-five cents that Daddy leave on the table for me to buy sweets, fall and roll under the cabinet and hide. I knock down a chair and it nearly hit Rally. I didn't even see him by the door.

"Gurl what do you!" he say.

I bawl until me voice gone and hiccups take over.

But every morning, I does still wake up early and look for Daddy. And I does still listen for me whistle.

Chapter 15

The Conversion

On the 13th of March, in 1979, the New Jewel Movement overthrow Gairy and make Maurice Bishop the Prime Minister.

Mammy say that Gairy is the best Prime Minister Grenada ever have. She say is Uncle who stand up for the poor farmers and them, and if it was not for him, how poor people would of starve. And she say, "If wasn't for Uncle, some of us woulda never know panty!" Mammy used to say. "You see how he name big and heavy! SIR ERIC MATTHEW GAIRY! You ever hear a big name so?" Mammy even had a big picture of him hanging up in the hall. But Daddy say that Gairy is a real wicked man, and how his Mongoose Gang used to beat up innocent people and throw them in jail for nothing.

And after the Revolution, it have soldiers driving up and down the place with guns. Daddy in the army too. He is a driver and he does come up and see us, driving the army jeep, with some other soldiers. A lot of them is Rasta. Daddy too. And when they passing Mammy does say, "Watch dem nuh! Dese good-for-nottin and dem. Dat's all dey good for!"

But Daddy don't stay in the army long. He say, after Rasta pick up gun and fight for the Revolution, how they turn against Rasta. So he leave the army, and he come back and stay in the little house.

Every morning, Daddy going in the spring, in the back of Celeste, and coming back with he hair dripping wet, and a lot a little pieces of things in it.

I wake up early early to go in the spring with Daddy. He half way down the mango row already. I grab me hulahoop slippers and dash down behind the house, by the avocado tree, through the Mango Row and the callaloo row.

The Mango Row is the boundary for Mammy land. It start right by the road with the Mango Flim - the one that ripe green-skinned - and it run right down to the ravine with a lot of Mango Coot, that only congorees burying theyself in, because people cutting style on them, and a Mango Sour – sweet, with pretty red and yellow patches - down the bottom of the land. And they does smell sweet! But the seeds sour as lime.

"Daddy wait for me! Ah comin with you." I shouting at Daddy. Me slippers still in me hand and stone jooking me bare feet. Whole day I does run about without slippers and stone don't hurt me feet so. But every little stone that touch me feet does hurt, when I just wake up. As if me feet does turn to putty in the night.

I mash a ripe mango. It so ripe the skin slip out and stick under me foot. "Oh geed!" I glad the mango don't have congoree in it. I stop and wipe me foot on the grass. The grass still have dew. I put on me slippers and clamp it with me toes, because me feet wet.

I meet Daddy down the bottom of the Mango Row. He picking up Mango Coot and putting them in he calabash.

"Moning Daddy," I say and hug he leg. Daddy don't smell like cigarette and cologne anymore. I could only smell the dew on the ground and ripe mangos.

"You wake up aready? You good?" Daddy ask and hug me with one arm.

"Ah want to come with you."

"Well let's go Princess."

I like when Daddy call me princess. I hold on to he

hand. We cross the ravine and walk up through Mr Nummy land. The sun just coming up over Piton Hill, and the sky starting to look yellow.

Daddy stop and pick some young cocoa. Then he stop again and pick some cochenille. He put them in he calabash. And Daddy only searching in the bush. He get some ripe bananas. He find water lemons between a thick patch of yam vine. Papa always bring some for me when he go up in the mountain. They look like passion fruits but they have soft, kind of spongy skin. And sometimes the white lady up the road does smell just like water lemons.

When we reach the spring, I sit down on a river stone watching Daddy grate he cocoa and cochenille, mix them up in he calabash and rub it in he hair. He don't talk a lot again, so I sit down real quiet, watching him. Watching the river water running down between the stones.

"You want mango?" Daddy ask me.

And even though Mammy tell us we mustn't eat mango first thing in the morning, because it going to give us shittings, I say yes. The mango smelling sweet! And it nice and hard, just how I like it. I suck it down to the seed. I lick the juice running down me elbow. I lick me fingers. And then I suck another one, and another one, until me belly start to make ruction. Then I run in the bush when the ruction ready to come out.

When Daddy finish sucking he mangoes, he tell me to wait there, and he go across the river, up the hill - where cocoa and banana trees cover up, so the sun can't shine under them - to dig yam. Daddy say is wild yam, but I glad is early morning and nobody seeing him, because he trespassing. If Mr Nummy see him, he go chase him with he cutlass.

When Daddy come back, he pour spring water on he head. Then he shake he head. And shake he head, until he

106

hair stick up in he head like a porcupine. And I wonder how come Daddy don't get giddy and fall in the river. And he shouting, "Jah! Rastafari! Jah Rastafari! Selassi I!" He does chant that every morning when he wake up, and Mammy does say, "'you doh see the boy gone mad! The boy gone mad, mad!" I does want to say, "who tell you Daddy mad?" But Daddy does sound mad in truth. He always looking as if he watching something, and he alone could see it. And he doesn't raise me up and throw me up in the air again.

Me and Rally were still staying by Mammy and Papa but we always going over in the house by Daddy when he home. Then Rally start staying by Daddy all the time and going in the spring with him. And Mammy say, "Bon dieu! Papa you doh see what the man do me Beta! Beta take out that ting in you head! Bon dieu!"

A lot of the youths in the village start throwing away their afro comb and shaking their dreadlocks. They leaving their mother house and building ghettoes. Gathering in a little house down the road, talking about Marcus Garvey and Haile Selassie. Blasting Bob Marley music and cooking ital. Smoking weed and chanting down Babylon.

Daddy start playing the guitar. And every night he practice for long long. And Mammy does say, "See if ah doh calling the police for him. All de boy doing is smoking marijuana and making a bundle a noise in people head!"

Then Daddy change he name to Rasta Goose. I can't call him Daddy again, because he say Daddy is a Babylon thing.

Chapter 16

In The Ghetto

Me and Rally in the *ghetto* for weself. We always in the ghetto for weself, because every morning, when Daddy come back from the spring, he does dress-up in he Rasta colours, he bad eyes, green and gold, we does call it. He does say. "I man making a *trad*." And we don't see him again until night time.

We don't go to school anymore, because when Rally start growing he locks, the principal say he not having no Rasta in he school, as if the school is his. And Daddy say he not cutting Rally locks, so Rally stop going to school. I don't have locks yet, but Daddy take me out of school too. He say we don't need no Babylon education. That he don't want no Babylon school brainwashing he youths. Daddy say that he going to give us a real education in the ghetto. So when all we friends going to school and getting brainwashed by Babylon teachers, me and Rally home in the ghetto liming, smoking weed and doing what we want. Sometimes we don't know what to do with weself. We would go and knockabout in people garden, picking coconut and golden apples, anything we could find. And smoke. And eat. And sleep. And when we wake up, we smoke again.

Rally never used to bother with Daddy before, but since Daddy make him lock up he hair, he want to do everything he see Daddy doing. He want to dress-up like Daddy. Smoke weed like Daddy. And so he playing big man. And I following him, because is always me and Rally. From since we little, is Lee and Rally. Rally and Lee.

Rally roll-up a spliff for heself, and he roll-up a little one for me.

Is the first time I smoking a whole one for meself. I have nine years.

He light the one he roll for me.

"Jus take you time and pull it so," he say. I watch good, how he suck on the spliff to show me.

I take the first pull. Slow. Just how I see Rally do it. But as soon as I pull, the smoke come out fast fast. It fly up straight inside me head. Slide down inside me throat. And cough start pelting out, one after the other, like popcorn jumping out of the pot.

"Not so gurl! Ah tell you to pull it slow!" Rally take back the spliff from me.

I still coughing.

"Watch me eh! Pull it so." And he suck on it again.

I take the next pull, smoke pass through me mouth and me nose. Me nose burning. Me eyes burning. I remember the same thing happen to Rally the first time he thief Daddy cigarette and hide behind the house to smoke it. But Rally could smoke real good now. I watch how he sip the smoke as if he sipping a Fanta through a straw. Pull in some air through he teeth and close it inside he mouth. He hold it inside he mouth, then he blow out the smoke through he mouth. And through he nose. And the smoke float out, like how the smoke does float through the chicken wire over Mammy fireside. But every time I take a pull, the cough hurting me chest. Everything burning. The ghetto spinning. And me chest hurting.

The sun stand up right over the ghetto. And Papa say that when the sun right over your head, is lunchtime. And so me belly grumbling. And the ghetto spinning.

Daddy build the ghetto right behind the little house, near the Mango Row. When me mother go, she take away she nice overseas clothes smell, she coksie shoes and them that I used to put on and walk around the house - cok cok cok, with me hands on me waist. She take the sweet stew chicken on the little two-burner kerosene stove in the little kitchen that sit down on four tall posts. She even take away she Cutex smell, that used to stay in me nose long long after she cutex she fingernails.

And I don't know what Daddy do with she things and them, but as soon as he turn Rasta, the house turn empty. Everything gone: the bed; the table and chairs; the pictures on the partition; the cabinet with all the glass sets and Pyrex dish and them that people gave them when they got married. Even the plastic vase in the corner, with the plastic flowers that fly mess-up on, gone too. Then one day some men come and break down the little house. They pack up the pieces of house on a truck, and go with that too. Daddy say the house is Babylon dwelling. And I wonder if me mother know.

When I wake up, the sun all over by Mt Craven. It heading for Carriacou, across the sea. Me belly grumbing real loud. And Mammy outside cussing. She always cussing and quarrelling, especially when Daddy not there.

"Ah doh know who give him permission to build house on me land. Ah doh want no Rasta on me land! Ah give those children mother the spot. Who give him permission to bring he Rasta business in me place?"

But Daddy say that the land is Jah land. That land don't belong to no man. If you ever hear anybody come on this earth with land. He say that no man don't own no land. Land is for Jah people to dwell and grow food, and give thanks.

The sun reach by Carriacou, getting ready to dive down in the sea behind it. Rally still sleeping and Daddy don't reach home yet.

I look in the little calabash to see if Daddy leave any change for us, even though it too late to go and buy buns by Auntie Sille. They always finish before she take them out of the oven. I wonder if Papa bring down some water lemons from the garden for me. Sometimes he does bring down Mango Julie or ripe figs, and call me when he think Mammy not looking. "Reenie? Come. Come and take dat." But Papa does forget Mammy have eyes all behind she back. He can't not do anything without Mammy seeing. She does creep up on him behind the house.

"What you bring ting for dem for? You doh see dem is big people now. Dey smoking marijuana. Dey doh goin to school. What you bring ting for dem for?" But Papa does stand up there with the water lemons in he hands, looking shame shame, but he does stand up there until I go for it.

Sometimes in the morning, Mammy does stand up by she bedroom window combing she hair. Rubbing coconut oil in she long Indian hair reaching down by she bambam, and combing it until it shining. Then she does plait one on each side, tie them up and pin them up in the back of she head.

I sit down in the yard. Me eyes puffy and me belly grumbling. I watching Mammy. We don't have to call her Mammy again. Daddy say to call her in she name. But since I have three years, I calling Mammy, Mammy, and Papa, Papa, so when I try to say she name, it doesn't come out at all.

And Mammy just stand up there, with she eyes hiding behind she thick, little glasses that make she eyes look *cokie*, and she face falling down around she mouth. And I could see she little feet shiny shiny with coconut oil, standing up there, right by the white enamel pail. The dent up one she does use every night. She have a new one wrap-up in plastic under she bed, for when she have to go in hospital. The door between she bedroom and the one

111

me and Rally used to sleep in, full of clothes hanging on it. And it leaning down as if it go fall off the hinges. The black trunk on she right, overflowing with new panties and nighties and dusters and all kinds of things that Mammy daughter sent for her from England, things that too good to wear. The trunk look like a big whale with the mouth open. Mammy have a grip on top of it to close it. And the grip full of more new things that too good to wear too. Just like the cupboards and she press, where the Home Sweet Home lamp lighting. All of them is for when she going in hospital.

Mammy stand-up there, holding the blind and watching, watching, until the whole sun sink down behind Carriacou. And dark night spread over she glasses. Then she bolt she window.

And every evening, when dark night coming, I listening for Mammy bolting she window. And I listening for Daddy Converse boots grazing on the grass on the bank, pounding the little track down to the ghetto. And I waiting for the little gladness that Daddy footsteps does bring.

Chapter 17

Knocked Out

Daddy having a Nyabhingi gathering, and Ras Joe is the first one to reach. Ras Joe from Mt Rich. He tall and he look just like a African carving I see in one of Auntie Liz book, with big thick lips, flat nose and big wide eyes that sink down in two holes on he face. He doesn't wear shoes at all, so he feet hard hard. And he toes spread out like the roots on *The Big Tree* down in the pasture.

Me and Rally waiting for Ras Joe to open he sack, because every time he come by Daddy, he does bring bake dasheen for us. They soft and sticky, and taste like earth, but I like them. He take out a small bag of weed and give Daddy.

"Dat is de real ting! Some real Sensimillia!" Ras Joe say.

"Give tanks. Jah bless!" Daddy say. He open the bag, pinch out a little piece, sniff it, then close he eyes and take another deep smell. He smile. "Give tanks to Jah!"

Then Ras Joe dip inside the bag again and he take out baked dasheen, yam and some tannia too. He give me and Rally a little dasheen to share, and he put the rest in a calabash, for later.

The pot of rice and callaloo bubbling on the fire in the yard. Daddy put a lot of seasoning in it, from he garden behind the ghetto. And he pull out two of those tall tall, weak looking ganja plants, cut up the leaves and put them in the pot too. So the ghetto smelling like coconut and seasoning.

The pot bubbling slow, and the yard full of Rastas,

from all over the place. The ghetto fence round so nobody could see inside. Bob Marley, Burning Spear and Culture, playing on Daddy big black tape in the corner. Not so loud. And them Rastas take out their spliff and lighting it up. Me and Rally sit down watching them.

They talking about the Revolution, and about the Prime Minister, Maurice Bishop and he boys. Daddy call them Babylon Boys. He say how them Babylon Boys and them don't want to see Rastaman progress. That all they doing is victimizing Rastaman, even though is Rastaman who pick up guns and fight in the frontline to put them in power. They talking about all the Rastaman, who the PRA arrest for smoking the ganja herb. How them Babylon Boys and them anti-Rasta. And then Daddy pick up the Bible and start to read from it.

"The Most High watching dem you know. Watch! Right here, Proverbs talk about these things dem boys getting on with. The Most High don't stand for no liars, no hands that kill innocent Brethrens, no wicked minds, evil doers or trouble makers! Why you tink dem boys fraid Rastaman so? Because Rastaman don't stand for no evil!" Daddy say.

I like to listen to Daddy. And all the Rastamen listening to Daddy too, as if he some kind of leader or something. And so Daddy looking serious.

After that, Daddy share out the *ital* in *bashies*. All man hungry now, after smoking their spliffs. They ready to *nyam* their ital, like hungry lions.

The first time I taste Daddy ital, I didn't like it at all, because it didn't have no salt and no taste. But Daddy does put a lot of coconut milk and seasoning in it, and me and Rally accustomed to it now.

Daddy put Rally share in a big bashie, because Rally does eat a lot. Especially after he smoke. He put mine in me little bashie and I waiting for it to cool down.

"Yes Ras! Dat ital real *irie* dread!" One of the Rastas say, when he taste the food.

"Jah! It have real vibes man. What!" Another one say.

Daddy finish he first bashie and he take some more. Sweat running down he face and falling in he bashie.

Sweat gathering on Rally forehead and he nose, like little rain drops, and getting ready to run down he face, like Daddy.

I eat mine real slow. I have to drink water after every spoonful because Daddy put a lot of hot pepper in the ital too. And I sweat too. By the time I finish eating, me nose running and me mouth on fire.

"Jah! Give thanks and praise!" Daddy shout, when he finish he second bashie of ital. He scrape off the sweat from his face with his fingers. Then he go to the side of the fence, hold down one side on his nose and blow hard. Then he hold down the other side and blow again. "Jah! Dat one was a wicked ital Ras!"

And all of them blowing their nose and saying.

"Yes I!"

"Real wicked Ras!"

"Fire burn!"

Then Daddy take out the chalice and light it up. He does only light the chalice for special gathering. Daddy face make two holes on the sides, when he pull on the bamboo tube and the water bubble. He close he eyes, hold he breath, and then he take he time and blow out the smoke. Then he pass it to Ras Joe. Then Ras Joe pass it to the next brethren. And the next, until they reach Rally. Rally couldn't wait! He pulled on the tube. The bubbles sound real loud. Then he give me.

Me belly making ruction and me head feeling as if it too big for me. And all them Rastamen watching me. I pull down me dress under me knees. I fix me hula hoop slippers. I never smoke from the chalice before. I like when is just me and Rally in the ghetto for weself smoking. I try to remember how Daddy do it. I don't want to cough up and choke in front all Daddy brethrens.

"Go on Fari. Take it," Daddy say.

I put the thin bamboo tube in me mouth. *I could do it. I just have to pull like Daddy. Make sure I don't suck up water.* I suck, as if I sucking a snow-ice, until I hear the water bubbling. But I suck too hard. Water shoot up and go right up in me nose. And it's as if it go inside me head too. And shooting up from right down in the bottom in me belly, to me chest. And I sure it bruise-up me chest, because it hurting real bad.

"Take it easy Fari! Take it easy!" Ras Joe say. He tap me on me back and he take the chalice from me.

"Easy Princess." Daddy say.

Me head spinning. I feeling giddy and sick. I want to vomit. Me head feeling heavy. It feeling light.

Rally sucking the chalice again.

The ghetto upside down.

Me eyes closing down. I get up to go inside the ghetto. Daddy holding me. Me feet feeling like putty. I lie down on the bunk. The ghetto spinning.

Brightness playing outside me eyes. I want the brightness to come inside me eyes. I try to open me eyes. They heavy. They not opening. I feeling as if it have gravels inside me eyes and stones on top them. I try to raise up me head but it too heavy and me mouth dry like paper. I not sleeping but I can't get up. Everything heavy heavy.

"Fari? Fari rise up."

I hearing Daddy voice but I can't open me eyes.

He shake me.

"Rise up Fari!"

Then me eyes open. I raise up me head and the

116

bamboo roof spinning. I lie down again. I feeling *bazodee,* like a zombie.

"Fari. De I aright?" Daddy ask me.

I sit up on the bunk. The light outside too bright. It hurting me eyes.

Rally moving on the top bunk. I close me eyes.

"Rise up Fari. Rise and shine." Daddy shake me again.

When I wake up again, I hear Mammy talking behind the house.

"Well he kill dem now! The boy kill dem poor chilren! Ah Papa God! Is the police ah callin for him jus now. You doh see the boy crazy! What he have to do the poor chilren and dem that for! Eh?"

Daddy say me and Rally was sleeping for three whole days.

Chapter 18

Back To Roots

We living in the back of Celeste now. Daddy get tired of Mammy cussing about she land, so he get a piece of land, all the way in the back of Celeste. He pick a spot on top of the hill, near the river and the spring. It only have two other houses over there, but they not nearby.

The land was real high woods when Daddy get it, but he cut down the trees, like the Motelbas, Glory Cedars and Cutlets. He cut down all the wild vines and bush. And me and Rally help him build the ghetto. We hold posts for Daddy to pound the nails. We pass the coconut branch. We go in the bush and look for *tash* from palm trees. Daddy put them under the bamboo on the roof, so rain wouldn't come inside. We help him build the bunks with bamboo and make the mattress with coconut branches.

And when we move, Daddy say not to call him Daddy anymore. He say is a new life we starting now. Is back to roots, so we have to call him by he name, I-Trad. He call Rally, I-Rally and he call me I-Lee.

When Daddy finish building the ghetto, he start to fork up the land. I-Rally climbing trees and chasing lizards in the bush, and I sitting down by Daddy watching how he driving the fork in the hard, dry ground, with all he might. Riding the fork to make the soil loose. Sweat dripping from he face, running down he chest and soaking up he pants waist. And when he turn over the soil, earth worms wiggle out, and congorees coil up in balls to hide from the fork. But sometimes when the fork catch one of them, it does make a crunching sound that does make me skin crawl.

Daddy not talking so much now. Sometimes he does ask me to bring some water for him. But he always looking as if he far far away, on some high meditation.

When he finish forking-up the land, he start praying for Jah to send some rain, so he could plant up he herbs. The rain come and the ground drink and drink. And Daddy say it looking nice and rich. Good ground for planting. And he say, "Thank you Jah!" And he plant he ganja seeds. And he make beds by the ghetto and plant sweet potatoes, dasheen, tannia, peppers and a lot of chives and thyme.

Twit. Twit. Twit. Twit. I lie down on me bunk listening to the little Ceecee birds in the tree, right outside the ghetto. I could hear the blackbirds and the peepeerits too. Rally know all the bird sounds and he does make me listen to them, just as he used to make me listen to the kites.

Outside bright already. The sun come out early. Bob Marley and the Wailers singing *Don't worry.* And Rally snoring on the bunk over me. I can't see him, but I sure he mouth open and dribble running down from the corner, soaking up the blanket he fold up as he pillow.

I get up, take two mangoes, and go out in the yard. Daddy up in the field already. He does wake up before the sun. He does even wake up before the birds, to go and work in he ganja field.

I sit down in the yard eating me mango and watching Daddy. He moulding the ganja plants. Pulling out every little weed he could find. He does even talk to them, as if they could hear him. And sometimes I does see him just standing up right at the top, just watching the field. It reaching all down to the bottom of the hill. He just watching it as if he could see them growing, right in front he eyes.

A lot of rain does fall and the ganja plants growing real fast. They reaching all by Daddy knee already. And they green and looking real strong. Every time I watch them, they looking bigger. And I like to watch how the leaf and them spread out for the sun. How they does wave when the wind blow. And after rain fall, how they does smell. And how they does look new.

I-Rally wake up and come outside with all the dry up bridle around he mouth. He stretch and look up at the sky. I know he looking to see if rain going to fall. But it don't have no rain clouds today. That mean we have to tote up buckets and buckets of water from the river to wet the field. Sometimes, me and I-Rally does do it for weself. And when the sun real hot, we have to wet the plants in the evening too. That does make I-Rally get real vex

Daddy finish weeding the plants, and he come down to the ghetto.

"De Princess aright?" He ask me. He washing he muddy hands in the bucket of water by the door.

"Ah good," I say, licking the mango juice from me fingers before it fall on me dress. *Rastaman vibration* playing now. Daddy turn up the volume. Then he come and sit down by me with he bashie of mangoes.

I still can't call Daddy I-Trad because he is me Daddy. But he say that this Daddy and Mommy thing is Babylon teaching too. And he don't want people to call him mister either. He say that come straight from slavery days, so he not putting no Mister or Mistress in front nobody name either. It could be the Prime Minister or the Pope! And don't let him start on the Pope. He say the Pope is the devil himself! All he good for is brainwashing poor people.

When I-Trad finish sucking he mangoes, he say, "I-man have to make a turn today." He suck out some mango thread from he teeth. "De I go give the ganja some water later eh. Wet dem before the sun get too hot. Irie?"

"Um hm," I say. I watch I-Rally. He don't answer.

Daddy always going on some mission. Sometimes he does bring us with him. One time he bring us in Grenville and we go in the photo studio and take out a picture. In the picture, I-Trad stooping down, with he Bible in he hand, and me and I-Rally standing up by him. I-Rally face looking vex vex. And I looking skinny, in me new polka dot dress that me mother send, and a green head-tie. And I looking as if I want to cry. The picture stick up on the post in the ghetto.

When Daddy go, me and I-Rally take we bucket and head down to the river. We have the whole river for weself. And Daddy not coming back now, so we have the whole day to do what we want.

We wet the ganja plants quick. We give them just enough so the stools look wet. It have a lot of ganja plants. Once me and I-Rally start to count them, but we stop when we reach halfway. We count about two hundred and something.

When we finish wetting the field, we go back down in the river. We take out we clothes, put them on a river-stone and we go in the river and bathe. Daddy does only bathe with spring water, but me and I-Rally like to bathe in the little basin in the river. Then we does rinse out with spring water.

I-Rally catch some little mullets. Then when he throw them back in the water, they wiggle away fast and swim for their lives.

"Lee come quick!" I-Rally call.

He does forget to call me I-Lee

"Bring the paint pan come! Quick!" He bending down by a river stone watching something in the water.

"Ah coming," I say, hopping from one stone to the

next, with the little paint pan that we does use to full up the buckets.

"Come and see that crayfish quick!"

"Whey?"

The trees over the river making dark shadows on the water.

"Over dey! You doh see it? One big *gandolie*. Watch it! Watch it! The claws big!"

I bend down, looking where he pointing.

"Hold the paint pan eh. Ah go ketch e backside!"

I-Rally push he hand in the water real slow. He aiming just like when he playing marble. He face set. He eyes on the crayfish. Then he make a grab. Pull out he hand. Push it inside the paint pan. And all the time I holding the pan good good, but as soon as I hear the crayfish claws start scratching up inside the pan, I let it go. I sure the crayfish go come out of the pan and bite me. I-Rally catch it quick before the crayfish get away.

"A! Wha happen to you gurl? How you coward so?"

"Well you know ah fraid crayfish aready, you know."

Everything does frighten me in truth. And I-Rally always frightening me. One time we in Edwards - Mammy land up in the mountain. Papa picking cocoa, Mammy gathering them up and me and Rally bringing them up by the little house, near to the road where Papa tie the donkey. Edwards dark! Even when sun was *eating pin* outside, Edwards still dark and wet. The nutmeg trees and them stand up tall and straight like soldiers. The mango, Lung and the grafted Julie, guarding the front. The coconut trees line along the road, like school children in assembly. The breadnut and breadfruit branches spread out wide, touching the cocoa branches and they blocking the sun. So I heading up to the house with me little pan full of cocoa and I listening for every creak or rustle in the bush. Even me own footstep on the dry cocoa leaves - that cover up the ground like a carpet - does frighten me. So I walking quick. I just wondering how far Rally reach when something jump out from behind the giant nutmeg tree going "YAAAHHHHHH!" Just like when me mother frighten me with Daddy mask. Me whole body freeze up, but me heart start to beat as if it go burst out me chest, and fall in the big drain like me bucket. I bawl out so loud, Papa and all run up to see what happen to me. And Papa looking so funny running up with he cutlass in he hand, me and Rally start to laugh. And Papa laughing too.

We go in the bush and hunt fruits. We come back with mangoes, plums and sugarcane. We full we belly. Then I-Rally roll up a spliff for heself. And I roll one for meself. I could do it for meself now. We smoke we whole one.

When I wake up, the sun over the trees on top of the hill. Is evening time and Daddy don't come back yet, so we start to cook. I break up some brambles from the behind the ghetto, and I-Rally light the fire with coconut shells.

I-Rally like to cook. And we always watching Daddy when he cooking, so we know what to do. He grate the coconut and peel the yam. I pull up some sweet potato from the bed in the garden and scrape them. Daddy say the best part is under the skin so he does not peel them. I cut up some callaloo and some seasoning, then I-Rally pack them in the big bashie.

Daddy stop cooking in pots. He use calabash to make pots and bowls to eat, call bashie. And he use coconut shell to make knife, scraper, spoon, cup, ashtray and all kinds of things. Once I hear Daddy say, "You see this coconut? Jah make it specially for Rastaman. And he use everything from the coconut tree. He build he ghetto with the coconut branch; make stool and bench with the trunk; light the fire with the coconut skin; roast breadfruit; wash up the wares with the fibre from the skin; use the coconut shell to make cup, spoon, bowl, ashtray and all kind of things. And he used coconut milk in everything he cook. And he does make oil with it too.

When the fire burn down, I-Rally make a circle in the middle, put the bashie on the hot ashes and fix up the coals around it. He make sure no coals toucing the bashie to burn hole in it

While the bashie on fire, we play the Bob Marley tape again. I-Rally picking the guitar strings. He putting he fingers how he see Daddy doing it and playing. I beating the drum and we singing. We singing loud. We alone in the whole place. Just me and I-Rally. Is always just me and I-Rally, since before we move. Because Lano go in England and Miss Kay stop Boyboy and Yvette from playing with us. She say we is bad influence. How we go make them smoke weed too. And nobody living near to the ghetto to hear us. Only the birds, the lizards, and the sheep and goats grazing in the bush. So the bashie bubbling and me and I-Rally singing.

I-Rally light another spliff and we smoke it together, like big people. Me head light and I feeling as if I in the ghetto, but I somewhere else. I want to laugh and I want to cry too. I sure Bob Marley singing right inside me head. I sing with him. *Pimples paradise, that's all she was now. What is pimples paradise? Pimples paradise?* The bass guitar echoing inside me head. The drums too. They vibrating and I waiting for the drummer to hit the silver thing – the thing that look like a plate on a stick. Daddy call it the cymbal. I real like the drums. I wish I could be a drummer.

I-Rally stop playing the guitar. He watching through the door. He eyes looking wild.

The bashie bubbling hard. The coconut milk falling down in the hot ashes, outing the fire. I want to get up to go and check it but I can't move. I-Rally hearing it too, but he don't move. After a while he go outside and uncover the bashie.

Me head go and knock about. *I in school doing dictation, waiting for Miss Charles to correct it. Walking up from school with Yvette, Marie, Lano and Boyboy and I-Rally, stoning pwadoo on Creft Hill. Oiling Papa head on the veranda. Combing Suzie hair and listening the radio. Me mother washing me hair in the yard. Mammy calling me to come and scrub she back.*

Mr Nummy donkey bray three times. I bet Mammy listening to the death news now. She does know when it's six o' clock when Mr Nummy donkey bray.

Dark night coming and I praying Daddy go reach back before it cover the whole place. And owls start to call. Dogs start to howl. Frogs croaking in the bush. Bamboo splitting from all the hot sun.

I-Rally does pretend he not frighten. Playing he real brave, but I know he real frighten too. Sometimes we does get real glad when we hear manicou hunters out in the bush.

I does lie down on me bunk quiet quiet, me eyes wide open, until I hear branch breaking through the track. But it have times when sleep does knock me out cold, and I doesn't hear when Daddy come.

Chapter 19

On The Bus

Me and I-Rally wake up real early. We going with I-Trad by one of he brethrens and we glad. But better yet, rain fall in the night, so we don't have to wet the field.

We don't even play in the river. We just bathe quick. And we dress quick. I put on me favourite dress, the same polka dot one I have on in the picture. A long time I don't wear it because we don't go out a lot. The dress hang on me as if me is a hanger. And it reaching right down by me little bony ankles, as if I shrink. It almost hiding me new leather slippers, that one of I-Trad brethrens make for me. I remember one day when I-Trad mark out me left foot on a big cocoa leaf, and put it in he bag.

I-Trad never go anywhere without he bag and he Bible. He pack it already, with sweet potatoes and yam from the garden. He does bring things for he brethrens and when he come home, he always have something in he bag from them too.

I-Rally have on he Jim boots and he new dashiki. And he bump all the way down to the bus, checking out heself. And when anybody look at him, he give them he *what you watching* look.

I walk behind, grinding pain because the slippers hard hard. And it hurting between me toes.

The big board bus with BIG SHOT paint up on the front, stop in the junction. I-Trad used to drive one just like it. It almost empty when we get in. I sit down in the middle row, by the window. And I-Rally take the seat in front of me, by the window. And I know people does sit down by their children, but I-Trad leave us and go all the way in front the bus. The lady in front have to move up by the driver, for him to sit down.

The next time the bus stop, two schoolgirls come in and sit down right behind the driver. Their long, oily plaits lie down on their white school shirts, like ropes. And I smelling the coconut oil on their shiny skin.

A man and two ladies sit down in the back of the bus talking.

"Well ah doh know what happen to dese children now-a-days nuh. All dey want to do is smoke weed and idle by de road."

"Yes mama! Ah have a boy dey, de ting turn him bazodee oui. He doh even goin to school now. Hmm," the man say.

I look back quick. The lady who talking big big! She taking up two seat for sheself. And she voice big just like her.

"Well mine want to kill me oui papa. He smoking the ting too! And when you see he smoke it eh, he eating everyting in de house. And ah can say nuttin you know! No sah! When de ting take him, he cussing all man an dey brother. Is de PRA ah callin for him jus now. You see how dey does round dem up and make dem join the Militia? Well is dem ah callin for him just now!" The other woman saying.

The bus stop again and a little boy climb up. He sit down in the same row with me. He smell like pencil shaving and rusty things, just like school. And is Monday morning, but he shirt looking dirty dirty and he khaki pants have mango stains on it. Under me eyes, I look across at he feet. He blue hula hoop slippers tie up with string and one of he big toes tie up with a dirty piece of cloth. And I wish he didn't come and sit down by me, because he smoke herring souse in he carrier stirring up me belly already. I turn me face to the window and I trying to hold me breath. And breathe through me mouth.

One of the girls behind the driver look back at me.

"You doh see dat Rasta girl behin dey!," she say.

The next one turn around. They watching me and laughing. All their front teeth black black. I turn to the window again. Watching the sea and holding me breath. Then breathing in through me mouth, out through me nose.

Outside the window, the sea spread out itself like a big blue blanket. It so big and wide, I start to feel as if it swallowing me up. And it looking as if it rolling pass the bus. And everything in the sea looking small. The fishing boats look like little nutmeg pods that floating on the water. The sail boats look like the little paper boats we used to tear out pages from we exercise book to make.

The sea breeze salty and fresh. I breathe. In through me mouth. Out me nose. Hold me breath. The sea breeze full up me head. I feeling giddy. And every time the bus hit a pothole, me belly falling down in the hole with it.

The girls look back again. We eyes bounce up. They cover their mouths and giggle. I wonder if they does brush their teeth. Mammy never used to make me and I-Rally brush we teeth. But we does suck a lot of sugar cane. And I-Trad make us use guava stick. But we don't use no tooth paste.

Sourness bubbling up in me throat, like Andrews Liver Salts, when Mammy pour it in water. On the other side of the bus, the little board houses running up the road, while the bus going down. Ladies in the yard washing, in front their dresses soaking wet. Children sweeping yards. Running around in old tear-up jerseys. No underpants. No panties. Some naked as they born.

I-Trad looking out the window too. The driver

looking across at him, and back to the road. I-Rally watching the sea.

"So what going on Fenneh?" The driver shout, as if he talking to somebody in the back of the bus. Daddy name was Fenneh before he turn Rasta, but he doesn't answer when people call him that name now. He just looking out the window, as if nobody speaking.

And I praying for the bus to reach where we going.

"So wha happen man, you stop speaking to people now?" The driver say.

I-Trad don't answer.

More sourness coming up in me mouth. I swallow it.

"Man wha happen to you man? Because you turn Rasta you doh even want to talk to people now. Well I never see!" The driver let out a big *stupse.* Then he look back in he mirror. He eyes bounce up with mine.

I breathe in. I hold it. Sourness in me mouth again.

"An what you do you children that for, eh? You doh even sening dem children to school."

I-Trad still don't answer. But he face starting to get real hard, as if he trying real hard to hold back he temper.

Everybody on the bus stop talking. And I feeling as if all of them watching me and I-Rally. I put me eyes outside on the sea. Me mouth full. I want to spit but I can't put me head out the window. The breeze rushing pass the bus too fast.

The girls looked back again. I-Rally turn he bad eyes on them. They look in front one time.

A lady in the back say, "Poor ting. Ah sure he does give dem de ting to smoke too. You doh see how she eyes dey in two hole!"

The next one say, "Me! No man doh takin me chilren and turn dem in no Rasta! Ah wonder whey dey mother is!"

I swallow again, but the sourness don't go down. I

feeling as if I in the sea and the waves boiling me. Me eyes start to get dark and I start to sweat. I force down the spit. Me mouth full up again.

When the bus stop, all me insides heave up and then drop down. When I see I-Trad get out I jump down quick. Before I even reach the bush on the side of the road, all the mangoes and ripe *figs* I had eat before we leave home, shoot out from me belly with full force.

As I wiping me mouth with the end of me dress, I hear I-Trad saying, "Live and let live man. Jah bless." Then he trod on. Bag on he shoulder. Bible in he hand.

Chapter 20

Ras Shanti

Me and I-Rally follow I-Trad through a nutmeg plantation. It dark and wet, just like up in Edwards. It have rotting mangoes all over the ground, with congorees inside them. And congorees crawling all over them, and making me belly sick again.

I-Trad walking fast, and he not talking at all. I wonder if he thinking about what the bus driver say.

I walking close by I-Rally. He walking fast too, so I have to run sometimes, to keep up with him. Me and I-Rally whispering to one another, as though we afraid the trees and the animals go hear us. He show me a bird with a red head and white chest. A woodpecker. He call it a pecker-o. And the little little one we see flying over some flowers, is a doctor bird. He and Lano used to shoot birds with slingshots. They used to shoot lizards too, with bows and arrows, with common pins stick on to the ends. But I-Rally don't do that kind of things again. I-Trad say Jah created the animals too and how they have a right to live just like us.

I feel glad when we reach a wide patch of grass and I see light. I tired and me belly grumbling. We pass a garden full of cabbages, lettuce and beets. Then we see smoke coming out from on top a hill, and a Rastaman waving at us.

"Dat's me brethren Ras Shanti," I-Trad say.

When I wake up next morning, I hear dum dum, du du dum dum. Somebody beating a drum. And chanting. I-

131

Trad does beat he drum like that every morning, when he meditating and giving praise to Jah.

I sit up and a foot dangle right in front me face. The toes on the foot open wide and the big toe pointing the other way. I-Rally foot.

I don't know the ghetto. It smaller than we ghetto. It have some bamboo shelf in one corner, with all different size bashies on it. It have a big bashie on a plank of wood, full of mangoes, guavas, rock-figs and one big ripe soursop. The soursop so ripe, the skin start to turn brown. It have a soursop tree behind Mammy house. Me and I-Rally used to pick them as soon as they ripe and eat them, licking the juice between we fingers and down we elbows.

Then I smell the sapodillas before I see them in the bashie. Me mouth start to make water for them. I-Rally don't like how it does make he lips stick together when he eat them. But I like them more than any fruit. I like how the flesh soft and sweet. And when they well ripe, I eating the skin and all. I even like the seeds, how they black and shiny. And they look like diamonds.

And then I see a rastaman sit down at the other end of the ghetto. He eyes closed and he look like a high priest. He skin black as coals. He big bundle of locks lie down on he back. Some little ones falling around he long hard face. And he big, broad nose look as if somebody stick it on he face by mistake.

When he open he eyes, he see me watching him.

"Princess de I rise up?" He say.

And I remember the rastaman waving at us from on top the hill. Ras Shanti. And I remember the special ital oildown he cook for us, with all kinds of things in it. And when we finish eating, he bring out the chalice and give I-Trad to light. Then I lie down on the bamboo bunk. And me eyes close down.

I look around for I-Trad.

"I-Trad make a turn aready Princess," Ras Shanti say, as if he could read me mind.

"He have to watch out for de herbs Princess. But he say de I could stay for a while."

I-Trad just leave us and go. We don't even know Ras Shanti. But I know I-Trad must be feeling we have to stay by Ras Shanti for a reason. He always saying how Jah don't make things happen without a reason.

Me and I-Rally really like it by Ras Shanti. We help him in the garden. It not so hot up in the mountain and the soil wet and black. I-Trad say that kind of soil good for planting. The grass always feel damp, as if the rain drizzling on it all the time.

We roam the garden and full we belly with fruits and sugar cane. In the evening, when Ras Shanti cooking ital for us, I sit down watching him.

"Princess, bring ah *I-bage* and some seasoning for I-Man," he say. And I run out in the garden and pull out the cabbage, I shake out the soil and break out the roots. I remember me teacher saying cabbage have fibrous roots. The roots look like fibre in truth. I pick some *poor man pork*, some chive and thyme and some peppers. And when he put them in the bashie the whole ghetto smell of seasoning and sweet coconut milk. And I can't wait for the ital to cook. Ras Shanti could cook real good, like I-Trad.

When we finish eating, Ras Shanti give us a spliff. Me and I-Rally share it.

The sun still hiding behind the mountain, when I wake up. And rain falling. The roof low down, so it sounding as if it falling right over me head. The wind sneak in through the bamboo and touch me shoulder and me face, like cold hands.

The ghetto smelling like ganja and mint tea. I sit up on the bunk and wrap up in the sheet, tight tight, like a cocoon. I-Rally still snoring.

"De Princess rise up. De I want some herb tea?" Ras Shanti smile and pour some tea in a little bashie and bring it for me.

"Dis go warm de I up. I-man make it special for de Princess."

Ras Shanti look hard and strong. I wonder if he have children. But even though I-Trad always telling me "Ask and ye shall be told. Seek and ye shall find," and I know Ras Shanti go answer me, I don't ask him.

I drink me tea and lie down. I pull me cover over me and curl up meself. I close me eyes again and I listening to the rain beating drum on the bamboo roof. All kinds of pictures start to flash in me head, as if I looking in a viewfinder: me, Rally, Daddy and me mother on the beach. Me mother frying bakes in the little kitchen. The Pyrex dish falling on my foot when we come back from Bathway Beach. Running and meet Daddy when I hear me whistle. Me mother waving and going inside a big plane...

I stand in front of the door. The sun dancing on me face. The rain stop. The plants look happy. The lettuce smiling. The corn nodding, as if they telling me good morning. The pawpaw leaf tickle me face. The sun inside me. I laughing and singing.

I-Rally and Ras Shanti not in the garden. I go outside and look for them. Behind the ghetto. Through the bush. They not there. Me head heavy. The breeze wet on me skin. I climb down the track to the river. It steep steep. I am afraid of precipice. The ground muddy. Slippery. I grip the big fat roots. Slide down in the mud.

I-Rally washing sweet potatoes in the river. He putting the pink potatoes in a bag.

I have on Ras Shanti shirt. It full of mud. I take it out and wash it. The water cold. I climb on the big flat stone to spread the shirt on a branch over the water. The stone wet. Slippery. I falling, falling, falling in a big black hole. Down, down. Sinking. Sinking like a big heavy stone. Me arms stick on me. I can't hold nothing. Mammy saying, "E damn good for you. Ah tell you aready water doh have branch." Me legs not moving. The hole big and black. It swallowing me. Daddy catch me. I hold Daddy neck tight tight. He smell like Pears soap and cigarette smoke. Ras Shanti raise me up the track.

I jump up on the bunk. I shaking and sweating. Me heart— Ras Shanti's drum. Me teeth knocking together. I looking round for I-Trad. Ras Shanti sitting on he stump like Haile Selassie.

"You irie Princess? De I have a bad vision?" Ras Shanti say.

"Um hm,' I say. I afraid to speak. I still shaking and the dream in me head. I want Daddy. I want to go home.

"I-man cook some special ital today."

The sun make inside the ghetto look like inside a mammie apple. I-Rally in front the door making a pawpaw flute. Ras Shanti chipping up ganja leaves in a big bashie and rolling out a lot of little spliffs.

Some baby robin singing outside. They sound hungry. I bet their mother digging up worms in the garden for them. A cow moo far away. I-Rally finish the flute and testing it out.

Me heart get a little quiet.

"You want a blow?" he ask me.

I shake me head. I don't feel like blowing no flute. He blow it. It look easy to blow. Not like I-Trad bamboo flute, that hard hard to blow.

"It sound bad eh! Ah go make one for you tomorrow eh," he say.

I don't want no flute. I want to go home by me Daddy.

Ras Shanti walk with us halfway through the woods. He give us five dollars to pay the bus.

"Jus follow the track down and de I mus reach the road," he say. "Jah guidance youth-man," he say, and he give I-Rally a bounce. Then he touch me head and say, "Irie Princess." And he leave us in the middle of the woods.

Me and I-Rally follow the track through the nutmeg plantation. I walking so close to I-Rally, if he turn he bouncing me down. Me ears open. Me eyes open. I on the lookout, as if I expect something to jump out from the bush. A nutmeg fall, me heart leap. A branch move, me belly fall down.

I-Rally bring the bag of itals Ras Shanti give us. He say he sure he remember the way, until we end up by the same mammie apple tree, three times. And then he start to look all round him for the road. And I start to get real frighten.

Then we meet an old man picking up nutmegs. He show us where to go. We walking down the track and I-Rally start singing Peter Tosh song.

If you just put your hand in mine, we gonna leave all our troubles behin'

We gonna walk and don' look back.

And I singing the chorus in me head - *don' look back.*

And I look back and see the old man shaking he head the way Mammy does shake she head to say "Poor tings."

When we reach home, I-Trad tell us how he catch a man name Buck in the ganja field. Buck is a real ganja thief. He does just wait for people ganja get big and thief them and go and sell. I-Trad say he walk up to him, real quiet. And I know I-Trad could walk in bush like an Apache. He say he take Buck cutlass from him, and give him one *planassing* in he backside. Buck gallop and bawl

like a donkey, through the bush, prickle and *zootie* and all.
And me and I-Rally laugh until we belly hurt.

Chapter 21

The Visitors

One evening, I-Trad bring a group of Rastas home with him. They from England and they have a reggae band name *I-Water*. All of them have dreadlocks except one. But they don't look like I-Trad or his Rasta brethrens. They dress up different. Their locks not thick and stick-up together like I-Trad locks. They long and they looking neat. Their hands look soft and their fingernails clean clean, as if they never hear about work in they life! And they smelling nice, like inside Grandma Clarice suitcase.

Drewry is the only one who don't have locks. He have Indian hair like Mammy. He skin white white. He face long. He nose long. He moustache covering he top lip and it looking as if it should be on one of them other Rastas, not on Drewry. Once, I-Rally find a lizard egg in the mountain, and he let me touch it. I wonder why the lizard lay she egg right on the ground there, between stones and roots and all kinds of hard things. Right where people walking. The egg so soft I pull back me hand one time, because I afraid I go burst it. And I watching Drewry and I wondering how come he end up with this band of Rastas, because he just like the lizard egg.

I-Trad cook a real big bashie of ital, with a lot of ganja leaves, that he send I-Rally and pick. All of them Rastas sit down in the yard rolling spliffs from the little bashie of ganja I-Trad give them. And they looking happy. After we eat, we sit down in the yard, under the full moon, playing music and singing whole night. I-Trad does not bring any and any body in he ghetto. And I like when he bring one of he brethrens and we just playing music and singing, because most time is just me and I-Rally alone. But sometimes, I wish he bring a Rasta sistren. Sometimes I does wonder how come none of he brethrens don't have a little Rasta child like me, so we could sing together.

All of them sleep outside by the ganja field. When they go the next day, Drewry say he want to stay with us for a while. And I-Trad say, "free up youself brethren. Irie."

"You want to come in the river wid us?" I-Rally ask Drewry.

"What? The river?" Drewry sit down in the yard watching the ganja field and smiling.

"Ah say, if you want to come in the river wid us." I-Rally say it loud, as if Drewry deaf. But Drewry still don't understand. So we take we buckets and we tell him to come on.

Drewry get up real slow. He hold on to a stump but he looking as if he don't have no balance at all. He looking flimsy as a plum branch, as if he go break if you touch him too hard. He take he time and walk down the hill. By the time he reach by the river, he breathing hard hard and looking as if he go fall down dead. I get frighten for him. I-Rally help him to sit down on a stone.

"Am alright. Am alright." Drewry say, but he still breathing hard, as if he just finish running a race. He sit down on a stone watching everything, as if is first time he seeing bush, and trees, and river stones. We leave him there while we wet the field. And every time we come back to full up we bucket, Drewry just sitting down there watching the river. Watching a lizard. Listening. Smiling. He can't stop smiling.

When he see us bathing in the river, he take out he shoes, roll up he pants and try to get up from the stone. I-Rally run and hold him before he fall. But he only saying,

"Am alright, am alright," but he not looking alright at all.

Drewry legs white and full of big water plugs! And every time he put he foot on the ground, he have to pick it up again fast, as if he put it on prickle! So I hold one hand and I-Rally hold he other hand, and we help him to go in the little basin where we does bathe.

Drewry stand up in the water as if he afraid of it. I-Rally pitch some water on him.

"*Bumbaclot*! This water's cold to ras!" Drewry say, ducking from the water. And he sounding like the other Rastas and them from the band.

I-Rally throw some water on him again. Then I throw some on him too. He start to laugh. Then all of us splashing water and laughing till me belly start to hurt. And Drewry looking red like a crayfish in hot water.

Drewry can't sing. He can't even play the guitar or anything. He tell us he just travelling with the band because he like reggae. And he like Rasta vibes. He like how Rastas live simple and natural.

Even though Drewry say he have twenty six years, we have to show him how to do everything. When we go in the river, I-Rally show him how to catch mullets. I show him how to wash he clothes. Drewry say he can't believe we have a natural spring right by we home. He could drink all the spring water he want for free.

Sometimes he does go down by the river with he notebook and he pen. He does sit down quiet, listening and writing in he notebook. I wondering what he writing. He like to listen to the birds and I-Rally does tell him their names. I does watch him walking about in the field, touching the ganja leaves. Smelling them. Sometimes he does lie down on the ground and roll in the sun with he short pants alone, until mosquitoes and sandflies chase him.

And so Drewry does make me and I-Rally laugh. He can't even shoo a fly, but he want to do everything he see me and I-Rally doing. He try to help bring up a bucket of water, but by the time he reach half way up the hill, the bucket almost empty. He want to help us cook, but he hands so soft, he can't even break up brambles to light the fire. And everything he eat, he have to run straight in the latrine. And I glad he have he toilet paper, because it have a lot of red ants in the coconut fibre I-Trad does use and I bet Drewry can't use bush like me and I-Rally.

Before Drewry come, me and I-Rally didn't have any friend. Now Drewry is we friend and we glad we have company. I-Rally don't even get so vex when we have to wet the ganja again. And I does not be so afraid again, when night reach.

Chapter 22

The Raid

The ganja field growing as if it making haste. They look like a family, waving and bowing together when the wind blowing.

The male ones tall as I-Trad already. They long and skinny, and the leaves look light green. I-Trad does pick the leaves and put in he ital when he cooking. The female ones look real strong. And they have dark leaves and a lot of seeds. But it have some with short branches, and their flowers look like dry corn beard. I-Trad say that's the real special ones. The cream of the crop. The Sensimillias. And he looking after them the best. He treating them just like the teacher and everybody in me class used to treat the new white girl from America.

When I-Trad home he always up in the field with them, as if he is their Daddy. He moulding them and pinching out the buds. He say that is to make the branch and them spread out and get thicker. And he still talking to them.

Then one morning when I wake up, I hear noise outside. I-Trad up in the field already. I-Rally snoring, and Drewry curl up in he pink blanket on the floor, in front me bunk. He look like a big baby. He mouth open just a little bit and I could hear him breathing. But he not snoring like I-Rally.

Is the first of July, 1980. The day before was Drewry birthday and I count fourteen days to go before I take ten years.

I peep through the bamboo. Light hit me straight in

me eyes. Early morning light does hurt eyes bad. Just like how the ground does hurt your feet early in the morning.

I could hear talking. Bush moving. The cocks up the hill crow already, but Mr Nummy donkey braying. I don't hear the baby birds tweeting outside. They get big now. Maybe they gone and get food for theyself.

I peep again. I don't see I-Trad. All I could see is green. The ganja field, the trees, the bush. And all them soldiers in their green uniform.

"I-Rally, wake up!" I shake him hard. Me hand trembling. And I feeling like me legs starting to tremble too.

"Mmmm. Man! Wha happen?" I-Rally groan. He roll over and just go back snoring again.

I looking for I-Trad, but I only seeing soldiers. I shake I-Rally again.

"It have soldiers outside!"

"Wha? Soldiers?" He jump up. Climb down from he bunk, over Drewry and run straight outside.

I stand up by the door and I looking for I-Trad. Me knees weak. Them PRA soldiers everywhere. All around the field. And they have guns. Then I see I-Trad. He stand up on the top of the field. He back to the ghetto. He stand up straight like one of them tall pillars under we little house. And he just watching the field. And two soldiers stand up pointing their guns at him.

I have to go behind the ghetto to pee. But I afraid to move. The soldiers moving about in the field now. Some rooting up the ganja plants. Some chopping down. Some dragging them and putting them in big cocoa sacks.

I sweating and I trying to squeeze me pee until I can't squeeze it again and I run behind the ghetto before I pee meself.

Drewry get up and he stand up by the door with he mouth open wide. He looking whiter than when he just come by us. As if he don't have no blood in he body. He looking sick too.

And I-Rally in the yard watching the soldiers real bad-eyes! I sure if he get a gun he shooting down the soldiers and them, just like in them western movies in Griffin cinema.

Just yesterday, the yard full of ganja. I-Trad say how most of them ready. How is time to reap the crop. When he cut them, he would put them in cocoa sacks and put them under the bunk to cure. Then put them on top of the roof in the sun. And me and I-Rally would have to watch out for rain; just as we used to do when Papa put cocoa to dry. Just yesterday, the ganja field swaying and nodding in the wind, and I-Trad talking to them and giving Jah thanks for the good crop. Now the field naked! The soldiers strip it naked. Only stumps that stand up there now. I-Trad never get to reap he crop.

I wonder if I-Trad know the soldiers who pointing the guns at him. I bet they fight together in the Revolution. I could see the soldiers talking but I-Trad not saying a word. He just stand up there staring at the field, with he head leaning on one side. I-Trad always stand up like that when he thinking real hard about something. I bet he talking in he mind. *Why you Babylon must victimize I-man so? I-man a dwell out here living a simple and peaceful life with I-man youths. I-man en trouble no one. I-man just planting a little herbs. The healing of the nation. Why you people have to victimize Rastaman so? Why all you can just leave Rastaman in peace eh? Why all you so afraid of the ganja herbs? Why all you so afraid of the words of Jah?* I-Trad always talking about Babylon oppression and Babylon victimization. I bet that's what he talking to heself about. What the soldiers doing.

We walk down the track with soldiers in front and

soldiers in the back. I-Trad walking in the middle. They let him put on a shirt and he shoes before they handcuff him. Me and I-Rally walking right behind him. And Drewry walking behind us with he sleeping bag under he arm. He walking like a little child that just learning to walk. He stumping he toe on all the roots and stones in the road. I swear he go fall on he face.

I feel real sorry for Drewry. He looking like skin and bones, and he have boils and sores all over he body, because mosquitoes and sandflies murder him. But I-Trad say he want to see ghetto life, so let him take the chafing. I wondering if the soldiers go lock him up. I wondering if they go lock up me and I-Rally too.

All the way down, I-Trad lock he jaw tight tight. He don't say a word. He eyes look like steel. He face hard like *The Lion of Judah.* He walking with he head up, and he looking straight in front him.

Me bare feet pounding down the stony track. All kinds of things knocking about in me head. Where the soldiers go bring us. If we going back by Mammy and Papa. If we mother go come back. If I-Trad going in jail. And I-Rally playing brave but I know things knocking about in he head too.

When we reach the house at the bottom of the hill, the lady stop sweeping she yard and she watching us. And I wondering why this big lady sweeping yard, because she have children. Maybe what people say about how she does spoil she children is true.

Then Miss Mavis come out in she pink duster and she bed slippers. Miss Mavis have a little shop in she kitchen and Mammy used to send me to buy an ounce of butter or onion when hers finish. I used to think how Miss Mavis real lucky because she have everything right in she kitchen. Sometimes she used to give me a free Joe Gum.

"Look at what the man do to these children nuh!"

She talking like people who come out in England. And she face looking as if she have stupse on it all the time. "Thank the Lord! Yes! Take them back to their grandmother. Poor little things!" She say, and she pull she duster around she chest, as if a cold breeze just blow.

The army jeeps park up by the stand pipe, by Auntie Sille shop. They put us in the jeep with I-Trad and one a soldier drive up the road to Mammy house.

Miss Kay by the road hanging up she clothes. The piece of clothes in she hand fall back in the tub. "Ah Lawd Jesus! Look at dese chilren trouble nuh Papa God!" She put she hands on she waist. She shake she head. I glad is a school day and Yvette and Boyo and them not there to see us.

I-Trad still don't say a word. He just looking straight in front him, at nothing.

As soon as we reach by Mammy, she start to bawl. She put she hands on she head, she stoop down on the ground and she start to bawl. As if somebody dead. But I know Mammay just pretending. "Me Beta? Me Beta come back! Come me Beta. Come by you Mammy!"

Papa stand up in he water boots, with he cutlass in he hand, and he mouth open.

The driver come out and let me and I-Rally out of the jeep.

"Granny, we bring back you grandchildren for you." He say. Mammy pull I-Rally and try to hug him, but he wriggle out from she hands. He not she Beta anymore.

Then Mammy eyes fall on Drewry, and all bawling stop. Mammy is the only person who could cry anytime she want and not a single drop of water come out of she eyes. She is the only person who could bawl down the place one minute and then next minute she finish. Just so!

"A a. Who is dat nice young man?" She say, watching Drewry.

Drewry try to smile but he look as if something hurting him.

"What happen to him? Come. Come Beta," And Mammy stretching out she hand to hold Drewry. Mammy don't even watch me.

Drewry looking afraid. He don't know what to do. He hear us talking about Mammy but he don't know her.

"Come Beta. Come let me see you," Mammy say. And she hugging Drewry as if she know him.

When the soldier drive off I-Trad just looking at me. I-Trad does speak without saying a word. He does speak with he eyes. They don't look like steel again. He just looking at me as if to say, *Don't worry, bout a ting, cause every little ting, is gonna be alright.*

And I watching the jeep going up the road to turn, and I remembering when Daddy used to bring me for a ride when he go up and turn. And me cry burst. All the time Mammy calling she Beta and hugging Drewry and doing as if she don't even know me, the cry gathering up. And I-Trad always telling me I have to be a strong princess. But something burst behind me eyes and all the cry start to fall down me face. I cry because me Daddy don't raise me up in the air again or hug me like when I was little. I cry because I afraid the soldiers and them go put him in jail. I cry for me mother. I cry because Mammy never call me Beti too. I cry for Drewry. I cry until hiccups start to heave out from me and me eyes swell up and close down.

Drewry get real sick. He roasting with fever. Mammy put him in me and I-Rally old bed. He look like a little boy in the big bed. She put a wet cloth on he forehead. She boil lemon grass and sugar-dish tea for him. She rub him down with she special coconut oil. She make soup for him and she try to feed him. But Drewry can't even swallow. He looking so sick, Papa only saying, "De boy go dead oui."

Drewry legs swell-up swell-up. More boils coming up. The sores look worse, even though I-Rally bring aloes to put on them. And every time I watch Drewry I feeling the hard dumpling in me throat.

When water more than flour, as Mammy does say, she call Doctor Rampasal. He say Drewry have dengue fever and he have to go in hospital. Mammy say, "What hospital? For dem to make him see trouble! Ah go see after him for meself. He doh goin in no hospital."

And Mammy see after Drewry as if he is she son. And even though I know Mammy only like Drewry because he is Indian, just like her, I glad. Because he don't have nobody else.

We spend two days by Mammy and I-Trad come for us. Drewry stay by Mammy until he get strong. Then he go back in England. He leave he pink blanket for me and I-Rally.

Chapter 23

Movement Time

Every morning, when I-Trad wake up, he up in the field, walking around and shaking he head. Sometimes he does just sit down with the dry stumps, picking up the soil and then letting it fall through he fingers. He hardly talking, so me and I-Rally leave him alone.

Then one day, after I-Trad meditate for a long time, he say Jah tell him is time to make a move. He say we going in St Lucia and stay with some of he brethrens.

First time in me life I going in a plane. Me belly boiling but I feeling glad.

I-Trad walking in front us. I-Rally in front me. He have he bag on he back, and he bumping away. I have me little bag with me two dresses, a head-tie, and me half of the pink blanket. I-Rally cut the blanket Drewry leave for us in two. He have the other half in he bag.

The plane smaller than the one we mother go away in. The air hostess stand up in front the door and she watching me coming up the steps. I don't like how she watching me at all. Every time we go anywhere, people always watching us watching us, as if they never see Rastas before.

I-Rally sit down by a window and I sit down by him. I-Trad sit down on the other side.

When the plane start, it so loud it make me jump. Then the air hostess stand up in the front saying, 'Welcome to Liat, The Caribbean Airline.' And she hardly even opening she mouth, as though she have tight lips. She have on purple lipstick and blue eye shadow, like me mother have on in the picture. She blue skirt don't have a single crease, as if she does not sit down on it at all. She pointing to the sides and in front of her when she speaking. She fingernails long and they the same colour as she lipstick. I-Trad would say how she not proud of she heritage. That is Babylon teaching that making her want to paint up she face so, spoiling she natural beauty.

When the plane start to go up in the air, I grip the side of the seat and me belly drop down in a hole. All when the plane reach up in the air, I still gripping the seat.

I look out the window. The houses by the sea in Pearls Airport looking smaller and smaller. And the sea looking as if it ready to swallow up the plane. I start to feel giddy, so I rest me head on the seat and close me eyes.

I open me eyes when the air hostess push the trolley with things to eat through the aisle. She don't smile. She watch me and I-Rally again, as if to say *where these Rastas and them going*? People always thinking Rastas nasty. But me and I-Rally clean and we looking nice, so I don't know what she watching us so for!

When the air hostess ask if we want a drink, we say "no thanks." But as soon as the "no thanks" come out me mouth, me belly gave one big rumble. And I sure she hear it, because she watching us as if she feeling sorry for us.

"You sure you wouldn't like a drink?" She ask me again. And I wish I could say "yes tanks", because I real hungry. But I just shake me head.

I close me eyes again and try to sleep but the plane making noise and me ears full up with air, like a balloon. Me mouth full up with spit. I swallow. Me ears clear up a little. Me mouth full up again. Me head start to spin. I press me head on the back of the seat and I keep me eyes closed tight, but the sickness boiling up in me belly. *Oh God! What ah go vomit in?* I-Rally look like he sleeping. I can't tell I-Trad because I afraid to get up. I elbow I-Rally. As soon as he watch me he know.

"You want to vomit?" he ask me.

"Mm hm." Me mouth too full to swallow.

Me eyes getting dark. I could hear I-Rally searching in the seat pocket. Me belly going up and down like the waves on Boucherie Beach. Every time I feel one coming, I pressing harder in the seat and I trying to ride it, so it won't boil me over. But the waves getting bigger. And rougher. And I feeling as if the plane upside-down. Then somebody put something in me hand. I open me eyes and the air hostess say, "You can use this bag." I look in me hand. A brown paper bag. A *paper bag! How that go hold vomit?* I put me mouth over it just in time, before the next wave hit me. Everything in me belly pour out! And what can't wait to pass out through me mouth, pass out through me nose. When I finish, me belly feeling empty and raw. And I feeling so sick and weak I start to cry. I-Rally take the bag from me and hold it until the air hostess come back and take it.

I glad when we reach the airport in St Lucia. I feeling so weak, the heat nearly knock me down when I walking down the steps. I-Rally take me bag from me. When a little breeze blow, I full up me empty belly with air.

We stand up in the line watching people going up to the counter and then leaving. When we turn come I-Trad give the officer we passports. The officer watch them. He say something to I-Trad, then he watch the passports again. Me and I-Rally stand up on the side waiting. I-Trad taking longer than everybody else. I wondering what the officer saying. And I wish I could sit down because I still feeling weak. And I real hungry.

Next thing I know, an officer take I-Trad and bring him in the back and a lady officer come for me and I-Rally.

She bring us on the side and tell us to wait there. I glad to sit down, but people only watching us and I-Trad taking long. I-Rally watching them back hard, but I feeling to cry and I wondering why I-Trad taking so long.

As soon as I see I-Trad face when he come back out, I know something wrong in truth, because he have on the Babylon victimization look.

Then just like that, we on another plane and I bringing up all the green groundnuts I-Trad give me to eat in the next paper bag I get in the seat pocket. Then we back on Pearls Airport.

When a man on the airport ask I-Trad what happen, I hear him saying how the immigration officer say they don't want no more Rastas coming in St Lucia to join the Rastafarian uprising. And how he and he youths just going to see some brethrens. He don't trouble nobody. But Babylon always fighting down Rastaman. How they always trying to keep Rastaman down.

Not long after, I-Trad say is movement time again. Another Exodus. Another movement of Jah people. We move to Ahoma, in Tivoli.

Chapter 24

More Freedom

Tivoli is a real Rastafarian Kingdom. I never see so much Rastas in me life!

When we just move, we stay by one of I-Trad brethrens. He have a big ghetto. He living with he wife and they have a lot of children. All of them is Rasta too and all of them looking same height. It even have a little Rasta girl, but we don't make friends because we don't stay there long at all. I-Trad build a ghetto up in the hills in Ahoma, where most of the Rastas living, and we go and stay there.

Everyday I-Trad going on more movements and he not coming back till late. Then next thing we know, he go and build another ghetto for heself. He say all top have to stand up on their own foot. And all tub have to sit on their own bottom. So he leave us in the ghetto for weself. As if me and I-Rally is a top or a tub.

One day me and I-Rally meet another Rasta boy name I-Jalee. He have thirteen years. He from Tivoli so he know the place real good and he know everybody. And everyday we going and knock-about with him. We always together. Smoking. Cooking. Playing music and *drevéin*. We like *Bim, Bam* and *Bambam*!

The three of us chilling in the bush cave we find in the woods. Smoking. It have big giant trees and vines tangle up together. And dry leaves cover up the ground like a carpet.

The smoke go straight down me windpipe. I give

back I-Jalee the spliff.

"Take it easy I-Lee. Dat piece real strong." I-Jalee say. I-Jalee always have weed. I don't know where he does get it from, but every time he come, he bringing a piece for us.

I-Rally spliff down to the nook. He have to pinch it to hold it. And he fingers look as if a rat bite them up when he sleeping.

I lean back me head on the tree trunk behind me. The sunlight squeezing through the branches and playing on me face. I close me eyes. The light tickling me and I listening to all the bush noise. I hearing everything. The baby birds *cheep cheep cheeping,* calling their mother. Their voices soft soft like their baby feathers. Once I-Rally let me touch one, and I remember how it feel just like cotton wool. And peepeerits sounding like school children quarrelling with one another. A lizard run through the bush and dash up on the tree behind a spider. A jumping jack boring holes in me ears. It so little, I don't know how it loud so! A bumblebee buzzing away, like a little choir.

I real like we little spot. I wish I could stay there forever, just sitting down on the ground, doing nothing. I-Trad say that is dwelling with nature. We does go every day and when the sun start to go away, we does go home and cook.

I-Chad does come by us too. He older than us. He have sixteen years. He half Indian like I-Jalee. He have thick *dougla* locks and they falling around he face and down he back like cattails. He skin is same colour as cornmeal porridge sweeten with brown sugar. He always half naked and he chest full of curly hair. I like when I-Chad come by us, because he does give us some real jokes and make us laugh for so. Sometimes I does watch him from the corner of me eyes. And when he catch me watching him, he does smile. And I does wish he is a girl, so I could have company too.

We cooking and playing music. I-Trad leave a guitar for us. And I-Jalee have a drum. I-Rally does make up music on the guitar. I like the bass and I does try to play it how I see I-Trad play Bob Marley Redemption Song - *bum bubum bum bum bum bum bum, bum bububum bu bu bu bum bum.* I does play it and play it until the guitar strings dig drains in me fingers.

And one evening, when the four of us there cooking and playing music, I-Chad big brother, I-Shaman, come by we ghetto. He and I-Chad look alike bad. But he skin darker, like wet cinnamon. And he locks bigger too. And he does tie them up on he head like a crown. I-Shaman ghetto not far from us. Sometimes I does see him passing, but he never come in we ghetto before.

Outside black as coals. It don't have no moon, so we in the ghetto with the fire lighting. The ghetto look just like the one we used to stay in before. It have two bunk beds and the bed where I-Trad used to sleep. I-Jalee does sleep on it now. It have a big shelf where we does put the bashies and things and two stumps and a stone, where we does sit down. I-Shaman sit down on the stone across from me.

All of us watch him when he pick up a piece of hot coal with he fingers to light he spliff.

"What!" I-Rally say. "How you do dat?"

"Practice youthman. I-man hand tough." I-Shaman say.

He hand must be real hard in truth, because even I-Trad had to use a piece of coconut shell to pick up fire.

I-Shaman pass the spliff to me. I still high because all of us smoke already. Me head so bad I could feel me eyes sinking down inside me face. But I still take it. Because when somebody pass you a smoke, you just take it. Smoking is like eating. You eat, you smoke. You smoke, you eat.

I-Rally still juking up the guitar. I-Jalee eyes closing down already. Mine too. Then I-Shaman sitting down by me. *When he move by me?* And whole night he watching me watching me. I don't like how he sitting down by me. I-Jalee and I-Chad does sit down by me all the time and I does not feel so. But I-Shaman make me feel as if I should get up and sit down somewhere else. But me legs feeling heavy and they don't want to get up.

It getting late. The darkness outside thick. I can't even see a single star. I-Jalee sleeping sound now. I-Chad gone already, but I-Shaman still there. I-Rally tired too, but he watching I-Shaman. He watching him real hard.

The next night I-Shaman come back again. And he sit down right by me again.

The fire get dead and the ghetto dim. The battery low so the tape start dragging. Making Bob Marley sing in slow motion.

I-Jalee not sleeping yet. First time, because he always the first one to knock-out. I-Chad gone. He does not say he going. One minute he does be in the ghetto with us and next minute he gone. And I-Rally eyes closing down but he still holding on to the guitar. I tired too. Me head feeling light.

I-Shaman light up another spliff even though all of us still high. He give me. I take it. Me head leave me and start to go and knock about. *In the veranda by Mammy and Papa. In we little kitchen with me mother frying bakes. It down by the river watching Drewry eating mango.* Something on me leg. *Oh God!* A hand crawl up and rest there. *I not in the hall by Mammy. I not reading me New West Indian Reader. Belle not on the floor by Rally. Look I-Rally right there sleeping on the guitar.* The hand still on me leg. The tape dragging still. I-Jalee sleeping with he head on the bunk. The hand still there. It move up some more. *Men like ladies with nice legs you know.* Then it hand move. It gone. He gone too.

The fire dead now. The ghetto dark. Outside black. I stoop down behind the ghetto. And I waiting for the pee to come.

Chapter 25

Force Ripe

I not in me bunk when I wake up. The sun not on me face. It hiding behind a big dark rain cloud. And I-Rally not snoring in he bunk over me. I look through the door. Me eyes rest on two little birds jooking-up something in the yard.

I sit up and I feel something sticky between me legs. And I smelling something.

The cloud move. The sun hit me. And the day before come back.

Outside not dark yet. I-Rally and I-Jalee gone by I-Jalee grandmother since morning. I stay home because me belly hurting me. So me alone home when I-Shaman come. I playing pick-up in the yard for meself. He come and sit down in the yard.

"De I want some sapodilla?" He ask me.

I real like sapodillas. I stop playing pick-up and I take a sapodilla. I split it in two and I suck the juice before it run down on me hands.

"De I want to see I-man yard?' I-Shaman say. "De I is a nice princess."

Rastas always talking about finding a little princess, a little virgin princess. I-Trad used to say that I would make a nice little princess because I could cook ital, and I could wash clothes good too. And I only have ten years.

Me head is not mine. It floating over me. The ghetto spinning. Crickets making noise in the bush outside. Frogs too. I-Shaman sitting-down in from me. He grinning. He missing two teeth. He mouth moving. I don't hear what he saying. Crickets and frogs inside me ears. They bursting me ear drum. Ear Drum? How come people have drum inside their ears?

I-Shaman standing up.

"De I could stay wit I-Man tonight Princess." He still grinning.

He unzip he pants. Rest it on the bottom bunk.

"Come nuh Princess. De I could sleep with I-man tonight."

He climb up on he bunk.

Me father does call me Princess. But I don't know the last time I see me father.

I stand up but is not me. Me head spinning. Me legs feeling as if they sleeping. I climbing up on the bunk. I-Shaman pressing heself on me. Something crawling over me chest. Over me bee stings on me chest. It pulling up me dress. I lie down stiff. It moving down to me leg. I have to brush it out, but I don't move. If I just lie-down stiff, it go crawl away. But it don't crawl away. It between me legs. It heavy on top me. I-Shaman on top me. He smelling like sweat and weed. Strong strong. Something hard pushing between me legs. I close-up me legs tight tight. It pushing me legs. It opening them again. The hard thing pushing between me legs again. I squeeze tight. I don't want that thing between me legs. Pushing. Pushing. He breathing in me face. The crickets inside me ears. Something wet between me legs. He stop. He breathing heavy heavy, as if he come out a run a race. He pressing me down. I want to push him. He sweat running down on me. I want to get up, and wipe meself. I want to wash up meself. But I don't want to move. I don't want that sticky thing to go nowhere else. So I just lie down there. I just lie down there with the crickets in me ears.

I could smell meself. I could smell he perspiration on me. I could smell the wet thing between me legs. I want to wash up. Outside, the cloud covering the sun again. I-Shaman not there. I take a bashie of water and go behind some bush behind the ghetto. I fold up me dress around me waist and stoop down. I pour some water on me. The water cold. I pour more. I don't want to touch meself there. I don't want to touch meself anywhere. I stay in the bush until the rain burst through the clouds.

The rain come down real heavy. I don't have to pour water again. I stoop down in the rain. I don't move. The rain soak me locks. It soak me dress. It run down me back, me chest, between me legs, and then the ground suck it up. I let it wash out the dirtiness I feeling.

I still in the bush when I-Shaman come back. He locks dripping wet and he bringing a bucket of water and a bunch of plantains. I stay in the bush. I don't want him to see me. I stay there until the rain stop and me dress start to dry again. I don't know what to do. I afraid to go home. I wish I-Rally come and look for me. But I don't want him to see me. I don't want I-Jalee to see me. I don't want nobody to see me.

When I come out from the bush, I-Shaman lighting the fire. He grin. I don't want him to grin for me. I feeling real shame. I just want to go back in we ghetto and cook and play me music with I-Rally and I-Jalee.

When I creep in the ghetto, I-Rally don't even watch me. He just go outside.

I smoke a whole spliff and I lie down on me bunk and close me eyes.

You is a nice princess, I-Shaman saying. And Mammy saying, *Watch her nuh! You doh see how she force ripe like a Julie mango.* I-Trad saying, *Jah doh make nothin that doh have to happen, happen.*

And me mother in she blue halter back dress watching me. I have a little brother too. I don't even know what he look like.

Since we little, is always me and me brother. Lee and Rally.

Me and Rally in Mr Glenford veranda. We have on same colour shirt, with triangles on them, and we long pants and sandals. Me ribbon in me hair. Rally in he black cockroach-killer shoes and looking vex vex. Mr Glenford holding he big camera and waiting for Rally to smile, for him to take out a nice picture for Daddy to send for we mother in Aruba. Me and Rally climbing the mango Julie tree up in Bologna Estate. Rally calling me to 'come and ketch the mango nuh gurl, ants biting me you know.' Me sticking out me little hands to catch it but dropping the mango on the ground because it hit me hands so hard and Rally getting vex with me and saying 'you han is a basket or wha? You only letting the mango and dem fall!' But he doesn't stay vex for long. Me and Rally playing in the road with Garry and he sister Shelly, with she big dougla hair that look as if comb never pass through it yet! They born in England and Papa is their grand uncle. Rally pushing Shelly on we little pink horse, the one that some white people who we mother used to work with, give us. And Shelly squealing 'faster, faster!' And me brother pushing her fast fast, down the stony road. And I closing me eyes tight because ah sure Shelly go fall and gashey she bambam, but she just squealing louder and louder and she brother Garry begging her to come off so he could get a ride too. Me watching Rally saddle up the donkey in the yard and Papa saying 'Yes, come on. Heave it up so. Yes! Dat's me boy! You gettin better dan Papa now man.' And Rally riding the donkey up the mountain and me running up behind the donkey, because I too coward to ride with him. Me and Rally putting the little chicken with yaws under a milk tin behind the kitchen and beating the pan hard hard, is either the chicken catch up itself and run by the mother or drop down dead! Me and

Rally chasing the big cock in the garden on Friday evening. Rally dashing after it in the bush with prickle and all - just like he does dash down the hill in the bush behind the cricket ball - so Mammy could purge the fowl out so Papa could kill it Sunday morning. And Mammy could cook it for lunch, with rice and dhal and stew callaloo. Me and Rally licking the bucket after Mammy made cake and scraping the pot outside in the yard when Mammy make sweet potato pudding.

When I wake up, I-Shaman in the yard waiting for me.

Chapter 26

Little Wife

Me alone in the river. I sit down on the big flat river stone by the little basin where I does go and bathe and wash me and I-Shaman clothes. Sometimes, it does have other Rastas bathing there, but when I hear them I does turn back one time. I does sit down under the cocoa trees and wait till they go.

The sun come up over the hill already, but the breeze still blowing cold cold.

I squeeze the two lemon in the bucket of water. I push down I-Shaman jeans pants in it. The jeans pants drink up the water as if it real thirsty. It nearly didn't leave none for me two dress. I leave them to soak while I scrape the cochenille and grate the young cocoa I pick from the tree where I pass to come in the river. And every time I pick the cocoa I remembering what Mammy used to say - how since this Rasta thing start, farmers can't get a pound of cocoa to sell, because they picking all before it burst out on the tree.

I rub up the mixture in me locks. It slimy slimy, and it have a lot of little pieces of cocoa in it that does stick up in me hair. Me locks still en form good yet. I-Rally locks nice and tight, and they growing real fast, but mine just stick up together. And they big and loose, as if they still en sure if they should lock-up or wait still. I leave the mixture to set just like Daddy. No, not Daddy. We can't call him Daddy again. I-Trad is he name now. He used to leave it in he hair while he go in the bush and dig yam and look for

163

mango.

I-Shaman jeans pants big and heavy. And they real hard to wash. They too big and heavy to rub. And I don't have no scrubbing brush to scrub them. When we used to go and watch Kung Fu movies in Griffin Cinema, I used to see the Chinese women pounding their clothes with their hands, then squeezing them on river stone. So I pound them on the river stone too. I pound them real hard, but I still can't squeeze them, so I leave them on the stone for the water to run out for itself. Me dress and them easier to wash. I rub and rub them so me hands could make the *squishy, squishy* noise like the lady who used to wash for Mammy. But it can't make no squishy noise without soap. Me and Yvette used to compete to see who could make the loudest squishy noise when we washing. Yvette used to win. She used to beat me in everything.

I look around first to make sure nobody there before I take out me home dress. Nobody around. Only me and the river, and the noise in the bush. A doctor bird float over a flower. Wings flapping flapping real fast. It giving the flower a injection with it needle beak. A dragonfly rest on the stone by me. I could see straight through the wings. It just stand up on the stone watching me. It just watching me just like people does watch me. But as soon as I move, it fly away. And I could hear a mama soleil in the bush too. I used to see them in Mammy land up in the mountain. They look like big giant beetles, with shiny, blackish-greenish wings.

Something tickle me toe in the water. A mullet. It dash under the stone and hide as soon as I move. And I nearly fall off the stone when I see the face in the water. The face watching me and I watching it. I watching it and it watching me as if it never see me before. Mammy had a big mirror on the dressing table in we bedroom. And every time Miss Kay daughter give me a new cornrow style, I used to run in the bedroom and jump up on the bed to see how I look in the mirror. And on Sunday morning before we go to church, I used to check in it to see if Mammy tie me ribbon good. The face in the water watching me still, with she swell-up swell-up eyes and she hard hard face. *Eh. You doh see Peeya! You doh see how she mouth lang!* Mammy used to say. Every time she watch me she had something to say. *Whey dat ugly girl come out? Wha happen to she eye? Dey deep deep. And how dey lookin wild so?*

The thump behind me made me jump. It chase the little girl in the river. And then I see the same old lady I does see sometimes. She sit down on a river stone bathing. She have on all she clothes. She dipping water with a paint pan and watching me. She make me remember Maymay who living near by Mammy, because every time I see her, she dragging wood, just like Maymay. And she there throwing water on sheself just like Mammy, when she was bathing behind the house.

The old lady watching me pick up the breadnuts that just fall down on the riverbank. She just watching me and shaking she head as if she feeling sorry for me. People always watching me watching me, and shaking their head when they see me. The lady in the shop down in the junction does shake she head when she see me. And the old man who does pass by the ghetto with he donkey does mumble and shake he head too. And every time I see him, I does see Papa. Papa heaving up the saddle on Melba back. Fixing the bridle in she mouth. Left foot in the stirrup. Sling the right one over. Sometimes Melba used to get vex and kick up a little and Papa would say, *eh eh. Well what taking you today?*

I put the breadnuts in me calabash. It have two breadnut trees in Mammy land so we used to get a lot of breadnuts. And Mammy used to cook them in a big burn-up lard tin behind the kitchen. And when they cook, she used to put them in a big bowl for us to share. We used to sit down behind the house sucking the salty water from the breadnuts. Sometime we used to bet on who could shell the most without eating them. But I like them so much I could not stop meself from putting everyone I shell in me mouth. And days after people still know that we eat breadnuts.

I drop the bundle of wood on the floor quick quick. A black ant biting me in me neck. I pinch it and mash up the little beggar. The ting little little but it biting hard hard. And the worse place to get bite is on your toe. When they bite you on you toe, you scratching forever. But it does feel nice!

The clouds and the sun playing hide and seek outside. It look as if rain go fall. And the ground hard and dry, but I still don't want the rain to fall.

I gather up the wood. I leave out some to make the fire to cook me breadnuts and I pack the rest neat neat under the shelf by the fireside. I scrape up all the ashes from the fireside and toss it out in the garden. I used to watch I-Trad well good when he lighting the fire. Dry leaf first. Then some coconut fibre over it. And brambles on top it. Then I pack the wood on top of it and I make sure I leave space for the fire to breathe. I-Trad say if the fire can't breathe, it won't light. The fibre spark up as soon as I rest the match on it. It blaze-up and then it out. I put some more fibre and I light it again. The wood a little wet and the wind not blowing inside so I kneel down on the floor and start to blow it. I full up me chest with air. I huff and puff and huff and puff like the wolf in *The Three Little Pigs* and I blow. Smoke nearly choke me. I fan and fan the fire with a piece of cardboard until it blaze up again. Then I leave it to burn.

Next I crack the coconut on the stone in the yard, hold it over me mouth to catch the sweet water. I lick me chin, and me arm before it run down and wet up me chest. I scrape the coconut with a sharpen piece of coconut shell. The wood turn to coals real quick. I clear out the centre and make a circle with the coals. Then I put on the bashie with the breadnuts and some green peas to cook first. Breadnut does take long to cook. I scrape the skin from the sweet potatoes but the yam skin hard so I peel it, even though I-Trad say when you peel them you taking out the best part. When the breadnuts get soft, I put in the sweet potatoes and yam. Then I pick some chive and thyme in the garden. Cut up some seasoning pepper and put them in the bashie. Leave it to boil.

The sun start hiding behind the tall coconut trees in the back of Fourtree. And the sky look just as if it on fire. Me alone in the ghetto and I glad. I always glad when me alone in the ghetto, until dark night reach. When dark night reach all the trees and them does start to walk; the stones in the yard does start to talk. When dark night reach all the day noise does turn black like the night. And me ears does open wider. Me eyes too.

I wish I could play *Pimples Paradise*. That is me song. *Rastaman Vibration* is I-Rally song. He know all the words. He have all the movement when he *skanking* to it. Pimples Paradise is me song. But I-Shaman don't have a tape.

The bashie bubbling too loud. I push away the coals a little bit. I don't want the ital to dry down before it cook.

I roll a spliff. Sometimes I-Shaman had some that roll already, but I could do it for meself now. I scoop up a piece of fire with a coconut shell and light it. I go outside and sit down on the big stone in the yard.

Pimples Paradise. Dat's all she wu us.
Pimples Paradise. Dat's all she wu us.

I practice holding the spliff between me fingers like them ladies in Griffin Cinema. People always saying I have big hands for a girl. I get me hands from me father. The three lines running down in the palm of me hands look like roads. I have double lines on me fingers. I double jointed so I could bend back me fingers real far. When me and Yvette used to play pickup in the yard, I used to hold the most stones on top of me hand.

The sun playing hide and seek. It peeping through the trees like it used to peep through the louvres by Mammy, then hiding behind the clouds and the trees.

Every ting got to be onto me.

Every ting got to be onto me.

I pull on the spliff. Suck in the smoke. I try to hold it long like I-Rally. But it does always burst through me nose. Me mouth. Me eyes and all.

She's gettin high tryin to fly da sky, shoo bee doo bee doo bee doo bee

An she's dancing when dere ent no song. Oo wo oo wo

Pimples Paradise. Dat's all she wu us.

I-Trad say is not Pimples Paradise. Is Pimpers Paradise, but I find pimples sounding nicer with paradise. And I don't know what is pimpers so I still singing pimples.

A tiger-colour butterfly fly over the garden. It rest on the sugar-dish flower. Another butterfly come and rest by it. They fly away together. Wings touching. *The butterfly and all have friend.* A donkey bray down the hill. The sun almost gone. Then it gone. The spliff finish. I go inside too.

The bashie still bubbling real slow. It simmering and the whole ghetto smell of ital. I sit down on the stone in the corner. Bubble. Bubble. Coals turning to ashes. Bubble bubble. Soft soft, as if it snoring. Me head light. The bashie spinning. The ghetto going round, dancing in slow motion. I rest me head on the glory cedar post behind me. Close me eyes. Me and I-Rally sitting down by the fire and Daddy playing *Ole pirates yes dey rab I. Sold I to de merchant ship* like we used to do. I could play the bass to it. *Tum, tudum tum tum tum tum tum... tum tududum.. tu du du dum dum.* But I-Rally have the guitar. I hardly see him. I wonder what he doing.

A bird in me ears. I fly up in the roof.

She's gettin high tryin to fly da sky, shoo bee doo bee doo bee doo bee

Me head dancing.

An she's dancing when dere ent no song. Oo wo oo wo

Me wings light. They light as me head. Flying. Fly over the shelf. Over the fireside. Hit the coconut branch. Up in the roof. The ghetto spinning. Bump! The branches don't have no window. I land on the bunk. The top one. *No! No! Not yet. Not time yet. Not the bunk yet!* Flap. Flap. Back on the stone.

Pimples Paradise. Dat's all she wu us.

Pimples Paradise. Dat's all she wu us.

The fire dead, but the ashes still hot. And me belly grumbling, but I don't get up. Dark night reach, so I fraid. I don't even get up and light the torch. I waiting. Then I hear it. Leaf crackling. Tump. Tump. Foot hitting ground. I know he footstep real good now. And when I hear it, me dark night *'fraid'* does go away. And me top bunk *'fraid'* does come.

I-Shaman drop he cutlass in the corner. He sack on the floor. I wonder what he bring. Sometimes he does bring home sapodillas from the big tree in he mother yard.

He reach for he big bashie of ital I take out for him. I take me little bashie and sit down on the stone. The only sound in the ghetto is I-Shaman teeth chopping up food. He missing some front teeth on the top of he mouth. Good

169

thing he don't have dumplings to bite.

I-Shaman sit down on the coconut stump stool. Sometimes he does tell me things, like his mother sick or if he see me father when he was passing. But most times I-Shaman does just sit down there quiet quiet, smiling. And I does just sit down there quiet too. I don't say nothing about the old lady by the river, or where the breadnut come out or about the mullet that tickle me toe.

I-Shaman let go a big belch when he finish eating. *Give Jah tanks*! The lamp light real low. I can't see I-Shaman good, but I know what he doing. Take down the bashie with the weed to roll a spliff. He always roll up a spliff when he finish eating. He sprinkling the weed on the bluggoe leaf. Not fig leaf. Fig leaf does split up too much. Level it out with he thick, rough finger. Lick he fingers and roll it up neat neat. Tie it with a piece of bluggoe string.

I take the spliff when I'Shaman pass it. I always take it when he pass it. When I feel high I does go places. When I feeling high I could full up me head with anything I want.

Up on the top bunk. Sweat smell pressing me down. Head full up. *Me mother bathing me in the yard. Passing me nice red dress over me head. We going in Daddy car. Going down Mt Craven by Laura and Hensley. Orange Fanta bubbling in me glass. Dixie biscuit.* Quick. Quick. Sweat smell roll off. I climb down the bunk. Creep outside. It dark. I afraid. But the thing between me leg. I don't want it between me leg. It making me belly feel as if I go vomit. I used to have me little basin to wash up in by Mammy. I wish I had me little basin. The cold water does make me feel clean.

Bottom bunk. Head gone and knockabout. Sleep knock me out. I dream the same dream. Me mother sitting down by the hibiscus in the yard cutexing she fingernails--red like the hibiscus flowers. And when I wake up, I could still smell Cutex nail polish.

Chapter 27

Rasta Sistren

The sun over the ghetto when I wake up. Easter coming, and the wind blowing nice and strong.

Me belly grumbling, fuss it hungry. And me right leg stiff as a piece of wood. A lot of little boils coming out on me body, but the one on me right leg is the biggest. It look as if it ready to burst. And I have to go in the river and sweep the yard, but I don't feel like getting up at all. I don't want to go outside.

Saturday is market day. I-Shaman gone and help he mother in the market. And it have *blocko* down in the junction later. I hear when the loudspeaker pass and announce it. I bet I -Rally going. He doesn't miss he blocko. He real like to dance. And he like when everybody stand up and watch him. He used to cork all session down by Scottie-Boy shop on Sundays. Scottie-Boy used to put the giant black speakers by the road and blast out the music.

One time some boys try to test I-Rally. "So dat boy tink he bad oui. Ah bet you ah could dance better dan him!" One boy say. "Well go on nuh! He go cut you tail for you!" Another one say. And just as if Scottie-Boy know what going on, because he put down a Bunny Wailer. *And any dance that you can cork, I can cork it tighter. I'm the toughest, I'm the toughest, I can draw better crowd than you, and you can never draw the crowd that I do. I'm the dub master. I'm the dub master.* And as if I-Rally was saving-up he bad moves in he pocket. He start pulling them out: one foot up, then pound the ground, then the next one up, then down. Arms pounding the air. Shoulders heaving. Locks jumping up and down, as he skank down the place. And everybody stand up watching him, and clapping.

I real like to dance too, but I just watching, because I don't like when people watching me.

When I-Shaman come back from the market, he say he going in blocko. I don't want to go, but I don't want to stay in the ghetto for meself in the night. So I go.

When we reach the junction I-Shaman go by he mother. She living just across the road from the shop where the blocko is. I don't go because he sisters and them does watch me funny. I corner meself by a bunch of banana trees by the road, and I praying for darkness to come and hide me. I don't want nobody coming up to me and asking me any question. I don't want people eyes crawling all over me like black ants.

The pasture by the Catholic church full of people. The road full of people. They only moving when a vehicle passing, then they moving right back in the road again.

Men knocking dominoes and drinking Guinness under the mango tree. Women holding children hands and drinking Malt or Coke. Children dress up in their nice clothes--the boys in jeans and jerseys and the girls in their halter-back tops and short pants - their hair dress up like Christmas trees. Some of them running around the pasture, playing catch me and ship sale. Some dancing and eating popcorn, sucking their salty fingers. Some licking ice cream cones quick quick, before it melt and licking what running down their hands and elbows too. Some sucking bright, rainbow *snow cones*, with condensed milk on top. And flies trying to get some too.

I stand up watching them, me mouth making water for some popcorn. And I wish I could lick an icecream cone too.

A Rasta sistren stand up with some other ladies in

the pasture. She have on a nice African dress and she have a scarf tied at the front of her head, like a headband. She locks fall down on she back and spread out like a fan. I see her somewhere before, but I can't remember where I see her. They talking and watching me. I wonder if they talking about me.

I look around to see if I catch sight of I-Rally and I-Jalee. Maybe he didn't come down yet or he up by the shop, right by the big speakers.

The Rasta sistren start walking towards me. I like how she walking, not dread-up bumping, like some Rasta women I see. She just walking like a real humble sistren. She looking real nice too.

I have on me same polka dot dress again. It washout now but I still like it. And I like how me green scarf matching the green dots on it.

The Rasta sistren stop when she reach by me. She smell like sweet coconut oil mix up with nutmeg.

"You aright little daughter?" The Rasta Sistren ask me.

She sound like somebody from town.

I nod and look away.

"I-Vonne is I name. What is de I name?"

She have nice teeth too. They look like Chicklets chewing gum.

"I-Lee," I answer. I take out me eyes from she face and rest them on the ground.

"De I living around here?"

I nod. I clamp me leather slippers with me toes.

"How old is de I?"

What she askin me dat for?

"De I don't have to be shy with me you know!"

Me slippers start to dig the dust.

"Eleven?"

I shake me head.

"Ten?"

I don't answer. *What she want to know how much years ah have for?*

"Where is de I brethren?"

Me brethren? Which brethren she talking about? Me brother, I-Rally? I want her to stop asking me questions and leave me alone. I look away.

A little girl run past me sucking a lollipop. A little boy running behind her. He trying to take she lollipop. She give him one hard slap. *That good for he backside!*

"De I just want to reason with the daughter."

The Rasta sistren watching me. And I watching me feet as if is first time I see them. How they looking dry dry and how me toes spread out in me slippers. I squeeze them together, so they line up straight, like children in assembly.

"De I having your period yet?"

What period she talkin about?

"De I know what period is?" She ask me.

I don't answer.

"Nobody ever talk to de I about you period?"

I shake me head again. I want her to go back in the pasture and meet she friends and them and leave me alone. But I like she voice. I like how she smelling. And I want to know what she talking about.

"De I start to bleed yet?"

I shake me head. Me skin start to itch as if I stand up in zootie.

"When de I start to bleed between your legs, that is the period."

Me chest heave. *Bleed between me legs? Blood have to come out between me legs?* I squeeze me legs together as if I holding a bad pee.

"When de I start to bleed, de I will have to wear panty you know."

Aw! How she know ah doh wearing panty? She could see trough me dress? I-Trad say panty is like pants, and how Rasta women should not wear pants, so I had to leave all me panties by Mammy.

"'And de I will have to wear pads too. De I know what a pad is?"

I never hear about wearing pads yet. I don't even know what a pad is. I just want her to stop talking about that kind of thing.

"And when de I start seeing de I period, de I could make a baby you know."

The zootie biting me now. I glad it starting to get dark.

"I see you and the brethren. I know de I living with him you know."

Me chest drop down inside me belly. I feel to run back in the ghetto and hide in the dark where nobody could see me.

"De I is just a little girl. Where is de I mother?"

What she go and ask me about me mother for? She make water gather up behind me eyes.

"De I must go back to de I father."

I want to run but me feet stick on the ground.

"Remember what de I tell you eh little daughter?"

She touch me on me shoulder. Me eyes full up with more water.

"Jah guidance daughter," she say. And then she go.

And as soon as she go, me feet unstick. And I speed up the hill and through the track, slapping all them broom bush and razor grass out of me way, with I-Vonne voice chasing me. *Blood between your legs... could make a baby... between your legs... between your legs... between your legs.*

When I reach the ghetto, me chest pounding hard. I could hear it. I sit down in me corner until it not sounding so loud again. I look in the bashie for a spliff. I get a little roach. I smoke it with a match stick so it wouldn't burn me mouth.

A little bit of light from the moon come inside the ghetto and keep me company. *I-Vonne is a Rasta sistren too, so how come she telling me all dem kind of tings. Maybe she not a real Rasta sistren. Maybe she is one of dem bald head Rasta I-Trad does talk about, who does just grow locks and pretend to be Rastas.*

The moon high up now. Slices of light line up in the ghetto. I feeling hungry but I don't move from me corner. Me leg hurting and me head full up with *blood ....baby...between you legs...de I mother... mother... mother?*

I could smell the black sage outside. I could smell the sugar-dish bush I does make me tea with. And the stink bush behind the ghetto. I does still see me mother by the hibiscus flower, cutexing she nails. *But how she Cutex smelling again?*

Chapter 28

Ah Want Back Me Daddy

I get up early, before I-Shaman get up. I limp down the track to I-Trad ghetto, parting the wet bush that hanging over the track so they don't hurt me legs.

The boils getting bigger and bigger. And everyday me legs looking more swell-up. The one on me right leg so big and full of pus, I frighten to even look at it. I don't know if I-Shaman know, but I never say nothing. Not even when he hurting them in the night. And I don't know what to do.

I don't know the last time I see I-Trad. But I see him in me dream last night. I wonder what he go say when he see me. If he go talk to me. Call me he little Princess, like when I was little.

When I reach by the ghetto, me heart start to beat fast. I stand up by the row of pawpaw trees that line up like a fence, in front of the ghetto.

The ghetto real neat. I-Trad does always take he time and do whatever he doing. He does always say when you doing something, do it good, or don't do it. So he coconut branch and them weave tight tight, so breeze could pass through easy but not rain. He bamboo roof so neat I sure it don't have a single leak in it. And he have bamboo spouting running around the roof to collect rain water in drums, to wet he plants in the dry season. And it have beds with all kinds of plants on both sides of the ghetto. He have chives, thymes, poor man pork and a lot of peppers. And them peppers looking nice and pretty. It have red ones, yellow, green and orange ones. Long ones, round ones. I-Trad does cook with a lot of hot peppers, so he always have in he garden. And he does not plant anything he cannot eat or use as herbs.

I just stand up there waiting to see if I see him. I don't know how to go in. The heavy pounding in me chest root me by the pawpaw tree. Then the pounding fall down, thump, in me belly when me eyes catch I-Trad. He stoop down in the garden. I don't know how he reach there. One minute he not there and next minute he there pulling out weed as if he was there all the time.

"Come trough nuh Princess."

I jump. *How he see me? He didn't even look round.* But I know me father have sixth sense. I come out from behind the pawpaw tree and I try not to limp, but me leg real hurting.

"I man see de I in I vision last night you know," I-Trad say. He don't even look up. He still stoop down there pulling up grass, he thick locks resting on he shoulders. And he sound just as if he see me coming. I-Trad always having visions and is just as if they does happen in truth. I see I-Trad in me dream and he see me in he vision too.

I sit down on a bench outside the ghetto. Me legs feeling as if needles jooking them. I can't say nothing. And I-Trad stay quiet too. Then he get up and come straight where I sit down on the bench.

"Let I man see de I foot." He stoop down in front me and take me foot.

How come he know? Maybe he de see me limpin.

I raise up me dress and show him the bad one. I could smell the puss. I wonder if he could smell it too.

"Come inside Princess," he say, after he look at it for a while.

Me heart feel glad but me eyes full up with a cry that waiting to burst. He call me Princess. I get back me Daddy.

I sit down on a stone inside the ghetto. I-Trad tear

out piece of cloth. He wet it in a bashie of water and wipe around the boils. Then he go out in the garden.

Me eyes roam round the ghetto. Everything pack up neat, neat on shelves. I-Trad have all kinds of tams and bags hang up on bamboo hooks.

I-Trad come back with some leaves and stoop down by the fire. Even this early morning, I-Trad fire lighting already. He have a bashie on the fire and I could smell the ganja tea. He put the piece of banana leaf over the bashie, for the steam to make it soft. Then he put the pepper leaves on a stick and pass them over the fire so they turn same colour as the ground. Then he put them on the boils, wrap the soft, warm banana leaf around me leg, and tie it with a piece of banana string.

"De I mustn't let water go in it eh," he say.

I look in I-Trad face for the first time since I come. He look different. He eyes look deeper. And he didn't have on he false teeth so he face sink down like holes and the bones under he eyes stand up high high.

I-Trad pour out some ganja tea for me, and sweeten it with honey.

"De I could relax here if de I want," he say. And he go back in he garden.

I sit there real quiet drinking me tea and thinking about all kinds of things. *How come me father leave us for weself. How come he living right there and I does not see him. How come he never come for me. How come we mother never come back for me and me brother.*

I want back me Daddy. I want him to whistle so I could drop everything and run and throw meself at him. So he could raise me up in the air and tickle me face when he kiss me. But I know he can't whistle again, because people can't whistle without their front teeth. And I wish I could call I-Trad Daddy, but he is not a Daddy now.

Chapter 29

Rescued

The wind push the flimsy blind aside and come inside. I pull me blanket around me shoulders. The early morning sleep hug me up tight and pull me in a nice place. I like that nice place. I want to stay there and let the sun play with me through the branches. I try to get up, but it hold me down on the bed. But the voices outside shake me up rough rough, and pull me out.

"WAKE UP! WAKE UP INSIDE DEY! COME OUT WIT' YOU HANDS UP!"

I jump up. *Oh Gosh! Who outside dey? What happenin?* I grip me blanket. I hold meself stiff like a piece of wood. I afraid to even move. The voice come out right outside, in the yard.

I Shaman snoring on the bunk over me. He don't even hear. *Why he doh keep quiet!*

"AH SAY TO COME OUT! NOW!" The voice say again. It right in front the door now. Me heart pounding loud. I sure they could hear it outside. I sit up on the bunk and wait for something to happen. For I-Shaman to get up. For the voice to come inside.

Voices all around the ghetto now and only the coconut branches between us. I want to look outside but I frighten to move. Just as if I stick down on the bunk.

I could see a shadow in front of the door. It holding something like a gun. Pointing it to the ghetto. A coldness pass over me and cold bumps spread on me skin.

"INSIDE DEY! YOU EN HEAR AH SAY TO COME OUT!"

I-Shaman jump down from the bunk then. He grab he pants from the floor and jump inside them real fast. Then he stand up looking around him as if he gone bazodee. He grab the bashie with the weed, pitch it in the fireside and kick ashes over it, like a cat covering up mess. Then he raise he hands over he head and walk outside.

I fix me nightie. Rub me eyes and wipe them with me nightie. They feeling puffy. I get up, but as soon as I put me feet down, the ground jook them like needles. I sit down again. The big boil burst and the pus dry up around it. I get up again. I limp to the door. I raise up me hands over me head and limp outside.

As I step out through the door, me skin start jooking again. Outside full of PRA soldiers. Just like that time when they came and cut down all I-Trad ganja and arrest him. They surround the ghetto. Their army suits make them look like the bush too. Like how iguanas does look in trees. And all of them have a gun.

"Move it, move it!" The same voice that shout to come out, say. The red-skin soldier who say it look as if he in charge. He face thin and hard. And he beard look like *cornbabe*. I bet people does call him Reds. He look like a Reds.

Reds eyes fall on me. It move on I-Shaman. Then back on me again. He look as if he trying figure out something.

I put me eyes on the ground. The grass feeling wet on me toes. I don't like how it feeling. And all them soldiers watching me.

I could smell somebody coal pit burning somewhere in the bush. In the morning you could smell everything. And everything does smell different. I could smell the pus on me leg too. "Put down you hands chile. Put down you hands." Reds say. He come up nearer to me and he watching me hard. Me face en wash yet and I sure I still have caca jé in me eyes.

"I know you. You is Rasta Goose daughter?"

I hold me eyes on the ground. I don't answer. Shame crawl over me like mad ants. And me arms fall down on me sides. They trembling bad. Me toes start to dig the ground. Me toenails long and they look dirty. Me fingernails dirty too. And me nightie old and flimsy flimsy, I sure they could see straight through it. I feel just as if I naked. I wish I could run in the bush and hide. I wish me Daddy come for me.

I-Shaman sweating and he eyes jumping all over the place, as if he looking for the chance to *break bush.*

Some of the soldiers come out from the back of the ghetto dragging some big ganja trees behind them. *Oh gosh! Dey get dem!* I-Shaman well hide he ganja between the peas trees and the black sage so nobody could see them. The soldiers drop the ganja in a heap and go back in the bush.

Then I hear voices coming from down by I-Rally and I-Jalee's ghetto too. Is not only us they come for. The voices coming from all over the place. Them PRA soilders all over the place. Chopping and shouting. And Rastaman chanting.

A bad pee hold me but I squeeze it in. I wondering what they going to do with us.

Them soldiers round up every ghetto. They root up and chop down every ganja tree. Then they gather us up and march us down the hill.

Stones jook me bare-feet going down the track. I wish I had on me slippers, but I didn't have time put them on.

I-Rally walk next to I-Jalee. He face set vex like a bull. When we eyes bounce up, he turn he head.

I look for I-Trad in the herd of Rastamen, but I can't see him. *Ah wonder if he looking for me too.*

We walk down the track, through the bush like sheep. Everybody on Tambran Hill come out from their house - like crabs coming out from their holes - to see what happening. Children in the yard shouting out "PRA! PRA! PRA! Ay Soldierman. MR PRA!" One of them say, "You doh see gun boy!" Some hailing up the Rastas they know. Others pointing and laughing. As if they get a big joke.

Me head full up with cinnamon tea and bakes frying in people kitchens. It make me belly grumble bad.

"You see dat little gal dey? She stayin wit a Rastaman oui!" A girl say. And she make the mad ants crawl on me again.

The girl who say it have a baby hook up on she waist. She breasts big big and they hanging down under she jersey, like them long pawpaws Papa plant by the Mango Row. She have a piece of comb stick in she hair. The baby don't have on no diaper; just a tear up vest. And snot running down he face. The girl look as if she only have about twelve or thirteen years. I wonder if the baby is hers or maybe she mother or she sister baby. But a lot of them young girls on Tambran Hill have baby already. Even I-Shanam's little sister have a baby and she only have fourteen years. The Rasta Sistren voice come back in me head again. *You could have a baby when you start to bleed between your legs you know.* I wonder if the girl start to bleed between she leg already. A stone jook me bad foot. It hurt me so bad it chase away she voice.

I limping real bad by the time we reach the main road. And me feet hurting. Two army trucks park up by the road, waiting for us, like monsters. And one amount of people gather up by the side of the road, as if they waiting to see a road race or a parade or something. People going

183

to work, children going to school, old people - taking purchase on walking sticks – and shaking their heads. And all them eyes on me again. Jooking me. Bruising me. Boring holes in me.

Me mouth taste dry and stale. I look for I-Trad again. And when I glimpse him, me chest swell up with a little bit of gladness. Two whole weeks pass since the time I went and see him. More boils burst out on me, but I just do what he tell me. I put ganja ashes on them. And some of the little ones dry up, but the big one just getting worse.

"Go in! Go in! Go in!" Reds shout. We pile into the truck. I-Trad stand up by the mouth of the truck. Reds push him to go in. He plant he feet on the ground, standing firm.

"Fire go burn all ah you Babylon!" A Rasta brethren shout.

Reds chuck I-Trad. "Jus go in the fucking truck Rasta!" he say.

I-Trad still don't move. But he face get hard. He eyes get deeper.

"Wha happen Rasta! You doh hear ah say go in the fucking truck!" Reds shout and he kick land on I-Trad leg. I-Trad nearly fall. But he hold on to the truck.

"Babylon victimization! Babylon go burn!" The Rasta brethren shout again.

"Hush you fucking mout and go in the truck nah Rasta!" Reds shout.

I-Trad climb in the truck. The Rasta brethren hush he mouth.

Inside the truck dark. They pack us like sardines on the two benches. I-Trad sit down by the end of the bench. And I sit down by him. I don't even watch I-Shaman. I wish he disappear, so the shame could go away too. I want I-Trad to hug me and call me Princess, like when I was little. But he don't say a word. He just staring at the darkness inside the truck, with he face like a lion.

I-Rally and I-Jalee sit down on the other side.

Then the truck start up. The cloud blocking the sun move and the light blind me eyes. The soldiers in the back of the truck pull down the tarpaulin. And I don't see light again for a long time.

It hot in the truck. And it so dark, I feel as if I could touch it. I press up closer to I-Trad. He smell like ganja and early morning. I want him to sing *every little thing gonna be alright*, like the first time the soldiers came for us. *Maybe dey go bring me and I-Rally back by Mammy and Papa again.*

Inside the tuck starting to smell stink with sweat and ganja. And I smelling the pus on me leg and I-Shaman on me.

The truck rumble down to the road, like a moving dungeon. It dipping in all pothole in the road. Bumping up and down, and swinging round them corners so hard, me head spin and me belly turn upside down. I grip the bench hard when I feel me tripe coming up. And good thing nothing come out! I clamp me mouth tight and I breathe in and out, in and out, through me nose. And pray for the truck to reach where we going.

Chapter 30

Locked Up

When the truck stop, a soldier raise up the tarpaulin. And I open me mouth and full it up with air. I feel giddy and sick, and glad we reach where we going. But we not in Celeste by Mammy and Papa. We in front a police station. The St George's Police Station. I remember it because once Mammy bring me there with her to see somebody she know.

The soldiers make everybody come out the truck and go inside the station. Then the police officers take over. They put me and I-Rally in the same cell with I-Trad. *Ah didn't know dey does lock up children too.*

I stay by I-Trad. I want I-Rally to come and sit down by us too, but he don't even watch me! He and I-Jalee like *Bim and Bam.*

I-Trad still not talking. It's a good thing, because I have a big cry inside me waiting to burst out as soon as somebody say anything to me.

Inside the cell hot too. Not like the truck, but I could feel the heat. And it smell like stale pee. The concrete floor have big stain marks in the corners. The walls dirty dirty and mark up with all kind of bad words. *Fuck Babylon. Fuck baldheads. Fire fee all bumbaclots. Rastaman oppression. Jah live!*

A skinny rastaman, one with a long, hard face, sit down in a corner holding he head. And he rocking like a little fishing boat on the water.

Another one, the one who does plant a lot of sweet potatoes and tannia, say, "I-man hungry to bumbaclot!"

Some of them rastas just there chanting, "Rastaman victimization. Jah live. Fire go burn Babylon. Fire burn Babylon! Jah! Rasta Fari live! Jah Jah know!" Others just sit down staring at the wall.

Time pass slow. I don't know how long we stay in the cell. It feel as if days pass.

A police lady come by the cell. "Come little girl. Come with me."

Me heart start to beat drum. I don't know what to do, so I watch I-Trad. *What she calling me for? How come she calling me alone?* I watch I-Trad again, but he still staring at the wall.

"Come, come with me darling," she say. She don't sound rough like a police. She voice nice. She sound as if she accustom talking to children. Me heart settle a little bit.

The police lady tall and she uniform neat neat. She shoes looking too big, but they shining like Papa's shoes, after he polish them. She have on glasses. She look like a nice police. She bring me in a little room with two chairs and a table.

"Sit down chile and wait for me here. Am coming back just now."

I sit down in the room. I wait long long. *What she leave me here for?* I want to go back and meet me father. Nobody can't do me nothing when I with me father.

Me legs feel stiff and it hurting. I raise up me dress and look. It swell up bad! And the big boil look as if it eating up me flesh. And it smelling bad.

The police lady come back with a plastic bag, a glass with juice and a pack of Shirley biscuits. She put them on the table

"Eat something chile. You must be real hungry!" And she look as if she feeling sorry for me.

I real like Shirley biscuits, but I shake me head. Mammy used to buy them when she went in Sauteurs to do Saturday shopping. Me and I-Rally used to bite off the edge of the biscuits and save the middle for last. It have a little house with flowers in the middle.

"You not hungry chile?" The police lady ask me.

I shake me head again. But me belly grumble real loud.

"Just drink the juice darling. You must eat something."

I real hungry in truth, but I can't eat that. I-Trad say how the body is the temple of Jah and how we must not put anything unclean in it. Shirley biscuit is not ital. And I don't know where the juice come out. I wish she did bring a mango or something, because I hungry bad.

The police lady sit down on the chair by me.

"Chile eat something. Is just biscuit and juice. It won't do you nothing."

The cry start to swell up. Me belly grumble again. Me mouth dry dry. And the juice looking nice. It in a real glass, like the ones Mammy have lock up in she cabinet. And it look real orange. Not dirty brown like Mammy lime juice. Me mouth run water, like the water running down on the side of the glass. I wish I could drink some.

"I have to ask you some questions eh darling. And after that, you go bathe and take out that old dress on you eh eh. I bring a nice little dress for you. And some slippers. Aright?"

The cry getting ready. I feel it behind me eyes. Waiting.

"What is your name dear?"

"Lee." I say. Me voice hoarse. I swallow, but me mouth dry so only air go down.

"You know where you are?"

I nod. I put me eyes in me lap. On me hands.

"How old are you chile?"

What she asking me all dat question and dem for? I don't answer. I put me eyes on me toes. They dry. Dirty. I push them under the chair.

"Who you was staying with in the hills? Your brother?"

Oh God! Eyes on the wall. The cry on reach on steady. And if I just open me mouth, it reaching on Go.

"Come chile. You could tell me you know. The soldiers and them tell me where they find you."

Cry burst. *Oh God!* I want to go back by me father.

She touch me on me shoulder. "Don't cry darling. Is aright. Don't worry. We go look after you now. We call you mother aready."

Me mother! Dey call me mother! Me mother coming? Me face wet. Me nose running. Me chest swelling up. The cry can't stop. Me shoulders shaking.

"Don't cry chile. We send a message for your grandmother. I know you grandmother good. She coming down for you."

The cry shaking up me whole self now.

"Watch me chile. Let me see your face," she say. She raise up me chin and wipe me face with she handkerchief. A white one with red and yellow flowers on it.

"How your eyes puffy puffy so? Your father used to give you the weed to smoke too?"

I don't answer. She press she finger under me eyes and then me face, as if she testing out bread.

"Ah bringing you by the doctor for a check up, eh darling? Go in that bathroom over there and bathe and change your clothes. Ah coming back."

The bathroom don't have no door. It have little, white square things on the floor. The wall look as if somebody start to paint it and then change their mind - like the bathroom inside by Mammy. Mammy bathroom

189

didn't have the little square things and the walls look rough like sandpaper.

The water feel colder than the river water, but I wet meself. I pick up the Lifebuoy soap in a dish on the little shelf, but I put it back down. I remember when Miss Kay used to bath us with it on Sundays. I pick it up again and rub it on the rag. *Me father won't know.* I use the bottom pipe. I put up me foot on the wall, but it still get wet.

I take out the things from the bag: a pink panty; with little flowers on it, a pair of hula hoop slippers and a dress. I put on the panty. *Me father won't know.* And I like the dress bad. It have a halter back and a lot of colours like the rainbow, going up and down, like upside down Vs. And it fit me real good, as if the police lady know me size. I know me father go like the colours, but he would not like me back expose so.

I rip out a piece of cloth from me old dress and wipe up around the boil. And I just banding it up with another piece, when the police lady come back.

"Lord have mercy! Chile what happen to you foot?" She come closer then raise up me dress to see better.

"Lord Jesus! Come on chile. Eat something quick. Ah bringing you in the hospital right now."

The cry start back again. A whole river full. It still flowing out when she put me in the police car and bring me up in the hospital.

Chapter 31

Rasta Girl

The hospital room smell like Jeyes, Dettol and sick people.

The nurse watch me as if she feel real sorry for me. She small and she look real young. She make me pee in a silver bowl – that shape like a bean. Then she make me lie down on a narrow narrow bed and tell me, "Stay there. De doctor comin jus now."

A man and a lady come by me bed. They look like brother and sister. The two of them hair black and straight. They have same round nose and brown eyes. And the two of them have on white coats. They from Cuba. I hear them speaking Spanish to one another.

The man doctor press below me eyes with he thumbs. He pull down the skin under me eyes. He shine a bright little flashlight inside me eyes. He say, "ahhh" and open he mouth wide wide, for me to open mine too. He shine the light inside me mouth. Then he stretch out he tongue for me to follow him, so I stretch out mine too. He shine the light on it. He press the cold thing he had hanging round he neck, on me chest and me back. And he breathe through he nose and out he mouth. I do it too. Then he and the lady doctor talk Spanish again. The lady doctor talk to the nurse. The nurse tell the lady doctor something. Then the lady doctor come back by me bed, as if she forget something. She raise up me dress and bend down and watch me legs. She tell the nurse something again. Then she and the man doctor go.

After they go, the nurse clean up the boils. She dress the big one and she tie a big bandage around it. She make me look as if I have a big sore foot - like the old lady on the hill in Celeste! Then the nurse put me in a wheel chair and push me upstairs.

As soon as the nurse push me inside the female ward, everybody eyes fall on me. And I feel them on me like mad ants. I small up meself in the wheelchair. The little nurse who push me up, go and talk to the nurse on the ward. Then she park up the wheel chair by the empty bed in a corner, and leave me there.

I don't want to stay there. All them people watching me watching me, and I know they go start to ask me questions too. *Ah wonder when me mother coming for me.*

After the nurse tell me that is me bed, she bring me in the bathroom.

"Let's cut that ugly hair on your head now!" She tell me.

And just so, she bring some scissors and just cut me locks. And I just sit down there watching the pieces of locks falling on the floor, like black cotton. When she finish, me head feel light! And I feel just as if the nurse strip me naked. *What me father go say when he see me? Ah wonder if dey cut I-Rally locks too?* But then I remember me mother coming and I start to feel glad too. I don't want me mother to see me with rasta hair on me head.

"Dat looking better now man," the nurse say. "Ah coming back just now. Ah going for a nightie for you."

I pick up me hair from the floor. I remember when I-Rally was little and Mammy make Jakko cut he hair for school. Mammy pick up all the hair, she put them in a plastic bag and put it in the drawer with she going out clothes. She say if you throw away you hair, bad luck go meet you. I hold the pieces of hair and wonder what to do with them. I don't have no bag to put them so I rest them by the sink. That's when I see the little girl in the mirror.

When we used to live by Mammy, I used to stand up on the bed and watch meself in the big mirror that stand up the dressing table. The one with the gold frame, leaning up on the partition. Especially when Miss Kay's daughter plait me hair in a nice style. But I-Trad say how mirror is vanity. I don't even know what vanity is. We just didn't have no mirror in the ghetto.

I watching the girl in the mirror and she watching me back. She not the little girl with ribbons in she hair, smiling for she Daddy, and for Mr Glenford to take out the picture. The girl in the mirror eyes down in two deep holes. They red red. And round them dark and puffy. She face looking hard. She nose too big for she face and she mouth black and dry. She front teeth rotten. And she look just as if something jump out from the bush and frighten her. She look as if she still frighten. That little girl in the mirror real ugly. That's not me.

The nurse see me watching meself in the mirror, when she come back. "Doh worry man, it go grow back jus now," she say. Then she bring me back in me bed.

When I wake up, is evening time. And it have a plate and a cup cover down on me dressing table.

"You wake up?" The nurse say. She come by me bed. "You take a real good sleep man. Come, get up and eat you supper."

I get up and sit up on the bed. She uncover the plate and give me. It have two thick slices of bread and some eggs on it. And the milk tea look watery watery; as if they just dash in a little bit of milk to change the colour. But me belly boiling with hunger, so I drink some. I forget all what I-Trad does say about body and temple and Jah, and I eat up a piece of bread. It dry, but it taste nice with the butter on it. But as soon as I swallow piece in the egg, I start to feel sick. And next thing I vomiting everything in the bed pan. Then I lie down and fall asleep again.

When I wake up again, I lie down on me bed watching round me. When the lady in the bed by me ask me if I want a biscuit, I say "no tanks." She sit down on she bed eating Crix and cheese. And she have a glass of orange Fanta on she dressing table, making bubbles. She have a lot of things on she dressing table: a bottle of Johnson's baby powder, a full bottle of Limacol, a bottle with plastic flowers, a pink soap dish with red flowers on it, and a little silver flashlight. The only thing on me dressing table is the toothbrush,that the nurse give me and me dress fold up inside the cupboard.

Night come. Morning come and it have a different nurse now. She big and she look real serious. I wonder if the nice nurse coming back.

"Come chile. Get up! Get up! Go and wash up to eat you breakfast!" The big nurse say. And she give me a little scratch-up silver basin. "Make haste chile!"

Ah know she de rough! You see how she face sour!

And me leg feel real stiff, but I limp go in the bathroom.

The nurse just dressing me leg when I see Mammy coming. She have on she blue going out dress, she white netted hat and she false teeth. And before the nurse even show her me bed, she start to bawl down the place.

"Bon jé oh! Look at what de man do me Beti nuh! Papa God! Dat man could ah kill you oui. You doh see how de man coulda make de chile lose she foot! Bon jé oh!" Mammy bawl. She cry. She pull out she handkerchief from she bag and cover she mouth. And she just stand up by me bed watching, with the handkerchief over she mouth.

I wish was me mother who come. But I so glad to see Mammy, me face start getting wet too. *And Mammy call me she Beti.*

The nurse finish dressing me leg. "Mammy, doh cry man. She in good hands now," she say. And she bring a chair for Mammy to sit down.

Mammy bring a cream soda Fanta, a pack of Crix biscuits and cheese for me. She put a bottle of Limacol, a bottle of My Fair Lady powder and a Lifebuoy soap in a green soap dish with flowers - like the one the lady in the next bed have. She bring a new rag and a pink and white towel for me too. And they smell just like inside Mammy big black trunk.

Chapter 32

Me Mother Come Back

As soon as I see nice, dress up lady talking to the nurse, and the nurse pointing me bed, I know is me mother what come.

Me chest heave up and then it fall down. I watch her walking to me bed. She have on a cream pants suit with a lot of pockets and buckles. She face round and pretty, and she curly hair falling around it. I want to jump down from the bed and run and hug her up, but I want to hide under the bed too. I don't want me mother so see me so. Me head looking ugly. Me eyes and them up swell up swell up.

When me mother reach by the bed she sit down on the chair quick quick; as if she woulda fall if she didn't sit down. Then she put she face in she hands and she start to cry. She hands look nice and smooth. She have on red Cutex on she fingernails and she rings look as if they squeezing she fingers.

I feel me eyes fulling up too.

"Oh Lord! Look what your father do you nuh!"

The two of us crying. I crying and I wondering how come she take long to come, because two weeks now I in hospital. And how come she never hug me and kiss me like people does do when they don't see one another for long.

I stay in the hospital for four weeks. And me mother come and see me almost every day. Then the nurse say I could go home.

Home is back by Mammy and Papa. Papa in the veranda as usual. He in he same old wrought iron chair. The chair almost naked now, because all the paint gone. And Papa looking old and thin, thin. He mouth twist to one side and he tongue so heavy, he have to fight to say, "A ...a. Ree...nee... you ... come ...home?"

Mammy say Papa had a stroke, and that's why he can't talk good. Papa can't move he right hand or he right foot. He have to use he left hand to move the right one. And I wondering who does scratch he back and pull out he socks for him now.

"Well give Papa a kiss nuh," me mother say. Papa smell like Limacol and Mammy nutmeg oil mix-up. And when I kiss Papa, he face scratchy scratchy, like prickle bush. He can't shave heself again. He can't even put on he clothes for heself. But Papa still have a smile for me. He head shake. He whole good side shake, when he make he twist-up mouth smile for me. And Papa make another set of cry start up again.

And Mammy there watching me as if she glad too I come home. All of a sudden, is Beti this and Beti that. But I know she playing nice just because me mother there.

I stay inside all the time. I fraid Yvette and Boyo and them go tease me and call me *sore-foot Lee,* like they used to tease Miss Nyo from down the road. Mammy say Miss Nyo have a life sore. She have it long long and it never getting better. And I frighten mine never get better too. It looking big big. And I have to go in the surgery for the nurse to dress it, and band it up, just like Miss Nyo.

Miss Kay is the first person to come and see me. As soon as I reach, she come over by Mammy.

"Lee, me chile! Let me see you nuh!" she say in she high squeaky voice. And she hug me she hard self; shiny and smelling of sweet coconut oil and petroleum jelly mix up. "Well watch what de man do de chile nuh! Look how he coulda make de chile lose she foot nuh papa God! Ah glad dey put he backside in jail you hear! Dat is wickedness man!"

All the time I in the hospital, nobody never say nothing about me father. I didn't want me father to go in jail. But I just glad me mother come back.

Then the white lady, from the big house up the road, come and see me too. I don't know how come. Because she accustom just passing in she car and just waving for Mammy. But this time, when Jakko stop, he go round and open she door for her to come out. And she didn't just stand up by the road, in front the veranda. She walk down the two steps, holding on to Jakko shoulder, pass through the veranda, and come right inside Mammy house. First time I see her close so. She right in front me. She so near by me, I could smell she perfume and she cigarette. I could even see all the lines and them round she eyes and she mouth. And if I want I could touch she soft doll hair too.

"How are you my dear child?" She ask me. She sit down on one of Mammy morris chair – the new one. She take me hand and hold it in hers. Inside she hands soft, but the skin look like the skin on one of them real tough chicken after Mammy dip it in hot water and pluck out the feathers. And it have a lot of brown spots on it.

And I sit down there, with me hand in the white lady hand and I wondering how come she come all in Mammy house to see me. And how come she looking as if she feeling sorry for me so. And Mammy there smiling as if that's the best thing in the world; this white lady in she house. She even tell the lady how me birthday coming next week.

The day I take eleven years, that July, the white lady stop in front we house again. But she don't come out this time. She maid, Betty, come out of the car with a big cake.

Only in story book I ever see cake like that. It different from the cake Mammy and Miss Kay does make. It smell like toffee sweets, and it have something soft all over it – like brown butter. None of us like the cake. Rally say, "You doh see dat is white people cake!" The only person who eat piece is me mother.

All the time I in hospital, Rally there by Mammy and Papa. The police and them bring him by them. Mammy say she don't know what we father do with she Beta, but how he turn into a beast. She say how all he doing is smoking marijuana and giving trouble. And how he want to kill people when he smoke the thing. He curse her up when she try to make him cut he locks. He is not Mammy Beta again.

I want me brother to be glad we mother with us, but he vex with everybody. He not even speaking with me. And I afraid of what I see in he eyes when he vex. We mother can't even tell him nothing. One day when he there getting on, we mother get vex and she tell him why he don't keep he backside quiet. Well who tell her say that? He curse her up well bad! He start to pelt words like big stones.

"Who you tellin to keep quiet eh? You doh see how you wicked. You leave us and go since we small. You make we fadda take us and bring us in the bush and you never come for us. He make *man* take me sister! How come you never come back for her! Eh? Who you telling to keep quiet! You doh see you wicked! All you studying to do is dress-up dress-up. Wha you come back now for? You doh know how ah hate you nuh!"

All of us in the veranda quiet. Mammy mouth clamp tight. She watching Rally and rocking on she sofa. Papa mouth open but nothing coming out. We mother crying. She whole self shaking, as if she feeling cold. And I crying too, because them words and them Rally pelting, hitting me hard hard; bruising up me skin. Bursting me head.

And every evening when we in the hall, I does get real afraid me mother go ask me about what happen. I afraid I go have to tell her *that thing* I don't want nobody to know. Sometimes, in the middle of putting she rollers in she hair, she does stop, watch me and just start to cry. But she never ask me nothing.

Three weeks pass. Then one Sunday evening, she in the veranda writing a letter, and she start talking.

"I have to go back now. I can't stay longer because I leave your little brother with them people. I have to go back to work," she say.

She stop writing she long, leaning-down words. And she talking to me but she not watching me – she watching she writing pad as if is it she talking to.

"You brother hate me. And all he doing is cussing and giving trouble. I don't know what to do with him. I can't leave him with Mammy! He go kill her. And Papa not strong again."

Me mother voice trembling. Water squeezing out from she eyes, running down she face.

"All you father just take all you and spoil all you in the bush and now I don't know what to do."

I just sit down there – in me dress that the Police lady did give me. Every Sunday I does put it on after bathe. And I watching me hands in me lap. Me nails clean now.

"I can't even leave you with Mammy. You see enough trouble already and I can't leave you here to see more trouble."

And all the time I know me mother have to go back because she leave we little brother with them people she working with. But I praying for her not to go. We father in jail. Mammy don't want me. I know that because one day I hear her talking to the white lady maid Betty. She there saying how she don't know where me mother go leave me because she not keeping me – not after man spoil me in the bush! She even say how she go to ask the white lady if she could take me and bring me in Canada with her. And I wondering why the white lady go want to bring me in Canada for, when she is nothing to me.

"It have a lady in St George's who used to be in Venezuela with me. She say she will take you to stay with her until I come back," me mother say.

I still watching me dress. I watching the upside down Vs until I seeing doubles and all them colours mix up together, like a big collage – like we used to make in Ms. Belfon class.

The week after I take eleven years, Mammy call the PRA and them for Rally. They take him and bring him in The Villa where they does put boys who behaving bad. And me mother pack up me clothes and bring me down in St George's by the lady she talk about.

Chapter 33

By The Lady

The house big. It have upstairs and downstairs. I wondering if they rich, because is rich people that does have upstairs and downstairs house.

"Come in, come in," The Lady say. And she smiling as if she real glad to see me and me mother.

She bring us up upstairs. A man and a old lady upstairs too. The old lady sit down on a Morris chair and she bottom spread out so much it overlapping on the sides. You can't even see the cushion under her. She look as if she would never be able to get up from there.

The man big and tall, just like me grandmother husband. It look as if everybody in that house big, because The Lady big too and she belly high high. She have pink sponge curlers in she hair and she glasses thick thick.

Me mother put down the bag with me clothes on the floor and sit down. I sit down on the chair The Lady show me – the one with the back cushion missing – and I put me bag on me lap.

It have four chairs in the room where we sit down. And it have a long table with a television and a big radio on top it, and books and records and all kinds of things pack up on the shelf below. It have a shelf over the television with a lot of little animals and little people on it. And a big clock, on the partition over me head. First time I ever see a clock big so. It have a long table in the room too, with four chairs around it. The table shiny like the floor, and it smelling strong like varnish. I wonder if the lady varnish it just because me mother coming. Every Christmas time and Easter time, Mammy does get somebody to give the house a good clean-up and varnish the floor. And when somebody from away coming by her too.

The Lady and me mother and the man talking about Venezuela – the people they know, the places they used to go. Then she start talking about how she meet the man. Mr Joe is he name.

And all the time they talking, I listening to them. And I listening to the clock going *tic tocking* over me head. *Tic tock. Tic tock.* I count the doors in the room: the front door, the one to go in the veranda and four others. Six doors! I wonder what behind the other four. The loud *DING* over me head make me jump. The clock saying half past eleven.

"Well put down de bag nuh," The Lady say. And she watching me through she thick glasses. "You en going nowhere you know."

I rest the bag on the floor by the chair. The Lady name is Claire. But I wondering how I go have to call her. *Auntie Claire? Misss Claire? Claire?*

I don't even know these people where me mother leaving me. The morning when we leaving home, Mammy just watch me and shake she head. "Go mama! Go let dem make you see trouble! Whey you ever hear strangers does take people children jus so? Go mama!"

When me mother say she have to go back, Mammy raise she head at me and ask me mother, "And whey you leaving dat one?" As if me is nothing for her. So I don't know what Mammy talking about. And Papa just there, quiet as a mouse. Since he have the stroke, he even more quiet. And he could hardly even move. He right hand just hang down by he side and he have to drag he right foot behind the left one, to walk from the bedroom to the veranda. Sometimes he does drag heself down behind the house for Mammy to bathe him. Papa does hardly eat food, but he does drink a lot of coconut water. Papa face and all drop down on the right side – so he can't even grin like a silly-billy again. So that morning when me and me mother leaving, and I say, "Ah goin eh Papa." He just stand up by the veranda gate watching me go down the road, as if he don't know what happening. As if he want to say, "Reenie, whey you goin wid dat big bag?" And all when I pass Miss Kay house going down, I could still see Papa striped pajamas on the veranda.

After the clock ding-dong twelve times, we go downstairs and eat. The fat lady stay upstairs and The Lady bring up she food for her.

The downstairs dark, even though the windows open. The bathroom and the kitchen downstairs. It have a big stove in the kitchen and a lot of cupboards. Two tables with chairs around them; one by the kitchen and one in the next room by it. They have fridge and all. *They must be rich boy!*

We eat rice and peas, stew chicken wings, with lime juice. And the food smell nice! And it taste real nice too. But I didn't like the lime juice. It too sour. Me mother does make real nice juice with the passion fruits and lemons in the garden. And she does buy ice down by Ms Mavis to put in it. I wonder if The Lady have snow ice in she fridge too.

When we finish eat, Mr Joe go back upstairs. The Lady say he going and rest.

Me and me mother sit down by the table.

"Well ah have to go now. It getting late," Me mother say. She have to go and get bus to go back up by Mammy.

"Behave youself you know. Don't give de lady trouble," me mother saying. "And listen to de lady when she speak to you. Do what she say. Don't give her no rudeness."

Me not a rude child. Is Rally what does give me mother rudeness! So ah doh know what rudeness she talking about.

Me mother dip inside she bag and bring out she handkerchief. I watching the floor. Some of the brown diamonds on the linoleum look wash-out, as if somebody scrub them out.

"You know ah have to go back, because ah leave your brother wit dem people."

Them people is Señor *and* Señora Pinto – the people she working with. Me mother say how Mr Pinto does treat Carlos as if is he own grandchild. How he always buying presents for Carlos and spoiling him. She say Señora Pinto not nice like the man.

Me mother have a lot of pictures with Carlos: he is a baby, with he nice nice hair; he playing with some white children; hitting a big blow up animal with a stick, in a birthday party. Me mother say that's a piñata – how it have sweets inside it. In one of them pictures, he in a big, fancy kitchen – eating something in a bowl with milk and making a monkey trick with he face. Me mother say is cornflakes he eating. But is not she he making face for, because she by the sink washing up wares – with she yellow gloves on she hands. Carlos eyes same like mine. And he look like we father even more than me.

Me mother go. I hear her outside, telling The Lady she going. I sit down by the table where she leave me. I squeeze me cry inside. I lock it up inside me chest. It swell up and me chest get heavy – as if it go burst and everything inside there go pour out on The Lady wash out linoleum.

The Lady bring me back upstairs. She tell me to bring me bag in the room – the one behind the middle door.

The room small. The bed narrow narrow, but it still don't have no space in the room to move. It have clothes hanging up on the partition and a little cupboard with perfume and cream and things to put in hair, on top it.

When The Lady say, "You go sleep here with Julie." I know she mean on the floor. *How dat bed go hold two people?*

"Pack you clothes on the shelf below," The Lady say, opening the cupboard door. "And I hope you could work you know, because all man have they share!" she say, before she leave me in the room.

I wonder what me mother tell The Lady about me. When she and the lady was talking, she did make me raise up me pants leg and show The Lady the sore. And when The Lady see it, she put she hand on she mouth and bawl, "Oh Lord have mercy! But the chile nearly lose she foot man!" She say how she daughter Marion – the one who is around same age like me – go bring me in the surgery to dress it. And I feel glad The Lady have a daughter round me age. Maybe we go be in the same school.

Chapter 34

It Have Work To Do

It didn't take long for me to find out what The Lady mean. The first morning, early early, she knocking on the bedroom door, waking up people. Is Saturday morning, but she there knocking the door loud loud, saying, "Come on, come on. Time to wake up!"

Julie groan. "Well Mommy!"

"What you mean well mommy! Just get up madam! You en see daylight already and it have a lot of work to do!"

Daylight? I can't see no light coming in the room. I don't even hear no cock crowing yet.

She go in the next, where Marion sleeping with the old lady.

"Get up, get up. Sun getting hot already and all the clothes sit down waiting." the lady say.

Marion groan. Julie still groaning and stupsing in she pillow – so The Lady can't hear.

Is a good thing I accustom waking up early. And the way The Lady saying it make me get up faster.

I fold up me bedding; three big, old dress and a sheet to cover with. I put on me home clothes and sit down in the hall, waiting. I have to go downstairs to brush me teeth, but I frighten, because the trapdoor close. First time I see a trapdoor in me life! I don't even know how to open it, so I waiting.

The clock ding six times.

The Lady come out from she room.

"Mornin Miss Claire." I say.

She have on a uniform. She working in the hospital.

"A a, you get up? Good! Because ah en having no lazy bones in dis house at all at all," she say. She taking out she pink sponge rollers from she hair.

"Marion go show you what to do. The house have to clean and you go help her wash the clothes. You could wash?"

I shake me head. "Um hm."

"Don't shake you head when people speaking to you. Answer properly,"

"Yes Miss Claire," I say.

"And call me Claire," she say. "Everybody does call me Claire."

I glad she tell me that because all the time I wondering how I go call her.

She finish taking out she rollers and she open the trapdoor. One big, hot, black hole there below there. Watching me! I glad when she put on the light.

"When ah come back from work, ah want to see the place clean! From top to bottom! And all clothes wash and dry! Sun blazing today!"

A bus horn blow in front the house and Claire shout out, "Ah comin, ah comin." She comb she hair quick quick. Pick up she bag and make haste down the steps.

Julie get up and go downstairs to make breakfast. She is Claire second daughter.

I go and brush me teeth and I waiting for Marion to get up and show me what to do. She is Claire last child.

Marion get up and she vex to burst. She have a vex face. The first time when she see me, she just watch me and roll up she big eyes. And she look like a big woman! Everything big. She face big. She breasts and them big big. She bottom big and stick behind her, like black ants.

Marion just give me a piece of cloth and tell me to dust down the chairs. She start to sweep from the back of the hall, by the cabinet with all the special wares; between Claire room and she biggest brother room.

I know how to sweep but I watching Marion. She move the Pyrex dish and them and wipe on top the cabinet. She wipe around the window. Fling the cloth over she shoulder and sweep again. Cobweb over Claire door. And she rubbing she nose and sneezing sneezing. Making a funny noise with she throat, jooking she ears and shaking she head as if she getting fits.

I rest the cushions on the floor, for me to wipe the chairs.

"What you put dem on the floor fuh?" Marion ask me.

And I want to give Marion a real bad eyes. *First time I doing dat. How she expec me to know?* But I hold back me bad eyes before she go and bring news for Claire.

"You have to put dem in the veranda to sun."

So I take them out and bring them in the veranda. First time I go in the veranda. The floor cold and it feeling wet. It have a room in the veranda too. One of Marion brothers sleeping there.

I could see all round from the veranda - the road below, and people going in the market, a man sweeping the yard across the road. He wave for me. He stop sweeping the yard and go through the garden with he broom in he hand. He wave for me again. He grinning all the time. I smile back for him. He look like a man and he look like a boy. He have a lot of growing moles on he face.

An old lady come out from the kitchen.

"James! Jamesie! Where you gone?' she call.

"Ah comin now Mammy," he say and he run back in the yard quick quick, with he broom.

I finish brushing the chairs, I dust down where the television is, the records, the shelf with all the ornaments. Me belly grumbling, fuss I hungry. Marion sweeping slow and she still pulling she throat, jooking she ears and shaking she head.

I well glad when Julie call us for we breakfast. I ready to go downstairs when the old lady come out with she potty in she hand. The potty full and she hand trembling for so. She is Claire Auntie. She name is Auntie Ethel.

"Come and take that from me chile!" she say.

I go and take the potty.

"Go and empty it in the toilet," Marion tell me.

I go down the steps real careful, because the potty full up. And I holding me breath because the pee smelling strong strong. I pour it in the toilet and put the potty in the bathroom.

When I see Auntie Ethel going down the steps, through the trapdoor, I sure she go tumble she big self right down to the kitchen. I stand up watching her put she foot careful on the steps and holding on to the floor – coming down one today, one tomorrow, until she reach the bottom step.

I eat me bread and cheese and drink me Milo tea quick. We still have the window and them to clean. And the concrete sink outside full of clothes soaking. And it have another big bundle waiting. But Marion sit down on the step eating slow slow. Tickling she ears with a mash up piece a feather and making that noise with she throat again.

Sun real hot when we ready to wash the clothes. Marion give me the little clothes – like panties, underpants and socks – to wash first. As if she testing me out – to see if I could wash in truth.

The four clothes lines in the yard full of clothes and me hands quail-up quail-up like a prune. We leave the little clothes to hang up last. I hanging up the panties and them, but Marion say, "Girl doh hang up panties by the road so!"

And I done hang up all she brother underpants and them on the line already and she didn't say nothing. So I don't know why she telling me not to hang up them panties there.

"Hang dem on de back line," she say.

When we finish hanging up the clothes, they look nice and clean, pin up on the line in all them colours. And so they smelling nice – flapping about in the breeze.

By the time we finish the windows, polish the floor and scrub the bathroom, is lunch time. Marion fall asleep on the step with she plate of food on she lap – the same step where she eat she breakfast.

I stay in the kitchen and watch Julie make bread.

Chapter 35

Feefee Eye Girl

July finish. I watch TV for the first time in me life. Before, was just the movies in the cinema, but I never see no TV in nobody house. August bring carnival time and we go and watch pretty mas in town. Then September reach and I have to go to school.

Since me father take out me and Rally from school, I never do no school work. I never even pick up a book. Only the Bible – and that's before we father take it when he leave us and go and stay for heself. How I go remember how to do arithmetic and dictation? I can't even remember me times tables. Them children go laugh me and call me dunce.

Claire put me in the Saint Paul's Government School. The school just down the road from the house, so it only take about ten minutes to walk it. Marion used to go to that school too, but she going in secondary school now.

Julie bring me to school the first day. She is Claire's second daughter. The first one not living home. She married already and she living in the country with she husband and their four children. Claire have two sons too.

Julie in the Militia and she dress up in she uniform. I have on me new uniform too - blue pleated skirt, white shirt, black shoes and white socks. Julie plait me hair in cornrows. She tie two red ribbons in it; one on each side. The bows and them so big, I look as if I have red wings on me head.

The school yard full of children. First day of school and everybody in their brand new uniform. First time some of them little ones going to school and they frighten. A little girl hang on to she mother dress crying. "Mammy! Mammy ah want to go wid you. Ah want to go wid you Mammy!" A little fat boy throw heself on the ground, bawling down the place. He roll. He kick up. He roll. He drag on the ground, in he new khaki pants. He mother leave him on the ground. She walking away fast fast, but I see she cry want to burst out too. A big girl pick him up and bring him inside. All when he inside he still bawling. "Mammy! Mammeeey! Mammy!"

Me new school don't look like me old school at all. Me old school nicer than it. It big and it have upstairs and downstairs. It have boys' toilets and girls' toilets and a big tuck shop. And we have a big pasture and the churchyard to play in too. But Saint Paul's school look like a big, long fowl run. It flat and it have wire round the sides – as if they build it for fowls and then they change their minds and make it a school. The classrooms and them open, so you could see all round. And you could hear the teachers and them teaching and children making noise and everything.

Julie bring me in the principal office and leave me there. The principal name is Miss Wallhead. And she have a real *man-head*. She hair short short, like a man. I waiting hear her talk to hear if she have a man voice too. But the voice that come out and say, "Let me take you to your class now," not like a man voice at all. It just like one of those little rubber animal toy people have on their cabinets, that soft and nice, and when you squeeze it, it does make a loud, squeaky noise.

Me heart go full speed walking through the corridor with Miss Wallhead. Fuss I frighten, I want to run back home.

213

We pass the classes with them big children. And all them classes open out open out – they don't have no partitions. And the teachers have to talk loud and everybody hearing what everybody else saying.

I hold me bag tight and I walk close close to Miss Wallhead. She stop by a class in the corridor. The teacher stop teaching and talk to Miss Wallhead. All them children head turn and they watching me. I hug me bag tighter. Put me head on the floor.

Miss Wallhead leave me with the teacher. Miss Phillip is she name. She fair-skin and she hair thick thick.

Miss Phillip send a boy for a chair. Them children still watching me. Some of them talking secret to one another and laughing. Me knees feel weak. *How come dey talking secret and laughing so? Maybe dey know about me. Dey know me father in prison.*

Break time reach. All them children go outside. I stay in me seat. And fuss I keep me head down, I get stiff neck!

"You not going for break Carla?" Miss Phillip ask me.

I shake me head. *I en going no outside nuh! For dem children to see me ugly sore and call me sore-foot! And picky head!*

And me name always changing. Mammy used to call me all kinds a names. When me father turn rasta, he change me name. Now Uncle Joe - that's Claire husband – say he rather me second name, Carla. And everybody in the house calling me Carla. So I have to use that name now. Sometimes I does even forget that's me name.

It have a lady in the yard selling things to eat. I wish I could go and buy a snow ice and a cake with the dollar Uncle Joe give me. But I frighten to even move. Them children watching me too much.

Some girls stand up in the corridor. Some of them look real big.

"All you, whey dat ugly *feefee* eye girl come out?" The biggest one say. All of them laugh. I small-up meself in me seat. Put me head lower down. I could feel the cry gathering up behind me eyes. I hold it back. Me father always used to tell me not to cry so much. *You must be a strong princess!* Well me not no princess. Princess does be ugly so? Me eyes still swell-up and down in two deep holes. Me face still look like the little girl in the mirror in the hospital. I sure that's what people does see when they watch me. And I don't even know what *feefee* mean, but I know I ugly.

I put me head on the table. I well holding me cry and praying for school to over, but Miss Phillip come and ask me, "What happen to you Carla?" And just so me well burst, and everything start to pour out. Me eyes get even more *feefee*.

The day drag slow slow, as if it didn't want to finish. Then three o' clock, the bell ring for school to over. I speed up the short cut. And whole road, *Dat ugly feefee eye girl ... feefee eye girl... feefee eye... feefee eye,* chasing me.

Chapter 36

The Revo Days

"FORWARD EVER!" Comrade Maurice Bishop shout in the mic.

"BACKWARD NEVER!" The crowd chant.

"FORWARD EVER!"

"BACKWARD NEVER!"

We Pioneer group in a rally in Government Park. The Park full of people. PRA soldiers everywhere. Everybody in some kind of organization: youth clubs, women's organizations, pioneers movements, the Militia. And they have on T-Shirts to say which organization they in.

And everybody listening to Comrade Maurice Bishop. He talking about 'wiping out illiteracy' and 'free education for all', with he big, deep voice pitching all the way on top of De Abro Hill.

Uncle Joe say how the Prime Minister have real charisma; how he have a gift for speaking. How he voice does compel people to listen to him – no matter what he was talking about. And everybody love Comrade Maurice Bishop. But Uncle Joel does shake he head and say, "This regime won't last. Mark my words. Watch what go happen!"

Is when I go and live by Claire, I start to see the real Revo days. Before that, all I know is Maurice Bishop overthrew Gairy; people start getting free milk and we getting free lunch in school.

Julie put me in the Pioneer Movement in school. We have meetings every Wednesday, after school. And that's how I does start to learn all kinds of things about the Revolution. I learn all the ministers and them names. All them different groups and organizations. And it have a slogan for everything.

IT TAKES A REVOLUTION TO MAKE A SOLUTION! If you not in the PRA (People's Revolutionary Army) you in the Militia, or in the NYO (National Youth Organization) or in the NWO (National Women's Organization), or the Pioneer Movement or something.

IF YOU KNOW, TEACH. IF YOU DON'T, LEARN! People start going to classes to learn all kinds of things. It have classes in me school every evening. All them big people, old people and all – who didn't go to school or leave school early, going to class to learn how to read and write, and do their sums. EDUCATION IS PRODUCTION TOO! NEVER TOO OLD TO LEARN!

EVERY STUDENT A WORKER. EVERY WORKER A STUDENT. Women learning to sew and make things. KNOWLEDGE IS POWER! People get scholarships to go in Cuba, to study to be doctors and dentists and engineers and all kind of things. And a lot of Cubans start to come in we country too. We call them Cubanos. We have Cubano doctors. Cubano teachers. Cubano builders and construction workers – building schools, community centres and houses for poor people. WORK HARDER. PRODUCE MORE. BUILD GRENADA!

IDLE HANDS WORKING IDLE LANDS EQUALS AN END TO UNEMPLOYMENT! So people working the land, planting food. Fruits not spoiling on the ground again because it have factories making drinks with all them mangoes, soursop, pawpaw, tamarinds, golden apples and things. Nobody idle again. LET'S JOIN HANDS TO BUILD A BETTER LAND!

I glad I join the Pioneer Movement. We going all over the place. We dressing up and doing all kinds of displays when they have rallies. We even do a display at Pearls Airport when President Samora Machel, the President of Mozambique, come in Grenada. He shake we hands and kiss all the girls.

We learn folk songs and dances. And on Saturday they say we going in the TV station to take part in a cultural program.

Everybody excited we going in the TV station! We singing and dancing, waiting for the transport to pick us up.

When I see a big army truck stop by the school, me heart stop too.

Everybody jolly. They never ride in an army truck before, so they can't wait to climb in. They beating the drum, singing, making jokes. And I sit down in the truck quiet quiet, remembering *that time* – darkness in me eyes; sweat smell in me nose; sickness rising up from me belly, fulling up me mouth – as the truck bump down the long long road.

And I dig up me hole in the darkness – in that place inside me – and I bury *that time*. Then I cover it up and stamp over it, just like me and Rally used to stamp over a chicken grave, when yaws kill it.

Chapter 37

Kissing Prime Ministers

"**W**ho want to be on TV?" Comrade Jones ask, one evening when we having Pioneer meeting. Everybody hand fly up. When he say is to read news on TV and you have to be a good reader, all the boys hands fly back down.

One time in class, Miss Phillip ask who want to read. I push up me hand quick quick, because I reading all the time now. I reading all book I could find in the house. But as soon as I open me mouth and start to read, all them children start to laugh and mock me – saying how I speaking like a *country bookie*. So I keep me hand right where it is.

"Carla, what about you?" Comrade Jones ask. "You don't want to read news on TV?"

I push up me shoulders, to say I don't know.

"How you mean you don't know?"

All them children eyes on me now.

"Anyway, if anybody want to take part I have to hear them read first," he say.

Comrade Jones bring he chair away from the group – under the big *cokeeoko* tree.

Comrade Jones is a schoolteacher but he is a Militia leader too. He short and stumpy. And he have a big afro. He face always looking serious, but he does make a lot of jokes in class. He is Julie real good friend. Sometimes he does come by her and they does stay outside talking for long long. And Claire does keep watching the clock and looking outside. Sometimes she does even go in the veranda and call Julie. Ask her, "So you not coming inside

219

den?" And Julie does say, "Well Mommy!" And even though Julie have twenty-three years, she still have to come inside when Claire call her.

"If anybody want to read for me, come over here," he say.

Most of the girls go up. I want to go and try too but I frighten. *Dey wouldn' want a country bookie to read news on TV. Ah sure dey go want a girl like Nicole Fraser, even though she dunce as a bat! She pretty and fair-skin. She hair long. And she does talk nice too.*

"Anybody else?" Comrade Jones ask.

Everybody looking round to see who going up next, but nobody go.

"Carla?"

I jump. "Yes Sur!" I say, trying to speak like them town children.

"Comrade. No sir here Carla. Come. Come let me hear you read," he say.

Me legs start to tremble. I frighten to even get up, but I can't tell him no. He is the teacher. So I go up.

"Sit down," he say.

I sit down. Me hands shaking like Papa hands when he was shaving.

"You don't like to read?"

"Mmhm," I say. I real like reading. Uncle Joe does make me read the newspaper for him. And when I don't know the word, he does make me spell them and try to pronounce them for meself. The girls in me class always reading Secret Seven and Famous Five books. I does wonder where they getting all those nice shiny books from. I wish I could get some too.

"Ok, read for me." He give me the newspaper he have in he hand; *The Free West India.* I hear the boop boop boop in me chest. I wonder if he hear it too. Is the same newspaper I read for Uncle Joe Friday – the one with the words he does make me pronounce, over and over and over. But as soon as I open me mouth to let them out, I start to stumble and trip over them, as if I walking down a stony, bumpy track I never walk before.

The next week Comrade Jones bring me, Nicole and one of the boys to the TV station. He say we have to try out in front Margaret Charter. She is the news lady.

Margaret tall and skinny skinny. And she talking as if she hoarse. Uncle Joe like she voice. He say it husky – that make me think about patch corn. The first time Uncle Joe see her on TV, he say how she sexy. And Claire watch him one cut-eye and say, "Boy ketch yourself eh. You don't see it have children around!" And Uncle Joel watch me and Marion and he laugh.

"Well what's wrong with sexy then?" He ask Claire. But Claire tell him to have some respect.

Next meeting, Comrade Jones tell me Margaret Charter choose me to be in the program. *Me? How come she choose me? I did still stumble over them words. How come she en pick Nicole? Me de country bookie reading news on TV! Me, wid me picky hair and me feefee eyes!* I couldn't wait to go home to tell Uncle Joe. I could not wait to see he big grin and the gladness in he eyes.

The first day, I take a bus for meself, to go in the TV station. Is the first time I take a bus for meself, but I remember where to drop out, and walk up the road.

The TV station in a big old plantation house, in Sandy Hill. The yard big and nice - with a lot of hibiscus, buttercups and lady-slipper flowers. It have a big flamboyant tree behind the house. And all the red flowers on the ground look like a red carpet.

I meet two other Pioneer boys there. I don't know them. The small one is Marcus and the big one name is Glen.

Margaret bring me in a room to read for her. She give me a page with what I have to read; she call it a script. She make me read it over, and over. Then she leave me in the room for meself to practice. I read it over and over and over, until I tired. And all that time, Glen and Marcus outside playing. I could hear them laughing and talking to the camera men. Asking them all kinds of questions. *How come is only me she making practice so?*

Marcus from Cuba. He is the youngest in the three of us. He only have bout seven years, but he real bright and he could read real good. Glen from up in the country, but he talking like a town boy. And so he show off!

Every Wednesday is same thing. I practice and practice and practice, while Glen and Marcus watching TV or playing. But no matter how much I practice, I could never say them words like Glen and Marcus. I trying real hard to speak like a Town girl, but Glen does still mock me. Call me *country bookie.*

But every Wednesday night, I downstairs listening to the news, and waiting for when Margaret say, "And now here is Carla Charles with the Pioneer News." And I does dash upstairs to watch meself on TV. But I does stay near by the trapdoor in case Claire shout, "what you doing dere? Go back down and do your work!" And I does watch meself on TV, with me feefee eyes and all, and I does wish me mother could see me.

One day, Margaret say we going to interview Prime Minister Maurice Bishop. *Interview the Prime Minister! Me! Wid me feefee eyes!* When I tell them home, hear Julie, "Well wait nuh! I never even meet the Prime Minister and you going and interview him!"

"That's my girl!" Uncle Joe say.

And Claire just roll up she eyes and say, "eh eh!"

The interview in Government House, where the Prime Minister living. It not far from the TV station. The house sit down on a hill and you could see Mt Gay and Tempe, down in the valley and Mt Panassus up on the other side.

We sit down out in the yard, in a semi circle. Comrade Maurice Bishop in the middle. Marcus on he left side. And Jackie Creft on he right.

Jackie Creft is the Minister of Education. She wearing a long, wide foot pants and a big dashiki. And she have on leather slippers - just like the ones I had, *that time*. She have teeth like the lady in the Colgate advertisement and she big eyes lighting up every time she smile.

I sit down by Marcus and Comrade Maurice Bishop there right there – in he khaki shirt jack, khaki pants and leather slipper too. Inside me full of bubbles. The Prime Minister sitting down right there, by me. He not just a voice on the radio or the TV talking to the nation now. I could hear he voice right there – he big deep voice coming out all down in he belly. And when he smile, I could see he nice white teeth shining between he bushy beard and he moustache. I could just reach over and touch he big, neat afro if I want. *Ah bet it soft and spongy.* Jackie have a afro too, but hers shorter.

Glen first to ask he question. Fuss he show off, he shake up heself like a rooster and put on a big voice that don't even sound like his. And he talking to the Prime Minister as if he know him so good. As if them is companion.

When me turn reach, Margaret turn and watch me. And just so me belly drop down under the chair! Me mouth get dry. Me mind get blank. All me words disappear from me head, just like when the teacher rub off the work from the blackboard. I even forget I have the paper with me questions in me hand. I watch Margaret. She smile for me. And she nod. And I remember what she tell me. Why she does make me practice so much. I used to think she curry favour. But I know is not because she don't like me.

Then I look at Comrade Maurice Bishop. He smile for me too. He peel back he big lips over he big white teeth, and he smile with he whole face.

"You're ready my little Pioneer?" He ask me. And this time he voice sound as if it come out from he chest, not deep down in he belly. It sound softer. And I smile too, look at me piece of paper and read out me questions.

After the interview we go inside for refreshments. Jackie pass round with a tray with drinks. I take the one that look kind of redish-orange. It look like real juice – not the watery juice we does make home. But when I take a mouthful, I feel to spit it back out. Is the strongest, bitterest juice I had ever taste. I have to force to swallow it because I don't know where to spit it out. I put down the glass in a corner and eat me cheese sandwich just so, because I too shy to ask for another one.

When we ready to leave, Comrade Maurice Bishop shake Glen hand. He shake Marcus hand. I watching he fingernails how it clean and neat – like Jakko fingernails. He toenails too. They round and neat neat.

When he reach by me, I stretch out me hand and I waiting for him shake it. But he don't shake it. He put he hands on me shoulders and he kiss me right on me face. Just like President Samora Machel, from Mozambique. He did kiss me too, when we go on the airport and do a display for him. And Comrade Maurice Bishop smell nice! Then he kiss me on the other side. And he beard tickle me just like how me father beard used to tickle me. Inside me bubbling up, like how Fanta does bubble up when you pour it in a glass.

And I can't wait to go home and tell everybody how the Prime Minister kiss me! I writing and tell me mother too.

Chapter 38

More Secret Again

I upstairs sweeping. Marion outside washing. Auntie Ethel downstairs watching the shop. Claire open a shop downstairs, in the front. Auntie Ethel does mind the shop, but she too heavy to get up all the time, so every time somebody come and buy, she calling Julie to come and sell.

I sweep three rooms already. But Uncle Joe still sleeping, so I leave he room for last.

The radio playing real low. A Jackson Five song come on. I wish I could put up the volume loud, because I real like them Jackson Five songs. I singing in the broomstick. Not so loud, because even though Claire gone to work, I don't want Auntie Ethel to hear me. And I dancing round the room, while I dusting down: the chairs, the TV and then the black shiny record player, the tables and then the window ledges.

I real like to sing and dance. And now I hearing all these nice songs I never hear before. When I used to be with me father, I used to only hear reggae. And I like them reggae too. But these songs and them does make me forget. I does forget about school. I does forget about all them ugly names them children does call me. They does make the work easy and sometimes I does even forget Claire home, until I hear, "Turn off dat damn radio and do you work!"

But sometimes when Claire gone to work and me alone upstairs, I does even thief a chance and put on the TV. They does show *The Land of The Giants* and *Voyage*

Under the Sea. But I always on the look-out, in case somebody come upstairs and see me. If Claire see me, she bawling, "Take off dat damn TV. Only ah TV TV TV! Take it off and get something to do". She always telling people to go and get something to do. She can't stand to see nobody sitting down - even if we finish all we work already. In the night, when me and Marion want to watch *Different Strokes* and *Gimme a Break*, and she can't say get something to do, she telling us, "Go in all you bed! All you have school tomorrow!" On Saturday, is "Go in all you bed! It have church tomorrow!" Even on Sunday evenings, when *Knight Rider* and *Six Million Dollar Man* showing, she barking in people head. "Go and do all you homework!" Claire always barking at people. The only person in the house she doesn't bark at is she oldest son – the one who always looking vex. He face always sour sour. He doesn't even talk to nobody. He does just grumble. And when he home, he does just stay in he room.

But every time Claire bark at me, I does feel as if she barking louder. And harder – like how a dog does bark at strangers in the yard. She bark does hit me hard hard, right on me chest. And it does hurt even more than Mammy bark.

I finish in the living room. I knock Uncle Joe door. He tell me to come in. Uncle Joe had a stroke, like Papa. And now he left side dead. When he just come back from hospital, he couldn't even walk or talk good. But now he does drag around with he stick. And he look as if he just get old real quick. He whole head turn grey. Uncle Joe eyes and all change colour. They used to look same colour as wet river stone – dark dark grey, but now they light grey and dull dull.

Before Uncle Joe had the stroke, I used to sit down on the bed with him, with the broom in me hand, listening to he stories about Venezuela. He say me mother is a good-looking woman. How nobody could dress-up like her. Once he tell me how I starting to look like me mother. *Me? Look like me mother? Me mother prutty. Me mother have nice hair and nice hands. I en no look like no mother.* And I like to hear Uncle Joe stories, but I always on the look-out – ready to dash if I hear Claire coming.

Uncle Joe not sleeping, but he still lying down. The room small and pack-up pack-up, with all kinds a things. And it smelling like sick people and hospital.

I wipe the dressing table, then go downstairs and empty the pail. When I come back up, Uncle Joe sitting up on the bed. I sweep the little space between the bed and the dressing table. Sweep under the bed. Claire does inspect the room when she come home. If she find any trace a dust, she starting to bark again. "What kind a sweep you say you sweep? Is so people does sweep? All the sweep you sweep, de place still full a dust!"

"Cong, si dong," Uncle Joe say. He still can't talk so good yet. He tongue heavy heavy. Sometimes he does roll a marble around in he mouth to help him to speak better.

"Ah en finish sweeping yet Uncle Joe," I say.

I don't want to sit down. If I stay upstairs too long, Auntie Ethel go call and ask me what I doing upstairs all this long time. She does call Marion too – when she stay in Uncle Joe room long. Any time Auntie Ethel can't see us, she does call us, as if she think we doing something wrong. We can't even go in front the shop! Especially if it have boys in front there. Even when we right in front she eyes, she saying, "Come on, come on! Go in the back! All you have vice in all you head too much! And is she who have vice in she head. Because we just want to listen to them rum man and them giving jokes and watch what going on."

So I don't want to sit down. The last time, Uncle Joe make me sit on he lap to hug me. He like to hug and kiss people too much. He always hugging and kissing the neighbours, just like the people on TV. He say where he come from, people does hug and kiss one another all the time. But every time Uncle Joe try to kiss Claire, she does push him and say, "Look here boy, behave yourself eh!" As if Uncle Joe is a boy. And Uncle Joe is she husband. But Uncle Joe does just laugh and kiss her again. And I could see she like it you know, but she just playing ting.

But when Uncle Joe hug me that time, he say how me boobies starting to come up now. And I didn't like how it make me feel at all. And when I sit down on he lap, it does make me feel as if I doing something wrong.

"Ah going and finish me work Uncle Joe," I say. I open the door to go, but Uncle Joe say, "Come and give me a kish."

So I go to give Uncle Joe a kiss on he face. But Uncle Joe turn, and he mouth go right on me mouth! And I feel this big, wet, slimy thing go straight inside me mouth. I feel to vomit. I pull away fast and dash out from the room. Down the stairs and straight in the bathroom. The bathroom is the only place I could go, without anybody asking me what I going there and do. I wash out and wash out me mouth. I gaggle. Spit. Gaggle. Spit. Wash out me mouth again. But I still feeling the wet, slimy thing in me mouth.

I wonder if he does do that with Marion, when she go and sweep he room.

I don't tell nobody. Everybody like Uncle Joe. Nobody go believe me. So I just dig up me hole and bury it with me other secrets and them.

And the day when I go home for me lunch and Claire son Jimmy tell me let's go in he room with him, because nobody else not home. I run back to school fast fast – me heart pounding me chest harder than me feet pounding the road. I don't even eat me lunch.

When I go home after school, Jimmy looking real shame. And I thinking, is a good thing he ask me first. Is a good thing he didn't just take what he want, like some of them men I does hear about.

So I buried that secret down in me hole too.

Chapter 39

1982

A lot of things happen that year. Uncle Joe get another stroke. Not long after he put he tongue in me mouth. And this time he get real sick. He tongue get so heavy he couldn't talk. And he never walk again.

Since that time, I stop all that sitting down in Uncle Joe room, listening to he stories. I's in. Sweep quick. And out quick. I bring a drink for him when he ask me. He food for him too. But I not sitting down in he room at all.

One morning, I hear Claire telling Auntie Ethel, "He gone you know." And I know she talking about Uncle Joe. But I still wondering where he gone, because he can't even move from the bed.

All the neighbours come and see Uncle Joe before La Qua come for him. The house full a people, but it still real quiet. No radio playing. No TV. And everybody talking quiet quiet, as if they think they go disturb Uncle Joe.

First time I in a house with a dead person. I fraid the whole house – as if it full a spirits. All when they put Uncle Joe in the hearse and go, I still fraid. I fraid to go upstairs. I fraid to stay downstairs. I fraid to go in the bathroom. I never like that bathroom. It under the outside steps inside there always dark dark. And I not boarding anywhere by Uncle Joe room!

Everybody go to the funeral except me and Auntie Ethel. Auntie Ethel sick, so Claire leave me home with her. I glad! Because I still fraid everything. I try to think about nice things – like running home to show Uncle Joe me report

231

book, when I come second in me class. How Uncle Joe looking real proud every time he see me on TV. Listening to he stories about Venezuela. But *that time* only pushing out all the nice things and shoving itself up in front me mind – just like a greedy child in the lunch line. And I still seeing Uncle Joe dead body, cover down under that white sheet, when La Qua taking him. Uncle Joe stay inside me head for a real long time.

After Uncle Joe died, Claire daughter Pam come back home with she children. The house full now. Claire shuffling people round the house like cards, to make space. She put them children to sleep on the floor in Auntie Ethel room. They knock up a room downstairs for Jimmy. And Pam get he room.

Pam in the National Women's Organization and she always out in some meeting or going away to some conference or some kind of workshop or something. So them children with us and everybody looking after them.

I still sleeping in the room with Julie. But sometimes, when one of Claire niece come by her, I have to sleep on the floor with them children. Jasmine is the oldest one. She only two years younger than me. I real glad for the company. But every time I sleep with them, me nightie always soaking wet when I wake up. And I does not pee no bed. Since I have three years I sleeping on Mammy bed and I does never pee the bed. And Auntie Ethel does make them pee before they go and sleep. She does even wake them up in the night and make them pee, but all man and they brother still peeing the bed.

So now, on Saturdays, is more work. More clothes to wash. To hang out. Pick up. Fold. More food to cook. And don't talk about wares to wash! But I always in the kitchen doing something. And is a good thing I could work. Nobody have to call me to come and help in the kitchen. I like to cook. And so Claire does cook some nice food, especially on Sundays.

On Sundays, after church, they cooking stew beef, or pork, bake chicken, macaroni pie and rice and peas, fry plantain and stew pumpkin or callaloo. Sometimes Claire does buy crabs from the market and Auntie Ethel does cook them with callaloo. Auntie Ethel does make the best soup I ever taste in me life. Especially she crab and callaloo soup. When we have crab, we leaving them for last, especially the real big *gandi* claws. Then all you could hear is spoon knocking crab shell and everybody sucking the sweet, juicy crab meat.

On Saturday, I watching Julie make bread. Then one Saturday she let me help her. And since that time, is me who kneading the ten pounds of flour, every Saturday and making twelve big, fat bread.

I set the yeast, and put it by the window – right where the sun shining - to rise. I pour out the two five pound packets of all purpose flour in the big bread bowl. Sprinkle the salt. Mix it up while I watching the yeast. I like to smell it. It bubbling up. Rising up to the top of the bowl as if it have life. Is a lot of flour, but if you see me! Mixing up the flour and the salt. Mashing up the lard. Rubbing it in the flour. Pouring water. Mix up. Pour some more. Mix it up again. Knead. Knead. Me hand feel as if it go fall off but I kneading as if me is a real baker-woman. And I like to feel the sticky dough between me fingers. It feeling like putty. I watch it swell up under the towel and full up the bowl. And when I roll them out, they swell up again. Full up the tins. Then I put them in the oven.

I sit down on the step tiefing a read from the Nancy Drew book me friend lend me. And timing the bread. Marion upstairs in the room jooking up she face. Or maybe she sleeping. Them children by the neighbour playing. We yard too stony to play in. And the road too busy.

"RONNIE! RONNEEEEY! Boy come and feed the pig and dem nuh! Since mornin you leave de poor beast and dem to starve!" Tantie May bawling out from next door. She only have boy children. Six boy children. And she always saying, "Ah doh know what ah do for Papa God to punish me wid all dese boy children! He en give me a single girl chile to help me out in the house. Who go help me when ah get sick? Who go look after me when ah get old and grey?" Ronnie is she last son. And she was always calling him to come and do this or do that. He have to thief a chance to play. And he always fretting because he have to listen out for Tantie May call him every minute. Then one day she bring a little girl home. And Ronnie get a break.

The shop busy. Everybody doing their Saturday shopping.

"Ah want to get two poungs a chicken wings... one poung a sugar, a poung a rice aaan, eeem... wha mammy say again boy? Em." Randy from up the road. He mother does not leave the house, so every time she want something, he in the shop.

"Ah tired tell you mother to write down what she want when she sending you in the shop! Tell your mother ah say to make a list next time eh! You hear me?" Julie say.

I wish I could help out in the shop. Sometimes Julie does let me help open up the plastic bags when she weighing out sugar and rice and things. But I wish she let me help her scoop it into the bags and balance them on the scale too. I want to sneak some full cream milk in me mouth when she not watching. But Auntie Ethel always chasing me and Marion from in front the shop. Especially if it have men drinking.

"Mmmm! That bread smelling real sumptuous man! Mmmm!" That's Deegan. I know him by he voice. He have a real deep, heavy voice. And he always using some big big words – especially when he drunk.

"Dere you go stay and bawl bread smelling sumptuous!" Julie say. "Carla don't let the bread and dem burn you know!" she shout to me.

"A a! Carla, is you who making that sumptuous bread dere? Bring a slice with butter for Deegan when it ready, you hear Carla?"

"Bring wha slice wid butter? Why you en buy some flour and go and make some instead of drinkin out all you money!" Julie tell him.

"Ah chuts woman! Just give me an eight a Jack Iron and some water and hush you mouth nuh woman!"

All where you see Deegan, he drunk. And Claire always chasing him from the shop because when he real drunk, he does curse real bad. When you hear he start to curse, he does curse all man and their brother. And their sisters too if they there. But I like Deegan. Anytime he see me down the road waiting for bus or walking home, he would call me and ask, "What's up Carla? Everything copacetic?"

I bend the page where I reach and close the book. I only have two more chapters to go and I want to finish before Claire reach home.

When I open the oven, the bread and them look fat and brown. They ready to come out. I line them up on the counter to cool. The whole kitchen smell of bread. I feel real glad. Claire and all say how me bread does come out good. Me mouth making water for piece. I wish I could cut a slice now. Butter it while it hot - so the butter melt and soak in the bread, and run down between me fingers when I bite it But Claire go curse. So I just watch them and wish them well.

And that is what I doing when I meet me little brother for the first time.

I hear when the bus stop in front of the shop. Claire come already. As soon as she reach I hear her calling them children to come home. I hide me book before she come in the kitchen and ketch me reading.

"Aa! What me eyes seeing dere! You didn't tell me you coming today," Claire say.

I peep through the door. The one that does swing between the kitchen and the shop. And I see me mother standing there with a little boy. I have pictures with that little boy, so I know him straight away. That's me little brother. I didn't even know me mother coming. Claire never say nothing.

I fly through that door so fast. Me chest full of gladness. I so glad I want to laugh. I want to cry. I want to jump up and down. But I don't know how to do it. The gladness leap out from me chest. It jump inside me head. It make me giddy.

"Carla. You get so big!" Me mother say. "And you hair grow back nice."

I want to hug me mother, like how them people on in movies does hug one another. But I don't know how to do it. So I just stand up there watching them. And me mother just stand up there holding Carlos hand, as if she don't know how to do it too.

"Carlos that is su hermana. Beso su hermana."

Me little brother holding me mother hand tight – as if he fraid she go leave him. And he sucking he finger hard.

"Carlos go on. Give you sister kiss."

Carlos smile. He dimples dig two little holes in he face – like the little holes them little *torties* does dig up in the dust under the house.

Then he come and hug me leg with one hand. He finger still in he mouth. Carlos have four years but he real little. I raise him up and kiss he little face. He laugh and press he face in me neck – like how I used to do when Daddy raise me up. He skin soft! And smooth! And he smelling nice – like baby powder, Vaseline cream and me mother perfume mix up.

I don't want to put down Carlos. I so glad to see me little brother, I just want to hold him, tickle him and kiss up he little smooth face. He just hold on to me neck with he little skinny arm. But Carlos never take out he finger from he mouth. Even when he laughing, he clamp it tight tight in he mouth.

I bring Carlos in the kitchen with me. I have to finish making the bread, but I don't even want him to go and play with Pam children. I want him for meself. He is *my* little brother who does speak Spanish and suck he finger hard hard – like a snow ice.

I well thinking me mother come back and stay. I thinking I going home with her and me little brother. But she stay for one week. And when she going back, she leave Carlos with Claire too. She say she can't keep him with her again. He big enough to go to school now and she have to work.

I wonder how come Claire taking Carlos, because she always saying how the house full up! But I not stupid. I know how she like to get me mother letter every month with the US money in it. I see how she does be in a real good mood and treat me nice nice, when she get the letter – the one with the nice, long, slanting letters on the front and on the back. And the Simon Bolivar stamp in the corner. I see how she does rip it open quick quick, to check for the money. Now I sure me mother have to put more money in the letter.

"Look after you brother you know," me mother say, when she going.

Cindy McKenzie

"Yea," *Me mother doh know how I glad for me brudda!*

Carlos could walk to school with me and Pam children. And watch *Night Rider* and *Solid Gold* with us, when Claire let us watch TV on Sunday nights.

"Make sure he eat he food eh. He only like to eat cereal, cereal." I hope Carlos like bread, because Claire does not buy no cereals. Is bread and egg or luncheon meat or fishcakes or something for breakfast. And the bread never enough yet. Claire does leave out three bread to share for everybody and lock up the rest in she room. Sometimes she does even slice them up and count out the slices for everybody, before she go to work. Sometimes you could see through the slices, fuss they thin!

"And you have to bring him in the toilet because he does see trouble to go off," me mother say.

Carlos think we mother just going and buy sweets for him. And he busy playing so he don't cry.

I do me Common Entrance that year too. I get one bad bellyache when I doing it, the teacher have to bring me out of the hall. Give me warm milk to pass the bellyache. But me belly hurting so bad I can't even sit down. So I don't have time to finish the exam.

I know I fail before the results come out. But I still sit down with Julie searching for me name in the newspaper. Me eyes make beast under St Paul's Government School, looking under C. And it have a lot of Charles under C. But no Carla Charles!

"Dat's it!" Claire say, when Julie tell her. "No more reading no news on no damn TV again. You go stay right here and study your lessons!"

So Claire like to take things from people, especially me. If you like the music on the radio, she taking off the radio. You like to watch *Night Rider*, she taking off the TV.

238

She even taking me book from me, when she ketch me reading. I does have to hide in the toilet to read me Nancy Drew. You can't let Claire know you like nothing, because she does get a special gladness when she take it from you.

I just go in the room and cry quiet. And I put away that hurting thing with all the others.

Chapter 40

The Prison Visit

Julie and Pam downstairs talking about me father. They don't know I there listening. Nobody does ever talk about him in front me. Is just as if he not even alive. I trying real hard to forget *that time.* So I have to try to forget me father too. But I always seeing me father in me dreams. And he always on me mind.

"I thought he in Hope Valle." Pam say.

"They move him from Hope Valle long."

"So how come is now he want to see her. After all dat time?" Pam say.

"A a. I don't know. So de man can't just want to see he daughter den."Julie say.

Want to see he daughter? Want to see he daughter! What Julie mean he want to see me? I en going in no prison nuh! I never see me father again, since that day the police lady take me and bring me in the hospital. So I fraid.

Me father send a pass for me to visit him. Is me who pick up the pass in the post office. But I didn't even know that, that pink piece of paper, that fold up and staple together – with *Her Majesty's Prison* – write on the front, is a pass.

Is July 1983. School on holiday. And I take thirteen years the same week Julie bring me up in Richmond Hill Prison.

We drop out in White Gun and walk up Richmond Hill. Is a long walk up the hill but is a real nice view. You could see the harbour and all them buildings in town from up there.

When we reach the prison gate, it have soldiers with guns all around. They don't even watch the pass because they know Julie. One of them walk down to the prison with us. He have a big AK on he shoulder. He and Julie talk while we walk the long stretch to the prison. It have barbed wire all around. It have a hospital on top the hill, on the right and a lot of pig-pens down the bottom, on the left. I could hear the pigs grunting and squealing. And the breeze bringing the pig mess scent all up the hill and right in me nose.

"Dat man is a real true Rastaman," the soldier say. "He en eating no food at all nuh man. Dem soldiers and dem in Hope Valle de try and force him to eat. I hear dey used to push de food down in he throat, but that man never back down. He still on hunger strike."

"So what he eating?" Julie ask.

"Only mango and ripe fig and ting yea man. Dat man real strong boy!"

I wonder what hunger strike is.

The soldier watch me good. "Dat is not de same likkle girl who was up in the hills wid him?"

Something dark cover me, like how a rain cloud does cover up the sun.

"Um hm," Julie say.

"She get big boy!"

People always saying I get big. Or how I get nice. As if they expect me to stay small.

Sometimes I does wish I could stay inside that darkness so nobody could see me. Because all how I try to forget *that time,* somebody always coming and talk about it and bring it back.

I wait to hear what else the soldier go say. And I saying me prayers in me mind. I well glad when we reach the prison before anything else come out.

Another soldier bring me and Julie up to the cell. The darkness still over me. And me belly start to do all kinds of things - it boiling up, stirring up, griping. Making ruction, as if it want to chase me to the toilet. By the time we reach the top of the steps, I sure I go have to run in a toilet.

The soldier bring us by something that look like a black hole in the wall. Not a single piece of light shining in the hole. But I could make out something in a corner. Me eyes get accustom to the dark and I see is a man. He look naked. He just stoop down in the corner. Head bend down. He whole body bend over, like a little old man. He not moving.

A little bit of light seep through the door. It crawl under the iron bars and take a spot on the floor. It chase out some of the darkness in the cell. And I see me father. Me belly start to bawl.

Me father still not moving. He eyes still on the floor, as if he fraid light go touch them. He just skin and bones. I sure I could count he ribs if he come by the light. Me eyes get more accustomed to the dark. And I see he not naked. He have on a piece of jeans pants. He don't even look like me father. He don't have no locks! He head scrape. But he still have he beard. It long. He look like the Ghandi man in the movie we class go and see in Empire cinema.

Julie trying to talk to me father but he don't answer. He not saying a word. He just stoop down there staring at nothing. Me chest get tight – as if something squeezing it.

But I know me father good. I know is a vision he have. That's why he have to see me. Maybe he remember is me birthday too.

When the soldier come back for us, that's when me father raise up he head. He look straight at me. And I see he face. It hard. And he eyes. Fire blazing from them two deep holes.

"Freedom soon come Princess," he say. But he say it real low. He voice weak. Then he say, "Take care of de I self Princess. Jah guidance."

And just so, all the darkness that covering me up, and all the crying in me belly, start to pour down me face. All on the bus it falling. All the way home, I can't finish crying. Fuss I crying, I can't even dig up me hole to put that one. So I just let it fall and soak up me clothes. And soak in the dust between the boards in the floor.

Chapter 41

Convent Girl

That August in 1983, Carla Charles under C in the newspaper. And next to it, St Mary's Convent write up big and bold! All them girls in school always talking about how Convent is the best school. And how you have to get a real high mark to go there. I can't believe I get enough marks to go to Convent! I can't wait to write me mother and make her feel glad.

St Mary's Convent in the heart of Town. It sit down on top of Church Street like her Majesty on she throne. With the cathedral right on the doorstep. And the House of Parliament on the left.

The first morning I walk up the steps, the yard look as if it blossoming blue and white. Everywhere I turn is girls in their pleated navy skirts and white shirts, white socks and white shoes. Everybody looking nice and new. And smelling sweet and nice too.

A tailor up by the post office make me skirt. It real neat but it too long. It reaching all down by me ankle. But is me shoes that fretting me. I sure they make them with cardboard and just polish it white, fuss it light and ugly! The bottom thick thick and the front square; just like them old fashion nurse shoes.

When Claire bring me in the store, I choose a nice pair of shoes I real like. But she say, "Um mm, No way!" And she buy these old, ugly shoes. Is just as if she can't stand to see anybody feeling glad. She does just have to take it away. So I watch the other girls in their nice sneakers. I only see one other girl with shoes like mine.

And I could bet she mother buy them in the same store at the bottom of Market Hill. I pray for mine to mash-up quick.

Claire leave me at the top platform and she gone. All the girls gather up there chatting and giggling and showing one another their new things. I have new things too. Me mother had send a new bag for me. And a pencil case with pens and pencils and rubbers that smelling like thing to eat. But I don't have nobody to show me new things. So I just stand up on the side for meself, feeling like a *titiree* in a river full of crayfish. I don't know anybody. None of them from me school.

I watching the girls coming in with their mothers, dress up and looking real highfalutin. Some fathers coming too. And I wishing me mother could come, so they could see how she could dress-up real nice too – with she soft hands and pretty long nails.

We have a big assembly in the school yard. Then a teacher call out we names and the class we going in. I in the classroom right at the top of the steps – in Form 1A.

A lot of the girls know one another, because they went to the same primary school. And they sit down together. Some of them only have ten or eleven years. They looking too little to be in secondary school. But they pass their exam the first time. *Ah bet me is one of the oldest in the class. They go tink ah dunce because I din pass me exam the first time.*

Everybody get quiet when the teacher walk in the class. She have on a muddy brown, long skirt, that drooping on one side. And she glasses thick thick. She look too old to be a teacher.

The teacher sit down at she desk with the register, and call out we names again. She is the teacher some of the big girls was talking about outside. I hear them telling some of the new girls to "Pray you don't go in Miss Kettle's class. She does shame people real bad."

"Lee McLean."

I jump when I hear the name. I still not used to that name, because everybody at home does call me Carla now. And I using Carla Charles in school. Then I bring in me birth certificate when I doing Common Entrance, and Charles nowhere on it. Me name is Lee Carla McLean. Charles is me father surname. Carla is me middle name. But now I have to use me first name and me mother surname.

"Lee McLean!" Miss Kettle call out again.

"Present miss." I try say it real soft. And I try to say it just like them other girls, because me is a convent girl now. I don't want them to call me a country bookie. But they still laugh.

One of the girls answer 'present,' when Miss Kettle call she name. Miss Kettle stop. She push she glasses down to the tip of she nose. Peep over them. She look like an owl.

"Present who?" She search the class for the girl, without moving she head around.

"I repeat! Present who?" Miss Kettle say, when she eyes find the girl. And everybody eyes on the girl too.

"Present miss!" The girl say. She in the back row, right in the corner. She look too big to be in form one. She grin and rock back on she chair. She skin black and shiny, like parch cocoa beans when you now shell them. And she teeth big and white like Chiclets chewing gum.

Miss Kettle raise up she eye brows and she watch Chiclets teeth real good. As if she memorizing her - what she look like; where she sitting down; how she sitting down. Then she start calling names again.

When Miss Kettle finish, she push she glasses up on she nose. Push back she chair. Stand up in front the class, with she arms behind she back. She tell us she is going to be we head teacher. And she will be we English Language teacher too.

"Remember, you all are not in primary school anymore. You are in secondary school now! And I expect you to behave like secondary school children. I do not want any talking in my class. And no running around like race horses. This is not a race track! If you want to run around like race horses you could go down to Queens Park. It is just down Cemetary Hill! You are young ladies so you must conduct yourselves like respectable young ladies do! You all hear me?" Miss Kettle look round the class at each and every face.

"You!" She say. And she point to a girl in the corner by the window. All heads turn round and look where Miss Kettle pointing. The girl she pointing look round, then look at Miss Kettle. Is the same girl who was turning back every minute, and talking, when Miss Kettle was calling the register. She hair plait in two and she have two big white bows. She look as if she was ready to cry.

"Yes you. Take your bag and come."

The way Miss Kettle talking make me feel to cry too. I small up meself in me chair.

The girl pick up she bag. It so heavy it nearly knock her down when she get up.

"And you! Yes, you with the titivation in your hair," Miss Kettle say. This time she pointing to the little girl with big, bright eyes. She hair short short and they plait in tight little cornrows. And she have a lot of clips in them. The little girl stand up real slow. She eyes open bigger, watching Miss Kettle.

"Come. Sit over there."

The girl sit down in the chair Miss Kettle pointing, right in the middle of the front row.

"And tell your mother not to put all that beautification in your hair. You not going to no fashion show. This is a school. You hear me?"

The little girl big eyes full up with water. Mine too. I small up me self some more. Keep me head down. Me eyes on me desk. It scratch up and have all kinds of things writ up on it. *Sam Loggie. Miss K is a PIG! Nikki is MBF!* I wonder what MBF mean.

"And you," she say. This time, is a girl in front the class she talking to. "Take her seat."

Oh God! Please doh let her call me. Please God! If I small up meself more, I go slip down under the desk. But I holding meself tense tense, as if that go make me *invisible*. I learn that word in them Nancy Drew books. So I learning a lot of new words now.

If Miss Kettle call me, and I have to stand up, everybody go watch me. Because me seat right in the middle of the class – right next to a girl with a big space in she front teeth and big fat plaits. *Ah bet is she grandmother who plait she hair.*

Me hair grow back now. Julie press it with the hot pressing comb and she plait it in three - one on top and two at the back, with two white ribbons in them. It could even go back in one.

Miss Kettle make some more girls change seats. "No sitting down by no friend so you could chatter like parrots." she say. "Leave all that for when you have recreation! When you are in my class, you keep quiet and learn your lesson! You hear me?"

Everybody say, "Yeessss missss."

When Miss Kettle finish all the smaller girls in the front and the bigger ones, who were older, in the back row. She leave Chiclet teeth right where she is – in the corner in the back – as if to keep her out of the way. And I know Miss Kettle go be watching her like a chicken hawk.

Chapter 42

The Revo Done!

Is just after lunchtime on October 19th 1983, and I could feel it have something in the air. Children running to their classrooms, talking loud loud. Even though the Sisters always telling us how Convent girls should be seen and not heard.

"Girls quiet please!" Miss Kettle shout. But nobody listening to her.

Some of the girls packing their bags already, as if school over.

"Settle down now girls!" Miss Kettle say again.

But everybody still talking. They not settling down. And outside sounding busy. Vehicles speeding up St John's Street, and up toward Cemetery Hill. A car pass up the back of the school. Parents who have cars does drive up there to pick up their children. Another one pass up again. Two ladies come up the front steps. *Ah wonder what happening? How come everybody else lookin as if they know what happenin so? And I en know nothin?*

"GIRLS QUIET NOW! And LISTEN to me VERY carefully!" Miss Kettle shout. And she slam the blackboard eraser on she desk. A piece of chalk jump up from she desk and fall on the floor. Miss Kettle glasses almost fall from she face. She push them down on the end of her flat nose and she watching us over them. She hand start to tremble.

Chiclet teeth say something and the girls in the back row giggle.

"I Said QUIET! You all don"t know what QUIET mean? Now pack your bags quietly and stand."

Books slapping books. Desk slamming. Bags, heavy with books, landing on top desks. Chairs making ruction with the floor.

I pack me bag quick and I stand up behind me chair, real quiet. I nearly put me finger on me lips too, like Teacher V used to make us do in pre-school. I not giving Miss Kettle no reason to call me no *ignoramus* or *nincompoop*. She like to call people that.

Chiclet teeth and them girls in the back row still chattering away.

"Stand up quietly. You understand what quietly mean?"

"Yeesss Miss!" Everybody answer together.

"Now do exactly what I tell you. Do you understand?"

"Yeesss Miss."

"Now take your bags and go straight home. I said STRAIGHT HOME! Not down in the Market Square and lime by the bus stop. You hear me! Take your bags, get on your bus and go home! Is that clear girls?"

"Yeesss Miss."

Everybody grab up their bag and is out the door. Some of the girls have to wait for their older sisters in the higher forms. Others waiting for their friends or their parents to pick them up. We know something happening but we don't know what.

A swarm of convent girls and Brothers' College boys and St Hillary girls flood Market Hill. I make it down full speed. I don't have any friend yet so I always walking by meself.

The Market Square busy. Children still line up outside *The Hungry Eye*, waiting for the popcorn to stop jumping up and down in the machine. The smell make me mouth water for some. I wish I have money to buy a bag too. So I could sit in the bus, popping them in me mouth, one by one, and lick the salt from me fingers.

I walk straight pass the little box shop, through the rows of buses and get on me bus. Miss Kettle voice still ringing in me ears.

The bus almost empty. The driver not in he seat. And I don't hear Joyce the conductor. She always on the bus talking with the passengers. And she have the biggest, loudest mouth I ever hear, so you must hear her before you see her. As a matter of fact, everything about Joyce big! As if God give her extra in everything, when he was sharing.

Something happening in truth, because the Market Square buzzing. Everybody talking about something. The same thing. They hustling around. And even though is just after one, the market vendors and them packing up their coconuts and yams and their *quail-up* callaloo that start to dry up already. The ripe figs, sapodillas and guavas sit down in the sun whole morning too. Their strong smell mix up with the pee scent that seeping up through the culverts.

The bus taking long to full up. People just stand up outside talking. They in no haste to go home. A lot of school children still walking about and liming. Children from Weston College and Jolly Hill Secondary. I wonder if Marion there liming too or if she gone home already.

A few people come in the bus. And I start hearing pieces of conversations. "House arrest…. Bishop…. PRA…. Going up on de fort." A woman rush inside the bus with she two children. "Le we go home you hear! I en like dis house arrest business nuh!" She put she head out the window. "People! All you come on the bus le we go nuh! Ah want to be in me house safe and sound. Driver! All you whey de driver gone? Whey you see ah want to go in me house dere!"

Ah wonder what happenin? Bishop? House arrest? What dey talking about? Maybe dey arrest him in he house. But how dey could arrest de Prime Minister? He is the leader of the people. How dey could arrest him? What dey arrest him for?

Then all of a sudden people start to rush onto the bus, as if somebody chasing them. Joyce appear and close the door. The driver jump in he seat and start up the bus.

"You see dis ting wha going on dey? I en like it at all. Someting real serious happenin and de people need to know." The driver say over he shoulder.

"You en hear how much soldiers up on de fort? You better make haste and come back because ah going up dey too!" Joyce say. She squeezing she big self between the seats to collect bus fare and punch tickets. Stretching sheself over people. Pushing she big bosom right up in people face.

The bus pass through River Road, Tempe, Mt Panassus, up the St Pauls road and up Mardigras. All along the way, people heading down the road. All kinds of people: construction workers, their clothes cover up with cement; school teachers and school children; road workers; shop keepers closing up shops and heading down too. Is as if everybody just leave what they doing and join the march. *Ah bet all of them goin in Town to see what happening.*

We pass soldiers going down full speed in their army jeeps too. And that make fright swell up in me chest – just like when they come and chop down me father ganja field and arrest him. And that time when they put us in the army truck and bring us in the station.

When I reach home, in front of the shop was full of people. All the neighbours and them gather up there, listening to the radio. I pass through the kitchen door at the back. I stand up behind the shop door, trying to listen. I don't even go and change me clothes. Is the kind of evening I know nobody bothering if I change me clothes or not.

The radio announcer saying something about *"unconfirmed reports" that Prime Minister of Grenada Carriacou and Petit Martinique, Comrade Maurice Bishop was placed under house arrest by some rebels in his own home.* Then the announcer say that people were coming from all direction. How the people joining up with the forces. Marching up to the Prime Minister's residence. How they going to free him.

I in the shop now. Nobody see me, because all man ears, eyes and everything on the radio.

Later the announcer say how *Maurice Bishop and some of his ministers were freed by the masses. How they taking him up to Fort Rupert.*

Everybody start to clap. "Yes man! Dat's we boy! Who the hell dey tink dey playing wid!" Linty from next door say. She jumping around and clapping.

Claire in front of the shop too. She didn't have work that day. And Pam home. Carlos and Pam children not home yet. I wonder how come they didn't send them home early too. I still don't understand what really happening but something in the air. I could feel it in me belly.

"A a. When you reach home?" Claire say when she see me. I don't wait for her say nothing. I fly upstairs. I never change me clothes so fast in me life.

When I go back down downstairs, Carlos and them reach home. More people gathering up outside. And all man ears glue to the radio. And they looking frighten and worried.

I upstairs changing Carlos clothes when the announcer come back on again. He saying how hundreds of people gather up and marching up to Fort Rupert. And how a lot of school children joining them too. And I wonder if their teacher didn't tell them to go straight home too. I does never lime about in town after school like some children. I well glad I home.

I change Carlos clothes quick and run back downstairs. The radio announcer saying how PRA opening fire on the masses. Everybody bawl out. *What dey shooting people for? How come them PRA turn against the people? One minute everybody is comrades and everybody love Maurice Bishop and next minute dey shooting down people!*

Miss Vicky start to bawl. "Oh Lord Jesus. Whey me children? Sweet Jesus keep me children safe you hear!" She stand up in the road with she hands on she head. She two daughters didn't come on the bus with me. One in the same school with me and the other going to Weston College. Marion not home yet either.

"Well ent dey tell dem to go straight home. What dey doing in town still?" Claire say.

The announcer start talking real fast. He saying how people running everywhere, running from the bullets. A lot of school children in uniform too. Dodging bullets. Running. Jumping off the high wall from Fort Rupert, up by the hospital. That make me think about the Caribs jumping off Leapers Hill into the sea, when the French chase them out.

"Oh Lord, God. Have mercy!" Miss Vicky bawling. "Sweet Jesus bring me children home safe!"

"Ah wonder if Michael go up there too?" Tantie say.

I holding Carlos on the toilet when the announcer start saying how Maurice Bishop, along with some of his ministers have been shot in cold blood, by the PRA on Fort Rupert. Everybody get quiet. Me blood get cold. I hold Carlos tighter.

Dat's not true. How dat could happen? Is not true. Why the PRA want to kill Maurice Bishop? Everybody love Maurice Bishop. He is a good Prime Minister. How dey could kill him jus so!

Tears burn me eyes but they don't come out. They go and hide in the back of me head and made it feel full up and heavy.

In front the shop still quiet. Nobody not saying a word. They just listening. Waiting to hear what coming next.

Carlos grip me tight. He screw up he little face and push. *Mmmmm.* I rub he back. He push again. *Mmmm. Mmmmm.* He cry out and something plop down inside the toilet. Carlos hug me legs while I wipe him. The paper red. *Poor Carlos.* Even though Claire does give him cod liver oil and prunes every day, he still seeing trouble to poo. I raise him up from the toilet and kiss him. I does never get tired kissing me little brother. I wish I could make the poo come out easier. And I wish I could make mosquitoes stop biting him so.

Outside dark now. The announcer gone. Tantie gone home. Miss Vicky daughters reach and they gone home too. Marion reach home. Julie and Jimmy too. But Claire oldest son, the one who in the PRA, not home yet. So she eyes making beast!

All man wake up early next day and sit down in front the radio again. The announcer talking about Maurice Bishop and what happen up on the fort. Then he say how the country under a state of emergency. How people should stay inside. There is a curfew on and anyone found outside after six would be shot on sight.

I don't understand what he mean about state of emergency. And first time I even hear the word curfew. But all I know is I fraid. And everybody looking frighten.

People start to pour in front the shop. Claire send Julie to open up. So much people in the shop, Julie call me to help her.

Everybody buying up rice, flour, milk and sugar, saltfish, Crix crackes and corned beef. All the saltfish and Crix and corned beef run out. Then all man and their brother gone home and take cover.

The road get quiet quiet. The only sound we hearing is soldiers passing up and down in their jeeps. And the radio.

We stay inside for the whole week. Claire not even letting us go in the veranda. First time we don't have to do any work - no sweeping house or washing or shelling cocoa or anything. I even pick up me Nancy Drew and Claire don't say nothing. But I read the same page about twenty times, so I put it down.

On October 25th, a loud explosion wake us up. I jump up and look through the louvers facing town. Julie jump up too.

We see smoke rising up in the sky.

"Dat look like down by Butler House," Julie say.

She run out in the living room and put on the radio. We gather round it again. Listening. Waiting.

The announcer talking, but he sounding frighten. He out of breath too. He saying how US troops landing in Point Salines, where the Cubanos building the new airport. We see helicopters flying over town. A big aircraft fly over the house. It so loud it sounding as if it right over the roof.

"Oh Lord. What is dis?" Claire say.

"Come on le we go downstairs you hear!" Julie say.

Carlos sitting down on me sucking he finger. He squeeze me neck with he other arm. I hug him tight. I know he fraid.

The radio start making noise. The announcer not saying anything again. All we could hear on the radio is the song, *Let them come, let them come, we go bury them in the sea.* Then the radio cut off.

The aircraft fly over the house again.

"All you lie down flat! Lie down flat!" Julie shout out.

Claire throw she hands up in the air and start to bawl. "Oh Lord! Well dey go kill us now! Papa God! Dey want to kill us! Lord God have mercy on us!"

And Julie shout "Mammy you can't hear to stay down!" Then Claire crawl under the table with us. She well fraid. I never know she afraid of anything.

Carlos fraid, but he like to hear the helicopters. He trying to sound like them. "Tatatatatata! Tatatatatatata!"

"Chile stop dat dey eh! Dat is not a joke you know!" Claire say.

Carlos rest he head on me chest. Suck he finger harder.

Carlos different from the other children. He always have on socks and shoes while everybody else running about in the yard bare-feet. He could not even rest he feet on the ground without he shoes. And he could not wear short pants because sand flies and mosquitoes go eat him up. And he love that finger! Claire put aloe on it to make him stop sucking it, but as soon as the bitter taste gone, he suck it right back in he mouth. The only time Carlos does take out he finger from he mouth is to eat. Sometimes, when he sleeping, I does pull it out. But he would just suck it right back in, as if he have a magnet in he mouth.

And Carlos does make me laugh. Sometimes when Claire bawl in me head, he does come and sit down by me and ask, "Que passé Carla?" And sing he favourite song for me. *La cucaracha. La cucaracha. Ya no puede caminar. Poque no falta. Poque no tiene, la patica principa.* And me laughing at him, singing with he finger in he mouth.

257

We stay under the table for the whole morning. We eat Crix crackers and corned beef for breakfast and everybody still hungry. By lunchtime, Julie say she going and cook. But as soon as she light up the stove, a helicopter pass and Claire shout, "Oh God! Turn off de stove quick! Turn it off! Turn it off! Dey go bomb up de house! Lord have mercy on us. Oh God have mercy on us!"

"Look Lady, keep youself quiet eh. You can see people hungry!" Julie say. I never hear Julie talk to Claire so yet. So I waiting for Claire to manners her up. But Claire stay quiet as a mouse.

Julie put the turkey wings on the fire. It season already. But the turkey tough, so it taking real long to cook. And Claire only shouting turn off the stove, every time a helicopter pass. So we have to eat Crix and corn beef again.

In the evening, after the sun gone down, we still downstairs. But we not under the table. And we not hearing the helicopters again, so we well say things cool down. But then we hear a voice on a loud speaker saying how they find ammunitions in the area so we have to evacuate immediately. The voice telling people to pack up what they need and go up to the road. And they telling people up the road to open up their house to take people in.

We pack up some food and some clothes, and head up to higher grounds. Everybody going up the road. Is like a exodus out of Babylon. Heading to Mount Zion.

Claire oldest son say he not going nowhere. He staying and watch the house.

We cram in by Claire friend. She have two rooms in she house. Nobody sleep except the little children. All of us sit down in the lady little living room with a lamp, wondering what going on.

Two days pass. Then the voice on the loud speaker pass again and say we could go back home. But that the curfew still in effect so stay inside.

When I go back to school, a few weeks later, I hear all different kinds of stories. People say how Bernard Coard and he men go against Bishop. How they kill Bishop because they want power for themselves. They say how they soldiers and them line up Bishop and the others against the wall on Fort Rupert and shoot them in the head. How nobody don't know where they put their bodies. How Jacqui Creft was pregnant for Bishop when they kill her.

A lot of American soldiers and peace keeping soldiers driving up and down the place. One day they come in we school. Them girls get excited when they see them American soldiers. They looking just like movie stars. They give out a lot of white leather sandals and packets of ration. I don't get sandals, but I get a pack of ration. So the granola bar nice!

And I wondering where they get all those white sandals from.

But all I know is, just so, the Revo done!

Chapter 43

Not Pregnant

I sit down on Mrs Grant veranda waiting for me mother to call. Claire don't have a telephone, so me mother does call by Mrs Grant on Saturdays. Claire would call her collect to say we there and then she would call back.

Mrs Grant veranda go all the way along the front and the side of the house. It have wrought iron railing all round too. It have all kinds of things all over the veranda: old cardboard boxes; pieces of wood; old shoes; a lot of dry up, half dead plants in pots. All kinds of old things.

She dog tie up in a corner of the veranda. And it have dog pee and dog poo all over the floor in that corner. Some of the poo look as if they there for days. The whole veranda smelling real bad. I wonder what Claire does think about Mrs Grant.

Claire stand up by the kitchen door talking to Mrs Grant. Most times Claire does come and call me mother for sheself. But today she want me mother to talk to me about me period. Me period started one Friday night when we on the veranda.

Since Auntie Ethel died, right after Uncle Joe, we have more freedom. The radio on one of the FM stations and they playing real good music. I leaning on the veranda wall when Marion bawl out, "Look a congoree on you nightie!" I jump off the wall and brushing me nightie as if it on fire. Then Jasmine say, "Carla girl, it have blood on you nightie!'

Just like that me period come. That thing between me legs. The bleeding that the Rasta Sistren did talk to me

260

about. It come as soon as I start going to secondary school. As if all the time it was waiting. Waiting for when I start to take bus for meself and go to school in town. As if it waiting for when I start to see all them Brothers' College boys and them, from on top of the hill.

Nobody ever talk about period by Claire. You just can't talk about things like that. But I know Marion seeing hers. And in standard six, a lady came and talk to us about it, in Family Life Education class. So I know what to do. And a lot of the girls in me class start theirs already. When I hear some of them say how theirs start since they have ten years, I say me prayers. I say *thank you Jesus for waiting till I have thirteen years.*

Me heart skip some beats when the telephone ring. Mrs Grant answer it and she call Claire. Claire talk to me mother for a while about Carlos and other things. I waiting in Mrs Grant sitting room.

Mrs Grant have a lot of nice things in she sitting room. She have two big sofas, a big TV, a big bookcase – pack up with a lot of books. She have a lot of pictures on the wall and vases with dry up flowers everywhere. But the place real nasty. I even feel like picking up a broom meself and sweeping all the dog fur on the nice burgundy carpet on the floor. I want to ask her for a cloth to wipe off all them dirty marks on the centre table. And so the place smelling like dirty dog. The only thing that smelling good is Mrs Grant beef soup.

And all kinds of things going through me head while I waiting. Especially what the Rasta Sistren tell me about how you could have a baby when you start to bleed between you legs. She didn't tell me how it could happen, but I know.

I don't even go near boys. So I don't know how Claire could think I pregnant.

261

"Come. Come and speak to you mother." Claire say.

"Hello," I say, when she give me the telephone.

"Hello Carla. How you doing?" Me mother ask.

"Aright," I say. Then I stay quiet. I wonder what me mother going to say next.

"Claire tell me what happen to you," she say. "What trouble you go and put youself in now?"

"Nuttin," Me voice almost fall back down me throat. I could hear me mother voice starting to get shaky already.

"How you mean nothing? She tell me you en see you period for six months and you saying nothing!" Me mother voice start to crack now.

I stay quiet. I don't know what to say. I waiting.

"You must be pregnant. How you could stop see your period for six months? People period does only stop when they pregnant!"

I could hear the cry in me mother voice. I know it real hard for her to talk to me about that. Most times when she call, she just speak to Claire. And if I with Claire, she go ask me how Carlos behaving. And how is school.

"Ah not pregnant."

"How you mean you not pregnant! So what happen to you period den?"

"I don't know. It just stop."

I know how people does get pregnant. How I could be pregnant? I don't even go near boys. Is school and home. Church and home. I can't even take part in nothing after school. I even had to stop learning to play tennis the same day I start up, because Claire say no staying back after school.

"Look at me trouble nuh. I working so hard, cleaning people house and mining other people children for me to send you to school. You know is me alone all you have. And you go and get yourself in dis kinda trouble already."

I move the phone to me other hand. Mrs Grant beef soup making me mouth run water for some. I wondering what she put in it that make it smell so nice.

"Well you go have to go to the doctor. Claire go have to bring you and take a test. You sure you didn't do nothing with a boy Carla? I don't understand how you period could stop for all dat long time. Look at me trouble nuh!"

"Mm mn."

"Well I hope so you know. I don't want you to do like me. That's why I working so hard to send you in high school. Don't make me shame you know Carla. Claire go bring you by the doctor. Ok?

"Ok," I say. I put down the phone. I know me mother go be worrying until me period come back.

Claire and Mrs Grant on the veranda talking still. I could imagine what she telling Mrs Grant. Bad girls that does get pregnant little *jamets*. Claire must be thinking me is a little jamet too. She always talking about bad girls - girls who does ban dey belly, when they makin chile, so nobody would know. Maybe she think I doing that too.

I wait for Claire to bring me by the doctor. But I know I not pregnant, so I not worrying at all. Claire don't even get chance to bring me by the doctor. The week after I speak to me mother, just as how it stop, me period just come back.

Chapter 44

Three Straw Men

I in the classroom finishing the last piece of me cheese sandwich, when all the commotion start. I done eat half break-time. Sometimes I does even eat half as soon as I reach in school. Claire always rationing the bread, so it never enough for everybody.

Me geography homework in front me, but I can't concentrate. Saturday evening as soon as I pick up me book to do it, Claire call me. "Come come. Put away dat book and go and help shell the cocoa." Even though whole morning I working. The house well sweep-up, the clothes wash and well fold-up. And the twelve big brown bread bake already and sit down in the kitchen waiting patiently for she to go and lock them up in she room. I even done shell me share already you know. And on Parents Day, when one of me teachers tell her, the only problem she has with me is homework – how me homework always incomplete. Claire still have the belly to ask me what I does be doing so, that I can't finish me homework.

Lunchtime always the noisiest time in Convent – with all those St Hillary girls out in the yard playing hopscotch and everybody pushing and shouting at Miss Shermie in the tuck shop. *A roti and a Coke please! A bread and cheese and a pennacool over here! A piece a cake and a juice for me, Miss Shermie! And doh give yuh girl no likkle likkle piece a cake dere you know! Fix me up nice.*

A few girls run down the driveway behind the school. Me seat near by the window so I could see everybody who passing. I don't know how I end up right in the back row with Patricia on one end and Carol on the other end – next to me. Maybe because am one of the oldest in class. I pass me exams late so I taking fourteen years.

Patricia in she corner with a real mess all round her: she empty lunch box; juice bag; biscuit and sweets packets on the window ledge; school books on the floor and a bundle of new books spread out on she desk. She running she own little business renting out Sweet Dreams and Nancy Drews for twenty-five cents a day.

Carol sprawl out on she desk, by the window sleeping. Carol does walk with she chest and bottom stick out like black ants. And she always talking about what she and she boyfriend do. Sometimes that girl does even start touching up sheself, right in the class, right in front of everybody, and saying how she feeling sexy. And all them goody goody girls and them does pretend they don't see or hear. And me too. I want to be like them. I just want to be an innocent Convent girl too.

Things heating up outside. More girls running down. Then back again. A lot of loud loud talking. Laughing. I remember the same thing happen last year, when a lady with a crooked leg came to see she daughter. She had little fingers on one hand too, as if they forget to grow. I remember how them children laugh and run and call their friends to come and see her. I remember how the girl never come out from she class.

The noise getting louder. *Maybe it have some crazy person by the gate.* I stick me head out the window, but all I could see is Convent girls running up and down, feet pounding the concrete like racehorses, in navy blue and white. *Ah wonder what happening outside?* I itching to run down by the gate and see too, but I say let me stay me backside right in me seat, because when you hear Sister

Carmen start calling out names in assembly, nobody could say I was there too.

Some of the girls start gathering by the window, looking inside. One of them pointing. I close me book. Look around the class. *Who she pointing at?*

Grace and Sheerece sharing their lunch and reading. I could smell their vanilla cake and apple. They always bring their lunch, well pack in their lunch bags. And they always have their heads in a book.

The girl who pointing cup she mouth and say something to another one. They throw back their heads laughing. *What they laughing at?*

The noise reach by the front door now. Girls pushing. Pointing. Whispering. Laughing. *What they pointing me for! Oh God!* Sweat prickle under me arms. Me throat get dry. A girl walking up to me. Me heart heave. *Oh God! What she coming by me for? What she want with me?* I know her. We used to go to the same primary school by Leapers Hill.

"Your father come to see you," she say.

And just so me insides drop down under the chair.

Me father come to see me? What she mean me father come to see me? How he could come to see me? Where he come out all this time? How he reach here? How he know which school ah in? What he come in me school for? Oh God.

Under me arm jooking now. And the girl stand up there watching me as if me father just like everybody else father and he does come and see me all the time.

"He outside to see you," the girl say. And she still stand up there as if she waiting for me to go with her.

Me heart start to gallop. Me belly shoot up in me throat, as if it want to choke me. And I want to run. From the time that girl say the word father, I know I should of run. I should of just take me bag and run. Run and hide somewhere. Anywhere. But I can't move. I just sit down there waiting. I don't know what I waiting for. I just waiting. *Oh God! What ah go do now! Everybody go find out about me now.* All the time I well hiding me secrets. Since that time, I dig up a deep deep hole and bury them so nobody go find them. And every time we go in the Prayer Room I does beg God not to let nobody find them. Please God.

The chair scrape the old, dusty wood flooring. I don't know how. Something lift me up from the chair. I don't know what. It put one foot in front the other, out the classroom door. Push me pass the toilets. Shove me out the other back door. Swing me to the left and down pass me classroom. Then pass the Prayer Room, until I reach the back gate. With everybody following, as if is some kind of procession.

The midday sun hit me right in me face. I blink. Big black circles spin around behind me eyes. Sweat run down between me breasts. Eyes jooking me skin like prickle worms. They jooking me shiny face, the back of me neck, me back - under me white school shirt. They even jooking me legs under me pleated skirt, that reaching below me knees.

Then me eyes fall on what causing all the commotion. The three men standing up on the other side of the road, at the top of St John's Street. Three Rastamen. And not just ordinary, everyday Rastamen you know. Three strawmen. And they just stand up there, posing like statues - leaning on their staffs.

The three of them have on clothes that make from some kind of straw. The two on the sides shorter and their locks sticking up like porcupine spikes. They have on long pants and something that look like a waistcoat. But the one in the middle different. He is the tallest one. He locks clump-up together in bunches – like branches. He have on a kind of farmer brown, and a long jacket over it.

Every piece of clothes they have on, from their bags down to their sandals make from pine straw.

Girls start to swarm round me like bees. More uproar. St Hillary girls squealing for their friends and their teachers to come and see! All you come and see! Even the Brothers' College boys start pouring down the hill. Pointing. Whispering. Laughing. And me ears ringing.

Lawd! Tha's she father!
Who father?
Which one is she father?
That Rasta have chile in convent?
What they have on there?
Lawd! Rastaman have chile in Convent oui!

Me head spinning fast. Just like Rally top. I used to watch him – how he used to take he time to ball up the twine round the tip of the nail, to the top of the smooth guava wood. Then he would spin it on any little patch of dust he could find in the yard. The top would spin so fast, but it would look as if it not even moving- as if it sleeping. Then slow down. Wobble. Wobble. Wobble. Then fall in slow motion. That's how me head feeling – like Rally top.

Well is ruction in the road now. Bus slowing down. Cars stopping. Drivers tooting their horns because nothing moving and people gathering up in the road. Passengers sticking their heads out the windows. People running up St John's Street. Down Cemetery Road. Some of them probably leave they pot burning.

And the same thing that make me walk to the gate jam me feet in the ground. Me head still spinning then sleeping like Rally top. Then me eyes leave me stand up right there, and float across the road to meet the one in the middle. The one with the deep deep eyes and the straight nose and the long knot-up beard – looking like Haille Selassie. Me father.

The last time I see me father is when I visit him in prison. That was two years ago. Then I hear that after the invasion – when them American soldiers set them prisoners free – me father *trad* up to the hills and he never come back down.

And all that time I trying to forget everything about *that time*. Every time I kneel down in church I asking God to rub off all that thing that happen to me from me mind. Like how the teacher does rub off the black board for the next lesson. But me father always in me head. He always sticking heself right in the middle of me dreams. And once, this girl in school just come up to me, out of the blue, and ask me if me father is a Rastaman. And if I was married in truth. And I just pretend I don't know who she talking to. But I dig up me little hole quick quick, and bury that before anybody else hear. But I could never forget how the shame crawl up all over me skin, like a big, ugly congoree. And no matter how much I try to brush it off, the thing just stick on to me.

PING A LING A LING! I jump. Children start running in to assembly. Some ignore the bell. It ring again. And again. I can't move. Only me eyes moving. They fall from me father and land on the culvert below me feet. I wish I could fall under the culvert too. Disappear.

Me father eyes on me now. I feel them on me. They just like magnets, because they drag me eyes back to him. He don't move. He don't say a word. He just stand up there like Moses, with he two disciples, burning me with he eyes. The voices around me sounding far away. Teachers calling the girls to come inside now. Senior girls rounding up the rest to go to assembly.

And somebody holding me. The same girl who come and get me. I want to jerk out from she hand. Push her down the culvert for making me shame so. If she didn't come and call me, nobody would know. Now everybody know this Rastaman, wearing straw and looking like a mad man is me father. Everybody going to find out I was a Rasta too; that I used to smoke weed. They go find out me not no innocent Convent girl.

Me tears taste like seawater. I can't see where the girl bringing me. I don't care. When I reach in me class I want to bury me head inside me desk, but I just rest me head down. The desk smell like ink and pencil and sweat. I cover me head with me arms and I let the cry come. All the cry that hiding inside me come out. I cry for me mother – for leaving me; for never coming back and get me *that time*; for leaving me by Claire and going back in Venezuela. I cry for me hole full of secrets that me father just come and dig up. The soft wood soak up me tears.

I remember one break time when Grace was crying on she desk, all the girls and them gather around her asking, *what happen to you*? Even one of the teachers came to ask her *what's the matter Grace?* Touching Grace's thick plait lying down on she back like a big cattail. She took Grace out of the class with her. Nobody ask me nothing. A light breeze drift up all the way from the Esplanade, up St John's Street and through the window, to cool down the afternoon heat, but nobody come and ask me anything. Me mother not the secretary in the Ministry of Education. Me aunty is not the Manager of no bank. And me uncle not the chief of police. I just that Rastaman daughter; that mad man wearing straw, who living up in the hills.

Out in assembly Sister Marie call out, "Now be quiet girls. Girls be quiet! Leave all that racket outside! Girls!" But too much excitement to be quiet. Sister Marie clang the bell again. Real hard. *I SAY QUIET PLEASE!*

I don't go to assembly. Me alone in the class. Then a girl bending over me shaking me. She pack me bag and take me out of the class. As I pass assembly, prickle worms crawl on me again. She take me to the Prayer Room.

After the library, the Prayer Room is me favourite room in the school. It small and cosy, with one chair in a corner and a lot of books on the shelves.

I take off me shoes and sit down in a corner on the soft, red carpet. The carpet still smelling new. The sun peep through the window, facing St Hillary Girls school. Little spots of sunlight dance about on the carpet. And on me skirt.

I sit down on the floor and cry until all I could see is red - like the carpet.

After assembly, the same girl come back for me. She have a nice face, big eyes, and she teeth look as if she used to suck finger. She look sorry for me.

"Sister say you could go home," she tell me.

I want to go home but I just want to hide in the prayer room.

We walk down Church Street and she leave me on top Market Hill. I take one look down the hill and I head up Lucas Street, pelting foot. People watching me funny. School not over yet so it look like I sculling school.

As the bus reach down in the Market Square, I see them again - the three straw men. They standing up right in front Voyager. Traffic stop. People breaking their neck, their foot, and everything else to see them straw men.

That evening, Clarie leave me alone for once. When outside start to get dark, they come and stand up outside the house. I hide upstairs. When outside get real dark, I peep again and they gone.

For the whole weekend I pray and pray for all kind of sickness to strike me down and for weekend to never finish. But Monday morning come, just like it does always come, after Sunday.

The convent girls gather up by the front gate and line up the steps like a firing squad, when they hear the Rastaman daughter coming. Me legs tremble. Me chest get heavy with fright. So I pull meself inside me, like a soldier crab. I could do it real good now. And sometimes, I does even forget to come back out.

Chapter 45

One Woman In The House

Is Christmas Eve and Town busy. Everybody dress up and out shopping or just liming. The streets full of people. The shops full of people. Women shopping last minute for new curtains and decorations. And maybe even a ham, if the money could stretch far enough. Mothers tugging children - hanging on to dress tails, pants loops, belts, bags, anything they could hold – so they don't lose in the crowd. Children gazing at the pretty toys in the shop windows and wishing. Some nagging.

"Mammy ah could get a doll? Eh Mammy? Eh Mammy? Please Mammy?"

"Mammy watch that bad police car nuh! Ah want one nuh Mammy!"

"You see how you is Mammy! You only buying ting for Pinky, but you doh buying nuttin for me!"

And the whole town look like Christmas. Lights blinking on the buildings and in the shop windows. Sparkly decorations hanging everywhere. Christmas carols and *parang* music playing all about. And people looking happy. Even people who don't have money could have a merry time, because Christmas in the air

First time Claire letting me go in town Christmas Eve, so I well excited. I put on me favourite three quarts yellow suit me mother send for me. But when I go downstairs, ready to go, Claire watch me from head to toe and say, "You wearing dat again! Where's dat nice corduroy pants you mother send for you? Put it on. You like dat damn yellow ting too much!"

273

Aaaa! I doh want to put on dat dirty brown corduroy pants nuh. The ting ugly ugly. The foot and dem wide wide, sweeping the floor when I walk! I en know where me mother pick up dese ugly pants! She always dress up nice nice, so I doh know how she could send a ugly old ting for me! So I praying for outside to get dark quick. And for me not to bounce up nobody from school in me old ugly pants.

Me and Jasmine follow Marion around town, squeezing through people and vendors on the sidewalks with their trays and tables heaped with all kinds of things for sale.

Marion only buying all kind of things. She buy biscuits, chocolates, apples and grapes. She even buy bras and panties. And I watching her and wondering where she get all that money from, because I know is not Claire who give her. But she always have money. And when she buy she biscuits and things, she does hide them in she cupboard, and eat them *petit fe petit fe.*

Jasmine have she Christmas money that she father send for her. She buy apples and grapes too. Every where you turn, vendors selling apples and grapes. And Jasmine give me a whole apple. First time I ever have a whole one for myself in me life! When Claire buy apples, she does slice-up one apple to share between all of us. And fuss the slice and them thin, you could see through them.

I watching people buying things and I wishing I could buy too? But I have me last twenty dollars and it's me bus money for when school open. So I leave it right in me ugly corduroy pocket and just watch them shiny Christmas things and wish them well!

We walk and walk all round town. Marion know all the streets. The only ones I know, even though I schooling in Town, is Church Street and Lucas Street. And I know the Market Square too.

We bounce up some girls from me school. Some of them with their boyfriends. They even holding hands, *big and bold oui!* I fraid for them. I wondering how they not afraid somebody go see them and tell their mother. Or tell Sister. Because Sister always talking about the reports she does get about some of them convent girls. And one time in assembly, she start talking about how some of us have double lives. *Some of you have school lives and outside lives. Let me remind you, that St Mary's Convent have laid an excellent foundation for many upstanding figures in society; this school has an excellent reputation and I don't want anyone - I will not allow anyone, to drag it down in the gutter. I want to remind you that a convent girl should be a convent girl no matter where you are – regardless of whether you are wearing this uniform or NOT.* And as I listen to Sister, I pull meself inside me, wondering if she know about me.

We hang around by the Market Square for a long time. Marion keep looking through the crowd. I know she waiting for some boy.

Music drift down from the *Top Of The Town* restaurant and bar, across the street. Lord Kitchener singing *Drink a rum and a punch a creama, drink a rum. Mama drink if you drinking. Drink a rum an a punch a creama, drink a rum. It is Christmas morning.*

The balcony full of men. And their eyes drifting down the street too. Whistling. *Psssseeping* the girls passing.

"Let us go upstairs," Marion say, after we wait and wait and she boyfriend don't come.

"Upstairs? Wha we going up dere for?" I say. "If somebody see us now?"

"Who go see us?" Marion ask me.

I never been up there. I know up there is for big people. And all those men there up there drinking. If somebody tell Claire now! She know Claire does know everything already! So I well fraid.

As soon as we step inside the entrance, darkness cover us. The steps steep and narrow. We have to squeeze pass people to get up. And upstairs real dark too. The walls paint in black and rusty orange. All the chairs and tables black too. And them men loud loud. Shouting at the girl in the bar.

"Two beastly cold Carib and a Heineken."

"Gimme a Guinness dey! An ah want a roti to go wid it too."

All the tables full of people, drinking, eating rotis, fish and chips, chicken and rice. And so all that food smells making me belly rumble. I wish I could buy a roti too and a nice icy glass of passion fruit juice.

Marion leave us and go in the toilet. Somebody whistle and *pseep*. When I turn round, is Marion they whistling at. Marion leave home in a dress but when she come out from the toilet, she have on she tightest jeans and a skin tight jersey top. She breasts stick out in front of her like twin mountain peaks. She bottom like two big, ripe breadfruit! And she buckle she belt so tight, she waist curve in like a number eight. Claire always asking her what she *gurting up she waist tight tight so for*? And Marion know the men watching her so she push out she chest some more. And swing she bottom harder.

Some boy come up to Marion and she stop and talk to him. Me and Jasmine wait for her.

Jasmine elbow me. "Look who coming up dey nuh!"

I look down the dark steps. Is Jasmine boyfriend coming up the steps with two other boys. Jasmine only have twelve years and she have boyfriend already. But he is she mother's friend's nephew. They always meeting up at beach parties and thing, so she didn't have to say he is she boyfriend.

He smile at us.

"Wha all you doing up here?" He ask. His skin dark like burnt cocoa. And he teeth glowing against it.

"We just waiting for Marion," Jasmine say.

He stay by Jasmine for a little while. He keep looking at he friends, as if he want to go and meet them but he want to stay with Jasmine too. Then when he go by them, he looking over at Jasmine.

Finally Marion boyfriend reach and we walk over to the Carenage. The water in the harbour shining like black glass. Rolling onto the wall. Little splash. Then rolling back. The fishing boats bobbing up and down together – as if they marking time. Behind the boats, further out, Christmas lights twinkling on the black glass.

I don't know when he meet us, but next thing I know, Jasmine boyfriend walking with us too. I walk well behind them everybody could see I not walking with no boy. But I know even if somebody see us, they go just tell Claire say they see *us* walking with boyfriends.

Marion boyfriend from River Road. He have about eighteen years and he working already. He bring us in Nutmeg Restaurant. And the place full of people, but he only hugging up Marion. And so he making us giggle with he jokes. When he laugh, he face make two deep dimples. And he have nice teeth.

Jasmine sit down by she boyfriend too. I wonder if they holding hands under the table. I wonder how it feeling. Once, when me confirmation class coming back from a retreat, me and a boy - who always watching me - hands touch in the bus. Inside the bus dark. He hold me hand in the dark. I remember how he hand feel dry and the skin feel rough. And I remember how I take back me hand quick when the bus stop and the light come on. And since that time, every time we eyes bounce up, he looking away.

Marion boyfriend buy chicken rotis and Fanta for all of us. And we stay in Nutmeg long long. And all the time I watching the red clock on the wall, because Claire done give us strict warning to, "Make sure all you back in dis house by eight o' clock. No later!"

"Marion, quarter past seven you know. Let's go home." I say.

But Marion enjoying sheself, so she not busy.

"It early still," she say.

When the clock say half pass seven, I start to get the jitters.

"Marion let us go home! You hear what Claire say already!"

"Girl chill out nuh! Wha you want to go home this early time for?"

The clock saying quarter past eight when we leave Nutmeg. Marion boyfriend show us a short cut from the Carenage to go up Lucas Street. We walk all the way up to Government House to wait for the bus.

I *pelt foot* up that hill eh. I leave Marion and them behind. Every time I see a bus coming, I telling Marion, but she never ready. Half past eight come and gone. Jasmine's boyfriend with us too because we waiting for same bus. But most of the buses too full to hold four of us, so we waiting long.

We don't reach home until about half past nine. I could smell Tantie ham boiling in the yard next door. I never see a woman like to do things late so. In the middle of the night she would be outside washing clothes!

We don't pass downstairs like we always do. Marion say let's pass up the front steps. I know she hoping Claire downstairs and we could pretend we reach home long.

Marion go inside first. I follow her, and Jasmine come in behind me. Jasmine mother watching TV. Carlos sleeping on the chair with he finger halfway out he mouth.

"How all you come back late so?" Pam ask, looking at Marion.

"We take long to get the bus. All them bus and them coming full up," Marion say.

I wondering where Claire is. What she going to do.

"You better go and tell mommy. She downstairs waiting for all you," Pam say. She looking at me and Marion.

"You miss madam, go and change you clothes and go in your bed!" She tell Jasmine.

Me belly boil like Tantie ham in the lard pan outside. Marion go in the room first, to put away she shopping. Then she take she time before she go downstairs. I go down behind her.

Claire in the kitchen seasoning meat. On Christmas Day they cooking everything – stew beef and pork and bake chicken and all kinds of nice things. As if it was the last supper!

"Mommy we come back," Marion say. She stand up on the step – the one before the last one to step into the kitchen. And I jam me brakes behind her. Me legs trembling.

"Good night Claire," I say. And I waiting.

Claire rinse out she seasoning from she hands. She turn round. Dry she hands with the end of she dress. Then she put she hands on she waist and she raise up she head. She watch Marion from head to toe. Then she watch me. Then Marion again, as if something puzzling her.

"You come back! You shouldn' come back! What you come back for? You go tell me whey all you come out from dis hour!" Claire say.

"Mommy the bus and..." Marion start to say, but Claire cut her one time.

"What bus and dem! No bus and dem nothing!" Claire say.

"But Mommy all the bus and dem were full up!"

"Bus and dem full up! Who you tink you talkin to? You tink ah stupid! Ah go show you bus full up!"

I see something bad in Claire face. That same thing that does make her glad when something like that happen, so she could get on. It make me want to run back outside and hide until Claire call me to come and put she curlers in she hair; until she fall asleep watching TV.

Claire don't tell me nothing. I stand up behind Marion and I don't know what to do with meself. Me knees start to wobble. I hold on to the side of the trap door.

Marion know Claire don't like people folding up their arms when she talking to them you know, but she stand up there folding she arms and puffing up she face – as if she want to take on Claire!

"Go and change all you clothes! Ah go deal with all you just now," Claire say.

I go back upstairs. I put Carlos in he bed. He finger almost fall out from he mouth, but he suck it back in quick.

I changing me clothes when Claire call me and Marion. Not Jasmine. As if she was not there too. And walking with boyfriend and all.

Marion go in the room. I stand up outside the door shaking.

Pam still watching TV. *The Love Boat* showing. Is Christmas on the boat too and everybody dress up and drinking and having a merry time.

The sitting room looking real nice. The new Christmas curtains up. They red with green flowers. All the cushion covers new too. The varnish on the oval dining table – where nobody does sit down to eat – not dry yet. It shiny under the light. The floor shiny too. Jimmy polish it that morning.

"So you think you is a big woman eh! You want to go and come when you want!" Claire saying.

Spasms shoot up in me belly when I hear the first lash fall.

"MOMMY!" Marion cry out.

Then a thump. As if somebody fall on the floor or hit the door.

Maybe Marion trying to hold Claire hand. Or maybe she grab the belt because Claire say, "So you want to fight wid me! Eh!"

PLAT! The belt hit again.

THUMP on the door.

"You playing woman!"

PLAT! PLAT! Belt hitting body.

"You not no big woman yet."

PLAT! THUMP!

"Ah TIRED tell you is only ONE woman in dis house! ONLY ONE!"

PLAT! PLAT! PLAT!

"Ah go teach you who is the woman of dis house!"

When the lady next door beat she daughters - and they always getting licks - they does bawl down the whole place. They does bawl for the Daddy they did'nt even know; their big brother who leave the house because he tired take licks; they does bawl for their uncle, their aunty and their *nennen*.

But no bawling coming from that bedroom. All I could hear is belt hitting flesh and the thumping. Marion not making a sound. She taking she licks like a lamb.

I waiting for me turn and is just as if the belt falling on me already. Claire never hit me yet. She does make me work like a Cinderella. She does shout and bawl in me head and call me names, but she never rest she hands on me yet. *Is not me fault we reach home late. I tell Marion how much times let's go home. What she go do me?*

When Marion come out from the room I nearly mess meself. *Oh God! If she do she own chile dat, what she go do me!*

Marion go straight in the room.

"Come in here YOU miss madam!" Claire say.

I push the bedroom door easy easy. The room even more jam-up than ever. And I could smell the bread and the Christmas cake that Claire hide up in she cupboard already. All the sweets and wafers me mother send for us lock up in that cupboard too. Ants eating them instead of us. And the room smell sour, like vinegar too.

"You lucky you know madam!" Claire say. "You lucky you is not me chile! But next time you come home dat kind a hour, you could jus pack you bag! You hear me! Jus pack you bag! Ah say is only ONE woman in dis house! Two hen can't stay in the same cage. All who tink dem is woman could leave dis house and go! You hear me madam?"

I want to say answer. I want to say "Yes Claire" but all me words just gather up and stick in me throat. I nearly pee meself. I sure Claire was going to murder me with licks.

When I go in the room, Marion on the bed in she panty and bra, eating she grapes. She arms swell-up and full of belt marks. All over she legs, she belly, she back, cover up with big lumps. I could see she well grease down with Vaseline, because she skin shiny, like the water in the harbour. And she big melon breasts heaving up and down, marking time, like them boats.

We sharing room now. Since Aunty Ethel died, Julie move to she room and me and Marion in the same room. We don't say anything to on another. Marion sit down eating she grapes. I make up me bed, lie down and say me prayers. *Now I lay me down to sleep, I pray dear Lord my soul to keep. If I should die before I wake I pray dear Lord my soul to take.*

I thank God Claire is not me mother. I thank God me is not she child.

Chapter 46

No Money, No Home

Is the second time for the week Claire send me to the post office. I stand up in the little wooden post office, next to the police station, watching the post lady flick through the bundle of letters. Me eyes make beast looking for me mother slanted writing and me grandmother small round writing. The lady hand me the ones for Claire. When I look through them again, me heart drop! None of them have the Venezuelan stamp or one with the Queen face on it.

"You get letter from your mother?" Claire ask me, as soon as I reach home.

"No Claire."

Claire breathe in real heavy.

"Last month, same ting. This month same ting!" She say.

Me mother started sending letters with a friend of hers who working on a cruise ship, the Cunard Princess. She used to even send little parcels with clothes and Carlos favourite cereals and sweets and things. The ship does come once a month and dock on the harbour overnight. That used to make Claire real happy, because every month, she getting she money on time. But in her last letter, me mother say her friend going on holiday so she would have to post the letters again. Claire didn't like that at all, because sometimes letters take weeks to reach Grenada.

"Well, all you will just have to go by all you grandmother until I get the money," she say. "I have all me expense. I have food to buy. How I go feed all you? I can't feed people children without money. I don't understand what happen to all you mother! How she expect me to feed all you without money?"

I in the kitchen in me school uniform listening to Claire. Something stir-up inside me.

"What you doing standing up dere still? Go and change you clothes. It have cocoa to shell!"

I go upstairs and sit down on the bed in me uniform. The thing still stirring up inside me. It start in me belly and it reach up in me chest. I sure that's how hate does feel. *God go punish dat woman. How she could say dat? Every month she getting she money. And she know letters does take real long to come from Venezuela. But she does always get it. And all the time she playing nice nice wid me mother. And when people come by her, and ask her who is that little girl, telling them "dat's my big adopted daughter" and putting she arm around me, stiff stiff like a piece of wood! Now just because the money late she getting on so. God go punish her. And all that work she does make people do, like some damn Cinderella! Every day shelling cocoa, shelling cocoa. People fingers cut-up cut-up. Now she find it hard to give me and Carlos piece of food, just because she en get money yet! God go real punish that woman! I don' know what me mother leave us with dis wicked woman for!*

The thing stir up so much it burning me chest now.

But Claire serious. Another week pass, and when she still don't get letter from me mother, she say we have to go by Mammy. Nobody say a word. Not even Julie.

She make Julie bring me and Carlos in town and put us on a bus going to St Patrick's.

Is the first time we come back since me mother bring Carlos down from Venezuela. And two years pass since that time.

Mammy and Papa in the kitchen when me and Carlos reach. The last time I see Mammy was when she came by me school to see me. She came to the courthouse and it is near to the school. That day when one of the girls tell me somebody by the gate asking for me. Me head started to hurt me one time.

Weeks after that time me father came by the school, every time I reach the school gate, fright does grip me like a pipe wrench. I does have to psych meself up, to walk up the steps; creep in the classroom; slip into assembly. And I praying harder than a nun, for nobody to ask me nothing about that day. But one day a girl come up to me and say, "Somebody say you used to live in the hills and you were married. That's true?" I nearly faint. The girl have short curly hair like a boy, and thick glasses. They make she eyes look like marbles. She friends and them gather around her, closing in, waiting for me to answer. Shame burn me skin. And then the bell ring. So I well relieved when the girl tell me the lady say she is me grandmother.

I meet Mammy sit down on the steps. She looked glad to see me. "Me grandchile going in big school oui mama!" She say. And before she go she put something in me hand. When I open me hand, is a crumpled up five dollar.

"A a! What all you doing here?' Mammy ask us when we walk in the old kitchen. She sitting by she old table and Papa on the sofa.

"Well mama oye! Who bring all you in me house? Ent dey put all you in Town. Ah taught all you was too good for me ole *jooper*!"

Mammy didn't know we coming. All the way up on the bus, I was praying that Mammy would be glad to see us, but I know one time that Mammy don't want us there.

Papa just there looking at me and Carlos and grinning like he old silly billy self.

"Claire send us up," I tell her. "Because she en get money for we mother.' I said.

"Well mama oye! All you mother take all you and put all you quite in town, by strangers. Strangers! Now look how dey chasing all you like fly!"

And I feel just like a fly in truth. First Claire shoo us away and now Mammy shooing us away too.

Carlos don't understand what going on. He hold on to me hand tight tight, with he two hands. He finger not wet anymore. Since Claire hold him down and rub he finger in *caca poule,* he finger does jam brakes as soon as it reach by he mouth. Then he does watch the finger as if it turn into a monster and hide it away quick.

Carlos jam up against me just like Belle used to jam up against Rally. Is the first time I sorry me mother leave Carlos.

When the sun going down, Mammy and Papa sit on the veranda with Mr Fin, just like when I was little. Mammy telling Mr Fin how the lady in town don't want us so she pack us back like dogs. And I don't understand how Mammy could talk about us, she own flesh and blood like that.

Papa on he chair in the corner, quiet quiet. He look like a stick man. He old stripe pyjamas hanging on him as if he is a hanger. He right arm rest on he lap like a piece of stick and he fingers look like brambles. He left hand scratching he bumpy legs, grup grup grup.

Me and Carlos in the hall. I take out me notebook to try and study me notes, because we have exams next week. The hall is still the same. The cabinet with the glass door in the same corner, full of dusty wares and cobweb. The radio still on top of the cabinet and me old doll Suzie stand up on a chair, with she mildew face and missing finger.

Carlos find Rally tin of marbles and he on the floor playing with them. Belle crawl up next to Carlos just like she used to do with Rally. Carlos put down the marbles and raise up the cat. He put her on him and stroke she orange fur.

I wonder where Rally is. Mammy say he is a stray way now. He does hardly come home and he stop going to school.

Sunday evening Rally pass home. He come to eat and go again. He look as if he not growing at all. He was shorter than me and he hair look natty natty, as if he growing locks again.

Rally never speak to me. But he glad to see Carlos. He bring Carlos in the road and play marbles with him. Then later, he just gone. Mammy say he always up the road by Miss Joyce.

I trying to read over me notes, but all I could think about is me mother and how Claire treating me. So I decide to write me mother and tell her about Claire. Claire does read all me letters, so I never get the chance to tell her what I really want to say. I don't even know what me and Carlos going to do. Claire never tell us when we could go back. How I go know if she get the letter? Now I go miss out me exams. Sometimes I don't like school at all, but I don't like to miss out a day.

And I know Mammy don't want me in she house. She like Carlos. She does hug him up, like she used to hug Rally. She does put him on she knees and sing for him. Carlos like that, but when she try to feed him she mash up food from she plate, with she fingers, he does screw up he face and wiggle away.

I just finishing me letter when I hear Mammy say, "Who is that in the road dere Fin?"

"Ah doh know," Fin say.

I peep through the louvres but I don't see nobody. I go out in the veranda.

"Whey you goin? Somebody come to you?" Mammy say.

The first little quarter of the moon out. It shining over Celeste like a dim flashlight.

It have a boy standing on the other side of the road in truth. I know who it is. Me heart leap. *What he doin up here?*

"Who standing up in the road dere?" Mammy ask me.

"I doh know nuh," I say. And I hurry back in the hall. Me heart start to beat fast. *What he come up here for? How he know I here? What he come all up here for? He want to put me in trouble. Lord!*

I peep through the louvres to see what Chris go do. He is Jimmy friend. He does come by Jimmy and he always watching me. He does help Jimmy do work around the house; grind the cocoa and fix things. And Claire like that. But one day she come home and meet me Marion and Jasmine downstairs watching Jimmy, Chris and he cousin, playing draughts. She start shouting at us. She chase me and Jasmine upstairs. And I don't know what she tell Chris, but he stop coming by Jimmy.

Sometimes Chris does wait by the bus stop and walk up part of the road with me. I know Chris like me. But he is a construction worker. He not going to Brothers' College or The Boys Secondary School. And I know if Claire ever see me talking to him, crapaud smoke me pipe.

"Is he what going up the road dere?" Mammy ask.

"It look so oui. Ah wonder who dere?" Mr Fin say.

I pull the curtain quick quick, just in time to see Chris walking pass the house. He walking slow and he watching the house, as if he could send some kind of signal like that.

Boop boop boop. Me heart fraid.

Carlos roll a marble on the floor. Belle spring under the chair behind it.

"Ah going outside for something eh. Stay here, ah coming back just now,"' I tell him.

"What you going outside for?" Carlos ask. I know he would not want to go outside with me because he fraid the dark. He roll another marble and Belle forget about the first one and spring through the bedroom door behind the new one.

I open the back door real quiet. Push it back, praying for it not to creak for Mammy to hear. I creep down the steps – the same steps I use to skip up and down when I was little, to bring a glass from the cabinet for Mammy or Papa shaving case for him. I tiptoe behind the old kitchen where me and Rally used to run behind chickens, and up through the garden where ground doves does scratch for gold dust in the cliff.

Outside just bright enough for me to make out Chris under the shadow of the damson tree on our side, and the Mango long tree on the other side. Chris there waiting for me, as if we plan to meet up and he sure I go come.

"What you doing up here?" Me voice tremble, fuss I fraid.

"I come and see you," leaning he head to the side.

"To see me? How you know I here?"

"I come by me partner Jude. He tell me where you staying."

Me eyes flick over to the veranda and back. I could smell the rotten damsons under the tree. Mammy used to make stew with them for me and Rally. But they so sour, nobody bothering with them anymore.

"Jimmy tell me what he mother do. Dat woman en easy boy," Chris say. "She real wicked."

Mammy bend over the veranda and looking up the road. She say something to Mr Fin. I move from one foot to the next.

"When you going back down?"

"I doh know yet."

Chris move closer to me. I move back. I wearing one of me mother nighties. It long – reaching all down on the ground. I fold me arms across me chest and glance at the veranda again. Mr Fin cutlass scrape the steps. He going home. Mammy does go inside as soon as he go home.

"I going back inside before Mammy ketch me," I say.

But as I turn to go, I see somebody coming up the road. Is the lady next door. When she reach by us I turn me face towards Chris so she wouldn't make me out. And the same time Chris hold me to him. I could smell he deodorant and sweat. And something hard press right below me navel. Me body close up. Cold bumps cover me. I want to pull away from him but the lady slow down, and she keep watching back, and shaking she head.

"I going back inside now," I say, as soon as the lady reach she gap. As I start to turn, Chris try to kiss me. He lips just have time brush mine, before I pull away quick. He mouth smell like hawks mint. I can't stand the smell of hawks mint at all.

"Whey you sister go?" I hear Mammy asking Carlos.

I dash down the yard so fast! I fly up the steps and bolt the door quick, before Mammy see me.

When I sneak in the hall, I nearly bounce up Mammy. She bringing the *Home Sweet Home* big lamp to she bedroom.

"Whey you come out?" She say, watching me over she glasses. The flame make she face look yellow.

"Ah come out in the kitchen for someting."

291

"You come out in kitchen! You tink ah born yesterday!"

I never answer her. Me and Carlos just go in we bed. The same bed where me and Rally used to sleep. I make him pee in the pail by the bed and say he prayers. And I say mine.

Dear Lord, please doh let Mammy find out. Please doh let her tell Claire about me. I didn't do nothing wrong Lord. Please doh let her tell Claire.

Chapter 47

The Letter

Bright and early Monday morning, Mammy wake me up.

"Get up, get up. All you have school. How all you go go to school? All you better go back whey all you mother leave all you eh!"

When I was little, I used to feel nice when the sun touch me face through the louvres in the morning. But this morning, I just feel like crying, because I don't know what to do. Claire get the letter but I don't know if we could go back yet. I don't even have money to pay bus, and I know Mammy wouldn't give me none. And I can't even ring me mother and tell her what happening.

When Carlos wake up, I bring him outside to brush he teeth. Mammy still getting on. She come in front the kitchen door where I stand up holding the cup of water for Carlos to wash he face. The same place where I used to stand up, bending over the drain to brush mine when I was little.

"Watch you nuh! You poopa take you and bring you in the bush. He make man jook you up like breadfruit. Decraycray you! You mooma put you all down dere. Me house din good enough! No sah! Now what you come back here and do? Ah doh want no chile dat man jook up in me house! Go back whey she leave you!"

"Carla, what is you poopa?" Carlos ask me, with he mouth full of toothpaste. I tell him is me father.

I does hear them girls in class talking about boys breaking their hearts. And I does hear people in movies talking about it too. But that is a different kind of break.

Because Mammy hawk out them words and spit them out so hard they hit me like river stones. Right in me heart. And I feel me whole self mashing up in a lot of little pieces.

I try to swallow the cry but me throat block it.

Carlos hug me leg with he wet hands.

"What you crying for Carla? Doh cry Carla," he say. Then he let me go quick and wipe he hands on he pajama and hug me again, with he toothbrush in he hand. And I see he ready to cry too so I try to hold mines back.

The only person I know who I could ask for money to pay bus, is me mother friend down in Sauteurs. So I get ready, dress Carlos, and we walk down to Sauteurs.

When we reach back home, Claire in hospital. She pressure high. She sugar high. *You see how God does punish people.*

Nobody don't say a word about what happen. Nobody don't ask me a thing. Is just as if nothing happen. Like if I accustom going and visit me great-grandmother.

But it different in the house without Claire. Everybody relax a little bit because nobody to bawl and shout in we head.

When Julie tell me I have to go and see Claire, I wish I could tell her no. That I not going. I don't like going in the hospital at all, but is what Claire do to me and Carlos that bothering me.

After school I go up in the hospital. The smell make me remember that time when the police lady bring me up there.

Claire in the bed, prop up with pillows. She not looking sick like some of the other ladies on the ward. She look just like she always look.

"Afternoon Claire."

"A a. School over aready? Is just lunch time," she say.

"We finish early because we have exams."

"Come come. Go outside and buy a malt for me. Then pass in the kitchen by matron. Tell her I send you and she go give you someting for me." All in hospital Claire have to find something for people to do.

I just have me big pencil case with me because we have exams. So I put me case under me arm and I turn to go.

"Leave your purse here," Claire say, making room on she crowd up bedside table.

Me belly flip. But I pretend I don't hear her. I walk faster.

"You en hear I say to leave it here? Whey you going wid it?"

Me belly feel sick. Bile fly up in me mouth. *Oh God! Why dis lady can't give people a chance. I can't leave me case. She go dig it up. And she go find me letter!*

I know Claire does search me cupboard home, because one time she find me *Sweet Valley High* book that I hide all in the back of the cupboard, under me clothes. "And who tell you, you could bring these kind a damn books in me house madam! Bring it right back whey you get it!" Everybody in me class reading *Sweet Dreams* and *Sweet Valley High* books. But Claire getting on as if is a crime, especially if she see the word *kiss* or *love,* or worse yet, *boyfriend*, on the cover. So I does have to hide in the toilet or read them in me bed with a flashlight.

The knot in me belly tighten. But I can't say no. I have to leave it. Is an order and I have to obey! So I put the case on the table. I could not even think of a reason or make up an excuse why I have to bring it with me.

I speed out of the ward. Skip down the steps, two at a time. Buy the malt. The lady selling the drinks chatting and turning and taking she precious time. I stand up there fretting. Me belly working up and I praying in me mind. When she finally give me the change, malt in hand, I dash down to the kitchen. Speed back up the steps to the ward. And I still praying for a miracle – for the doctor to pass or the nurse to go and check she pressure – so Claire won't have time to dig up me purse. *Please God! Please God! Doh let her open me purse!*

I out of breath when I reach back. I trembling. The malt and the container that the matron give me shaking too. Claire on the bed watching me. Then me eyes fall on the table where I leave me pencil case and I nearly faint right there, when I see what sit down on top it, watching me.

"I see you write you mother letter again!" Claire say. "How come you en post it yet?"

Well how dis woman so? What she have to go and dig up people ting for?

"Ah posting it today." I say. And I still praying, because I know how Claire is.

Playing brave, I pick up me case and reach for me letter.

"Leave it wid me. I will give Julie to post when she come later."

Oh Jesus! Lord! Me skin full up with cold bumps, as if an early morning blast of sea breeze just hit me. And I don't know how me legs still holding me up, because I feeling weak.

I want to tell Claire to give me me letter. I want to ask her why she can't leave people alone. I wish I brave enough to just grab the letter and run, but I don't say a thing. Because I don't know which one worse – giving Claire me rudeness by disobeying her or obeying her and leaving me letter there for her to open and read.

I walk out of the hospital begging *Please God! Please don't let her open me letter* could see her propping up she glasses on she face, unfolding the letter. And I know I in real big trouble.

When Claire come out from hospital and she don't say nothing about the letter, I well thinking God answer me prayers. Everyday I thanking God for that miracle.

Then me left breast start hurting me. Days it hurting and I not telling nobody. It hot and red and I can't even wash me clothes, fuss it hurting. So I tell Julie and she tell Claire. Claire bring me by the doctor.

After the doctor press and squeeze up me breast, he push the longest needle I ever see in me life in the breast that hurting. When he pull it out, pus come out too.

"How old are you?" The doctor ask me.

"Fifteen years." I answer.

Then he go and ask me, "Did your boyfriend bite you when you making love?"

I nearly dead! I watch the doctor, with he greasy Indian hair, he face full of growing moles and I wish I could take the needle and push it in he skinny, hairy arm! *How he could ask me dat question right in front Claire.* Now he go make her believe is that what happen in truth. I don't even have a boyfriend. I don't know how I get the abscess.   I can't remember knocking me breast or anything. But that is all Claire need to hear. I spend one night in hospital after the operation and weeks listening to Claire throwing words for me about how I wortless. And underneath. And how I go get what I looking for.

A whole month pass. Then one of me mother friends was going back to Venezuela, and I have to bring a package for her to bring for me mother. Me mother send a confirmation dress for me but it is too small, so Claire say send it back.

"And make sure you get the letter from Pam eh," Claire say, before she go to work. *What letter she talking about? How come Pam have a letter for me mother? Pam does not write me mother. Maybe Claire leave her letter with Pam? How come she didn't just give me for sheself? Maybe Pam writing to tell me mother about me breast.*

Pam hand me a fold up envelope. It not new. It crease up and it have dirty marks on it, as if it pass through plenty hands. *So she can't put the letter in a better envelope then! Why she sending dat old dirty envelope for me mother?* I unfold   the   envelop   and   when   I   see   the   slanted handwriting staring back at me, me mouth get dry! *Oh God! I know that handwriting. Oh shit! That's me letter. God didn't answer me prayers at all. Claire well open me letter! All dat time she well have me letter!*

I drop the letter on the bed. I wait so long to get the chance to tell me mother all the things I longing to tell her. I sit down watching the letter on the bed and me whole body start to tremble. I read my letter.

April 1986

Dear Mommy,

I know that you must be wondering why I am writing you again so quick, but I had to write another letter because Claire does read all my letters.

Me and Carlos are up by Mammy. Claire send us up because she did not get letter from you. She say that she cannot feed people children without money. I know that you think me and Carlos are happy by Claire because you don't know what kind of person she is. But Claire is not a nice lady at all. She just take us so she could get the money you sending for her every month. When you send things for us, she always hiding them in her room. Ants eating up all the sweets and biscuits you sent for us and when I want to wear my new clothes you send, she is always saying that they are for big women and that I think I am a big woman too much.

And I always have so much work to do. Every evening we have to shell a whole set of cocoa and now all my fingers cut up, cut up from shelling cocoa. Sometimes my friends ask me what happened to my hands - they always have dirty cuts on them and sometimes I can't even write properly because my fingers sore. When I have home work to do I could never finish it, because as soon as I pick up my book, Claire telling me to put away my books and go and do work. Then I always falling asleep on my books. Even in class I feel too tired and I can't concentrate on my work.

I always have to borrow money for school because what you send for me finish before the time. Sometime I have to take out from me bus money to buy lunch, because Claire always measuring the bread like ration and it is never enough to share for everybody. So I does eat my lunch in the morning when I get to school And you know what she did? The last time when Auntie write me and send £10 for me, she take it because she did not get your letter yet and I had to go and ask your friend for money to pay bus again. And she always quarrelling when the letter late and then when she get it she pretending to be nice to me. And she want to make people think she looking after us out of the goodness of her heart, but she is a real hypocrite.

I don't want to stay by her anymore. I want you to come back for us. I am looking after Carlos but he want you to come back too. I tired seeing trouble. I want you to come back.

Don't write anything about this in your letter to me here because Claire will read it. When you write back, send the letter in care of my friend Tanya Charles, Victoria Post Office, St. Mark's and she will bring it for me in school. Please write soon.

299

Cindy McKenzie

Your loving daughter,
Lee

I don't know how long I stay there with the letter in me hand, remembering things. Claire throwing words about taking `people children'. Getting a good report at Parent Day, and Claire telling me head teacher how she surprise to hear this report because I was `a little liar'. And that lady Claire does work with telling me how kind Claire is to take me and me brother, and look how nice I growing up and how I must not be ungrateful.

I wonder if all of them read the letter. *Oh gosh!*

Me head hurt with all the things banging around in it. I wish I could go back to that day in the hospital. I don't know what to do. I wonder what Claire planning to do. What she want me to do with the letter. But I not lying. Everything in the letter is true and I really want me mother to come back. So I take a pen and I write - *P.S. Claire open this letter and read it. I know that she will be writing to you about it. I know she will tell you I am lying, but I am not telling lies. You have to come back and get us because she will make it worse for me. Please write back soon and post the letter to my friend.* And I put it back in the old crease up, dirty envelope, and I put it in the package.

Claire tell all the neighbours how I does tell lies. How I am a wicked little girl. They think she is a nice lady. She take two children who was nothing to her into her home, even though her house full. To them I am an ungrateful little liar.

I not a rude child, so I still respectful to Claire. But that thing I feel for Claire growing, like the boil that nearly make me lose me foot. It getting bigger and bigger. It fulling up with pus. It getting ready to burst.

300

Every day I asking me friend if she go in the post office yet. Three weeks pass. Then she bring the letter from me mother.

April 1986

My dear daughter,

How are you and Carlos doing? I hope that you are ok. I got your letter and I am so sorry. I did not know that you were seeing so much trouble by these people. The lady was so nice when I asked her to look after you. I never thought she would turn out like that. I wish I did not have to leave you by people but you know that is me alone who working to mind you and your brothers. You all have no father. Work is hard to get in Grenada and I don't have no education to get a good work. When I come back where will I get money to send you to school? That is real problems for me now. I can't come back now and I can't send you by Mammy to stay so I don't know what I will do.

I will try to send a little extra money for you and ask your grandmother if she could help out, but you must take care how you spend the money because things hard over here and you know how the money low. You shouldn't have to take you bus money to buy food because every month I sending enough money for the lady to look after you all. Anyway you have to grind it for a little longer because I cannot come back now. I want you to finish school so you could get a good job and if I come I don't know how I will get money to send you to school. Look after yourself. Don't go and get in trouble with boys. Study you school work. Don't be rude to the lady. When you in people house you have to grind and do what they say.

Kiss Carlos for me. I am so sorry that you have to see so much trouble my dear child. Please look after yourself.

Cindy McKenzie

Am sending a little extra change for you to pay back your friend.

Your loving mother
Gloria

Chapter 48

Going Back Home

Sometimes, in the night, when I finish all me housework, and before I fall asleep on me homework, I does imagine me mother arriving in a taxi take me and Carlos. I like to picture her marching up to Claire and giving her a piece of she mind, for the way she treating us. Other times, I does picture me and Carlos waiting for her on the airport. Then watching her walking down from the plane, in she fancy clothes and high heel shoes. And me and Carlos running up to her; hugging her up and smelling she sweet face powder and she overseas smell. But it don't happen so.

Six months pass after the letter. And the day me mother come, we don't go on no airport. And she don't come in no taxi. She come on the bus, just like any other passenger.

Is Saturday, and I finish all me work already. Julie and Claire in the kitchen cooking. Carlos and the children in front the shop playing. The shop close down now, because people too damn bad pay.

I know me mother coming for us. She come back from Venezuela already. And Claire say she coming weekend. She didn't come Friday so I know is today she coming, because buses don't run on Sunday.

When the bus stop and Carlos see we mother, he little face light up. As if Christmas come. He dash on her nice beige pants suit, with he little sweaty self. *Oh gosh, he go dirty she clothes.* I run to take him so I could wash him up, but he grip on tight.

"Leave him, leave him," me mother say. She take out a handkerchief from she bag – a white one with little birds on the edges – and she wipe Carlos face.

"Carlos? Que pasa? Que pasa Carlos?" And Carlos crying and holding she leg tighter.

Months now I praying for me mother to come back. Six months pass since the letter. And every day I praying harder, because Claire only throwing words for me, saying how I does tell lies. How I ungrateful. And I just start form four and I hate school ever more! Geography too confusing. Spanish too hard. And I just can't get maths. The only subject I like is literature. I want to stay in class all day with Scout and Jem in *To Kill A Mocking Bird* and lime with Rosalie Ghidaree and Shellie in *Green Days by the River,* but the bell always ringing too soon. So I always feeling I behind the other girls. And I always worrying and afraid somebody go dig up me secrets. While all the other girls going to birthday parties and enjoying school, Claire not letting me go nowhere. I can't even go to me school garden party. Only once she let me go to a party and that's because a girl from class, grandfather ask her permission for me to go with her. I spend the whole evening in a corner, watching the other girls dance with their boyfriends and wishing I brave enough to get up and dance too. And at literary competition, I sit down in the hall pining, because I wishing I was one of the girls dancing on stage. But I fraid to go to dance class, because I too fraid people go see me scar the sore leave on me leg, and ask me all kinds of questions. And when the nurses come in school to give the Rubella vaccine, I overhear a girl saying how they ask her if she sexually active. I didn't know what that mean – if it mean did you ever have sex or are you having sex. So I never take the vaccine.

So all these months, I wishing and I praying for me mother to come back. Now she right in front me and I don't know what to do. I want to run and hug her, like how people does hug up one another on TV. I want to hug her and tell her how I happy she come back. But I feeling as if I need to run in the toilet instead. Things start to stir up and kick up in me belly – like when you eat too much different things and you puff! And I don't know how to do things like that. So I wait for her to do it first.

When me mother finally unlatch Carlos from she leg, she come and put she arm round me. And she kiss me. But she arm feel stiff round me shoulders. And I realize she don't know how to do it either. Good thing Claire come and save us.

"A a. Come in. Come in," Claire say.

"How are you Claire?" Me mother say.

They say it same time.

"Come Carlos," Claire say. And she hug Carlos to her. "You see how he get big and nice!"

Aa! Since when she does hug Carlos? You see how she playing nice, just because me mother come. Always playing nice when people come, after how she does treat people. God go really punish dat woman oui!

"Come. Come. Stop dat prancing about dere now," she tell the other children.

Them children just playing in the yard you know. But she can't even stand to see children play!

Carlos latch back on to we mother again. He sit down on she lap and he little arms round she neck like handcuffs. Claire calling him to go and eat with the other children, but he not going nowhere. He cling on tight tight. He not letting go at all. We mother have to feed him.

We eat rice and peas with stew chicken legs and pumpkin for lunch. I even get a full glass of passion fruit juice. I go miss the food. But I sure me mother go cook

305

some nice food too. I could help her cook. And I could make bread now.

"Come Carla. Go and get you things ready. Pack up Carlos toys," Claire say, as soon as we finish eating. She can't even give people a chance for their food to go down. And she know we things pack already you know. Since we know me mother coming, she make me pack. I just have Carlos toys and me school books to pack now.

Oh gosh. I go have to change school. I can't come all down here to school! I never even think about changing school. All the time, I so glad me mother coming back, all I thinking about is getting out from Claire house, with all she work to do and all she pretending. I can't wait to go home. I know Mammy don't like me, but she won't interfere with me now, because me mother here. Everything go be alright now. Rally go come back home. And he go teach Carlos how to play cricket and make flexi kite. Me and me mother go cook together, in the little old kitchen. We go wash clothes together, in the sink behind the house. I go hang out the clothes and watch out for rain. And in the evening we go sit down in the veranda with Mammy and Papa, and watch the sun going down. But best of all, I can't wait to see what we mother bring for us!

I bring we bags downstairs. Then I go and bathe Carlos and dress him. I dress too, and I ready to go. But me mother sit down chatting with Claire about Venezuela and the people they know, as if them is best friends. I don't want me mother to be friends with Claire, but I know me mother don't want to show Claire no bad face. So is she turn to pretend. She have to sit down there and pretend none of the things I tell her really happen. She have to pretend Claire is this nice lady who was so kind to take in she children and look after them. And I just want to go, because I feeling like I bursting to say something.

I go and tell Julie I going. She in the kitchen washing up the wares.

"So you leaving us eh madam. Look after youself you know," She tell me. I like Julie. And I does feel sorry for her. She is a big woman and she working but she still have to do what Claire say. And Claire does still talk to Julie as if she is a child. If is me, I leaving Claire house and go.

Marion outside washing still. Marion does spend a lot of she time vex, so me and her never get close. She just finish school and she waiting for she exam results. I wonder what she going to do after.

"We go see eh? Ah going now."

Marion say "mmhm." She don't even raise she head from the sink.

I don't get to say bye to Jasmine, because she spending time by she father. I make Carlos tell the others bye. And we ready!

"Claire, thank you so much for looking after my children for me. I don't know what I woulda do if you didn't help me out," me mother say.

In social studies classes, I learn how food, clothes and shelter are the basic needs of human beings. Claire provide food and shelter, that me mother pay for. But Claire behaving as if she do if from the kindness in she heart. Saying how she did not mind doing it. How people have to help out one another. And me chest fulling-up with that thing I does feel for Claire - that thing that does ride me chest like sour food. And I want to just go before I burst, because I know I not brave enough to empty out that weight on me chest.

"Say thank you to Claire for looking after you and your brother." Me mother say. But she don't use me name. Maybe she don't know what to call me either. Everybody by Claire calling me Carla, but me mother used to me first name, Lee. And I does write Dear Mommy, when I writing to her too, but I don't know how to call her mommy. I never call her mommy before. When Carlos call her mommy, I try it out in me head but it not sounding right. I could not call her Gloria either. It just don't sound right. *How I go call her when we go home? Maybe I should stop calling Mammy, Mammy and call me mother mommy instead? I want her to be me mommy.*

"Tank you Claire," I say. I force it out. It hurt me throat. It hurt me heart. *What I thanking her for? I just want to go home.*

"So when we seeing all you again? Don't give us back you know!" Claire say. And she sound as if she really want us to come back and see her.

But five years enough for me. *She tink I coming back here! She en seeing me again nuh. Not even me back!*

I practice how I go call me mother. *Mommy. Maybe I should call her Mom. No, dat's how children on TV does call their mother. Mommy. Mommy.*

Chapter 49

Back Home

Sunday morning, and outside bright and hot; just as if the sun have a special shine. It cover the whole of Celeste with a bright, happy kind of glow. Is the kind of Sunday that does pass nice and slow and put people in a good mood - cooking their Sunday food; taking it easy; sitting down a little bit. Laugh a lot. The kind of Sunday for bathing outside in sun-warmed water and children playing shop under the house - weighing up dust, sand, flowers and all kinds of things, on leaves, with stick scales and stone weights - to make mud cakes with bougainvillea icing. Then laze about under mango trees, belly full and *niggeritis* taking over, until the sun give them chance to play in the road.

We in the kitchen. *Billie Jean* playing on the little black cassette player me mother bring from Venezuela. Sometimes Mammy does take off the radio, saying how we making noise in she head. Even when it playing real low.

Mammy on she same little bench, with she plate of green fig, smoked herrings and chutney. She mouth still going like a little tractor, but it moving slower now - as if it running out of gas.

Papa on he seat - by the little table with the plastic table cloth, near the window. He can't even go down in the garden by the house anymore. He just there quiet quiet, looking out the window and smiling that smile that never goes away.

I on the sofa grating cheese for the macaroni pie. And Carlos sit down watching me and pinching the cheese from the bowl.

I don't know where Rally is. He have seventeen years now, only one year older than me, but so he feel he is a big man. He leave school and he coming and going as he want. Me mother can't tell him nothing. He staying all about, but he does come home and sleep sometimes. And he always vex. He vex with me. He vex with we mother. He vex with Mammy. The only time Rally doesn't look vex is when he playing with Carlos. Those times, he is he old self again, especially when he showing Carlos how to pitch marbles or spin a top.

Me mother in she little corner cooking. I still don't know what to call her. *Mommy* does come in me head. It does come and lime on me tongue, then just sit down there waiting to see what I go do with it, how I go do it. And I does weigh it up, roll it around and hold it there, waiting for the right time. But when I try to say it, it does just stick on me tongue.

The outside kitchen still look the same, but me mother well clean it up. And she fix up the corner with the long table, next to Papa little one, for she to use. She move out all old things: old bottles - with all kinds of things in them: rusty pans, with rusty nails, hooks and pins - full with dust and cockroach eggs. She take out all the rusty baking tins and all them new pots that only cockroach using to mess up in, from the shelf below the table. Sweep out all the dead flies and cockroaches, scrape out more eggs and all the wood ants from under the table. She spread a table cloth on the clean table and put she little two-burner kerosene stove on it. And she pack up she things, neat and nice, on the shelves.

Mammy have a kitchen inside the main house now. It have cupboards, a new gas stove and a little fridge that her daughter send from England for her. And it have a proper sink for washing up wares, right by the little window looking down in the garden. But just like all the new clothes Mammy have pack up in the big black trunk in she room, and all the pots in the kitchen she never use, the kitchen just there - collecting cobweb and dust. But Mammy give us early warning not to even think about using it. She have an inside bathroom too. She say it's for when people come and visit. But me mother does use it. And I does bathe Carlos outside in the bath pan of water that the sun warm up. But I too old to bathe outside, so I using the bathroom too.

I could see the heat rising up from the yard. The pail of water Mammy put outside go warm up quick. She will bathe Papa with half of the water, then bathe sheself with the rest.

I grease the Pyrex dish and pour the macaroni pie in it. The fire lighting in the coal pot outside. I pick up the dry clothes from the line already, so they won't smell of smoke. And I tie me head too, so my hair won't smell smoke. Since Mammy won't let us use the stove, we have to bake in the drum oven outside. Papa made the over from an old drum that used to collect rain water. He cut out the bottom with a cutlass and a hammer, bore some holes around it, then he push wire through the holes to make the rack.

The first time I bake bread in the drum oven and Mammy taste it, if you hear her! "A a, you could make nice bread oui! Who teach you to bake nice so?" And that was the first time Mammy words don't hit me like stones. But when me mother offer her food, Mammy would watch the plate over she glasses, squinge up she face and say, "Eh eh! What is dat? All you call dat food?" Papa would eat a little bit sometimes, when Mammy not there to see him.

But me mother would still take out a plate for Mammy and leave it there. Then Rally would eat it.

Up the road, Miss Joyce calling Boyboy to go down by Aunty May for piece of ice to put in the juice. Miss Kay stew chicken smell coming all over in Mammy kitchen and make me mouth water. And I could smell Miss Dora cake baking next door.

The coals burning nice and the coconut shells stop pouring out smoke now, so I spread them out on the piece of galvanize on top the drum. I put the pie and the chicken in the oven and then sit down in front the kitchen to keep an eye on the oven and read the new *Sweet Dream* book I been hiding from Claire. No Claire to say, "Put down dat damn book and go and get work to do!" So I reading to me leisure. I in the kitchen shelling peas, me book on me lap. I behind the house waiting for the sink to full up to rinse the clothes, I reading. All in the toilet, me book going with me.

So I sit down there reading me book in peace. I don't interfere with nobody you know. But Mammy start up. Is me second Sunday back. And when we just reach, Mammy playing nice nice, pretending she glad we come back. She always singing for Carlos. He is she Beta now. But she only throwing words for me and jooking me mother for confusion about everything.

"A a. You doh see her! She turn scholar now oui! All whey you see her she have a book in she hand! Papa oh!"

And just so I feel the same thing I used to feel for Claire – that damn ugly thing swelling up inside me chest, that does make me wish I could curse up Mammy backside well good and proper! And I see the same thing swelling up inside me mother too, because she chest start to heave up and down when she stand up in front Mammy. And I know she chest full up and ready to burst, just like when mango get over ripe, and start to ferment and swell, until it burst open and spit out all the sour juice.

"What wrong with you Millie? What we do you? What we do you, you hate us so! Your own grandchildren! Eh? Your own flesh and blood! What we do you?"

Mammy look up at me mother. She sucking she cheeks – in and out, in and out – like a little mullet.

Papa watching he hands in he lap. He mouth open.

"I come from your daughter. The only daughter you have. The ONLY chile you make! She what make me! The same daughter who take up all she children up in England, and leave me here. Me alone she leave behind, for you to make see trouble! You tink I forget all the trouble you make me see?"

Mammy rocking now. Just like that time when she daughter came from England and she start to talk about Mammy putting her in ants nest.

Me mother clench she hands by she side. She trembling. She trembling with everything Mammy do her when she was younger. She trembling with all the things she still going through now, all the things she feeling: anger for the time Mammy unplug the fridge just because she put some fish in it; frustration, because Mammy only throwing words at her because she don't have she own house; the worries she having with Rally; and sadness, because everybody else like to have their grandchildren around them, but Mammy behaving as if she is nothing for us. And I know she trembling with guilt, for what happen to me too.

"And you see her there," Me mother say, pointing at me. "Watch her! You see her! She come out from me! You hear me! She is MY child! My child! What she do you, you hate her so? You en find she see enough trouble

313

already? Eh! Why you doh leave her alone. She just reading she book. She en interfere with you!

Me mother chest heaving so much she have to sit down. And she still trembling.

"I never see a woman who hate she family so! You getting old Mammy! You should be glad you have us with you. Look at Miss Kay! Eh! She little house full. Everybody. All she children! All she grandchildren! And all of them living good. But I don't know what happen to you! You have curse! You must have the devil in you!"

Mammy still rocking like one of those little dogs people have stick up on the dashboard in their car—the head going up and down. Up, down. Up, down.

Papa still watching he hands, as if they not his. As if is first time he seeing them in he life.

I sit down there watching the fire until I seeing red. And inside me feeling red too. I well say when me mother come back and we go back home, things go be alright. I know how Mammy is, but I really thought she would be different because we mother there.

"Carlos. Come nah." Rally call from outside. He does always just appear when food ready, as if he timing the pot.

Carlos jump down from the sofa and dash outside to meet him, just like I used to do when I hear Daddy whistle. Before *that time*.

Two years later
Estranged from her mother
Lee is...

Epilogue

Back In The Ghetto

Sun peeping through the coconut branches and the bamboo door in me father ghetto. Just like it used to peep through the holes in the galvanized roof in the little house. The first rays feel soft and nice on me face; making me smile this happy little smile, even though I don't feel like smiling at all.

I wake up before day break, because I still fraid nights. Nights does bring darkness. And when darkness come, it does bring all kinds of things with it. It does bring worry; so me head does get so crowded, it does spin with all kind of thoughts. It does bring hunger; as if it gathering it up whole day so when night reach, it could hit me with it full force. So me belly making ruction and me head feeling light. But the worse thing is the fear it does bury deep down inside me, making shadows creep up on me and making me feel as if somebody watching me through the coconut branches. Especially when me alone in the ghetto.

Most times I does curl up on the bunk with a Danielle Steele romance from the library. Other times I does try to loose meself in a Sydney Sheldon thriller, until me piece of candle melt right down to the nook and make a wax pool on the mud floor. Until sleep creep up and knock me out.

The day I went by me father ghetto he didn't even ask me a question. And I didn't have to explain nothing. Is just as if he know I was coming. He just look at me real meditative, like he does, kind of shook his head and said, "De Princess know I-man home is de I-home. De Princess could stay as long as she want." Just as if he talking to heself. As if I not really there.

The bunk hard and me blanket too thin, so the bamboo digging me back. I take the blanket from Mammy's big black trunk. I take two sheets and some pillow cases too, because Mammy would never give me if I ask her. But fuss the trunk full, she never even miss them.

The sun climbing over the trees now and light seeping through all holes and every space it could find, and flooding the ghetto with the kind of rays that does hurt eyes.

Two sets of snores coming from the back room: One set have a steady rhythm, that I know is me father's. The other set loud, and have a deep kind of gargle and a chocking sound. That is from me father girlfriend. I wonder how the two of them fit on that little bunk. I wonder how the two of them come to be together.

The cocks finish crowing from the soursop tree in the back yard and me uncles start up. "Wha wha whhhat de mudercunt you you tink you doin? You can fu fu fucking hear ah say doh touch me mu mu mudercunt ting." They still pelting bad words at one another.

Ms Girlie mackerel in tomato sauce drifting from she kitchen, coming and tease me hungry belly. Sometimes she does give me a cup of hot water for me to make some tea, to go with me Crix crackers. And if I lucky, I does have a piece of cheese to go with it.

The road start getting busy too and I does listen to the people passing. The bunch of construction workers talking about woman.

"Boy sooo dat girl tink she smart eh!"

And them children walking to school and playing in the road.

"Boy gie me me damn ting nuh. Ah go tell mammy about you when ah go home eh."

And I does want to go and sit down under the coconut tree in the yard, where me uncle does cut the grass neat neat and every morning he sweeping it clean clean. I does want to watch the morning passing, but something does hold me and tie me down in the ghetto. Sometimes that thing does lock me up inside for the whole day. And it does make me mind wander on things. Me mother, living just up the road, but how we don't even talk. And I don't know the last time I see her. Me brother, knocking about and doing he own thing.

Other times, me mind does linger on me schoolmates and them. I does imagine those who working in banks or teaching. Who going to college. Who gone in America. What they go think if they see me now – back in the ghetto with me Rasta father and he crazy girlfriend. And that thing does make me watch meself and just feel to stay lock up inside the ghetto for days. I know that thing real good you know. It does not come in the night with the others at all. It does come in the big, bright day light. That same thing I does feel every time I go to the shop for me tin of condensed milk and Crix. Or down Sauteurs in the post office for me letter from me grandmother in England. That thing they call *Shame.*

The bamboo creak and me mind come back in the ghetto. Teeth grinding. A loud groan from the back bunk .

"You aright Princess?" me father ask.

Just as he say it something move inside me. Just a little flutter. It feel like me mother sweet, warm, milky custard. The first time I feel it, it scald me tongue, just like when the custard just come out from the pot. I had to leave it to cool down first.

I rest me hand on me little round belly and I keep still, waiting.

"Princess you aright?"

I stay quiet. Waiting for more of that sweet, milky custard to cool down.

"the sun sets to rise again..."

Lee's journey continues ...

Glossary

bambam, bamsie	backside
bashie	bowl or pot made from a calabash
bazodee	stupid, dazed, stunned
beta	Hindi word for son
belgamot	bergamot
beti	Hindi word for daughter
Bim and Bam	bosom buddies (from Trinidad comedy duo)
blocko	street party
bluggoe	starchy fruit like a large banana, used as a vegetable
bon jé	good Lord
break bush	to run off, escape
bridle	dry dribble round the mouth
bumbaclot	a vulgar swear word
bwaden leaf	bay leaf
caca poule	fowl shit
caca jé	dried mucus at the corner of the eyes
cockeeoko	flamboyant tree
cock sparrow	womaniser
cocoyaya	stupid person
cokie	a cokie-eyed person has a squint
coksie	shoes with hard noisy heels
cornbabe	corn beard
coucou pé	calf (part of the back of leg between knee and ankle)
crapaud	toad
congoree	millipede
doodoo	darling or sweetie
doomsie	ripe, juicy
dotish	slow, stupid
dougla	mixture of East Indian and negro

drevéin	to knock about, roam aimlessly
gashay	to graze or bruise
gauldin	egret
gandolie	a big crayfish
geegee	eagle, chicken hawk
ghetto	small hut usually built with coconut branches and bamboo
gospo	sour seville orange
hula hoop	flip flops (slippers)
ital	Rastafarian name for natural foods
jackey	piggy back
jamet	a bad loose woman
jigger	itch
joeg	carry
jooking	poking at someone, stirring up trouble
lallie	moss
laquas	dirt from the body, muck
masantoes	kerosene torches made using a bottle and a wick
maco	an inquisitive person
morrocoy	tortoise, land turtle
mybone	a small wasp
nana	to raid something - esp without pemission, but not considered as serious theft
nennen	Godmother
niggeritis	lazy feeling after eating too much
nyam	to eat
parrie	liming, hanging out
pirha	very low stool
planass	hit someone with the flat of a cutlass

poor man pork	big thyme, Spanish thyme, used to season fish
pwadoo	beanlike fruit with hard pits covered by sweet, fleshy pulp
quail up	wrinkled
renk	strong unpleasant smell
shortknee	a type of traditional mas band
skanking	type of dance originating in Jamaica with Ska music
snowcone	shaved ice with syrup served in a paper cup
soumaché	a shrub used for clensing the skin
stupidee	stupid person
stupse	a sound of annoyance
ta	something moulded into a flat shape and used for playing games
tambran	tamarind
tash	part of the branch of a palm tree
taytay	woman's breast
titiree	tiny fish
tootoo	shit
torties	tiny turtle like insects found in dust
trad	walk or go on a movement
yaws	tropical skin disease which affected chickens
zabouca	avocado pear
zebapique	bitter herb
zootie	nettle

Extra

That Hand (*Created from Chapter 6 - Under the table*)

*Is the same hand, the one that does pull vine for the rabbits
and tie out he mother goats
The same hand that does help Mammy to do little things
round the house
Move a heavy bag from the yard, clean the windows
Chop up firewood and pack them under the fireside
Hold Melba for Papa to fix she hoof*

*The same hand that does teach me brother to make a
compass
And tear up old sheets to make tail for he flexi kite
Carve out a bat from a coconut branch
Mould hot melt up plastic and squeeze up a compo
To play cricket in the road
That same hand, the colour of he mother cocoa tea
Before she put milk in it and some flour to make it thick
Fingernails full of mud
Palms tough as leather*

*Is that same hand, when me brother on the floor playing
with he marbles
Belle stretch out watching him as if she want to play too
When Papa gone in he bed.
And Mammy gone to funeral down in St John
Is that same hand that creep up under the table
And sit down on the chair by me
When I reading me New West Indian Reader
The kerosene lamp flickering
Moths falling inside*

The flame eating them up

Is that same hand, stale sweat smelling like hot pepper
burning
With charcoal fingernails
That crawl up on me like a congoree
And inside me burning
Me book trembling
And ah want to pee.
But ah fraid to move
And me brother still on the floor with Belle
And ah wondering if he see
Papa gone in he bed.
And Mammy down in St John
And I just seven

Acknowledgements

I must give thanks and show gratitude to:

A very special thank you to Richard Worth - for the space and the financial freedom to explore and nurture my creativity. For without those gifts, this book would not be.

Sallian McLean – my all time friend and supporter.

Marcelle Toussaint - the very first person I entrusted with my very first draft, who always believed.

Louise (Tona) St Louis - my very ardent reader and fan, who has never stopped pestering me about publishing.

Patsee Phillip – my constant and most vibrant source of energy and support.

Judy Antoine (Ama) - for insight and quiet wisdom.

And everyone who has given time and thought to my words; out of support and sincere love for literature.